Tomorrow Is Another Day

A Tomorrow Is Another Day Novel

T.R. Prouty

For Lindsey,
My co-conspirator, without whom this novel wouldn't exist.
My sister, my other half, my best friend.
The buttered toast to my gravy and my person.
I love you, Nilla Wafer.
-T.R. Prouty (AKA, your "Nelly")

DJ's Journal
KEEP OUT

Chapter 1

TWO NEW FAMILIES moved down the street from me
—the Greens and the Stars. I hadn't met either of them yet,
but it turned out I was related to the Stars. My family had
never talked about them, so how was I s'posed to know? My
mom hated Marti, her sister, but that didn't surprise me
because my mom hated pretty much everyone. When I heard
the Greens had a daughter my age, I decided I was going to
make my move and try to be her best friend.

After I shoved my big feet into my beat-up sneakers, I
slammed the battered front door of my house and took off
running. The salty breeze typical of Crab Cove washed over
me and almost distracted me from my efforts to step over
every single crack in the sidewalk. I made my way down the
block as fast as I could, which wasn't very fast at all. A hand
came down on my shoulder from behind with a *SLAP*!
Halting, I slowly turned my head and saw the long, fake,
purple nails of my mother and winced as I looked up.
Though she didn't know where we were half the time (and
couldn't care less), she claimed she hated when us kids "ran
around like heathens" because it made her look bad. One of
my mom's perfectly-tweezed eyebrows arched, fury burning

in her eyes when I met them. Out of habit, I took a deep breath to think of what I was going to say. But it didn't matter because she spoke first like she usually does.

"DJ! Just where do you think *you* are going?" Her brash voice was out of place in the otherwise quiet town. Besides my house, that was.

"I'm going to the neighbors', to meet Monica Green. She's five, too, and I want to be her friend." I didn't have any friends.

Her face twisted in disgust. "No way, DJ! You are *not* going!"

I should have expected this. Everything was always "no" with her.

"Why, Mom?" I whined, my hope extinguished.

"Because!"

"Because, why?"

"DJ, I cannot put up with your foolishness! And *you* certainly aren't going to *anybody's* house!" She sighed and placed a hand to her forehead, like telling me why would be too exhausting.

"But—"

"—no 'buts,' DJ. *I'm* going to the Greens, and I want us to seem like we have *some* class. Do you not remember me telling you that each of these mothers are *top* models? I don't care so much about Marti, but Megan Green is a fashion designer. Do you know what that means?"

She paused. My blank expression apparently was not the right answer. I tried not to stare at how flashy her outfit was. She looked like something from the zoo in that zebra print.

"They are *rich.*"

"Okay…"

"And they have access to *stilettos*." She raised her eyebrows when she said the last word, trying to make sure I

2

knew it was a big deal.

"What in tarnation is a stiletto?" I asked, scrunching my face up as if I had just smelled rotten tuna.

"You're going to be *pooping* stilettos if you don't shut your hole!" She stomped one of her high heeled shoes against the pavement and waited for me to go back home.

"Fine!" I groaned. It was no use arguing with her. She always won.

Tears burned in my eyes as I trudged back to my house. I didn't understand why I could never do anything. I was always too little, too dumb, too embarrassing. Plopping down on the stairs, I looked out the window across from me with arms crossed and lips pouted. That was when I noticed a redhead and a brunette in matching pink and blue outfits walking toward the towering mansion of Monica Green.

One minute I was trying to figure out who the two little girls were, the next I was lying on the floor with my mom standing over me. I rubbed my eyes and yawned. How long had I been out? When did she get back home? She was screaming and going on and on about why I wasn't listening and why I didn't answer her.

I finally pulled myself together to squeeze out a measly, "Huh?" but that just made her *more* mad.

She gave me the eye roll that let me know I'd annoyed her and started to yell at me for falling asleep on the floor again. I couldn't help it if the bottom of the stairs was the comfiest place in the whole house! Then she pointed at the carved-in writing and numbers on one of our corner living room walls, filled with cobwebs. It was out of sight from most people, unless you knew to look for it. For whatever reason, my parents thought that having our daily schedules carved into a section of our wall was better than having them written on the fridge like normal people.

I crumpled my face, then realized what she was getting at too late. Maybe I should have paid attention to everything she was rambling about instead of getting lost in thought and tuning her out.

"You *know* what I mean. It's four o'clock on the dot. Go milk Ol' Bessie!" Her hands slapped against her thighs, making a clapping sound that told me it was time to move it.

I stood and went outside, grabbing the rusty milk pail that sat by the back door on my way out. As I stepped into our backyard, a large and ugly plot of land, I saw my sister Rochelle running past. Her muscles were so huge that she looked like a big barreling bulk of meat charging at me. She claimed often that she was training for her boxing tournament, but I think she just wanted to get out of chores and used that as an excuse.

Before I knew it, she plowed right into me. My heart leapt out of my chest as I fell to the ground, feeling something smush beneath me. I clenched my fists, balling them up to keep the rage inside. The whole yard was nothing but dead patches of dry grass spattered green. It was that, and the gag-worthy smell, that let me know she had pushed me right into a fresh Bessie cow patty. *Bessie really needs to be in a pen,* I thought.

The idiot had the nerve to blurt, "Oh wow! There's some strong winds ova here," like nothing happened! I was a *person,* not the wind!

The back door slammed against the house as it opened. I turned in the direction of the sound to find my mom with one hand to her forehead and her eyes squinted. Kind of like a pirate looking for land. She dropped her hand and started to close the distance between us, muttering about how she could "literally hear us kids a mile away." In a cartoon, there would be steam coming out of her ears right now.

"DJ!" My mom gasped, her timing perfect as always. "Get up now! I can't believe this. Are you in your one and *only* good dress?"

"Uh—"

"Get out of that cow pat!" she snarled, so I hurried up, using the pig pen nearby for support.

"Go change." She scrubbed a hand down her face as she sighed, and it looked like her skin was melting off. I knew better than to laugh.

Rochelle was making her way back around to where Mom and I were standing. My mom couldn't see her, because she was leaning against the pig pen.

To clarify, we don't actually live on a farm. My mom complained to my dad that bacon and milk cost too much money, but he didn't want to give them up. So he brought home Bessie the Cow and one pig that just slopped around in this pen all day. Let me just tell you, that pig is not doing his job. I hadn't seen him crack out one piece of bacon since he got here a few months ago, just a little baby with a patch around his right eye and a chip in his left ear. My mom complained that she was not killing him, but I didn't know why she would even say that. That was a little extreme. Just because Beans (my secret name for him) hadn't given us any bacon didn't mean he deserved to die!

"What are you staring at?"

"No!" I screamed, and a puzzled look crossed Mom's face before she turned her head over her shoulder.

"Oh, crap!" Mom shrieked as Rochelle knocked her off her balance and flipped her straight into that pig pen.

"Rochelle, I am going to beat your butt so hard…" My mother gritted her teeth and frowned down at her clothing. I didn't know what to do. Was I supposed to change? Did I still need to milk Bessie? Where even was Bessie? A few of my siblings cleaning the yard and outside the house stopped to stare at the commotion. This kind of thing didn't happen to my mom; she was never below anybody. She stood and took a deep breath before gathering herself. She shook mud off her hand, and it slapped against the ground as Rochelle continued on.

"I just invited *Megan Green* over! I can't look like this!" She waved her hand up and down her body, and I followed it with my eyes. Her normally perfect hair was frazzled, and her skin-tight pants were drenched in Beans's slop. Mud caked her long fingernails.

With a loud groan, she lifted herself out of the pen, and her voice boomed across our yard. I straightened up. My siblings followed suit. "Everyone! Go get changed. NOW."

My brothers and sisters swarmed toward the house, behind my mom. A snort came from behind me. His eyes met mine, and I hesitantly looked at the house before turning back to him.

"Beans sit," I whispered sneakily. Beans just blinked.

"You can do it buddy." His nose poked through the fence.

"Sit," I repeated. His little curly-Q tail wiggled.

"Like this." I was mid-squat when my Mom's voice boomed like a cannon, and I nearly jumped out of my skin.

"I said *now!*"

I fell smack on my tuchus! *Again!*

Scrambling to my feet, I whispered, "We'll work on that later."

I retrieved the milk bucket that I apparently didn't need to use and followed the others back inside the house. Trailing along behind them like the caboose of a train, I swung the bucket as I went. They needed to stop slogging and pick up the pace. Once inside herself, Rochelle hollered for the kids who had been inside to get dressed, too. She hated taking orders, but she loved giving them. Kind of like our mother.

All fifteen kids now assembled, we headed to our rooms to change, and I tried not to get lost in the tide of the ocean that was my family.

Chapter 2

OH YEAH... Did I mention I had fourteen siblings? Don't even bother trying to keep track of them all. I barely could, and I had lived with them my whole life. The oldest two were twins, Emma and Emily. Then there were the triplets, Brad (the *WORST!*), Stacey (the weirdo), and Ashley (one of the prettiest girls in my family)—she was a real goodie-two-shoes. The next oldest was Orange... No, not "Orange," like the fruit, but said like "Or-on-jah." She was almost six feet tall and basically only said "whatever." Rochelle and Shaye were next in line. Then it was Ty, Tearston, and Tiffany. All of them had blond hair and blue eyes, though you could still tell all of them apart. If you knew them, that was. Otherwise it was just a big blur of blond and blue. DRUMROLL...I was next! D. J. Tipper. My hair was so blond it looked white, and my eyes were baby blue. I was told I was too chubby, but I just really liked Little Debbies. Josh was after me, and even though we looked alike, I couldn't stand him! Joe and Jillian were the babies of the family and were yet another set of twins. They stood out in our family because they had brown eyes and brown hair, like our mother.

"Are you kids dressed yet?" my mom hollered. We

rushed downstairs in a great stampede. I squeezed myself against the wall, so I wouldn't get trampled by the monstrosity that was my family. My eyes were peeled to the steps, trying not to miss one and fall to my doom. All of a sudden, a flash of movement passed when Rochelle pushed Stacey down the stairs. Under my breath I muttered a "thank you" that it hadn't been me, despite how rude it was to be glad someone else took that tumble. Rochelle snorted.

"Rochelle," my mother spoke through gritted teeth, grabbing the rail at the bottom of the steps; I had to stop, as did the rest of the mob. "Do you want me to pull you out of *all* your sports?"

Silence.

"Answer me!"

"No, Mom." Rochelle rolled her eyes when my mom was too busy looking over the rest of us, no doubt making sure we were dressed properly. I believed everyone should know how to match their clothes if I did. I think the teenagers didn't do it on purpose. Especially Rochelle. She had no fear or respect for my mom whatsoever.

Begrudgingly accepting our appearances, Mom went to one of the front windows to peek outside. Every one of us crammed against the window to see what was going on, too. I stood on my tiptoes but everyone kept pushing and shoving me out of the way, so I only was able to see bits and pieces. But lucky for me, my ears could hear just fine. I'd had a lot of practice when it came to listening behind closed doors. I heard a big "ew" outside, followed by a man's voice.

"Some crummy place, babe. Sure you want to do this?"

"Yes, darling," said a woman. "We have to be polite to everyone."

"UGH! I bet they don't even have a hot tub. Or a football game playing right above it."

I wished I could see who the voices belonged to. Not knowing things always made me nervous.

"Oh, honey. It's just *one* time. Plus we are meeting up with the Stars next."

"Move, I can't see!" Brad complained, shoving Ty out of his way.

I sighed, shifting my attention back to Mom. It was clear she had heard everything they said, but she smoothed down her shirt and sniffed. When she rolled her eyes up, I wondered if she was about to cry. I'd never seen her cry before.

"They just wanted to be nice… They didn't like me after all." She touched a pinky to the corner of her eye, as if she was picking at her makeup. But I think she was really trying to hide a single tear that was about to fall.

They knocked on our door, and Mom fumbled to close the blinds.

"Mom?" I asked. "What are you doing?"

"Shh!" Mom held a finger to her lips, and I stopped talking. She breathed deeply and stepped outside. I stepped in front of the door, so I could hear them talking. Orange groaned and flopped onto the couch.

"Let's go out instead," Mom said quickly, her voice fading further away. "I'll take ya to my favorite restaurant."

"Oh," the couple replied. "Okay then."

"They're on the move!" Rochelle blurted, drawing my attention to where she was standing, peeking behind the blinds. Ashley had just come downstairs, babies in hand. We all shuffled our way out the door, and I followed Shaye and Josh as they approached Mom's bug. As if we would all fit in that thing at the same time! Did she plan on leaving us at home? My mom clearly hadn't thought this through.

Fighting for a spot in my mom's car, I pushed Josh to the

ground. I was older than him. I should get to go. A sputtering engine broke up Josh's attempt to fight me back, and I turned to see my dad's jeep pulling up in a cloud of dust. He hopped out, abandoning the jeep at the end of the drive instead of parking next to the Greens. His orange ponytail and long beard swung in the wind like two flying squirrel tails. He was a workaholic even though he loved our family. Almost every day, my dad worked from six a.m. to eight p.m. Unless, of course, a football game was on. He only worked that much to get away from my annoying mom.

He began to walk over, but my mom paled at the sight of him. I wrinkled my face in confusion and stopped waving at him when Mom hollered, "You hillbilly! Get off my lawn!"

He stopped and spit in the grass. I grimaced, and my mom shuddered, her eyes roaming over the stains all over his factory uniform. He did a double take at the lady in the gray pencil skirt, whose auburn hair gracefully danced in the breeze.

My dad's jaw dropped, and he rushed to the woman's side. He kissed her tiny hand and said, "Enchanté, mademoiselle."

She nodded appreciatively, but the man beside her scoffed. His curly hair flopped over his eyes as he shook his head. I couldn't tell if he was confused or angry, because I couldn't see his eyebrows.

"Get away, Dude!"

How did he know my dad's name?

"How dare you? Do you know who they are?" my mom interrupted. I had abandoned the car and sidled up behind her. She lowered her voice and whispered to Dad, "These are the Greens."

He ignored her and brushed her aside like he was swatting an annoying fly.

11

"Dude? It's you, man!" Dad raised his arms and clapped the guy on the back. "I haven't seen you in years. Did you get a job at the steel factory yet?"

Wait— This guy's name was "Dude," too? I wrinkled my nose just thinking about it. My mom did the same. I could not believe that not only one but two people had babies and decided it was a good idea to name them "Dude."

"Yep," said Dude Green, "and you know, it's no biggie man, but this lady right here is a fashion designer of her own company *and* a top model. Don't mean to brag, but...she's *mine.*"

"No way! You lie!" yelled my dad. "You couldn't have ended up with...*this,* and me with Bessie the cow and that hillbilly!" He motioned over his shoulder toward my mom, who was the opposite of this woman. My mom was curvy and flashy. Her makeup, clothing, and everything about her drew the eyes—but not necessarily in a good way. This lady was slender and naturally beautiful. Nothing about her looked fake. When she walked, she walked on air.

"Oh, Dude, but I did!" He chuckled, both hands firm on his hips, his smile blindingly white.

"You two *know* each other?" asked my mom with a pinched up face. She stepped in between the two of them, leaving me and the pretty lady a few steps back. I stared at her, thinking I had seen her before, but she noticed me staring, and I embarrassingly averted my eyes back to my mom and dad.

"Oh yes!" said my dad. "We knew each other from ages three to fifteen, pretty much! We grew up in Peru together."

Where is Peru?

"Where is Peru?" I asked.

My mom shushed me and told me to quit eavesdropping.

"But, Dude! You never told me you moved here or that

12

you got married. And you didn't tell me it was to *Megan Carter!*"

"Eh, eh, eh," said Dude Green. "It's Megan *Green* now."

"Oh. Yeah." My dad sighed.

"Okay, whatever." My mom dismissed them with a wave of her hand. "Let's just all go to the restaurant, and we can get to know each other better—or, uh, catch up there."

"Whatever," grumbled Orange. I jumped, not realizing she had snuck up behind me.

"Don't do that!" I hissed, and walked beside her to my mom's car. We all had to split up into the different cars, and I was going to go with my mom. She sped down the road and headed to where we all knew was my mom's favorite restaurant:

The China Buffet.

When we pulled up and got out of the cars, Mom kept shushing my siblings repeatedly. The whole world could probably hear them. I gave my siblings a dirty look for being so loud and annoying. Someone shoved me, but I had no clue as to which buffoon it came from. With all of them pushing through the doorway, it took me a while to get inside, where Mom was speaking in hushed tones to the hostess. The owner came out of the backroom immediately.

"Deniese!" he exclaimed, taking in all of us children and the Greens. "My number one customer! Come on in."

We got this huge, and I mean *HUGE* table, slightly away from the buffet lines. I followed Rochelle, my mouth watering at the variety of foods to choose from. I stood on my tiptoes and tried not to spill anything but accidentally strung corn throughout all of the Chinese noodles and vegetables. While I was looking around to see if anyone noticed, something slapped against my cheek. It was a wet noodle.

"Rochelle and Dennis June!" my mom hissed, turning around from her spot ahead of us. "Stop throwing food for crying out loud!"

I peeled the noodle off my face and decided against eating it, due to the dirty hands it had come from.

"Dennis started it." Rochelle snickered and walked to the next line while I narrowed my eyes at her.

I know what you're thinking. *Wait a second,* Dennis *isn't a girl's name!* Yeah, well, apparently it was. My real name was Deniese, after my mother, but one day she referred to me as "Dennis the Menace," and it stuck like a bad song you couldn't get out of your head. "Dennis" was unfortunately really close to "Deniese," and I think most people honestly believed that was my real name. Being too much of a pain to try to convince them it wasn't, I caught me calling myself Dennis more and more each day.

Megan and Dude Green were out of view as I grabbed a roll, and I wondered if they had already finished filling their plates and returned to the table. I was glad they weren't hearing this, because it was embarrassing. A lady at the line I just left was complaining about corn being in the noodles, and I stared down at my shoes, my cheeks heating up.

"Rochelle! Do I have to put the leash on you?" my mother scolded, even though Rochelle was a full-grown teenager and hadn't worn a leash in over a year. But she was an animal, so my mom kept it in her purse whenever Rochelle went somewhere with her.

"No, Mama," Rochelle sneered.

"Then stop pushing Stacey into the fried chicken tray. NOW."

"Yes, Mama." Rochelle pulled Stacey away from the fried chicken section, then shoved her. She fell, and her plate clattered to the grimy floor. Despite the fact that Rochelle

14

was a middle kid, she was stronger than an ox. Maybe even stronger than my *mom.*

"Ow! Mom! Rochelle threw me onto the floor!"

"Rochelle!" my mother growled.

"What?" she spat. The next thing you knew my dad was running through the buffet and into the kitchen. It was right beside where I was standing, so I could hear every word.

"Is it on? Is it on?"

"Yes, Dude, the football game is on," answered a man. He sounded like it was perfectly normal for my dad to go back there, despite the contradicting looks on passing customers.

"Sah-WEET!" my dad yelled. I stepped out of line and stood in front of the open kitchen door, so I could eavesdrop better. He was dancing excitedly.

"Dude?" my mom called, oblivious that he had gone in there.

My dad rushed past me and cut in line beside my mother, frowning but saying nothing.

Chaos broke loose. We kids kept getting up and cutting in the line, not bothering to say "please" or "excuse me." After I pushed in front of a lady to grab a fortune cookie, I returned to the table. Setting my plate down, I picked up my fork and dug in, already needing to reach for a napkin at the mess I was making. The babies threw their food and wailed, irritating me. Ashley left them, finally done with being the "babysitter" and getting a chance to fill her own plate, and no one else bothered to tend to them. People stared at the number of children sitting at the table and whispered about whether or not we were all my parents "*real*" kids. I glanced up from my plate to realize there were two empty seats with empty plates. Attention, everyone...! Megan and Dude Green had left the building!

I looked toward my mom who ran her hands through her hair and whimpered, noise and movement all around her. She placed a hand to her forehead, and I knew we were stressing her out. But she lowered her hand and glanced around the restaurant.

"Where are they?" she snipped. Her eyes searched each kid, but nobody answered her. Most didn't pay any attention.

"Dennis June!" shrieked my mom. "You scared them off! Didn't you?"

"No! It wasn't me!" I dropped my fork on my plate. "I didn't do anything, and I am *not* going to the grounded room!"

"I will tell you what to do and when to do it. I *know* you scared them off, because everything bad that happens is *your* fault!"

"But I didn't do *this!* It was Rochelle." I threw her under the bus like she always did to me. It probably was her anyway. She was the one pushing people and throwing food.

Rochelle gave me the glare that let me know I was in for it, then spit at me and climbed across the table. Here we were, a five-year-old and a teenager rolling across the plates. My eyes widened and my stomach dipped as I neared the edge of the table. Rochelle landed another painful punch, and I was trying my best to dish it back in front of my cheering mother. She was just as bad as the kids in the schoolyard when a fight broke out. I couldn't believe she was letting this happen to me. Why wasn't she breaking us up? What was *wrong* with her? A plate dug into my back, and I winced as I struggled to push Rochelle off. Noodles matted my hair, and soy sauce soaked my hands.

"That's it! Deniese! Get your family out of my restaurant! Everyone is complaining!"

I held back Rochelle's fist and saw the owner motioning toward the other tables, which were full of open mouths and wide eyes. Heat rose to my face as my dad came out of the kitchen and approached the table. He must've snuck off to watch the game again.

"What's going on?" he blinked stupidly.

Rochelle climbed off the table, and I followed suit.

"Apparently we're leaving," my mom snapped at him, throwing her hands in the air. She gave him a dirty look and grabbed her purse.

"What do you want me to do about it?" He dumbly glanced at us kids. Pain swished in and out of my body, the bruises already coming on from the fight. I lowered my eyes in shame.

We were almost all out the door when Joe and Jillian asked for one of those toys in the vending machine, and I turned around, feeling too beat up to take another step. My mom was already in a bad mood because she was probably never going to eat here again.

"You want a quarter for *that?*" my mom began, her eyes bulging as if they had asked her for a gazillion dollars. "If you're asking me for money...I know you ain't askin' me for money," she rambled on. "But if you want MONEY, get a frickin' job!"

"Mom, they're only like three years old," said Ashley.

"No back talk." My mom turned around, pointing a finger at us all. "Or you *all* go in the grounded room."

Chapter 3

WE HEADED HOME. Mom had blamed me for the fight, and I didn't have the energy to argue with her. She went on and on about how it was the cheapest restaurant in town, and how she couldn't go there now. Ashley kept saying she was worried about us skipping out on the bill, but Mom told her she wasn't going to pay when she didn't even get to finish her meal. So why did it matter if it was the cheapest restaurant?

I wished we hadn't gone home, because we all got sent to our rooms. It was a really crappy arrangement too. Let me just tell ya about it:

- Room One: This was the nursery. It had Joe's, Jillian's, Josh's, Ambrosia's, and Stacey's cribs and beds.
- Room Two: Ashley, Emma, Emily, Orange, Tiffany, and Tearston all had bunk beds. I LOVED to hide in there— Tee-hee!
- Room Three: Mom and Dad slept in here. Do NOT enter!
- Room Four: This was my room! I was stuck in here with Rochelle and Shaye.

- Room Five: Brad and Ty were in here. I didn't think they should get all that space, but apparently because they were boys they got to have the room all to themselves.

Besides the bedrooms, we had a kitchen, and we ate at a gigantic picnic table outside. The bathroom was a little ways away from that. I didn't understand why we couldn't have a bathroom inside our house like the people did on TV. I hated walking outside in the middle of the night to pee!

But there were worse things than going outside to pee. Like my room. The reason it was the worst? Stacey used to be in our room, and Rochelle hated her as much as she hated me. But ever since she came home from the hospital with a baby (Ambrosia), she had to sleep in the nursery with her. Now Rochelle's anger was all on me. Everything was fine and dandy when I wasn't the one getting picked on all the time!

Ambrosia. That was a dumb name. I said so and got sent to the grounded room for it. Apparently that was a mean thing to say. All I knew was that Stacey kept getting fatter and fatter, and uglier and uglier, then one day she peed all over the kitchen floor and everyone lost their marbles. She went to the hospital, and I said that was a stupid thing to do. Nobody went to the hospital because they peed their pants. Maybe the grounded room, but not a hospital.

Everyone was *so* mad at Stacey because she was getting fat. I wondered if that was why everyone was always getting mad at me? I better lay off the Little Debbies. Anyway, after she went to the hospital, everyone was happy. I think when she was in the hospital, she told the doctors she was sad she was getting fat, so they gave her a baby to make her feel happy again. She brought home this warm ball with banana yellow fuzz and just a bunch of pink skin. And you know what? It worked. Those doctors knew what they were talking about! That baby motivated her to lose like twenty pounds, and nobody was mad at her anymore (except for Rochelle). I kept meaning to ask Stacey how she lost the weight. Maybe I needed the doctors to give me a baby.

I think everyone liked Ambrosia, but I didn't. She screamed all the time, was always hungry, and she pooped her pants like every two hours. Ambrosia was called my "niece" because she was my sister's baby. They told me that I was her "aunt," but that she wouldn't be calling me that because we were too close in age. I didn't want her to call me that anyway. Why would I have wanted to be called a bug all the time? I mean, I don't know about you, but being called something ugly that gets squished under shoes every day was not exactly a good thing! If I had to go by Dennis, and I got to have a title, then I wanted it to at least be something cool. Like "Puppy Dennis."

I tucked myself into bed, and everyone was asleep by 8:30 p.m. Everyone but me, that was. I squinted through the dark to see if Rochelle was *really* sleeping. A wave of pain descended my back as I wrapped the covers up to my neck for extra protection. Who knew what she was going to do to me tonight for ratting her out in the restaurant? Mom still blamed me, but it was all the same to Rochelle. I had the bruises to prove she had already won, but knowing Rochelle, there would be more to come. On the bright side? I wasn't in the grounded room.

Feeling a tickle on my face, I scratched it, only to be met with a bunch of nasty-smelling foam. It was then I realized that I had been sleeping with my mouth open, and some of it had gone in my mouth. I spat it out immediately, thinking, "Yuck!" It smelled like olives and was disgustingly bitter. I lurched up and grabbed the door handle with my clean hand. Fumbling my way through the dark as quietly as possible, I slipped on my sneakers at the back door. Then I started the trek to our outdoor bathroom.

Going to wash my hands, I slid on something and grabbed the sink, barely catching myself from falling. Reaching for the light switch, I saw the words "DJ was here!" spray painted in a whitish-green foam on the dirty floor. My mom's bottle of shaving cream was empty in the trash bin. Oh no. Could I explain to Mom that it wasn't me, that Rochelle was setting me up because she was mad? There was a good chance she wouldn't believe me, and I didn't want to risk it. So I grabbed a bunch of toilet paper and wiped up the mess as best as I could. Then I flushed it down the toilet, praying it wouldn't clog and overflow.

Looking at the bathroom door, I considered going back to my room, but Rochelle was in there. I paced around the bathroom, wringing my hands before deciding there was only one thing to do.

I slept on the stained, lidless loo.

That was, until sometime in the middle of the night when the bathroom door slammed open, and Rochelle kicked the stall door in. I stood up and braced myself by pushing my arms against the sides of the stall, but she pushed me until my butt fell into the toilet, soaking my pajamas with germy toilet water. Cringing at the thought of it, I flailed my arms, trying to get momentum to heft myself out of the bowl. She slapped the now-closed stall door, and her footsteps and laughter faded away.

Dripping wet and sniffling, I inched out of the stall. When I went to shut it, I noticed a piece of paper flapped from the movement. It was small and covered with scrawled out chicken-scratch handwriting. Taped with ugly gray duct tape. I peeled it off and stared at the words, beads of water trickling to the floor. It read:

"Dear Turd,
You ratted me out, which we all know I
HATE. So give me your lunch today, and
maybe I'll stop picking on you. Snicker,
snicker! Did I really say that? I didn't mean
it. Give me your lunch or else.
—Rochelle."

I made my way inside and peeled off my wet clothes, pushing them into a pile on the floor and shoving them under my bed. After putting on a different pair of pajamas, I went to the kitchen and grabbed the brown paper sack that said "DJ" and took it back to my room where I placed it under Rochelle's bed. Hopping back under my covers, I wearily stared at the ceiling. *Maybe my friends will be able to help me.* Yeah, right. If I had friends. This town was filled with nothing but bullies, boys, grownups, and siblings. I hoped Monica would go to my school.

School. I didn't exactly have the best rep there. Last year I went there for preschool, and it did not go well. Everyone blamed me for everything. The *preschooler!* My teacher believed it, too! I was sure Monica Green would want to be best friends with a tambourine player who had two demerits and a total of five hours and twenty-five minutes taken out of my recess time. Ha! Good thing I was a kindergartener this year and a big girl. If Monica didn't know about those things, I should be fine. Right?

Chapter 4

"SIX THIRTY! First day of school, my favorite day!" my mom hollered as she walked through the house, getting ready as she went. "The best day of *all* the days! I am *tired* of you leeches!"

Everyone but Joe, Jillian, Josh, and I got up and got dressed. I snuggled up in the warmth of my blankets. The big kids had to go to school an hour earlier for the more "advanced" work. Nothing I'd seen them do had ever really seemed *that* hard, though. But I got to sleep in, so I was not complaining!

"Get up, DJ!" My mom flung open the door and flashed the lightswitch on. I screeched and pulled the covers up over my eyes. Was she trying to blind me? Even Shaye and *Rochelle* had the decency to get dressed in the dark. Her high heels clicked as she made her way over to my bed and ripped the covers clean off. I grabbed at them like my life depended on it. *My cozy warmness!* I'd never get back to sleep now.

"Nobody can take you to school today." She piled several bobby pins into her hair and patted it down, getting out her little makeup mirror to check and make sure she did it right.

Her hair was *huge.* It looked like a whole swarm of bees could live inside.

"Get up, take the bus, and wait an hour at the school, or walk. I don't care." She turned on one heel and in one fluid sweep walked out the door. How rude was she? She didn't even turn the lights off. I groaned and slid out of bed and onto the floor like the lazy lard that I was. If she "didn't care," then she should have turned the lights off. Or better yet, she shouldn't have come in at all. I would have gone back to sleep.

After I reluctantly got ready and shuffled into the death rays of the sun, I waved at Beans then got on the bus with kids packed like sardines in a can. There were barely any seats left, and don't even get me started on the noise. Who talked that loud in the *morning?* Purple streaks in hair, sports attire, facial hair. It was terrifying. Who were all these people? The bus started to move, and I jolted, grabbing onto the nearest seat and trying not to fall into some random guy's lap. Glancing over my shoulder, I gave the bus driver the stank eye and hoped he saw it through the little mirror he used to watch us. I held onto the seats as I went and saw some smirks. So I lifted a hand to wave and smiled.

"Hello, big kids."

They all stared at me like I was some kind of a creeper. Fire bloomed in my cheeks, so I quickly slid into an empty seat and slouched down. Zipping my hoodie up as far as it would go, I tucked my face into it.

The drive was short, and the bus came to a screeching halt outside the school, where Jellyfish Avenue met Sea Kelp Street. I didn't know what to do, so I waited for everyone else to get off. With students filing out one by one, I was suddenly the only person left. As I stood up, I grabbed my backpack and inched my way out, the bus driver judging my every move with his squinty eyes.

I followed the big kids into the building, but the mean principal strolled over to me immediately. There was only one classroom, and we all would be in there together. But because of "legal" reasons, he said that little kids weren't allowed in yet. He made me go outside and sit on the sidewalk, telling me to wait it out. I didn't know his name but he was *so* rude, and I hated him. One of these days he would regret making Dennis June Tipper sit outside.

A white car rolled to a stop in a parking spot near me, and I held a hand over my eyes to shade them from the sun. Our teacher, Mrs. Sanchez (the third) stumbled out, balancing a load of workbooks. I didn't know who Mrs. Sanchez the first was, and I never met Mrs. Sanchez the second. All I knew was there was a bunch of family drama.

"Deniese! What are you doing here?" she asked, shutting her car door and swinging her satchel. Mrs. Sanchez hated my mom, and my mom's name was Deniese.

I didn't want her to hate me too, so I told her, "Everyone else calls me Dennis; you can, too. Or DJ."

"Answer my question, Dennis June." Deep frown lines formed around her mouth.

I didn't know how old she was, but she was going to look like a prune if she didn't stop making that face. Whenever we made odd faces at home, my mom always scolded us by saying our faces would stick like that. "No one could drive me to school today, so I had to take the bus."

"Okay, whatever." She grabbed her key out of her pocket and passed me. I stood to follow, but she shut the door before I even turned around. I mean, she could have *let me in!*

Huffing, I flopped my backpack back down on the sidewalk. I read through the information packet they sent my mom about me because I was bored and had nothing else to do. It had big words on it, but it basically said she was paying a lot of money for me to go here. I didn't know why. Everyone thought this school was so fancy, but it was actually the worst! Why did people have to pay for school anyway? Nobody even wanted to go. Every time I was at school I just thought about how I wasn't even having a good time.

Maybe Mom sold kidney beans like the guy who got arrested on the news a few nights ago, and that was how she could afford for us to go to school here. It was beyond me why somebody would pay thousands of dollars for something you could buy at the grocery store for ninety-nine cents. Unless you went on a Tuesday. Then you could get them for seventy-five cents. I knew that because my mom went on "Discount Tuesdays," and that was when she bought her canned "Mystery Meet." Yes, m-e-e-t. Not meat.

As soon as they unlocked the door for the younger kids, I rushed into the building. When I got to the classroom, all the big kids were finishing up their advanced "morning work." Mrs. Sanchez was arguing with the brunette I saw walking to Monica's house yesterday. She had pushed her way in front of me to get in here first, and apparently she was asking if she could come early and sit in during the older kids' classes. She was smaller than me, with chicken legs. Let me just tell you something, sister, you *can't* come early. Mrs. Sanchez told her as much before she saw me and pointed to a seat. She then told me to sit in it. It was the second seat from the right in the first row. I wanted to sit in the back with the "cool kids," but apparently the back was only for the older children. On the bright side, if I was in the front row, at least I didn't have to stare at anyone's buttcrack! A flashback of pre-school entered my mind, when

I sat behind Mark Melon and had to stare at his buttcrack every day. Why'd he have to be such a scrawny kid and wear baggy clothes? Breaking out of my flashback, I looked around nervously to see if anyone looked like a "Monica."

"Dennis!" I turned and saw Rochelle near the back, shooting me an evil glare. "Where was the lunch?"

"I left it under your bed?" I asked with a frown, my chest tightening.

"No talking!" Mrs. Sanchez scolded, and I faced her and her eyes that were peeled on an attendance sheet.

The cutest boy ever, Tommy Waltzer, walked in. I smiled at him but he walked right past me, thinking he was too cool to talk to me because he was a pre-teen. He shook his sandy hair out of his eyes and took his assigned seat near the middle. I watched every single person that entered the room and waited. Just waited…until finally.

"Monica Green, you may sit over there." Mrs. Sanchez's tone was way more polite than the one she had used with me and the previous students.

Monica Green was beautiful. Her hair, the color of a fresh penny, went down to her waist. The sun streamed through the window, highlighting her pink satin shirt and creating a halo around her. Eyes the color of grass on a summer day brushed mine for half a second as she took in her surroundings, and I prayed that she would sit next to me so I could be rich and famous like her. But she sat on the other side of the room, with the twins that walked to her house that day. Some girl named Katrina Star sat by me, and I knew she was my cousin. With her long legs and tall stature, she had to have been a few years older than me. I hated her instantly. She stole that seat from Monica. She stole my hopes and dreams.

I sized her up. She was flawless. Porcelain skin and raven

black hair. Thin as a rail. Why couldn't I look like that? She saw me looking and frowned before scooting her chair as far away from me as possible. She hated me and thought I was ugly. I already knew it. My fingers got caught in my hair when I ran them through it, and I caught her staring at the rat's nest it was. We were going to be *enemies.* Papers rustled, and Mrs. Sanchez approached the chalkboard as I pulled out my doodle book and scribbled:

"Katrina? What kinda name is Katrina? You're better than her, Deniese! Katrina eats bugs? Nah. I need something better. I got it! K.E.R. It stands for Katrina Eats Raccoons!"

I drew a smiley face beside a big angry raccoon and grinned maliciously at my masterpiece. Until Mrs. Sanchez cracked her ruler on my desk.

"Deniese, since you intend to ignore everything I am teaching, would you care to share with the class?"

"Um, not really." Flames attacked my face. She made me stand up and proceeded to read what I wrote, out loud, to everyone. My heart raced, fearing I had just humiliated myself in front of everyone—including Monica. Katrina bursted into tears, but it sounded so fake. I got sent to the principal's office where I got a demerit and sentenced to detention after school.

I had detention with Rochelle and Stacey. Rochelle got a clothing violation for wearing a belly button shirt to school, and I honestly had no clue what Stacey got in trouble for. I could only assume it wasn't really her fault though. Stacey got blamed for everything, like me. Mrs. Sanchez didn't let us talk the entire time, but Rochelle kept chewing wads of gum and sticking them under her desk. She was so gross.

When we got home, Mom stormed into the living room, fuming mad.

"Where were you?" she demanded.

"Detention," responded Rochelle, snapping her gum and grinning.

"All of you?" My mother put both hands on her hips and frowned at us. "It's the first day of school, for crying out loud. Stacey, I have a real job, I'm not a babysitter. Go take care of Ambrosia. Rochelle, go to your room. DJ, ugh—" Mom didn't finish her thought before going upstairs, so I did the dishes to try to get on her good side. It didn't help.

"I did the dishes," I told her, peering into her room. Nobody dared step foot inside. Her TV blared with people yelling in Chinese and dramatic music. I didn't understand why she got to have her own TV, *or* why she always watched shows in a language she didn't speak.

"What do you want, a reward? Get out of my room," she snapped. She never even glanced in my direction, instead flipping her magazine pages. It was like she was desperately searching for answers. I padded down the hallway, hoping I hadn't ruined her mood for the rest of the day.

"I'm sorry. I know you hate it, but I just picked up the pom-poms, and it felt right. Not all cheerleaders are bad," Shaye said as I approached our bedroom.

"That is just *sick,*" Rochelle growled.

I tiptoed inside. Cheerleading equipment littered the floor. As I hefted the pom-poms into my own hands, I weighed them carefully. And you know what? They did feel just right.

"Save it. You're a good for nothing wanna-be. I'm going

29

out with the gang tonight." Rochelle turned around as if she sensed my presence behind her. Her eyes lowered to the pom-poms in my hands, and she barked out a laugh. "Bunch of sick traitors in this family. It's a shame really. You'll blend right in, Shaye. Dennis, you're going to have to get a heck of a lot prettier if *you* wanna pull the cheerleader act off." She scoffed and slammed the door on her way out.

My mom's scream jolted me awake, causing me to sit up in bed. I fell asleep thinking it was going to be a long wait until supper because she was so wrapped up in that magazine.

"I just got off the phone with the principle of your school."

Rage bubbled beneath my skin. I hated that mean old bald man. He made me sit on the sidewalk all morning.

"Why are you being mean to some poor girl named Katrina?" Deep creases indented her forehead, and she looked pained.

I almost laughed. This was *rich* coming from *her*. She was mean to everyone who didn't meet her approval all the time. She shouldn't be so upset over a small problem like this.

"Mrs. Sanchez says she's worried you are going to get into trouble like you did last year." She kept looking over her shoulder, like someone was coming to get her.

"Why are you acting so weird?" I asked.

"Excuse me?" Her eyes pinned mine down, and if looks could kill, I'd be dead right now. I swallowed in fear. I knew she could hear it. I expected her shoe to come off, for her to send me to the grounded room. But instead she sighed and said, "Whatever, I have your father to deal with... He did it again."

My heart sank to the ground, and my mouth went dry, an uncomfortable sweat washing over my whole body. "No." I let out a shaky breath.

"He knows I'm not happy with him from the phone call I had with him. He picked up another shift at work to avoid me today."

"Mom, you have to stop him," I blurted.

She nodded then glared at me, as if suddenly remembering I wasn't allowed to tell her what to do.

"Do we have to accept this?" I asked, biting my nails. She threw up her hands and turned to the door.

"There are no refunds. It's not like clothes or a toy you don't want."

I followed her downstairs and clung to the banister. Mom set her jaw and stared at the door, and my dad opened it as if on cue, grinning from ear to ear. He saw me, and his smile grew even wider—if that was humanly possible.

"DJ! I am so glad to see you. Just wait till you see what I brought you." He spoke like a gameshow host offering a million dollar prize.

"I know what it is, Dad, and I don't want it." I pouted.

He stepped aside and placed an arm gently around a small blond girl, ushering her in. She looked enough like us to blend in with no questions. "Deniese, set another plate at the table for Krissy here." He straightened his spine to make himself look bigger. I didn't know if it was because he was proud of himself or if he was scared of my mother.

The young girl smiled and looked around our house wide-eyed.

My mom looked at him and frowned, then turned her gaze to the little girl. She huffed, "Fine. I suppose I can arrange one more plate. But *no* more, Dude. I mean it." She shook her head and delivered the message like it was a threat.

He paused as if he was considering her words. "I cannot promise that," he finally decided.

"How could you adopt *another* kid when we already have *fifteen?*" Mom's voice was practically dripping with poison. Tonight was going to be horrid. For *everybody.*

"I love kids, and you are *so* good at taking care of them," he said calmly.

My eyes nearly fell out of my skull. So did my mom's.

"No, I am not! And I certainly don't want *any* more. I never even wanted a single child. This is all you."

"But look at how cute she is," he offered.

My mom refused to look at her, as did I.

"No more." She pointed a finger at him then stormed off.

"Okay, you have my word," he called after her. But his fingers were crossed behind his back.

I narrowed my eyes at him.

"Deniese June, why don't you show Krissy where the nursery is?" He turned to me with a smile, and I didn't move. So he pleaded with praying hands and a childish pouty face.

"Follow me," I told Krissy, and spun on my heel. I climbed the steps, my legs like heavy weights. Having just climbed down these, I was *tired!*

"How old are you?" I asked at the top of the steps.

"Four," she squeaked. "Are we going to be in the same room?"

"No." I stopped and turned to look at her. My life was bad enough. I wanted to fit in with the older kids and with Monica, who was my age. I didn't need a baby following me around. I wasn't very good at math, but if I was her friend, it would probably drop my coolness by at least ten points out of one hundred. That was like more than half!

"I'm five. I sleep in a big kid room," I told her. She frowned. We reached the nursery.

"This is it."

She stared at the door and rocked on her heels a little bit before folding her arms across her chest. "Come with me."

"No." I considered what to say next since she clearly wanted to know why. "That's a baby room."

What if my mom saw me hanging around her and made me go back in there? I hated Rochelle, but I didn't want to be thought of as a baby.

"You're mean." She pouted and opened the door. Guilt coursed through me like toxic sludge, and I decided I would go with her. But she slipped inside and slammed the door in my face before I had a chance to.

Turning on my heel and making yet *another* trek down the steps, I sank into the couch. After a half hour, I went to the kitchen, where bowls and trash littered every counter *and* the sink. The fridge door was left open, and it reeked of moldy cheese. I pinched my nose before I shut the fridge and called for my mom. She didn't answer. Following the chaotic sounds of screaming kids, I found my family outside. Seated at the custom-made picnic table, my parents and most of my siblings had already begun digging into the meal. If you didn't eat fast in my family, you didn't eat at all.

"What's for dinner?" I asked, squeezing myself between Josh and Tearston. Josh smashed his hand into his food with a disgusting sounding squish that sent my skin crawling. He smeared it all around his plate, and I waited for my mom to go on a rant about being "wasteful" and how "there were thousands of starving children in Africa." But she didn't.

"Mystery Meet, now have a seat," hollered my mom brashly. She didn't make eye contact with me, but she smirked to herself. Such talk was considered "stupid" if it came from anyone but herself. But if she came up with it, she was convinced she deserved a Nobel Prize or something. I rolled my eyes and frowned at the slimy brown meet sitting in a huge glass pan. I had to lean so far my belly was on the table top, but I grabbed the spoon and flopped some slimy gravy "meet" onto my plate.

"In all my readings, meat is spelled with an 'ea', not two 'e's," I spoke up.

"What readings?" snorted Brad. "You can't read."

"I can so!"

He narrowed his eyes at me. "Quit being a liar, Dennis." His disgusted glare was like daggers going through me, and I hated him even more than usual. He stabbed his meal with his fork.

My mom smiled widely at him and said, "Don't let it trouble you. Dennis lives in her own fantasy world. She probably believes she can read."

It sickened me to my core how much she loved Brad. I got nothing but hatred from her, as did most of us. But Brad was her angel. Her golden boy. In her eyes, he could do no wrong.

"This is gross," Ashley chimed in. "Is this really spelled with two 'e's'?"

"Ew! It is?" asked Shaye.

"What kind of meat is it, really? Is it fish? Beef?" My dad poked at his serving, and it jiggled like jello, the sight of it curdling my stomach. There was a muffled stomping sound, and my dad straightened in his seat, a pained expression crossing his face. I bet my mom shoved her heel into his shoe. That's what she did when she was mad at him but didn't want people to see. She'd always get back at him under the table.

"Shut up," my mom scolded, before turning and throwing a threatening glance in my direction.

I looked down at my plate and kept my eyes there, trying my best to crawl into my invisible shell. My siblings' voices flooded my eardrums as they all broke out into disgusted retaliation at what was apparently new information, even though they'd been eating it for years with no issues. *Am I the only person who reads the labels on food?* I kept quiet, knowing I had started this war, and hoped my mom would forget that part.

"Eat it!" my mom demanded. "Or don't eat at all!"

"Whatever, whatever, whatever!" yelled Orange.

"Orange, please use real words, honey. We can't understand you." My dad gaped at her before failing miserably to wipe the slimy gravy from his beard with a napkin.

I bet that thing was full of germs! It was more of a rat's nest than my hair.

"Go to bed, you dirtbags. It's my money. This is *my* house." My mom stabbed a finger against her ginormous chest. "I will serve what I want!"

My siblings jumped up chaotically and headed for the house like a swarm of termites flocking to wood. Even Krissy, despite being new here. Something about Mom's voice always sparked fear. Fighting back my nausea, I picked up my spoon and shoveled a huge glob into my mouth, not even bothering to chew before I swallowed—it kept me from tasting it. I scampered off the bench, trying not to trip over my shaking legs. On that note, I headed directly for my room.

"Great, now we have to go to bed because this idiot can't keep her mouth shut," Rochelle snarled at me when I entered our bedroom.

"It's pretty late anyway." Shaye offered me a small, pitying smile.

"Uh, no it's not."

"It's after dinner," I whispered. "That's late."

"Three a.m. is late. You're such a baby Dennis." Rochelle climbed into her bed and chucked all of her covers onto the floor. Probably just to make a mess.

"It's okay, DJ. I need the extra sleep." Shaye grabbed her pajamas and headed for the bathroom.

"Can you stop by the pigpen and tell him goodnight for me?" I asked.

"The pig?" Shaye asked. I didn't want to say his secret name.

"Yes."

"Why?" Rochelle demanded. I kept my attention on Shaye. I wasn't talking to Rochelle.

"I forgot. Something bad might happen if he doesn't know I said 'goodnight'."

"You're a freak," Rochelle snarled.

"Will you do it?" I pleaded with Shaye. "It would kill me if he died."

"He'll *die* if you don't say 'goodnight'?" Rochelle scoffed.

"He *could!*"

"Sure. I'll tell him." Shaye gave me a sad smile and turned the doorknob.

"Stop pitying her, you traitor," Rochelle growled. "We oughta put her in the nursery and let that new kid stay with us."

My stomach heaved as I crawled into bed. This was exactly what I was afraid of. I wrapped myself up in my covers extra tight. I didn't know what time it was when I finally began to drift off, but I was just getting into a deep sleep when my mom slammed our door open.

"It's not true!" my mom's voice bellowed through the darkness. "Now go to bed!"

Rochelle was so silent I thought she was dead until she snored. Shaye and I, however, were upright, and I was sweaty, my heart racing.

"What?" I let out through gasping breaths.

My mom flicked the light on and looked around. "Oh. Wrong room. Sorry."

I rubbed my eyes to make the spots go away before exchanging a nervous glance with Shaye. Mom left, closing the door behind her, and Rochelle reached under her bed and chucked a shoe across the room. It hit the wall with a *thud*.

"Turn that light off, I'm trying to sleep here."

Shaye got out of bed and padded over to the lightswitch. How did my mom's screaming not wake Rochelle but the light did? What a freak. I rolled back over and tried to sleep.

The following morning was a Saturday. I enjoyed not having to get ready for school and was planning on sleeping in, but last night still freaked me out. Shaye was already up, preparing to do her chores. I stopped her before she left and whisper-yelled, "Psst!" at Rochelle.

"What the heck do you want from me?" she groaned, rolling over and flinging her legs over the side of the bed. She sat there but didn't budge to stand up.

"Do you guys know why Mom came in here last night? Why was she saying things 'weren't true' ?" I leaned forward in my bed, all ears.

"She was probably just sleepwalking again." Shaye shrugged and left.

"You woke me up for this crap?" asked Rochelle, wrinkling her eyebrows.

"Do you know any secrets about Mom? Or why she

sleepwalks?"

"Ha! I know a *lot* of secrets about Mom. She sleepwalks every time a new kid is added to the family."

I paused, thinking. "That's weird."

"Yeah, well it's probably pretty traumatizing for someone who hates kids to be surrounded by them twenty-four seven. Especially when new ones keep crawling out of the woodwork. She didn't even *birth* this one." She shoved her feet into a pair of slippers, and I did a double take.

"Uh, whose slippers are those? 'Cause they ain't yours." I frowned at them, trying to remember where I had seen them.

Rochelle looked down at her feet. "Oh no. I'm in for it."

"What?"

"These are *Mom's* slippers," she told me. Then she threw them at me, and I jerked as they hit me.

"I don't want them!" I stepped back from them like they were a poisonous snake. She ran to the other side of the room and stood on top of Shaye's mattress. I picked up the slippers and chucked them at her feet.

"Take them back!" she hissed.

"I ain't taking those! I don't want to die!"

Rochelle picked up the slippers and muttered, "Follow me."

Did Rochelle seriously just invite me to go somewhere with her? A voice inside my head told me not to, but my curiosity got the better of me, and I followed her down the steps and outside, around to the backyard. She approached our neighbor's fence and said, "Watch this."

My gaze followed the slippers until they were up and over the side, where they lightly thudded to the ground.

"Run," she said.

"What?"

"Just do it." Boy did she run fast.

I shouldn't have trusted her, but I followed her around the back of the house. She was too ahead of me, and I lost her. The door slammed open though, so I knew she went into the house. *Smart,* I thought. So I did the same. Out of breath, I made my way to the living room and flopped down onto a seat, cringing at the crunchy sound of potato chips. Gross! *Really?* Who *does* that?

A few minutes later the doorbell rang. My heart stopped, but I didn't know why. Something told me this was not going to be good. It rang a few more times. Even though it made the same sound, it somehow grew angrier and angrier with each *ding*.

"Is *anyone* going to get that? Ugh!" My mom flopped sluggishly down the steps, her hair a mess and no makeup on. It was so unlike her.

"Hello?" she asked groggily, reaching the door and flinging it open.

"Deniese. How many times have I told you now? Keep your crap out of my yard!" a woman snapped, and my mom's slippers hit her feet. My mom's frown was audible. Not because of her slippers, but because of who it was.

Alissa Waltzer—Tommy and Timmy's mother, was about my mom's age. My mom had declared her to be her mortal enemy. Every time she saw her out and about, she went on and on to me and anyone else who would listen about how she had stolen everything from her. In reality, she had only stolen one thing: Bob Waltzer. If it wasn't ironic enough, Bob Waltzer was my *dad's* worst enemy. They competed with each other over everything. Even their wives.

Bob dated my mom way before I was born, and my dad said they met because he stole her away from him. My parents tried to make this story sound cute, but it really wasn't. My dad regretted being with my mom. I could tell by how much he favored practically any other woman that he didn't want to be with her. The real truth? He only dated my mom to beat Bob, and now that "win" was a loss. Alissa was rich and hated our family because we were "slums," whatever that meant. I hadn't looked it up yet. Creeping closer to the two of them, I eavesdropped on their conversation.

"I'm telling you, I didn't put anything in your yard."

"Are these or are these not your slippers?" Alissa unfolded her arms and pointed toward my mother's feet.

"They are."

"And your explanation?"

"I don't have one." Mom shrugged.

Alissa peered over my mom's shoulders, and her eyes met mine. I ducked down immediately, but it was too late.

"You might want to ask one of your heathens then. I'm sure my sister enjoyed meeting all of them. Normally I would have thrown a bonfire and chucked those ratty slippers of yours right in there, but I feel generous today."

The length of my mom's pause made me uncomfortable, then she said, "What are you talking about?"

"Which part?"

"Your sister. I'm sure I hate her as much as I hate you." Mom snorted.

"Oh, Megan? Megan *Green?* Yeah. She's my half-sister. I saw how fake you were acting to impress her, and, honestly, it was just embarrassing."

A hint of blush flooded my mother's cheeks. "Get off my property," she hissed through gritted teeth.

"My money's on *that* one by the way." Alissa smirked, pointing an accusing finger at me before turning and walking back to her house. My mother shut the door, and I tiptoed to the stairs, my white knuckles clinging to the banister.

"Did you touch my slippers, Dennis?"

I froze, and the words seemed to linger in the air for an eternity. "I did not." This was kind of a lie, but also not. *I* didn't throw them over the fence!

"Then who did?"

"Um, I don't know," I stammered.

"Rochelle!" my mom hollered threateningly, and Rochelle came clodhopping out of the kitchen.

"Yah?"

"Did Dennis touch my slippers?"

"I believe she did, Mother." Rochelle painted as serious of an expression as she could muster onto her lying face.

"What?" I shrieked. Heat bubbled inside of me, and the anger was about to spill out everywhere. I tried to take deep breaths.

"You are in big trouble, missy." My mom clucked her tongue as she looked down at her slippers, sliding her feet into them.

"But I had nothing to do with your slippers!" I whined.

"I have to get food before I deal with you. I'm running on a cup of stagnant coffee and zero sleep. Don't move from this spot."

Rochelle stuck her tongue out at me and crossed the floor, beginning to climb the steps.

"Don't you move either, Rochelle!" my mom hollered from the kitchen.

Rochelle stopped dead still and muttered, "Does she have eyes in the back of her head? How can she see me if she's not even out here?"

My mom returned reluctantly.

"What's that?" I asked.

"A burrito."

"Where's it from?" It smelled heavenly of seasoned meat and nacho cheese.

"I honestly have no idea." She shoved about half of it in her mouth and started chewing. She swallowed before spitting, "Is this because that Katrina kid was riding her bike with Tommy yesterday?"

"Huh?" I managed to reply.

"You like that boy, right? You hate that girl. Did ya throw my slippers in his mom's yard to stir the pot?" She took another bite and chewed with her mouth wide open. The sloshing noise made my toes curl in agony.

"You like Tommy Waltzer?" Rochelle snickered. "That is rich!"

I shoved Rochelle, and she shoved me back. I fumbled backward on a few steps before catching my balance and stopping at the end. Rochelle followed me down and grabbed one of my ears, jerking me back toward her.

"Girls!" my mom yelled. We kept slapping and kicking each other. New bruises began forming over the ones that were fading. Rochelle snickered like nothing I tried inflicted any pain on her.

"Stop hitting me!" I bellowed.

"Stop being an idiot!" she yelled back.

"Well, this is so much better than a movie. I can't believe the ignoramuses that actually pay for this entertainment when it's right in your own house," my mom muttered. I didn't know if she was being serious or sarcastic.

Rochelle slapped me upside the head, and I grabbed my left ear. Finally having enough, my mom let out a groan and intervened. She wedged herself between us, pushing us each to a different side. With all the hands flying about, her burrito escaped her grasp and hit the floor with a wet slap.

"Girls! Rochelle Frogster Marie Tipper! Dennis June! I am trying to eat my burrito—for crying out loud!" Letting out a huff, my mom stared at the wasted burrito, and we got going again.

"Yeah, Frogster Marie!" I mocked, sticking out my tongue. Frogster. Wow. My mom must have been drunk when she named her. Yowza!

"Like Dennis June is so much better!" Rochelle shot back.

I raised my nose snootily. "My name's not really Dennis."

"It's not?" asked my mom, looking away from the burrito and smirking. Rochelle laughed, but the look my mom shot her implied that my mom was the only person who was allowed to think that was funny. She told us to "shut our holes," and Rochelle was sent to clean Beans's pen. I had to clean up the half-eaten burrito. The way I saw it, we both were cleaning up after pigs!

Chapter 5

IT WAS TEN THIRTY p.m. on a Tuesday night, and everyone was sleeping. I kept my eyes peeled in the darkness as I waited for Rochelle to make her escape. Rochelle snuck out almost every Tuesday around this time. She finally reached under her bed and started cramming her feet into her untied sneakers.

"What are you doing?" I asked.

She let out an "Ooomph!" sound as she dropped her body to the floor.

"I know you're sneaking out," I told her.

"How'd you know?"

"You do it every Tuesday. But the question is...where do you go?"

Her shadowed figure rose off the floor. "Uh...I go to the, uh, Taco Bell. I grab all of them fifty cent burritos, so I can um..." She paused like she had to think about it. "Hide them in peoples' lockers at school and create the rottenest stench ever. Yeah. That's what I do."

"Really?" I asked.

Her smile faded. "Yeah. Really. Gonna put one in Sanchez's desk, Katrina's locker, and Stacey's locker. I was going to put one in yours too, but now you know. So I can't." She scratched her head.

"Oh, I see. I think." She was so weird.

"Isn't it awesome?"

"No, it's mean!"

"Shh!" she hissed. "You're going to wake Shaye up. Do you want one in yours, too?"

"No!" I exclaimed.

She glared at me.

"No," I whispered, quieter this time. I lay back down in bed and let her go. She wasn't going to put a burrito in my locker, and she told me a secret. Thinking about that as I went to sleep, I actually smiled for once.

The following morning, I walked into the classroom, beating most of the younger kids there. Rochelle glanced up from her desk and nodded at me. I nodded back and waved, but when I did, Mrs. Sanchez thought it was meant for her. As she walked up the aisle of students, she said, "Top of the morning to you, too, Dennis!"

Everyone laughed, and my cheeks grew redder and redder. Mrs. Sanchez stopped at Boop Dawson's desk to help him finish up his "advanced" older kid work.

I'd always wondered if that was his real name. I'd never heard him called anything else.

Reaching in my backpack, I used this time to put a note on Monica's desk. I wrote it this morning. It was one of those ones that asked if she wanted to come to my house tonight to play, then said to circle "yes" or "no." When Monica finally got to school, I saw her pick up the piece of paper. She squinted at the words, and her mouth moved, but she frowned and rubbed her forehead. Flipping the paper upside down, she moved her scrunched up eyes over it again. *What was she doing?* Finally, she stood and threw my note in the trash. My heart sank.

I was depressed over my failure and scribbled other notes to give her to try again. But I kept crossing everything out. If she threw my first note in the trash, she obviously didn't like me. Tears welled in my eyes, so I kept doodling and tuning out Mrs. Sanchez. She was going over the alphabet with us younger kids, and I had already finished my paper forever ago. Who *didn't* know the alphabet?

"What's this?" asked Mrs. Sanchez. "Where's your worksheet?"

"I already did it," I muttered, not bothering to look up.

"Are you passing notes?" she asked, suspicion dripping from her tongue.

"No."

"You're lying, so you're not getting any recess today, young lady."

"But, Mrs. Sanchez!" I whined, looking up. Bags the size of Texas hung beneath her eyeballs.

"Stop whining! Or do you want a demerit too?" She huffed a breath to blow away a messy blond curl.

"No, Mrs. Sanchez." I turned my gaze back to the baby alphabet work and stared at it even though there was nothing more to do. Why was I being punished for finishing it *early?*

The whole school day just ended up being horrible. As much as I hated exercise, I walked home to avoid further humiliation on the bus.

It started to downpour, and a semi driver floored past me, spraying me from head to toe with muddy water. My worn overalls were drenched, and even though it was hot and muggy, I shivered. Gripping my backpack straps so tight my fingernails cut into my palms, I finished my walk home. The rain finally let up by the time I got home and found the door locked, which we rarely did. I knocked and waited for what felt like a billion years.

"Dennis!" gasped my mother upon opening the door. She ushered me inside. "What happened to your *good* clothes? Why are you so late?" If I wasn't so upset about all the other horrible things that happened today, I may have actually laughed. How on earth would my grass and bleach stained hand-me-downs be considered "good clothes"?

"It started raining real hard, and a semi splashed me."

"What?"

"I walked home," I told her, answering her second question.

"Well, that was stupid."

Yeah, no duh. I held in an overwhelming desire to roll my eyes.

"I have half a mind to send you straight to bed."

"But it's only four o'clock—" I crumpled my face up.

"Four o'clock? Go milk ol' Bessie!" she demanded, and flung an arm up before letting it slap to her curvy thigh.

"It's not my turn. It's—" I thought and counted on my fingers. Of course. "Brad's." Her favorite child. My heart sank for the millionth time.

"Brad?" my mom asked, turning to the couch where he was slouched like a potato.

"Yeah?" he asked, not bothering to look up from the television set. He stuffed cheese puffs into his face, and I just stood there, wondering when we got the money to buy cheese puffs. Better yet, why was he the only one getting to eat them?

"Is it your turn to milk Bessie?" asked my mom.

"No, it's Dennis's."

"It is not!" I blurted. I kept shifting my gaze between the two of them, waiting for my mom to tell him to get up and

47

move his lazy butt. But instead…

"You heard the boy," she said. "Move it."

"He's lying!"

"Dennis is lying!" His eyes remained peeled to whatever trash he was watching—a bunch of women bouncing around in bikinis. Disgusting.

"You cannot be serious," I muttered.

"Are you talking back to me?" A hand went to her hip as she narrowed her eyes.

"No." I dropped my backpack and went outside with the rusty pail.

Afterwards, I began my homework on the floor of my room. I pulled out the sheet on "writing your name five times" and let out an annoyed sigh. This was dumb. I wanted to read a book. Not write "Deniese June" every day for the rest of the year.

Rochelle's foot dug into my hip. "What are you doing?" she asked.

"Homework." I didn't look up at her. She was probably just looking to start another fight.

"Good. You can do mine, too," she told me.

I cringed. "I can't do math."

"It's not math. It's English."

My heart skipped a beat at the mention of my favorite subject, but I ignored it.

"Why would I do your homework?" My yawn threatened to turn into a groan. I was sick of being used.

"Because you have to."

"No, I don't." I put my completed work back in my pack and folded my arms.

"It's payback time."

"For what?" I barked out a laugh.

She kicked me again. "What did you say?" She squatted,

so we were at eye level, and I cowered.

"Fine, what's the assignment?"

"We have to write a paragraph about our favorite book." She grinned maliciously.

"What's your favorite book?" I asked.

"I don't have one."

"How can you not have one?"

"I don't read." She glared at me.

"Right." How silly of me to think she bothered herself with such frivolous things!

"Excuse me?"

"I mean 'fine'. I can write about *Pippi Longstocking,* but that's the biggest book I've read."

"Sounds dumb, but Sanch will probably like it." She slapped me on the shoulder. "Sanch" was what the big kids nicknamed Mrs. Sanchez. I wanted to call her that. I made a mental note to do so someday.

A loud thud sounded, and we both turned toward the hall. I sprung up to investigate and found Orange lying at the bottom of the stairs.

"Orange! Are you okay?" I hollered, flying down the steps as fast as my oversized feet could take me. I stubbed my big toe on a loose floorboard and cried out, "Hot tamales!" The blinding white pain seared through me like a knife! *Why did nobody fix that?*

"Grandfather?" Orange asked dramatically, staring at our ceiling. "Is that you?"

"You can *talk?*" I blurted, my eyes widening to the size of saucers. My big toe throbbed, so I remained where I was. "Wait," I said, pausing, "do we *have* a grandfather?"

"What's going on?" asked my mom, storming to the bottom of the staircase.

"Orange fell down the stairs!" I pointed. "And she can

talk! She said something about our grandfather!"

"You don't have a grandfather," my mom bluntly replied, bending down and asking if Orange was okay.

"Whatever, whatever, whatever!" Orange cried, a hand draped over her forehead.

"Save it, I know you can speak English," my mom told her. "And frankly, I think that you teenagers are stupid with that talk."

Orange scrambled to her feet, and muttered, "Whatever," before she stomped up the stairs. Her door slammed. My mom set her jaw and clenched a fist. I clung to the railing and sucked my stomach in as she stomped up the stairs just like Orange had. Nobody wanted to stand in my mother's path when she was angry. I stared up the stairway, wondering if Orange was getting cracked for slamming her bedroom door. Not that she'd ever tell anyone.

That weekend, when I stepped out into the road to kick rocks around, I got run over by a car. Okay, so nobody really believed my wording and said I was exaggerating. Maybe I was, but the car definitely made contact, and it was *my* story. So if I wanted to say I got run over, then I got run over. I screamed when I saw the car coming, thinking, "Today's the day." I was going to die at the hand of some crappy driver in a sloppy jalopy while my mom stood on the porch and *watched.* This was my fate, the death of DJ Tipper. ~~Nobody would care.~~ Okay, maybe Beans would.

"That was epic!" Rochelle yelled.

I grabbed my hip where the driver had nicked me and lifted my shirt. A black mark smudged my clothes, but nothing appeared on my skin...*yet.*

"That's just like the monster trucks on TV. Total ten out of ten. Don't you think, Ma?" Rochelle laughed, nudging my mom's elbow.

My head swirled, and I stumbled to catch my balance as my mother's reply rang in my already ringing eardrums: "Eh, I give it a seven."

The car's tires screeched and stopped a few feet ahead. Some of my other siblings had come outside to see what the commotion was about.

"Make a U-ie! Make a U-ie!" Rochelle started chanting, and Brad joined her.

"What is *wrong* with you freaks?" I screamed from the middle of the road. This was an outrage! The car did in fact swing a U-ie, so I grabbed my pounding heart and squeezed my eyes shut as tight as I could get them. I just froze. What kind of an idiot stood in the middle of the road and didn't move when a car was coming? I wanted to run, but I couldn't. It was like my feet were stuck in thick, wet tar. The car screeched to a halt in front of me.

When I realized the car wasn't going to hit me again, I forced my eyes back open. The driver's door popped open, and a woman with sunglasses and wild curly brown hair climbed out.

"Guess who just got out of prison?" she sang. Her black tank top clung to her skinny body as she moved toward our house. Brad and a few others ran inside at the mention of "prison," but Rochelle chuckled and loitered around. I was trying to pull myself back together enough to make it to the sidewalk.

"Me too!" my mom hollered back at the woman, who had left her car in the middle of the road with its door open. Lucky for her, we didn't have much traffic through here, but *still*. My legs were jello as I stumbled closer.

"Are you pregnant again or are you just getting fatter?" the woman asked my mom flatly.

I fell into the grass and felt sick. Partly because of everything that just happened and partly from pure shock. Was I about to witness a murder? *Nobody* talked to my mother like that. But my mom just shrugged at the comment. "I don't know. Could be both."

"What?" I whimpered. Nobody heard me. Who was this for my mom to let that just *slide?* My writhing stomach threatened to plunge up out of my throat, and I dry heaved.

"Who's the father?" the lady had the nerve to ask. She leaned toward Mom like she had a right to this information.

"Dude, of course!" My mom gasped and glared at her. But then she crumped her face, shrugged, and decided, "Eh, could be Bob Waltzer."

"Excuse me! Does anyone care that she just *ran over me?"* I yelled, pointing.

Both of them turned in my direction, and the lady said, "Shut up, Dennis. I was using you for target practice."

"What?" I feared for my life. How did this criminal know my name? And I was her *target?*

Then she chuckled and took off her sunglasses before crouching threateningly. "What's the matter? Don't recognize me?"

My blood went cold. I did recognize her.

My grandmother was Beverly Hill. Yes, that was her *real* name. Hating pretty much everyone but herself, she *especially* loathed children. Probably even *more* than my mom did. She liked to harass people with her cane that she didn't even need. Wonder where it was today?

She rose.

"Let's go hang out with some people at a club or something," she muttered to my mom, trying to muffle her words, so I couldn't hear.

"Better yet, guess who's in town?"

"Who? You know I hate surprises." She wrinkled her face, then frowned. "Like *you* were, example A."

My mom gasped and slapped her shoulder. "Your other daughter, Marti."

"How?" Beverly's eyes looked like they were searching for gold. She gripped my mother's arm.

"She moved here," my mom explained.

I didn't think her residence required an explanation and wondered if my grandma had been drinking beer like my mom did sometimes.

"Is Bev here? Did she make it?" a sense of urgency filled Grandma's voice.

"Uh, hello?" I rolled my eyes. Why didn't anybody care that she hit me with a car?

"Be quiet, DJ." My mom waved a dismissive hand.

"Did she also jump the border?" Grandma asked, her wild curls flopping and her eyes going all crazy looking.

"Mom, enough about Bev," my mom whispered, but Beverly was determined. She ignored Mom's comment and continued her tangent.

"Okay, I will have to find a way to secretly contact her and get her an escape to freedom."

I thought back on the last time my grandma came to visit. My mom prepared us all in advance, saying she had something wrong with her brain. I think she said it was similar to a split personality disorder. Apparently, she switched between Beverly (her real self) and "Bev" (her imaginary self), but she claimed Bev was a real person and that they were friends. All I knew was she told me she was Beverly one day, and then the next day she introduced herself to me again, but as "Bev," acting like she never saw me in her whole life. She talked about herself in third person all the time. It was all really confusing to me, but my mom preferred to switch between telling her she's crazy, and just "going along with it."

"Why don't you just lay low so you don't go back to jail?" My mom patted her on the shoulder in a patronizing way.

"We may have to use you as bait." Grandma continued to scheme, her wild eyes staring at nothing.

"Mother," my mom hissed, "use the little one instead. You know, Dennis." She nodded in my direction.

"Mom, I can hear you!" I gasped. Was she being serious?

She smirked, like this was a game. "Dennis, you would really be helping your grandma out and, well. Better you than me."

"What if I go to jail?" I didn't know what they were planning on doing to free a "Bev" who didn't exist, but I did *not* want to go to jail. My mom said it had rats and everyone had to pee in a toilet in the middle of the room.

"Then that would be one less kid on my hands to worry about." Mom laughed.

I was sweating through my shirt, and fiddled with my hands.

"I'm pulling your leg," she finally clarified, but she could have said that much sooner if you asked me.

"Speak of the devil. There she is, coming from her *castle.*" Mom rolled her eyes.

Two people walked up the sidewalk, and upon squinting, I learned one of them was Katrina. Puke!

"Hello, Mother. Deniese," said a woman who looked *just* like Katrina but older. Much older.

"Shut your face, Marti," my mom huffed. Marti blinked her beautiful big doe eyes, dumbfounded. They were the color of a rich sapphire. *Fitting.*

"Whoa, Sally! Is that *your* house?" gasped Beverly,

pointing at the classy white with gold trim, vintage, Victorian manor. Flowers of every color of the rainbow spattered the antique place's landscape, bringing its pristine ancientness to life.

"Why, Deniese. I am so sorry if I am intruding. Yes, that's my house, Mother. I didn't know you'd be here! I saw a car in the middle of the road and got concerned." She brushed her sleek black hair behind a dainty little ear.

"Did you bring me a homecoming gift?" asked Beverly, eyeing Marti's hands. They were empty. My mom gave her a dirty look, probably as confused as I was about her "homecoming."

Katrina glanced in my direction, so I stared at the grass.

Marti's porcelain skin blushed. "No, I'm sorry, I didn't expect to see you." Her voice was soft and soothing. How was she my mom's *sister?* She looked nothing like her, and her voice clashed horribly with my mother's brash outbursts.

"You could've at least brought me a gift though. You're clearly rich enough." Grandma rolled her eyes back to the mansion and smiled. "Well, at least one of my daughters turned out right, anyway."

My mom scoffed and shook her head.

"This one can't seem to figure out how to use birth control!" Grandma motioned a thumb over her shoulder to point at my mom. What was she talking about?

Marti blushed. "I have plenty of children, too. I sent you announcements for each of their births."

"I don't care about that kinda crap. Fishing for money and compliments if ya ask me." Her face was pinched.

"That's why I didn't tell you about mine," my mom piped up, brightly.

"Ha! Like you could have afforded to pay for all of the stamps!"

Marti looked between my mom and my grandma hesitantly. But Katrina grinned at the drama before directing her attention back to me. I scooted out of her view.

"DJ," Katrina whispered, stepping behind her mom's back. I didn't answer her.

"Come here." She coaxed me with a finger.

I stood, hesitant, at first. But my curiosity got the better of me, and we stepped a few feet away from the adults.

"Do you live here?" She wrinkled her nose like it was a pigsty.

Speaking of pigs...

"Ew, is that a *pig?*" Her eyes widened, and I followed their gaze to where the little cutie was rolling around in the mud.

I'd never had an urge to smack someone with a shovel. But I did that day.

I think she was happy that I lived dirt poor, and somehow she managed to drag Beans into it like the two were related.

"What's it to you?" I asked, fully aware of how rude I sounded. I assumed she knew I wasn't going to give her the satisfaction of a direct answer, because she changed the subject.

"I heard we are getting a big project, and all the grades will be working together for it at school."

"Really?" I took a step closer. I wanted to know everything about everything.

"I wanted to make sure things were cool between us in case we are partners." That was at least partially a lie. She hated me, so she wouldn't want to make things "cool." And did she not just ask me if I lived here? If she didn't know, she clearly wasn't expecting to see me. Or she did know and just wanted to rub salt in my wounds.

"I doubt we will be partners." I would never pick her as

my partner in a million years.

"Sanchez is *picking* partners. Must be some project."

The adults broke away from one another, and Marti was ready for Katrina to follow her home.

"See ya later, Dennis." Her smile looked more like an evil snake's sneer.

I faked a smile back as she returned to her house with her mom. Things were definitely *not* cool between us.

Chapter 6

STUMBLING TO MY SEAT with half closed eyes, I had nearly forgotten the events of this past weekend. When movement flashed outside the window and Rochelle climbed in, I jolted awake. I winced as the pain from the car incident hit me all at once. I had a purple bruise forming on my hip, real nasty-like. It added to my collection of old yellowish ones.

"I made it! No tardy violation for me, Sanch!" Rochelle blurted, stumbling over the tops of desks.

"Doors exist for a reason, Rochelle. And actually, you missed all of your morning classes. You will be in detention after school. Congratulations." Mrs. Sanchez did not sound like she was in a good mood this morning.

"Um, Sanch?" I asked, turning toward the back of the classroom where she was passing out papers, and raised my hand.

"Yes, Dennis?" She frowned at me. I didn't know if it was because I called her "Sanch" or because she was already irritated.

"I heard we are getting a huge partner project."

Katrina glanced in my direction, all traces of her smiles

from this weekend gone.

"Well, whoever told you that must hate you because they lied right to your face."

Correction. Mrs. Sanchez was *definitely* not in a good mood this morning. I let out an angry huff and frowned at Katrina, who refused to make eye contact with me. Her cheeks reddened.

"So, no project?" I asked, refusing to take my gaze away from Katrina.

"No, there will be a project. But it's groups, not partners."

"How many people?" I asked.

She sighed. "Four or five."

"I would like to work with Mon—"

Mrs. Sanchez cut me off, "Can you let me do my job, Deniese?"

"I'm sorry Mrs. Sanch—"

"Groups! I will be picking them." She paced to the front of the classroom and sat down at her desk. A loud fart sounded, and Mark Melon busted out laughing. Mrs. Sanchez pulled a whoopie cushion out from under her and chucked it in the trash. She didn't crack a smile *or* frown. She wasn't playing games today. Taking a deep breath, she began reading names off a paper. As I listened, I grew irritated when she read Monica's name and mine didn't follow. Especially when not just Haylee and Hallee Star but also Krissy were the ones listed with her. The same Krissy who was a preschooler, who I thought would make me look like a baby. Who would ruin my chance to be friends with Monica. The universe was not being fair.

"Dennis June," Sanch read, and I snapped out of my thoughts so I could hear who I would be working with. "Rochelle, Stacey, and Mama's Child."

What the *dump?*

"What the dump?" I asked, out loud.

"Excuse me?" Mrs. Sanchez nearly fell out of her chair. I hadn't meant to say that quite so loudly.

"Why did I get put in a stupid group of losers?" I asked.

"Cause you're one, too!" Rochelle hollered from the back of the class, her hands cupped around her mouth. She smirked, completely unashamed.

"Who in the world is *Mama's Child?*" I blurted over the outburst of laughter, then threw my hands up.

"A new student!" Mrs. Sanchez straightened.

I turned around and searched my classmates frantically. There were a lot of people I didn't know here, and no one looked offended enough to indicate they were Mama's Child.

"That's not a real name," I said.

"You all know Mama's Diner on Shell Street. Well, our new student is her daughter. We aren't able to legally disclose her name, so we call her 'Mama's Child'." Mrs. Sanchez acted like that was completely normal.

"My mom says that place serves toe jam as gravy." I blurted out my thoughts as they entered my brain, not bothering to censor them first.

"Dennis June!" Mrs. Sanchez huffed and shook her head. "You have detention after school for that comment. That is not nice, nor appropriate, or even relevant to what I just said."

Familiar heat creeped into my cheeks. I hated getting scolded in front of everyone.

"You *lie,* Dennis!" gritted a twangy voice, and I turned to see who was calling me a liar! A girl so short her legs dangled off her chair bore holes through me. Her sneakers were more beat up than mine. Her purple shorts and blue shirt were so tight that she probably outgrew them last year. I didn't see how that was possible with how small she looked. There was, however, a rubber duck on the shirt. I liked that. She shook her curly red afro. Where did she come from?

"My mom says that you Tippers are so ugly cause ya lie so much," she slurred.

"Mama's Child! You have detention with Dennis tonight!" Mrs. Sanchez slapped her ruler on her desk. I growled, trying to control my rage.

"Stacey is not going to be happy with you two, *or* Rochelle," Mrs. Sanchez informed us. Mama's Child and I stared at each other from across the room. I folded my arms and looked away.

Rochelle was nowhere to be found in detention, and it was just me and Mama's Child. She stared at me, and it was starting to really creep me out. Despite countless empty desks, she chose to sit right smack beside me. I looked at her when I thought she wasn't looking, but she was *always* looking. She slowly chewed on the pencil she asked me to loan her. I gagged. That would be so germy I'd get sick for sure. One touch was all it would take. No way would I take that thing back now. I decided I would try to avoid eye contact with her for the rest of detention. But I kept hearing slurping sounds.

The pencil laid gnawed up on her desk, and she had switched to biting down on an eraser. None of this stopped her from staring at me, though. What was her problem?

"How old are you?" I whispered.

"Five," she said, sprawling out five fingers. "And how old you be?"

"How old 'I be'?" I wrinkled my nose.

"Ya," she whispered, nodding.

"I'm five." Was she really five, or was she copying me out of spite? Then again, she couldn't know when she answered first. Or could she? She passed me a note, and I opened it up.

"Hay Denis
I jus wan tew tel yew dat I lyke yer ove
rals
Mamas Chyled"

It took me a while to decipher her handwriting. Things were misspelled horribly, and letters were written backwards. She didn't even spell her name right. What was her name?

"What's your name?" I whispered.

"Mama's Child." She chomped on her eraser some more before giving in and shoving the entire thing in her mouth like it was gum.

"I mean your real name."

"It's a secret," she stammered, spitting the eraser back onto her desk with a slobbery thud.

"Tell me what it is," I whispered. I had to know. It was eating me alive!

"Shhh!" Mrs. Sanchez hissed, glancing up from grading papers.

I whispered even quieter, "What is it?"

"I can't tell you."

"Why?" I pushed her.

"I don't wanna."

I frowned.

"Write me a note." She pointed at my notebook.

"Why?"

"I like you."

Squirming in my seat, I grimaced. She stared at me

intently, picking up the pencil and gnawing on it some more.

"You like me, or you *like* me?" I asked.

She quirked an eyebrow, tilting her head as she spit a splinter of wood on the ground before scraping at her tongue with her finger. "Write a note, dummy," she whispered when she finished.

How insulting! I'd write her a note, all right.

"Hey, I just wanted to tell you that

you can't spell worth a dung pat. I

need to know, do you stare because

you have a crush on me?

—DJ "

I had never had *anyone* stare at me like that or tell me they "liked" me. Nobody had ever wanted me to write them notes. Rochelle said something the other day about some girl having a crush on another girl, and it made no sense to me. But maybe Mama's Child had a crush on me! The only person I stared at was Tommy Waltzer, and I *liked* him. It seemed smart to not write who it was written to at the top. If someone found it, I didn't want them to think it was sent to her and be mean about it. That would embarrass both of us. I crumpled the paper and threw it at her. It hit her face, but she picked it up off her desk. She unfolded it and stared at it, crumpling her face.

"No throwing paper! What is that?" asked Mrs. Sanchez, standing and marching toward our desks.

"Dennis wrote you a note," Mama's Child stammered. What? Oh no. *Oh, no, no, no, no, no, no!* I reached for the note, but Sanch snatched it out of Mama's Child's hand.

I tried to take it back but she held it up high.

"Let me just read what you *wrote to me*, Dennis June."

Mrs. Sanchez skimmed the paper, growing more furious by the minute. "How dare you insult my spelling?"

"I didn't—"

She shot me a dirty glare after reading on and buttoned up the top button on her blouse. "I'm calling your mother. You need counseling."

"What?" I frowned and tried to look at the note, but she once again moved it out of reach.

"I'm calling your mom. Ms. Pumpernickel will watch you." Mrs. Sanchez walked toward the door and opened it, calling for her replacement.

Ms. Patti Pumpernickel was our librarian. I thought that was a stupid name.

It hit me on the way home that Mrs. Sanchez thought I thought *she* had a crush on me! I was mortified. Why would Mama's Child betray me like that? Did she hate me? My life was going to be even more miserable now. I jerked on the doorknob and opened our door.

"DJ, do you have something to tell me?" asked my mother, appearing in front of me. I stopped dead in my tracks as an outburst of laughter distracted me. In front of the TV set, as comfortable as Bessie after milking, sat my grandma. Exactly how long was she planning to stay with us? It'd already been a couple weeks.

"Uh, not really?" I slipped my hands into the pockets of my overalls.

"Mrs. Sanchez called saying you wrote her a very disturbing note." The corners of her mouth turned down.

Brad walked past, looked at me, and laughed before climbing the steps.

"What are you laughing at?" I called after him.

He snickered. "You being in love with Sanch!"

"You *told* him?" I cried. "That isn't even true! I wrote that note to Mama's Child, and she told Mrs. Sanchez that I wrote it to her. Everything just got misunderstood."

My mom shook her head and grimaced. "Rochelle and Stacey are working on your project. I just got a call from Mama's Diner. I thought maybe one of you brats was causing a ruckus, but it was that kid Mama's Child. She said she'd be over another day because she's sick."

She wasn't sick when I saw her.

"If she's sick, it's probably from chewing on that pencil," I muttered under my breath.

"What?"

"Nothing."

Loud wails came from the nursery, and my mom groaned before heading up the steps.

"Dennis!" Rochelle hollered. I tugged on my backpack straps, followed her voice to the kitchen, and found the two of them sitting on the kitchen floor, papers surrounding them. Rolled up tissues protruded from Stacey's bloody nostrils.

"I'm sick and tired of you leaving me with all the work!" Rochelle growled, throwing her hands up.

Ignoring Rochelle, I asked Stacey,"What happened to your nose?"

"Apparently I wasn't working fast enough," she spat at Rochelle, even though she was talking to me.

"Get to work, DJ, or that's going to happen to you, too." Rochelle shoved a notebook and some papers toward me, so I begrudgingly took a seat on the floor.

"What's the project even about?" I asked, realizing I had completely ignored it in class.

"Hopefully not *Pippi Longstocking*. I got a C on that paragraph you wrote."

"Considering I'm five years old, I'd say that's pretty good." I lifted my chin smugly.

"It's crap is what it is." Rochelle jerked forward, and I winced, but nothing came of it.

"It needs to be sort of a biography. We pick a person that we know, and we write about their life." Stacey read from a sheet, scanning the document with her finger.

"Where's Ambrosia?" I asked.

"With Mom."

"She wasn't when I saw her. But she was going upstairs." I motioned toward the living room with a thumb.

"Are you serious?" Stacey sighed and dragged her feet out of the kitchen.

"Let's do it on Mama's Diner." Rochelle snorted once Stacey was gone. "That freak Mama's Child is in our group. I heard they serve horse meat."

"They do not serve horse meat," I told her.

"Do you have a better idea?"

I thought for a second, and a lightbulb bursted into my brain. "Why don't we do it on Monica Green?" I could interview her! Then we'd get to know each other and become best friends forever.

"Why are you so obsessed with her?" Rochelle snapped.

"I'm not. She just interests me. I heard she's really rich. So she's probably a celebrity."

Rochelle barked out a laugh. "You sound like you're in love with her. You're so dumb, Dennis. She's not famous. Why would a five-year-old kid be famous?"

"It was just a thought," I whispered. "I just want to be her friend."

I crawled deep inside my shell while Rochelle and I scribbled to come up with ideas for a whole hour. Stacey returned a few minutes ago, and Ambrosia was on her hip, fussing. It was really annoying, and I grabbed my ears, thinking nothing could be louder. Until the front door slammed open. All three of our spines straightened.

"Dude, how *could* you?" My mom's words were shrill and deafening.

"What's going on?" Stacey asked.

"I'm gonna investigate." I stood, wanting to be the first to know.

"It's Krissy's twin! You have no idea how long the agency has been trying to get her to us. They hate separating family, and they've already been apart for two months." My dad trailed behind my enraged mother, a little girl following at his heels.

"I don't want *it.*" My mom didn't even look back at them. Did she seriously just refer to her as an *it?* And why were there so many twins around here? I wanted a twin! On second thought, no. That could get annoying *real* fast, and being that I already had sixteen siblings, I was fine being a single pringle. I just wished we would stop adding new people. Our house was getting cramped, *especially* with only one bathroom and one table! Looks like I wouldn't be getting a drop of attention now. Not that I got any but the "bad kind," anyway.

Mama's Child hadn't done *squat* on our group project. Rochelle refused all of my suggestions, and decided we'd do it about my grandma, Beverly. I didn't think it was a good idea, but we were getting behind and needed to do something.

Every day I ate alone in the cafeteria, sitting in my casual, usual seat. And every day I scribbled ideas in my notebook for the project. At the table across from me, Mama's Child sat and ate alone, but did nothing. Like today.

She stared at me as she bit into what appeared to be a taco. It was in a wrapper, but cold air came off it. It disgusted me as I bit into my peanut butter and jelly sandwich. I glanced at the empty seats surrounding me and frowned.

A few tables away, Monica sat giggling with Haylee and Hallee, and Krissy and Dominique (her twin sister). I longed to sit in that golden area with her, but a rock in my stomach kept me anchored where I belonged. Trying to think of a way to make friends, I glanced at Mama's Child suspiciously. She eyed me like a vulture sizing up a dead carcass on the side of the road. No way'd I invite her to sit with me after the crap she pulled with that note last week. I had a pretty strong feeling she wouldn't be inviting me to sit with her anytime soon, either. So we both sat there staring. Every. Single. Day.

After putting the trash from my lunch back in the sack, I mapped out some of the basics about my grandma. Tearing out a new page, I wrote down that she was old and had brown curly hair. I wanted to write that she was crazy, but that would be mean, so I didn't. Anger marinated inside me, and I glanced up, meeting Mama's Child's eyes. She clearly wasn't doing anything, but then again neither were Rochelle and Stacey. *If you wanted something done right, you had to do it yourself*, I thought and returned to my furious scribbling.

Under "hobbies," I listed that my grandma liked to ram things in her sloppy jalopy car, she liked to jump borders, and she was an "escape artist." (It would be inappropriate to mention prison—boy, would she have been mad at me!) Lunch was about to end, so I quickly scribbled that she watched TV all day and enjoyed harassing the world before packing up my stuff.

Deep down, I knew that we were going to get a horrible

grade on this project. But what could I do? I was only one person, and if I told people that I (a five-year-old) was doing all of the work, they would never believe me. Because nobody believed you when you were little.

It was the day of our project presentation. I got onto the bus—early again. My mom told me she was slammed at her salon, so she couldn't take me, and my dad had already gone to work. The big kids glared at me, and some of them were talking about me having a crush on Mrs. Sanchez. Which was disgusting, because uhm, ew!

"Hey, Dennis!" called Brad, making kissy faces at me. "Excited to see Mrs. Sanchez today?" His best friends, Chad and Derek, gave him fist bumps.

I slumped into an empty seat and stared out the window. How cool would it be if I had invisible powers right now? Nobody would know I was on this bus. If I had invisible powers, I could eavesdrop all the time, and nobody would yell at me because they wouldn't even know. I made a mental note to come up with a plan to make this possible.

"Wait for me!" someone hollered outside. The bus doors opened again, and a red afro appeared.

Mama's Child.

She slid into the open seat beside me, and dirty looks shot our way. We were the "freaks" of our school.

I glared at Mama's Child, the one responsible for my humiliation.

"What are you doing?" I asked.

"What? Am I not allowed to sit with my good friend, Dennis?" Her bottom lip turned down into a pout, but it didn't feel sincere.

"We're not friends. And we never will be." *Not after you started these rumors,* I thought.

She ignored my comment. "Hey, Dennis!" She poked my side. "I have an awesome idea." She wiggled her eyebrows.

"Your ideas would be horrible. You do nothing but get me in trouble." I turned my shoulder to her, so I could continue my stare out the window.

"No!" she exclaimed, grabbing my shoulder and turning me back around. "This is for real a good one."

The look on her face made my stomach churn. "I want to know what it is before I agree to it."

"Well, since you and I be on the bus today, I thought we could play a game."

"What game?" I raised an eyebrow.

"Truth or dare!" she sang in her hillbilly voice. Her lips curled up into a grin that reminded me of the Cheshire Cat. I hesitated, narrowing my eyes at her before deciding that this was actually a great idea. I could embarrass Mama's and take some of the heat off me.

"Okay, let's do it."

"Me first!" yelled Mama's Child, and I shushed her. She lowered her eyes at me and whispered, "Truth or dare, Dennis?"

I couldn't very well say "dare," because I didn't want to risk being embarrassed again. "Truth, Mama's Child, I pick truth."

"Okay, Dennis." She brought her hand up to her chin like she was really thinking hard before saying, "Your truth is to tell me your deepest most darkest secret. Somethin' you ain't never told another livin' soul!"

I could only think of one. But it was the one I wasn't supposed to tell… My stomach curdled, and I broke out in a cold sweat.

"Come on, Dennis! We're almost at the school!" She kept slapping my leg to draw it out of me. Like doing that would make me talk faster.

I blurted it as quietly and as quickly as I could. "My grandma was the one who murdered Mrs. Sanchez's mom."

Her eyes brightened and widened like a fruit fly's. "Do my own ears deceive me, Dennis June?" She cupped a hand to her ear and leaned up against me. "Did you really say what I think you said?"

I stared at the freckles plastering her skin. She even had them on her eyelids. "Ye-yeah," I stammered.

"My mama said they ain't know who done that! It was last summer! You're a silly goose!"

"She said she knew how to make it look like an accident. She's good at escaping...things."

Her eyes widened further. "What?"

"Shhh! It's very hush hush." We came to a halt.

"Oh, okay, Dennis. Ya can count on me!" Something beeped, and she gave me a sly smile as we walked off the bus. She shoved something into her backpack.

"What was that?" I asked.

"Nothin'." She ran to the sidewalk and flung her backpack down on the ground. I went to the other side of the building to wait for my class, but I kept watching her. *What* had she put in her backpack? Did she steal something from me? I didn't think I had anything *to* steal. Maybe it was a toy or something for school? Maybe it had to do with our project that I thought she barely paid attention to?

When I could finally enter the classroom, snickers swirled. People were still making fun of me about the Mrs. Sanchez thing. I glanced at her desk as I took my seat, and she muttered, "Don't look at me, Dennis." Her cheeks were red, probably embarrassed by the whole ordeal and just as angry as I was.

"You really should stop staring at her like that." Katrina

giggled. I rolled my eyes and scooted my chair away from her, toward the desk on my right where Mark Melon sat and made belching sounds and fart jokes most of the day.

He stuck his pencil up his nose and said, "Sup, Dennis?" I scooted my desk back toward Katrina with a loud, huffing sigh.

The groups began to present, and I couldn't tell you who most of the projects were about. Ashley's group did okay, but it was so boring. Monica's group did amazing. I was really jealous of Krissy and their last-minute addition, Dominique. Dominique could have been in my group, and I would have willingly traded places with her. Their presentation, or at least what Monica said, was like hearing Shakespeare. Monica's younger brother, Cameron, presented with his group, and it was meh. He was a preschooler and looked very confused. I don't think he said one word the whole time. He kinda just stood there.

Brad's was totally full of crap that he made up while eating breakfast this morning. Ugh, and Katrina's? Hers was a piece of cow dung. I pinched up my nose the whole time because it stunk so bad. It smelled like...like...half-eaten raccoons!

A million butterflies flapped inside me when it was finally my turn to go up. Rochelle, Stacey, and Mama's Child walked up with me, and we began our presentation. My legs were a little shaky, and people were smirking. I didn't know if it was because we were doing bad or if it was because of the Mrs. Sanchez thing. But then Mama's Child said she had something to present for our project. I stared at her, wondering what she possibly could have known about my grandmother that I hadn't already written down. She hadn't lifted a finger during this whole assignment. Then she pulled out a small metal box and pressed a button. A voice crackled to life.

My ears could *not* believe what I was hearing. It wasn't. It couldn't be. It *was!* My voice, on the bus, saying my deepest darkest secret. Spots swirled in front of me, and Rochelle and Stacey stood still, totally dumbfounded.

"Play it. Again." Mrs. Sanchez stood up rigidly, and fury enveloped her like a fire-breathing dragon.

"Mama's…" I muttered through chattering teeth, staring at her in shock.

She hesitated. "No. I can't. I promised Dennis I wouldn't tell anyone her deep dark secret. You look mad. Am I in trouble?" A sly, innocent look crossed her features, and I wanted to slap it right off. She *knew* what she was doing. Everyone was quiet and stared at me.

"Play it again, or I'll take it and play it myself," Mrs. Sanchez threatened. Her voice shook, and I trembled.

Mama's Child pressed play, and the whole class listened to what I couldn't believe was me saying, "My grandmother murdered Mrs. Sanchez's mom."

The teacher was silent for a minute before looking up at me and breathing, "Dennis. This grandmother, the one in your report, was the one who killed—" Her voice broke, and she took a second to get the words out. "—my dear mumsie?"

I looked down at my feet, my knees threatening to buckle.

"N..n.n…no," I stammered.

"You lie, Dennis!" Mama's Child twanged, pointing an accusing finger at me. It was like she'd slapped me across the face, and my cheeks were red enough that it looked like it, too. Why was she being this person?

"You told me in truth or dare! You can't lie when you're tellin' a truth!" she slurred, spit flying out through the gap where a tooth had once been.

Rochelle chuckled even though this was anything but funny. "Beverly's gonna kill you next, Dennis," she gritted.

Everyone in the class let out gasps and ooh's. Mama's Child still had the box in her hand.

"Did you get that, Mama's Child?" asked Mrs. Sanchez.

"Every single word," she answered, looking at the box in her hand. She was a backstabbin' snake!

"You three come with me," Mrs. Sanchez ordered.

"Why doesn't Stacy have to come?" I protested, but Mrs. Sanchez ignored me.

"Class is dismissed for the day."

Rochelle looked at me then at the windows. She bolted for an open one and crammed her body out of it, dodge rolling onto the ground. I tried to rush toward the window to watch her go with the rest of my class, but Mrs. Sanchez grabbed the back of my shirt collar and dragged me to the front office.

Mrs. Sanchez opened the door, tossed me onto the nearest wooden bench, and glared at me. We were waiting for my mom to show up. Mama's Child put up a fight, but Mrs. Sanchez confiscated the box and had her mom come pick her up. I turned to look out front, and my mom approached the glass doors of the entry turned toward the office and entered.

"What the dunk did you do this time, Dennis? This had better be important. I was in the middle of—oh crap."

"What?" I asked.

"I was giving some lady a perm, but she's been…that was…two hours ago. Well, she is *not* going to be happy." My mom placed a hand to her head and glanced back toward the doors.

"Mrs. Tipper," Mrs. Sanchez interrupted.

My mom faced her. The principal came out from a back room, sat at his desk, and rolled his eyes when he saw my mother.

"Yeah?" she asked.

"We're here because of a legal matter, a serious issue."

My mom inched toward the glass doors before snatching the handle and saying, "I didn't do it! I didn't do anything!" She reached the parking lot, got in her car, and sped off.

"I'm honestly not surprised," muttered the principal from behind the desk. He smelled like he had tuna breath, even from over here.

"Come with me to the police station," Mrs. Sanchez demanded, looking down at me.

"The *police station?*" I cried. "But what about my mom?" I pointed a finger at where her car had been a few seconds prior.

"Don't worry. Knowing *your mother,* I'm sure they have a helicopter tracking her constantly."

My eyeballs nearly dropped out of my skull.

"I'm sure they will find her shortly. Your whole family is probably getting arrested until they decide who is innocent and who's not."

"What?" My entire world turned upside down. What happened when my mom found out that this was all my fault? That this happened because of something I said? What happened when my *grandma* found out? She was still staying at our house!

I followed Mrs. Sanchez to her old car, and I didn't know what I was supposed to do. It wasn't like I was the one who wronged her! She was the adult here, so I was obligated to go with her, right? But I didn't want to. She opened the car door, and I got in, dumbfounded.

"Put your seatbelt on, this isn't your mom's car."

Crumpling her face up in a sneer or sob, she drove out of the parking lot and talked about all kinds of legal mumbo jumbo.

"There's probably a good chance you'll go to juvie, Dennis." This part caught my attention.

"What?" I gasped, a lump closing my throat. I tightened a hand around the seatbelt. Could that really happen?

"And honestly, I'll come to visit you."

"That's nice of you," I said, grasping at any kindness from another person I could. "You'd really—"

"—to drop off your homework!" she cut me off, her lips curling into a villainous grin. She pointed up, and said, "This is for you, Mom!"

I scooted as close as I could to the door, clutching my seatbelt for dear life.

"Oh, I cannot *wait* to see your family behind bars!" She chuckled. "Especially your pregnant mother. She'll look like a real cow in those stripes!" I knew Mrs. Sanchez was mean, but wow. She was totally a different person outside of the classroom.

Wait a second.

"My mom is prego?" I asked.

"When isn't she?" She laughed.

I leaned forward as far as my seatbelt would stretch and slapped her. I didn't like my mom, but she was still *my* mom. The car swerved a little as she pulled into the parking lot of the police station.

"That is assault, and I could file it," she spat. The car came to a stop, and she cut the engine.

Sirens pierced the air as multiple cop cars flew through the streets. I turned my head every which way to look for them, but Mrs. Sanchez barked the order, "Get out."

She grabbed me by the arm, and the gravel skidded

across the pavement as she jerked me in the direction of the ugly gray police station.

Chapter 7

I WAS THE FIRST member of my family to arrive. They placed me on an uncomfortable plastic chair beside an open room. Looking inside, I decided cops probably interrogated people like they did on crime shows in that room and found myself glad they put me in this chair. When I knuckle-tapped on the wall behind me, it felt paper thin, just like our walls at home. I wanted to know everything that was going on, so I had no intentions of moving from this spot.

Shaye was brought in what felt like an eternity later, and I wondered why I had to come immediately and nobody else did. She was mumbling something about Harvard and her permanent record. Ashley was brought in, pushing a few of the toddlers in a stroller. Her face was red. Poor thing. None of those kids were even hers, but she always got stuck babysitting.

"Sorry about this, Ashley," I piped up.

She stopped the stroller and turned to face me. "I hate you for this, Dennis. Everyone hates you. I try to be nice to you, but this is just beyond embarrassing. Derek Green heard all of that. He will never like me now." She frowned, tears welling in her eyes. The words shot a guilty pang to the pit of my stomach and pierced daggers through my little heart. Especially since they came from someone who was normally so kind.

A cop shoved Brad in our direction, and he scoffed, "Hey! Watch my hair, guys!" Brad was too lazy to do anything, but he made time to put globby goo in his hair every day.

"This is just downright *wrong!*" I recognized that voice immediately.

"Dad!" I cried as the cops ushered him in. But he was too preoccupied by all of the chaos.

"I'm missing Burrito Monday for this. I need to get back to the factory. I can't just abandon the guys like that!" he roared. He rarely raised his voice at anyone, but apparently burritos were very important to him.

Stacey pulled up her pants, a cop following close behind her.

"Were you on the crapper when they found you?" I asked loudly, and her cheeks turned into two red tomatoes!

"This is so cool," Krissy said to Dominique. They were sitting a few chairs away from me.

"We are in huge trouble. Don't you get that?" I asked.

I swung my legs, wondering how long this would take. What if I had to use the bathroom? Would they take me to a place with the toilet in the middle of the room? I pulled my feet up and hugged my knees, remembering the other thing my mom mentioned about prison—rats.

Speaking of Mom, a cop flung her into the room, huffing.

"I didn't do anything!" she yelled.

The cop folded his arms and frowned at her. "Then why did you *run?*"

"I didn't run, I *drove.*"

"Ma'am."

"I'm pregnant with triplets. Have mercy!" She pleaded with shaking prayer hands before grabbing her stomach. I hoped she was lying. Not about not doing anything, but about being pregnant with triplets. *Please no,* I thought to myself over and over again.

"I'll get you, you no good rat face Dennis." The eerily chilling voice gave me goosebumps. I turned, and my grandma Beverly was standing on the other side of me, deep creases embedding her forehead and the corners of her mouth. When did she even get here? It was like seeing a ghost.

"I didn't mean to—" I began nibbling at a thumbnail. What if she was gonna kill me? Muffled booms of voices shifted everyone's attention to the windows looking out toward the parking lot.

"Rochelle just punched a cop!" whooped Ty. "Did you see that, Orange?"

"Whatever," she muttered, before picking at her nail polish.

"I wanna see!" I said, cramming my way through. I was anxious for any excuse to get away from my grandma. Brad and Ty pushed me back, but I kept elbowing them to no avail.

"Sweet! He totally just tased her." Brad gaped in awe.

"I want to see!" I groaned.

"Get outta here, Dennis. You're a baby." Brad shoved me, and I was tired of getting pushed around so much. Like a dog with its tail between its legs, I returned to my plastic chair.

"What's wrong with her?" I asked the popo sitting next to me, the one guarding Rochelle.

He glanced in my direction and scoffed. "Don't worry

about it."

"Why is she shaking and laughing?" I asked.

"Tranquilizer," he grumbled. "S'posed to calm people down, but your sister's wiring must be outta whack."

I stared at him, and he frowned.

"What's a tranquilizer?" I asked.

"None of your business, kid."

"Are you the popo she punched?" I didn't see any bruises.

"Do you have to ask so many questions?" He scowled.

"I like to know things."

"Don't we all."

"Is that your badge?" I pointed to his chest. It was shaped like a star, just like in cartoons.

"Yeah. What else would it be?" Annoyance laced his words.

"It's shiny."

"It is."

"What does 373863 mean?" I cringed at the fact he had six numbers on his badge.

"What?" He followed my gaze. "Uh, it means my name is Pete."

"Why doesn't it just say '*Pete*'?" I wrinkled my nose at this stupidity.

He pulled out a walkie-talkie.

"Is that a walkie-talkie?" I pointed at it, my eyes growing wide. I'd always wanted to use one of those!

He didn't answer.

"Can I try it?"

Pete frowned and stiffened, taking a second before speaking. "Absolutely not. This is for professional matters only."

I hesitated a second before trying again. "How 'bout

now?" I asked, leaning toward him.

He held out a hand to stop me and groaned. "Kid!"

Out of nowhere, Rochelle slapped the cop's arm, and he yelled, "All right! That's it!" He stood, grabbed her arm, and took her down the hall. Where were they going?

"Can I come too?" I called after him. He was cool.

"Absolutely not," he answered, not bothering to look back at me before turning a corner.

"Let's start the interviews." An old cop came out of the room beside my chair, and my hand went to my racing heart.

He scowled, placing his hands on his hips. "Get in here, Dude Tipper."

My dad walked past me and into the room. Noticing the door was left cracked open, I scooted my chair over to hear better, and it creaked and groaned with each movement.

Josh pointed at me. "You farted!"

"Did not, it was my chair!" I hissed. He stuck his tongue out at me, so I stuck mine right back out at him. Then the interview started.

"Where were you on the night of Mrs. Sanchez's murder?" asked the cop.

"When even was that?" my dad asked.

Papers rustled, and all I could hear was something about an "aw top sea" and last summer. What was an "aw top sea"? Unable to hear clearly, I scooted closer without it looking too suspicious.

"Did anyone in your family have a motive to murder her?" asked the cop.

"Yes."

"Who?"

"I've said too much," my dad sighed dramatically.

"You've said too little." A fist pounded against a desk.

"I could always be bribed—"

"—sir you could get in a lot of trouble talking like that."

"I'm missing Burrito Monday for this!"

"What?" A mixture of anger and confusion laced his tone. I peeked inside the doorway they hadn't bothered to shut. There were papers strung across the desk and a low ceiling light dimly lit the room. My dad's chair screeched back, and he shined the light in the cop's face.

"I know you have donuts in the back room!" he yelled.

"I'm not giving you donuts for information, that's ridiculous," the cop responded flatly.

"Then I know nothing." My dad sat back down, and the light swung back and forth. I nodded in approval. He was so smart. I wouldn't tell him anything either if there was a chance that *I* could get donuts. Those were delicious! I liked the kind with the yellow custard in them, what were they called…bots and cream?

"I know you know something!" the cop yelled. Nah. It wasn't bots and cream.

"I plead the fifth!" yelled my dad. *Boston cream*! That was it!

Just then, Megan Green and Monica entered through a side door I hadn't noticed before. They had a white cardboard box with them. *"What's in the box?"* I wanted to ask, but didn't.

"Hi, Monica!" I called.

She waved at me—*she actually waved!* Hope sparked in every fiber of my being, and it was enough to nearly make me forget why I was here. What did I do now? How many seconds had passed? Was it too late to wave back without looking weird?

"We just wanted to stop by and bring you guys some donuts!" Megan told the cop at the desk, an old man with a thick moustache and a fancy hat. Something about his firm face and wise eyes made him appear in charge. Or maybe it was the hat because he was the only one wearing one.

"Oh, how kind!" he said. "There's even little sheriff stars drawn on them!"

He wheeled around in his chair and stood, coming from behind the desk.

"How are you, cutie?" He reached down and tousled Monica's hair. It was so silky looking and shiny that I wanted to play with it. When I reached a hand up to my own locks, my heart sank as my fingers caught in my nearly-white rat's nest.

"You are straight up *lying,*" my dad raved, exiting the room beside me. His gaze didn't leave the cop questioning him. "There are only *two* things that smell that sweet." My dad counted on his fingers. "And it's donuts and Megan Green!" He lowered his voice and muttered under his breath, "I bet you have them both, you dirty cops."

"Excuse me, sir?" The interviewing cop's face flamed red.

Megan Green and Monica walked past my dad to exit through the side door. I waved this time, but she didn't see me.

"Would ya look at that?" my dad asked, his eyes following Megan and Monica. He threw his arms up then dropped them to his sides.

"Bradford Tipper," said the interviewing cop, discarding my dad and motioning toward my brother. Brad walked over to him at a sloth's pace.

"Would you mind stepping inside—"

"—I'm not going in there."

"Fine, we can talk out here."

Excellent, I thought. But the silent groan on the cop's face told me he didn't feel the same.

"Is this about the librarian, Ms. Pumpernickel? I swear I don't have a thing going with her."

"What?" asked the cop.

Brad wrinkled his brow. "This isn't about Patti— I mean, Ms. Pumpernickel? Cause that's just a rumor!" Brad was getting all red in the face.

I tried to contain my laughter. *I* had started that rumor to get back at him for making me milk ol' Bessie! Tee-hee!

"What are you laughing about back there?" the cop asked, staring down at me.

"Dennis is dumber than a brick," Brad offered. "Just ignore her like everyone else does."

"I am. I'm sorry." I tried to contain my laughter.

"What kind of events do you recall going on last summer, son?" The cop rubbed his stubbly chin and folded his ripped, muscly arms.

"I did a lot of partying with this girl named Nicole. We had some good times before she moved to Crab Cove." He sighed wistfully.

I straightened in my chair and wrinkled my nose.

"That's where you live, idiot." The cop stared at him. "Do you think this is a joke? Are you as immature as your sister over there?"

"Hey!" I whined.

"This isn't Crab Creek?" Brad gasped.

"There is literally no place in California that I know of by that name."

Brad hesitated, thinking. "So she lives *here?*"

"If this is Nicole Green, then she's your neighbor and goes to school with you."

What was Brad's problem? Did my mom drop him on his head when he was a baby?

"This isn't Crab Creek Private School?" he asked,

motioning over his shoulder.

"Now, why would there be a school named after a town that doesn't exist?" the cop flung his hands up.

"Yeah, Brad. You're being dumb," I spoke up.

"That's enough out of you," snapped the cop. He pinned his hawk eyes on me, and I shrunk back in my seat. He was almost as scary as my mom.

What felt like a thousand voices fluttered over the sardine-packed room, and I didn't know what I should listen to and what my brain should toss to the junk pile. Lots of my siblings talked to officers about parties they attended that summer, and the cops wrote notes down on little pads. Officer Pete came back out without Rochelle, and I overheard him telling Mrs. Sanchez, "We're probably going to crack more than your mother's murder tonight."

She patted his arm and looked *happy.* Grinning ear to ear, she cheered, "Yay! Tipper dirt! Dig up all you can get!"

Standing, I pretended to stretch my legs and eased closer to the action.

"So what you're saying is that your mother and grandmother were scammed out of money by the deceased multiple times?" a woman police officer asked Tearston.

"Everything is a scam with the Sanchezs. Have you ever seen the workbooks she requires—and sells—for homework?"

The lady shook her head.

I remembered those workbooks! They were basically a blank notebook you had to have for her class. It had special places to fill out your name and such, but nothing too fancy. The stupid part was that she binded the papers herself. They always fell apart, and no two books had the same number of pages. So you never knew when you'd have to pay for another one, not to mention what one you were going to get.

She just gave you a random one off her giant stack. My mom always complained that they were a scam and that if she was buying something, she should at least get to see the product in advance. But Mrs. Sanchez made it mandatory for us to buy them, so we had no choice. Those workbooks were a rip!

"Get this—" Tearston leaned closed to the cop. "—one time, when she was in preschool, Dennis June got a workbook that was only the front and back cover. There weren't even any pages!"

"I remember that!" I chimed in. The two of them turned around, and the cop lifted an eyebrow but wrote this down. It felt good to be welcomed for once. Relief flooding over me, I stepped into their little circle.

"I told my mom, and she cussed Mrs. Sanchez out on the phone. Then Mrs. Sanchez said she would never do such a thing. She acted like it was all *my* fault. That I was a 'baby who couldn't be trusted,' and that I ripped the pages out myself!" Livid from just *telling* the story, I couldn't stop myself from flailing my arms all around as I did.

"Well…that tells us about *your* Mrs. Sanchez, but not really much about her deceased mother." The woman frowned. "Do you know if your family had issues with *her?*"

"They have issues with *every* Mrs. Sanchez," Tearston told her, the two of them talking it over without me.

"I didn't know the other two—" I began, but they talked over top of me, and I let out a sigh. I wanted to be interviewed. This was starting to be almost fun.

"Our old neighbor who lived in the alley behind us hated them, too." Tearston went on about the old neighbors. I didn't remember them very much.

"Did you know their names?" asked the police officer.

"They don't live there now. They never really left their house though, if you can call it that. I never saw them. My grandma helped them pack, loading up all their stuff for them. She said that their skin was too sensitive for the sun and that they couldn't come outside. Said they'd fry right up like an egg."

I wrinkled my nose at the thought. Couldn't they have just worn sunscreen?

"Interesting." The cop wrote all of that down.

"Actually, I think the mailbox might have said 'H. Bell' or 'H. Bill'. Something like that."

Snooping, I slipped around to the front desk to gather more information. Did they have trench coats and magnifying glasses in here? I could totally be a detective.

That Officer Pete was at a computer, and someone on his walkie-talkie told him to pull up information in the database on "H. Bill" followed by an address I couldn't hear most of. I stood on my tiptoes, put my hands up on the counter and watched him type. Some pictures of a Mexican-looking guy in a sombrero popped up. It said his age and his known relatives. Did they have one of those pages of me? A circle spun in the middle of the big clunky computer's screen, and Officer Pete slapped the top of the box as he grumbled indistinguishable words.

"Is that a fake mustache?" asked another cop, leaning over and pointing at the screen. The load circle had vanished and the picture of the man was on again.

"Looks real to me," I murmured.

"It totally is." Officer Pete barked out a laugh. The two of them read through some jargon that was on the screen.

"Read me the kids' names one more time." The cop chuckled, sipping on what smelled like bitter coffee. The slurping noise and his lip smacking was making me uncomfortable.

"Sarti Mtar, Teniese Dipper," Pete droned.

"Wait, did you say Marti Star?" asked the other cop.

"No, I said Sarti Mtar— Wait a second."

"Sarti Mtar, Marti Star? Teniese Dipper, Deniese Tipper? Dude, Heverly Bill is Beverly Hill! They just switched the letters of the names around!"

"Genius," Officer Pete remarked, a smirk playing on his lips.

"Is my name in there as Jennis Dune?" I asked.

"Aye! What are you doing back here?" demanded the other cop. He scowled as he stood up, nearly spilling his coffee all over his pot belly.

"Where'd you get all of them pictures?" I asked. "And why's my grandma dressed up like a man?"

"Get outta here!" he urged, rushing me away from the counter and back toward all the commotion. The cops must have decided to just give up and do all the interviews out here at once. I scanned my options, and another officer interviewing Krissy and Dominique caught my attention. Why were they getting interviewed and I wasn't? I walked over to find out.

"Ask me questions instead," I told the tall, thin officer, tugging on his pant leg.

"We are trying to get an unbiased opinion." He frowned down at me.

"What does that mean?" I asked.

"Girls, do you like Mrs. Sanchez? How does she go over in your house?" he asked.

"My new mom hates her!" Krissy blurted.

"Is that so?" He gave them a forced smile. "Weren't you just adopted?"

"Yes, we were! Yes, we were!" Krissy puffed out her

chest. I was beginning to notice that she liked to repeat herself.

"The mean old lady hates our teacher." Dominique pushed Krissy out of the way.

"Who is she?" He furrowed his brow, but I knew they were talking about Grandma.

"We went in lady's purse. We saw lots of money and cards." Krissy's eyes were wide.

"Were you guys thiefin'?" I pumped, my ears on fire. My mom hated thieves.

"We saw it, we really did!" Dominique went on, ignoring me.

"What were the cards?" He chuckled lightly and smiled at them like they were the cutest things he ever saw. It made me sick.

"One had a monkey on it, one had lady on it, and the other had a man!" Dominique was practically bouncing with excitement. Her and Krissy were so hyper and laughing up a storm that I wondered if someone had given them sugar. My stomach growled, and I squeezed it into a fat roll. I could really go for a Little Debbie right about now.

"Were these birthday cards?" the man asked.

"No, they were this big!" Krissy showed him the size with her fingers.

"It's the same thing that our mommy shows you guys when you stop her for being bad on the roads." Dominique pointed to my mother, who was ranting about something I couldn't hear from over here. She had her eyebrows raised to the ceiling and a nasty frown on her face.

"Oh, licenses!" he said. "What were the names on them?"

I stared at him with as much confusion as Krissy and Dom had. Was this dude *dumb?*

They looked at each other before Krissy finally said, "I

don't know, good sir. I can't read yet, can you?"

"I can."

"We have them in our undies!" Dominique snickered. Krissy joined in, too. I sat on the floor because this was going to be awhile, and I wanted to be next.

"Hand them over please, and I'll look at them." The cop walked over to a little box that was hanging on the wall and pulled out a pair of gloves. He stuck them on his hands and returned. It made a pleasing snapping sound. I liked that.

"Can I have a pair?" I asked.

"For what?" He frowned at me.

"I want to be a detective."

"Too bad," he said.

I crossed my arms and my legs, sitting crisscross applesauce.

"You want our undies?" laughed Krissy. Dominique bursted into giggles as well.

"The cards, not your underwear." His face grew pale.

"Cha-ching!" said Krissy, reaching down the back of her pants and sliding the card up her crack.

"We're like Mommy at the store!" Dominique reached down her pants and did the same thing, the two of them laughing hysterically.

I gagged, and the cop did too, wincing before he grabbed the cards with his gloves. What was it with little kids and sticking stuff down their pants? That was infectious!

"Here is lady," said Krissy, pointing at one card.

"This one is man," said Dominique, pointing at hers.

"You guys are going to get cracked for stealing those," I told them.

"Don't tell, Dennis. You're being mean." Krissy pouted.

Dominique just kept laughing, but then she stopped and gasped. Her eyes turned from frantic to rage. She turned to

Krissy and grabbed her shoulders, asking, "Where is monkey?"

"Uh, I lost him," she answered.

"No, sir!" Dominique hollered.

"He ain't in there, Dom!" Krissy yelled, fishing in her pants.

"Try harder!" Dominique demanded.

I didn't know who felt sicker, me or the cop.

"He's there! I think I felt 'im," Krissy said, wriggling her hand around.

"That is so gross! Stop it!" I wanted to crawl into a hole, I was so embarrassed to be related to them.

"Let me look!" Dom said, looking down the back of Krissy's pants. "Squeeze!" she told Krissy.

A piece of plastic clattered to the floor. The cop's face turned a murky green, and I didn't blame him.

"He fell! There he is! There's monkey," Dom said, and Krissy bent to pick up the card. She handed it to the cop, and he grabbed it reluctantly, muttering, "Thanks." I don't think he really needed that card.

"Looks like we got Heverly Bill, Beverly Hill, and Mad Monkey #001."

"Mad Monkey #001?" I asked, standing and walking to his side.

"It's a membership for Bob's Karaoke Club," he explained.

"That's what that says?" asked Dominique.

"Yes, you girls can go back to your mom now." He started to take the cards to the desk where Pete was, but Krissy yelled, "We ain't done yet!"

He stopped and turned. "Yes, you are."

"But you stole the cards!" Krissy was about to throw an all-out tantrum.

"Gimme that monkey!" Dominique wailed and catapulted herself toward him. After grabbing the card out of his hand, she shoved it back down her crack. The cop stood there like he didn't know what to do.

"Is the monkey really worth it?" I lifted a brow at him. Dominique slapped my arm, but I ignored her and the sting.

"No," he said.

"Then I would just walk away while you're ahead," I told him. He did just that.

"I love this monkey, Dennis!" Dominique glared at me hatefully.

Nonsense went on and on, but nobody asked *me* for my opinions. A bunch of the Star kids were brought in, and Katrina's older sister Cherry pranced in wearing jungle red pants and a black frilly top. She looked like a model. I wanted to be a model.

Everything she said made me uncomfortable. No matter what the cop said, or what he asked, she always felt the need to lower her voice, bat her eyelashes, and croon the word *officer* at the end of her sentence. The cop ate it up, though, and was hanging on her every word. After she left, I went up to that same cop, lowered my voice, and batted my eyelashes.

"What are you doing?" he asked, looking down to meet my gaze and frowning.

"I wanted to know if you wanted to interview me, *officer.*" I said the word exactly how I remembered Cherry saying it, but it seemed to have the opposite effect.

The cop shuddered. "Ew! What is wrong with you, child?"

Embarrassed beyond measure, I slunk back over to the familiar—but now dreaded—plastic chair.

My mom was telling a cop that she "couldn't possibly have been involved" because she was at the doctor. Something about thinking she was pregnant again, which didn't sound *that* unbelievable. The cop looked around the room, sizing up all of us kids, and I think he came up with the same conclusion I did.

Ms. P (Ms. Pumpernickel) came in to deny everything Brad had brought up, and she told the cops that their "relationship" was a rumor, too. What was more embarrassing was that she mentioned *I* had started it after she told me we weren't friends. I had forgotten about that completely, and that wasn't the reason I started the rumor. But thinking about it now, you know what? That did tick me off. She should have been my best friend when I asked her. How rude!

I heard bits and pieces of the muffled conversation between Ms. P and a cop, but could only make out something about Bob's Karaoke Club, an article in the library, and *The Legend of Broccoli Waltzer*. I had heard about that legend before. The teenagers claimed he was a lost boy that haunted the Karaoke Club. I had never seen a ghost before, but I got a little spooked thinking about it.

"What's going on?" Tiffany raised her voice, and once again I bounced to a different dilemma. "Are they arresting grandma?"

"Beverly Hill, you are under arrest for the murder of Mrs. Sanchez the second," announced a cop.

"Why did she do it?" someone asked.

"Yeah, Grandma, why?" I asked.

She frowned at me bitterly, a cop forcing her hands behind her back. "She was a no-good-for... You know darn well what she was. She shacked up with my boyfriend while I was in prison." She growled as the cop tightened the cuffs on her.

"You had a boyfriend?" I asked. "Who is he?"

"I'm not telling you, rat face. You can't keep your trap shut," she muttered.

"And the reason you pretended to be Heverly Bill was…?" asked the cop.

"It has to do with things in Mexico that are none of your business," she spat, hocking a loogie to the ground.

"Well, now that *that's* settled," said Officer Pete, "let's go investigate this '*Legend of Broccoli Waltzer*'."

"So we're free to go?" Shaye stood across the room, her eyes shifting hesitantly.

The cops looked at each other and shrugged. "I guess," they finally decided in unison.

"Y'all just busted a murder, and now it's just *over?*" I asked. Was I the only person who thought this was a big deal?

Everyone grabbed their things and filed out of the building, and my face crumpled like a piece of paper. I tightened my hands into fists. Apparently I was the only person who thought this was a big deal. You had gotta be kidding me! This was the biggest thing that had ever happened in my life, and I was there, but was I *really*? It felt like hundreds of cops interviewed people, but nobody gave a hoot about what *I* thought! Instead, I ran around like a chicken with my head cut off, trying to eavesdrop and get someone to listen to me. Nobody ever listened to me. Maybe I *did* have invisible superpowers after all.

I caught a glimpse of a few cops huddling and heard them coming up with a plan to go to Bob's Karaoke Club. I looked around. *Would anybody even notice if I went, too?* So I made up my mind. If people were going to treat me like I had invisible superpowers, then I was going to use them.

Playing detective didn't have to end just yet.
I was going to follow them.

Chapter 8

AS I FOLLOWED the officers to Bob's Karaoke Club, I couldn't help but wonder if the *Legend of Broccoli Waltzer* was true. I knew Bob, of course, but I knew very little about this Broccoli guy. The cops approached Bob Waltzer, the owner of the place. He looked over some pieces of paper they showed him, then reluctantly let them in. I staggered my entrance enough to where they wouldn't see me approaching.

This was my first time in this place. It was very dim and retro. A disco ball hung from the ceiling, and big black speakers that were larger than me surrounded the place. As I made my way over to the spacious singing area, the aroma of nacho cheese and grease filled my nostrils. It reeked in here. I wanted to play with the microphones, but that would blow my cover. And I was a detective, so I couldn't risk *that*.

Bob and the cops' voices were muffled as they searched the back rooms. I kept myself as flat against the walls as possible. Slinking around like a burglar, my back hit something hard, and it made a slight knocking sound. I winced and turned around to see what damage I had caused and found a low-hung frame swinging. Nobody came out to investigate. *Smooth, DJ.* The picture frame was crooked, and I felt an extreme urge to straighten it, so I did. It read "Karaoke Champion of the Week" and featured a picture of my smiling mother. She was wearing a low-cut top that was showing off *everything.* I stuck my tongue out and whispered, "Yuck!" My mom couldn't sing worth a dung pat—she sounded like a dying cat—so I suspected favoritism. After my mom's comments about Bob possibly being her (hopefully fake) baby's father, I wondered if they had a thing going on. The thought of it made me nauseous.

Footsteps sounded as the officers came out of one of the back rooms with Bob. I crouched behind a ginormous speaker system, and they asked him to show them the upstairs.

Bob frowned but said, "Uh, okay…but nobody's been up there in years. It's just for storage. Are you sure?"

The cops insisted, so they started moving. I didn't even know this place *had* an upstairs. After the footsteps faded, I creeped around the corner and started sneaking up the steps, picking my knees and feet up high and trying to stay as quiet as possible. The place appeared normal, almost like the upstairs was a house and not a club. There was a door at the top of the stairs, and nasty old cobwebs draped the corners and railings. I prayed they wouldn't touch me and cringed.

Bob's keychains rattled as he opened the door and let the cops enter. Then he followed.

"Who are you?" a cop demanded. Someone shrieked, sending a panic through me. I picked up the pace and crept around the corner. All the cops and Bob had entered a room to the left, and I got down on all fours to look inside.

"Who are *you*?" called a boy.

When Officer Pete shifted out of the way, I saw some

heathen with long brown hair and a mangled beard. Something very babyish about his features made me think he couldn't be any older than Brad.

"I'm Bob Waltzer, the owner of this joint, you hobo. How did you get in here? Did you break one of my windows, you dirtball?" Bob's voice was laced with either rage or panic, and he paced around the room, as if he was checking for damages. Or maybe stolen items.

"Hobo?" The boy's voice dripped with offense. "I'm your little brother, Broccoli!"

Broccoli? That was *Broccoli Waltzer!*

"*Broccoli?*" Bob's composure melted into a pile of pudding. "Where have you been all these years? Mom and Dad thought you were kidnapped! *I* thought you ran away! You look so...*old!*"

"I'm a lot younger than you! I was locked in some crappy house with some dude named Heverly until last summer, then I made my escape when he moved. I had nowhere to go, so I came here."

"You could have *told* me!" Bob demanded, before turning to the cops and saying, "I promise I didn't know he was staying here. Is he in trouble?"

Pete wrinkled his eyebrows, his eyes wide. He stepped between the two of them and cleared his throat. "Um, no. It's more of a general conspiracy in the community, so we felt the need to investigate."

I could not believe this. Broccoli wasn't a lie. He wasn't even a ghost! He was a person. A real person! My first day as a detective, and I was witnessing the return of *the* Broccoli Waltzer! A rustling sound came from somewhere beneath the commotion, and everyone got quiet. Naturally, I creeped inside to investigate. Officer Pete found the source and opened a door off the side of the room, and a person was hiding in there!

"Now, what is this?" Bob yelled, glaring at Broccoli. "How many people have been stowaways in my club? I knew somebody was thieving my nachos! The books never match up!"

"It's just my girl—my friend," Broccoli stammered, his eyes shifting nervously. "Nobody else, I swear."

"Rochelle Tipper?" asked Pete.

"Rochelle?" I asked a little too loudly.

Everyone turned, their eyes falling on me.

"Who is this?" Bob shrieked upon seeing me, his hands grasping his head. He looked like he was about to have a meltdown. His face kept switching between the color of snow and blood.

"Dennis June!" Rochelle yelled. "What are you doing here, you freak?"

"What are *you* doing here?" I hollered back.

"Hey! It's that kid from the station! The little snoop!" The pot-bellied cop pointed at me.

"You are trespassing, little girl. You need to leave," groaned Pete, lifting his head to the sky.

"I'm here as a detective! Rochelle is the one living in the closet!" I pointed at the closet she just tumbled out of.

Lie after lie and secret after secret unravelled in front of me. What was Rochelle doing here? And what was she doing with Broccoli Waltzer? Bob was losing his mind, begging the cops not to send him to jail because he had no idea they were staying here, even though the cops already said they never planned on arresting him. Everyone forgot about me again, but I was glad. I could keep eavesdropping this way.

"Broccoli, we need to get her back," Rochelle told him, speaking very hush hush beneath the other conversations. It was quiet, but seemed very heated.

"Who?" I scooted right beside her.

Rochelle shoved me, and I flew backwards a few steps.

"What's the problem over here?" demanded Pot Belly, straightening to his full height and flaunting his authority. Rochelle handed him a piece of paper—a photograph. I tried to stand on my tiptoes, so I could see what was imaged.

"I need to report a missing person," Rochelle told him.

"Who?" I asked.

She frowned at me, then turned back to the cop. Pointing at the photograph, she leaned forward and said, "This is my daughter, Lil' Shelbi. She's two years old."

Whoa Nelly.

It had been weeks, and Rochelle had forced me to keep my trap shut about what I heard. I couldn't believe she had a daughter. How did I not know she had a daughter? She wasn't married, so I thought the only way she could have gotten a baby was if she went to the hospital, where they make them, like Stacey. I told her as much in our bedroom while Shaye was at cheerleading practice.

"How do you have a baby?" I stared at her, looking for answers.

"I am so not going to be the one to give you *that* talk." Rochelle straightened up in her bed and glared daggers through me.

"But you're not married. You're not even that old. You can't drive a car."

"You don't have to be married or know how to drive a car to have a baby, Dennis." She narrowed her eyes at me. "I thought I told you to drop this. Have you been telling people this stuff? 'Cause I'll kill you."

"I haven't told anybody," I said quickly. "I'm not stupid,

though. I know babies don't come from storks!"

"What do you mean by that?" An uncomfortable expression crossed Rochelle's face. Rochelle rarely looked uncomfortable about anything, no matter how gross it was.

"Well, if you're married, then God puts babies in your belly and then you just have them. You don't know how many or when you're going to get them." But she wasn't married and didn't have a big belly. She's always had a six pack of abs.

Her lip curled into a smirk on the left side, and her eyes brightened. Probably because she was surprised I knew all this already.

"And if you're not married?" she asked.

"Then you can go to the hospital, like Stacey did. She told them she was getting sad because she was fat."

Rochelle snorted. I didn't see why this was funny.

I continued, "And then they gave her a baby. They make them there. I bet they grow them in a lab like the people that tried to clone sheep on TV. It's like a baby factory. Then they give them to people. Or you can adopt them, like Dad does. That's for the babies that nobody wants, so they live in factories or orphanages for years until somebody feels bad enough to take them home."

Rochelle's shoulders shook all over, and she grabbed her stomach.

"What's so funny?" I frowned.

"Nothing. That's exactly how babies are made, Dennis." She smiled and rolled back over on her bed. It felt good to be right.

"Do you think Mom will be mad that you have a baby? I mean, is she going to live here with us?" I thought for a second. What if Rochelle demanded that she slept in here instead of the nursery?

"She got over it with Ambrosia; she'll get over it with me."

"Ambrosia and Lil' Shelbi are almost the same age," I stated. "I like the name Shelbi a lot better."

"Well, Ambrosia never stood a chance. Her dad's name is Boop, after all. Stupid." Rochelle flipped through a comic book before groaning and saying, "Ew! Why do they have to put *words* in here?"

What would the book be without *words?*

"Boop isn't Ambrosia's dad. Stacey got her at the hospital," I said.

"Sure, she did." There was that irritating, puzzling smirk again.

I turned around in my bed and flopped down on it. Staring at the ceiling—that had some weird stains on it, by the way—I never felt more confused.

My parents went to the courthouse for another thing they call a "trial" today, even though it felt like this all had already dragged on forever and a day. Mom said it had something to do with Grandma and "withholding information," but I couldn't keep from worrying that they might go to jail. The two of them went several times, but she never let us go with them. When they went to these, Ashley was always in charge. She was being nice to me again. I think she may have actually forgotten that it had been me who brought everything up in the first place. Even though I knew she didn't mean it, I still thought about her words that day. *Everyone hates you.* With my life and the fact I still ate lunch alone every day and had no one to play with at recess, I was starting to believe she was right.

Mrs. Sanchez was at school most of the time, but a few days here and there *Mr. Mcloofin* had to teach us. That was our principal's name. I found that out when he introduced himself his first day teaching us. I didn't think he knew much. He always made us just sit quietly and do boring worksheets. I may not be good at math, but I knew how to write numbers, and I knew how to add one plus one.

Today was another one of those days where Mrs. Sanchez wasn't at school, and Ol' Mcloofin was teaching. Maybe Sanch was eavesdropping on my parents at the courthouse. I shook my head at my wandering thoughts. It was reading time for kids in preschool through sixth grade, so we were reading a book by Dr. Seuss, and I had already read it a million times. Mr. Mcloofin made us read aloud, saying that it helped us learn. Mama's Child held the book and squinted at the pages.

"Red Fa, fee... feesh, bluh... bloooo, fa. Fa—"

"Fish!" I groaned, and Mr. Mcloofin shot me a disapproving scowl, but why was she taking forever to read four words?

Maybe she was pretending not to know so she could get attention. Or maybe she was taking forever so she would waste Mr. Mcloofin's time, and we wouldn't have to do anything else! That was smart. Maybe I should do that, so I wouldn't have to endure this baby work. After careful consideration, I decided against it. I couldn't butcher a book like that.

We focused on reading for most of the day, and some of us even continued during our indoor recess. Haylee and Hallee had a book that was thicker what most kids our age read, and it caught my attention. Hallee was asking Haylee what certain words meant and how to say them, and some of it sounded familiar. I looked at the cover. *Pippi Longstocking*.

I crossed over to the playmat they were sitting on."That's

a good one," I told her, pointing at the book.

Haylee closed it and narrowed her eyes at me, raising a suspicious eyebrow. "*You've* read this book?"

"Yes. I liked it, but it wasn't my favorite."

"You've read *all* of it?" she asked. I didn't like her tone. Pausing in offense, I stated, "Yes."

She frowned and pursed her lips tightly. "By yourself?"

"How else would I read it?" This was annoying verging on insulting.

Her and Hallee exchanged a glance, and Hallee shrugged before telling Hallee, "This book's too hard. I don't like it."

"Hey, guys! I'm reading too!" Monica chirped, her dress poofing and a book clutched to her chest. My heart stopped. She sat down and folded her legs crisscross applesauce.

"What are you reading?" I asked. She gently set Dr. Seuss's *The Places You'll Go* on the floor, tucking her legs beneath her delicately.

"It's a tough one," Monica huffed, faking wiping her brow. "I can't read most of it. I asked Mr. Mcloofin to read it to me, but he got mad."

I frowned at the book. It wasn't a tough one from what I could remember. But I wanted to fit in, so I settled for, "Yeah, some of the words are tricky."

After recess, Mr. Mcloofin decided that we kids would be taking tests with our reading. Apparently when Mrs. Sanchez returned, we would be reading out loud to her one by one. My nerves bundled inside of me excitedly. People would finally believe I could read (cough cough) Brad! Thinking of Brad made me think of my siblings, and my thoughts drifted to Rochelle.

I glanced back at her and thought about her missing baby. How did it end up missing? Why did nobody know about it in the first place? She said that Mom would get over it like she did with Ambrosia. She probably should just tell them, though. My dad would be over the moon if he knew a new kid would be joining the family. He was even being nice to my mom right now and acting like he really loved her. At first I thought it was because he felt bad about Grandma and the fact they had to go to the courthouse all the time. But then I noticed him rubbing her growing belly, and it made me more and more nervous that we would be getting some new siblings soon.

One time, when I prayed at night, I told God we had enough babies and that He should give them to other people instead. Then I apologized because I shouldn't tell Him what to do. He might get mad at me.

My parents came home from yet another hearing at the court weeks later. My dad felt so bad about how upset my mom was that he even took the whole day off work. He told me he was going to the grocery store, so she wouldn't have to, and I passed the word on to my mom. But she wasn't happy. She made me sit beside her on the couch until he came back. I liked knowing things, but I didn't want to hear about her Chinese soap operas, *or* her nasty comments about how we "didn't have money" and that Dad was "buying the whole store." But it was unusual for her to talk to me unless it involved yelling, scolding, or demanding me do things, so I sat there and stared at the door with her until he finally returned.

She leaped up immediately to investigate the grocery bags as he brought them in, and my dad made some corny joke about how he was "literally bringing home the bacon." My mom's eyes took on a threateningly violent gleam.

There was a pause.

"Are you *kidding* me?" Her eyebrows shot up, and her

hand snapped to her hip.

My dad backed away a little, and he paused before fumbling, "Uh, you don't want to kill the pig, so…"

How dare he talk about Beans that way? "Beans doesn't deserve to die!" I piped up, but my mom ignored me and tore into my dad.

"Did you seriously buy milk from the store when we have a cow?" she growled.

"Why would I want to drink milk from that cow? And besides, did you see the missing child on the side of the carton? Look at that little angel. It's so sad." He pouted his bottom lip, holding up the carton of milk. I crowded up against my mother so I could see.

"Well, let's see the little rat that convinced you to spend money we don't have," she retaliated. Snatching the carton from his hand, she turned it to the side with the photograph.

"It says her name is Lil' Shelbi and that she's only two years old!" My dad looked like he was about to cry even though he didn't know the kid. Wait, did he say *Lil' Shelbi*?

Uh-oh.

Mom squinted at the text. "Why does this say to contact the police *or* Rochelle Tipper?"

Dad rubbed his beard, and my eyes drifted to the floor, suddenly losing interest in this argument.

"Dennis, what do you know about this?" Suspicion dripped from her voice.

"I dunno."

"Dennis…" Her hand curled under my chin, forcing me to meet her eyes.

"You need to ask Rochelle." My heartbeat bursted like fireworks in my chest.

Mom dropped my chin. "Rochelle!" she hollered, and kept hollering until my sister finally came downstairs.

"Yeah?"

"What is this?" She held up the carton.

"A carton of milk." She had mastered lying. No trace of nervousness laced her being at all.

"Why in the Bessie dung patty would they contact *you* about this kid?" My mom stabbed an angry finger at the carton.

Just then, the phone rang, and Rochelle rushed to it, gripping it like it was a water bottle in the Sahara Desert. My mom and dad stared at her, and I did too. I couldn't make out the other end of the conversation, but Rochelle said, "I'm sorry! I'll be there right away." Who was she apologizing to?

"I have to go," her voice wobbled. They let her go. They seriously just *let her go*. If that was me, I would've been sent to the grounded room for a week!

My parents resumed their argument about the groceries like nothing happened. I snuck out the front door and looked both ways down the road. Beans squealed from his pen, and I turned around. He had his snout up against the pen, like he was talking to me.

"I'm coming back, Beanie!" I cooed at him, like he was a baby. He was *my* baby. Beans snorted and huffed and puffed.

"Fine. Just one quick pat pat-aroo!" I glanced over my shoulder, then crossed the distance between us and gave him a pat on the head. He rubbed his wet nose against my hand, giving me little piggy kisses.

Hoping I hadn't lost her, I rushed back to the sidewalk, and finally saw Rochelle in the distance on her bike. I took off running so I could snoop on her. It didn't take long for me to lose my breath and feel like I was dying from the exercise. So when I saw a bike my size abandoned on the sidewalk, of course I borrowed it. I would return it. Eventually.

"Dennis! My bike!" someone screamed.

I nearly wrecked the bike trying to turn my head to see who it was. You'll never believe it—Mama's Child. I had just stolen Mama's Child's bike.

"Dennis!" she hollered after me, trying to run, but she was too slow to catch me.

"Sorry!" I called back at her. "I'll bring it back!" But was I really sorry? I mean, I think we were kinda even now.

Rochelle dropped her bike in front of a rickety old cottage. I had no idea what street we were even on. Hiding behind an overgrown shrub, I popped a squat and waited. An elderly woman answered the door, and her embedded wrinkles seemed to deepen further than I thought possible. Her outburst traveled all the way over here.

"Rochelle! Just what in tarnation are you trying to pull here? I try to be a good grandma and take in your kid until you graduate highschool. That was our deal, and I don't recall a graduation announcement in my mailbox!"

Did she just say *grandma?*

"Why did you lie and say you didn't know where she was? What if they had arrested me for kidnapping?" The woman's voice shook with a mixture of anger and worry. I moved a little closer so I could hear better, leaving the bike by the shrub.

"Lil' Shelb looked so cute in the miniature boxing gloves I got her. I realized that I want her back." Her voice cracked and faltered.

I had never seen Rochelle so concerned about anything in my entire life. As far as I knew, she hated more people and more things than my mom even did. This was a strange shock for me.

"I just. I don't know. I panicked! A missing person ad was the only way to get the information out at this point. What if people thought I just gave her up? What if *she* grows up thinking that? I love her."

The woman frowned, adding to her many deep wrinkles. She muttered something I couldn't decipher, then turned back into her cottage. Rochelle didn't follow her. When she returned, a chunky little toddler with two fat pigtails trailed beside her, dragging a small sack of what I assumed were her belongings. I watched this all unseen and thought, *Man, Dennis. You could be given a reward from your detective skills some day. That is, if you don't become BFFs with Monica and get rich and famous from being a supermodel.*

"You no longer can call me Great-grandma Microwave," the woman frowned at Rochelle. She muttered something else to Lil' Shelbi and slammed the door. Rochelle and the kid looked at each other for a few seconds.

"Come on, let's go home." She hefted the chunky tot into her arms, propping her on one hip and pushing her bike.

When I looked into Lil' Shelbi's face, I saw pure, one hundred percent rotten. A gnawing sensation in my belly told me she would grow up to be just like Rochelle, and they didn't call it the "terrible twos" for nothing. I waited a few seconds before I turned to get the bike, so Rochelle wouldn't see me following her. A hand grabbed my wrist, and I nearly peed my pants. Finding Mama's Child at the end of the arm, I shrieked and grabbed my chest.

"Don't do that!" I hissed. I was going to have a heart attack.

"You thief! You stole mah bike, Dennis!" Mama's Child's missing front tooth made her voice sound funny, and I wiped her spit off my cheek. I rolled my eyes. It wasn't looking like I would be getting home anytime soon.

My mom was furious! Even with me getting home much later (thanks, Mama's Child!), I could still sense the tension as my mom stabbed her salad with a fork. She was eating on the sofa, and I wondered where she got the food. If she went to a restaurant, I would've liked to have gone. I also liked salads. Especially if they had lots of cheese and croutons.

"Rochelle!" she bellowed, then continued chomping on the lettuce that was flopping around inside her wide open mouth.

"Ugh, Mom. What?" Lil' Shelb followed her down the stairs.

"Why don't we just put her in the grounded room? We're running out of space here."

"My child is not living in the grounded room." Rochelle glared at my mother like she had just committed treason.

"Well, I ain't taking care of one more kid. You are getting a job."

"I don't want a job!" Rochelle's eyes filled with flames. But my mom was even *more* livid.

"You shoulda thought about that when you decided to have a baby." She chomped on her salad obnoxiously.

"Lil' Shelbi can sleep in my room with me."

"I am not getting put in the grounded room!" I rushed over to where they were talking.

My mom's eyes snapped in my direction with a threatening warning glare. "Dennis June, must you listen to *everything*?"

I didn't answer, and she rolled her eyes, turning back to Rochelle.

"Dennis can sleep on the floor if she has to." Rochelle crossed her arms and glanced between us.

It was decided that Lil' Shelbi would be staying in our room, but that she'd have her own little mattress. I'd get to keep my bed. Not having to worry about that, my mind wandered elsewhere.

Thinking about how I didn't have any friends and that Lil' Shelbi didn't know me, I decided to be nice. Look at what happened with Krissy and Dom! I blew them off like they were babies, and now they were friends with Monica! I tapped Lil' Shelbi's shoulder.

"Hi, I'm DJ," I told her, but she just stared at me, a stone wall.

"Can I call you Lil' Shelb, like your mom does?"

"No!" She stomped a fat foot.

Okay, so that was a bad move. I tried again. "Your pigtails are really cute."

"Mommy!" she screamed over and over. I grabbed my ears. Rochelle flung the door open and rushed to her side.

"What's wrong?" Rochelle asked gently.

Shelbi pointed at me and started crying. What the dump?

"Dennis! Quit harassing my daughter!"

"I was just being nice!" I whined. "I want to be friends with her." *Just picture it—Monica, Lil' Shelbi, and me riding our bikes or walking down the street together. Could Lil' Shelb ride a bike? Maybe if we put training wheels on it?*

"Ew, no." Rochelle looked at me like I was scum.

"But she's my niece, like Ambrosia. Is she going to call me 'Aunt DJ'?" I fiddled with my fingers and glanced at Shelbi.

"Lil' Shelb is too cool to be your friend. She was *born* cool. You weren't. Quit trying." She wrapped Lil' Shelbi up in a big hug and sat down on her bed with her. The toddler bursted into a fit of giggles. The two of them seemed so happy together.

I went to my bed and sat down, feeling lonelier and sadder than ever.

Chapter 9

MY MOM RUINED CHRISTMAS time for me. Christmas was my favorite holiday, and how could it not be? Santa, Christmas music, no school. I was over the moon when we were on break. School was getting more interesting, but also more miserable. When we got placed in new reading groups after our testing, I ended up with Haylee, Katrina, Tommy, and Timmy. Haylee was the only girl my age, and I did enjoy sitting by Tommy. But Katrina was the worst, and I wanted to be in a group with Monica. Unfortunately, she was with Mark Melon, Marcus Delon, and Mama's Child. I didn't know the other kids besides them, so I just referred to the whole group as nothing but M's. My thoughts shifted, and I considered inviting Monica over to play games or sing songs, but I didn't know her phone number, and I was too scared to ask my mom.

My mom. The ruiner of Christmas. I went outside to milk Bessie, and a big ol' truck with a fence around the back lurked in our yard. Some man was forcing Beans to get inside the truck bed, so I banged on the side of his door and asked him just what in tarnation he thought he was doing with my pig. My Beans.

"Listen, kid, I bought this pig off your mother. Now quit banging on my truck!" The old man spit black stuff into our yard.

"Beans doesn't want to go!" I cried.

"Who is Beans?"

"My pig!" I gripped the fence of his truck and stuck my face up against it. Beans's snout wiggled, snuffing.

"This is my pig now. I don't have to answer to you. I already paid your mother. Now git!" He slapped his truck bed and hopped into the driver's seat, slamming the door.

The man's tires stirred up a bunch of mud and splattered it all over the yard. I glanced at Beans's empty pen. Then I started running after him, my milk pail swinging. I threw the pail at his truck, and it dinged it pretty good. Beans squealed and snorted, trying to get back to me, so I kept pushing myself to run faster and faster.

"No!" I wailed as loud as I could. I made it to the edge of our property, but the man's truck got smaller and smaller until I couldn't make it out anymore. Our backdoor creaked and slammed, but I didn't bother to turn around. I sat in the grass and cried my eyes out, thinking the tears were never going to stop. Purple talons grabbed my arm and jerked me up out of the grass.

"Dennis June! That man paid us good money for that pig. What is wrong with you?" My mother was red in the face, and she huffed.

"That's not just 'that pig'. That's my Beans!" I pointed at my chest, tears streaming down my cheeks.

"What?" Confusion crossed her face.

"I named him! It's not his fault! What if they kill him because he doesn't know how to make bacon?" I bawled, and my knees bent, forcing me to cower back to the ground. My mother kept pulling on my arm to drag me back to the house, but I refused, and I dead-weighted it, letting my body drag through the grass. I didn't care if my clothes got ruined.

"That's how people get bacon, Dennis! You're too young. You don't understand!" My mom groaned as she pulled my chunky body.

"Get up!" she hissed.

"No!" I ripped up grass.

"You have to get up. Now!" She jerked me up in one powerful sweep, and I stood, wailing. Pain seared like she was going to rip my arm out of the socket. When she glanced at me, something changed in her eyes, and she loosened her grip.

"It wouldn't hurt if you would just listen and go inside!" She was breathing heavily, so I followed her inside.

"What happened to your clothes?" asked Shaye, her eyes widening.

"Some man stole Beans!"

"Who?"

"She's upset over the pig." My mom's heels clicked against the floor, and she pulled a can of soda out of the fridge. I went to the living room and flung myself down on our empty couch. It seemed like all my siblings had Christmas time plans, but my Christmas was ruined. It could not get any worse.

It got worse.

A few days later, the news was on. My parents were both home, and I thought it was odd that my dad wasn't at work. The news people were talking about the Mrs. Sanchez murder trial. One of the men used a bunch of legal terms I didn't understand, and my grandma was on the screen in handcuffs. My mom placed a hand to her forehead and let out a loud sigh. Then I recognized the lady from the rickety old cottage.

"That's Great-grandma Microwave!" I yelled, pointing at the screen and standing.

My mom immediately turned to me. "How do you know about her?" she quickly questioned.

Sensing I wasn't supposed to know her for some reason —and not wanting to get sent to the grounded room for it—I explained, "I just know her name, I don't know her. Why is she named Microwave? That's not a real name."

"Because your great-great-grandma is an absolute idiot." My mom turned back to the screen, puffing strands of unusually messy hair out of her eyes.

"Is she really my great-grandma? She would have to be really old."

"She is, but your great-great-grandma is *much* older."

"She's *alive?* What does she look like? Is she all wrinkled up like a prune?" I hopped on the couch between her and my dad and got right in my mom's face, excited for answers.

"Dennis, I'm trying to watch this." She shoved me, so I flopped backwards and tried to sit still. My dad snored, and my mom shot him a disgusted glare, as if he could see her.

"Why is she on TV?" I asked.

"Because she's Beverly's mom and she's giving a statement."

"Why aren't *you* on TV? That's your mom!"

My mom shot daggers through me, and my dad coughed, but he wasn't sick, so I think he was faking it. And apparently also faking being asleep. "We were acquitted, Dennis June. We'd like to keep it that way. I was not involved in that mess, and I don't want to be now. What would people *think?*" The way she said those last few words had me wondering the same exact thing. What *would* people think? Was everybody going to think of us as criminals? I didn't want that. I wanted to be the hero.

"Beverly Hill will be returning to Mexico, where she is a citizen. She will be imprisoned for an undetermined length of time. There have been several warrants out for her arrest there, related to some armed robberies of Taco Bell restaurants." The news man's eyes widened.

Grandma was going to Mexico?

"Grandma is going to Mexico? Are we ever gonna see her again?" I asked.

"I have no idea." My mom frowned, then stood to turn the volume up. My dad followed, and banged on the top of the box to get the picture clearer. I didn't understand how that would help, but apparently it did.

Glancing at each other and whispering, my parents turned and looked at me. Then my mom said, "Listen, Dennis, I don't think Santa is going to be coming this year. I don't want you to be disappointed."

How in the world would I not be disappointed? First my grandma got arrested for killing somebody. Then I lost my pig—my *BEANS*—followed by my grandma being sent to *Mexico!* Now Santa Claus wasn't coming? I actually was looking forward to going back to school at this point because I didn't know how much longer I could bear staying in this house.

Returning to school after Christmas break was the worst. Santa, in fact, did not come to our house. But it sounded like he went to everyone else's. Were we considered bad now? And if we were, how long would it last? Santa always gave coal to bad kids. So what did it mean if he didn't give you anything or show up *at all?* Everyone else was doting all of their new clothes and toys. Staring at my worksheet with a familiar tightness in my throat, I told myself not to cry. At recess, Mama's Child told me that Santa didn't visit her because she was poor. I told her that he used to visit us even though we were poor and that I thought he didn't come this year because she got my grandma arrested, and now my family was doomed. She just frowned at me and walked away. I guess she didn't have anything to say after that.

I worked up the nerve to go to Monica's house a few days later. It was kind of chilly out, but it hadn't been all that bad. My jeans and long-sleeved shirt were keeping me warm, and the only place cold was my right big toe. That was because I had a hole in my shoe.

I rang her doorbell, but then my stomach rumbled and my pulse pitter-pattered. This place was somehow ethereal—a glittery, easter-egg yellow, and *hu-MON-gous!* Elaborate white-crystal pillars cradled the elaborate awning covered in vines of delicate, lively little pink flowers. Just touching the (probably real) gold doorbell seemed a crime. I was dirt poor and a "nobody." Monica was clearly a "*somebody.*" Hustling around to the side with garden plants, I crouched down and gritted my teeth, tensing every muscle in my neck. *You shouldn't be here. Nobody even likes you.*

I told the voices in my head to shut up and collected myself, taking a deep breath. When I gathered the courage, I rang the bell again. This time I waited for someone to answer. Footsteps came from inside the house, and it wasn't long until Megan Green opened the door. I smiled, but she frowned as she looked down at me. She let out a sigh. It didn't sound angry, more like she was saddened to see me. What had I done wrong? Maybe I shouldn't have come.

"So you're the person who's been ding-dong ditching us." She looked an awful lot like Monica, the same penny-colored hair and sparkling green eyes.

I didn't know what to say.

"What?" I frowned, and my cheeks reddened at my delay in response.

"I'm calling your mom. I'm disappointed in you, you know. You kids need to understand that this kind of thing isn't funny. It's an annoyance. Wait here," she told me, before turning back into her house and closing the door.

I stayed still, my cheeks growing redder and redder. What was I waiting on? It was killing me to not go inside and look around, but she told me to wait here, so I did.

I only rang her doorbell twice. I'd hardly consider that ding-dong ditching. Nervous, I looked around, at the garden, at the neighbors yard…then I saw her. Hiding in the bushes, snickering.

Mama's Child.

She must've been the one ding-dong ditching! When she noticed I'd caught her, she got up and took off running, ripping through the trees and people's backyards.

"Mama's!" I hissed, but she didn't turn back.

The door opened, and I snapped my attention back to Megan.

"Your mother will be here in five minutes if you want to take a seat on the steps." Megan's blank expression confused me. She had said earlier that she was disappointed, and she was enough so to call my mother on me. But she didn't yell, didn't even raise her voice in the slightest. It was so different from my mother's anger that I honestly didn't know if she *was* angry at all.

I waited for what felt like an eternity in silence.

"Dennis June!" my mother hollered, rolling down the passenger side window. "What is wrong with you?"

My mom parked her car and told me to get in the back seat and wait. She left the window rolled down, and Megan approached the car. Mom apologized profusely to Megan about me being so disrespectful. It was *just* a doorbell, and I only rang it *twice!*

After a few minutes, Megan was smiling and chuckling a little, as if she had completely forgotten the whole thing. My mom grinned ear to ear, but when she got in the car and we drove home, she let me have it. She didn't hit me or anything, but she kept ranting on and on about how embarrassing I was being and that "these people's opinions matter!" Well, didn't my opinions matter, too? Weren't we all the same deep down? What really made them any different from me?

When we came to a halt at a stop sign, she sighed.

"You're not going to that Back to School Dance this fall. I cannot allow it. You have to be punished, so you will learn."

"Wasn't losing Beans punishment enough for a lifetime?" I gritted my teeth, tears brimming in my lids.

She stiffened, and the color drained from her face. Turning away, she gazed out the window, cleared her throat, then her eyes fell to her hands. "I don't know what you're talking about," she croaked.

"You do—"

"—you have to learn," she murmured, but refused to look at me. We were back in motion.

"But Mom!" I whined. The dance would only be the coolest thing *ever*. Every grade would get to go to it. It was going to be shortly after school started next year, and it would be the first dance I'd ever get to go to! I said a silent prayer that my mom would forget about all of this by then and that I would still get to go. With Lil' Shelbi and Mom's new baby(ies?), I assumed she'd have a lot more chaos going on.

"Megan does not want you ringing her doorbell! Did you know that she's pregnant? Pregnant people don't like to be bothered!" My mom clutched her swollen belly with one hand as she pulled up to our house.

I groaned obnoxiously. "Why is everyone having babies? Katrina said *her* mom is pregnant, too. It's getting really annoying. It's making me hate babies."

My mom stopped the car and turned off the ignition. She turned to face me and said, "I have never agreed with anything you have said so strongly in my life. Maybe you are my daughter after all."

I walked up our dirt path slowly, then headed for my bedroom. What would I wear if I could go to the dance? Maybe something sparkly? How would I afford it? My mom wouldn't buy anything special or expensive. I didn't remember us having any fancy hand-me-downs, either. It didn't sound like it would be a formal dance, but I wanted to look like a princess. All the big kids would be there, and Monica and the other kids my age would probably be wearing clothes that their fashion-designing, model moms gave them.

Lil' Shelbi shot me the stank eye as soon as I opened the door to my bedroom.

"Do you even like living here?" I asked bluntly. "Is it better than living with the Microwave lady?"

"We not friends!" she screeched like a heathen, spinning around in circles and jumping on everyone's beds.

"I oughta call you Tarzan instead of Shelbi." I narrowed my eyes at her as she threw me into a sensory-overload with all her screaming and jumping. It was like one tiny ball of energy blurring across my vision every five seconds, with about five sirens going off. That was the simplest way I could describe her.

Chapter 10

TODAY WAS THE LAST day of school, but more importantly—it was my birthday! I turned six years old today. I cringed, because I *hated* the number six. This morning, I got dressed and ready for school, snagging a quick breakfast. It was pretty busy, and my mom was running late for work, so we all kind of just senselessly ran around, trying to eat and get dressed and make it to where we needed to be on time. Nobody mentioned my birthday. I assumed that was part of a surprise or something related to a birthday present. Acting like I didn't notice, I lingered a few minutes in the kitchen and waited for everyone to yell "Happy Birthday!" But they never did.

At school, we got a class roster at the beginning of the year with birthdays on it, but nobody told me "Happy Birthday" there, either. Not the Greens, not the Stars, not my own family. Mama's Child didn't glance my direction once. Mrs. Sanchez didn't act like anything was different or special today, but that didn't bother me. *Everyone must be in on it. Maybe Monica will be, too!*

Sitting in my casual usual lunch seat, alone, I pulled out some cheese and crackers and started eating. People walked by, heading to the lunch line to grab their trays, putting coins in the vending machine, or chatting it up about how it was the last day of school. Excitement filled the air, and finally the day felt a little more special. But I didn't hear anything about my birthday. Just comments about going on vacation or having sleepovers.

Then out the corner of my eye, I saw Monica walking in my direction, and did a double take. I tried not to stare because I didn't want to scare her off. She was probably just going to walk past me to get extra food or throw something away. Maybe she had to use the bathroom. But then she set her backpack down on the top of my table, unzipped it, and pulled out a small box. She slid it across the table with a demure smile and said, "Happy Birthday."

I was in so much shock that I couldn't even swallow my cheese crackers before she walked away. Gulping, I stammered, "Thank you," but it came out all breathy, and she didn't hear me. She sat back down at her table, and I wiped my hands clean on my shorts before opening the box. Inside was a little keychain shaped like a yellow stereo. It had a small square disc attached on a string that read "*NSYNC." I squealed because they were only like the coolest band around right now! My older sisters listened to their music and gushed over the boys in the band. My brothers tried to pretend they were just as cute. They were not.

Mrs. Sanchez stormed over to my little island of isolation and ripped me out of my seat by my arm. She told me I was going to go to the principal's office for my actions, and Mr. Mcloofin told me I was in trouble for "causing a ruckus in the lunchroom." I was so excited over the gift that I didn't even care. Mr. Mcloofin. I couldn't stand that *meatball*! He was so mean, gave me the side-eye like every day, and was always treating us like babies even though I was *six* years old now. My stomach lurched at that number.

I had to clean the chalkboard after school, and when Mrs. Sanchez told me I could go home, I was thrilled. I was getting a little worried that I would miss my own surprise party.

"Can I have a ride?" I asked her.

She frowned, more disgusted than usual, and spat, "Not a chance." Grabbing her satchel, she unlocked the door, and after we were both out of the building, she locked it back up. Walking home, I didn't feel quite so exhausted from exercising because I was too preoccupied with my little stereo keychain. I kept popping the little CD into it so it would play the few seconds of the song.

When I got home, nobody even said "hey." I shrugged like it didn't matter, but then I noticed there wasn't a birthday cake. No surprise stu, no noodles, and no ice cream.

"DJ?" my mom asked as I sat on our couch, playing the CD on a loop.

I looked up at her, hope rising within me. Maybe it was time for a cake she had hidden somewhere?

"Who the dung did you rob to get that stereo? You know I love *NSYNC, but I can't have you thievin'! My triplets are due in two months, and I don't want you getting me in trouble."

"I didn't steal it. It was a birthday present." I popped the CD in again so it would play the song. I smiled at this, the only good part of the day.

"You liar. Go to your room!" My mom pointed up the stairs.

What the dump? It was *my birthday*. Monica Green had given me this.

A few tears escaped my eyes, drowning me in my sorrow

as I walked up the steps and headed for my room. Flopping face down on my bed, I let it all out. Loud and clear. In between the sobbing, though, a strange noise loitered. Something like heavy breathing. Then somebody whispered, "Happy Birthday, Denny."

I shot out of bed and scanned the empty room. A pile of clothes in the corner of the room shifted, and out popped a familiar red afro.

Mama's Child.

I screamed, but she hissed, "Shh!" and approached me, something shiny in her hands. It looked like foil—greasy hamburger wrappers, probably from her mom's sketchy diner.

"I've been waiting for you since school let out." Her voice was calm, like this was totally normal.

My voice still high and much too nasal, I asked incredulously, "Why?"

"Open it."

I unwrapped the package and looked at her in confusion. "This is a cheeseburger," I said after we stared at each other in silence for a while.

"I'm sorry I told your secret."

Flames of fury bloomed inside me, but I quickly extinguished them and ignored this total lie. There were more important issues at hand.

"How did you get in my house? And did you call me *Denny* earlier?" I hurled the questions at her, and she just smirked her Cheshire Cat grin. "The games are over, Mama's Child. Get outta here!"

"I thought we were friends!" She raised both hands in defense.

"Mom!" I hollered.

"Denny!" she whined.

"Mama's Child broke into our house!" I didn't care that I was being a tattle tale.

"I'm goin'!" she yelled, rushing back to the clothes pile and digging around.

"What are you doing?"

"Getting my frying pan!"

"Why do you have a frying pan?" I demanded.

"How do you think I got in here?" she asked, fishing around in dirty clothes before hefting up a small pan. Then she ran out of my room, and I followed, trying to keep up with her pace. As she flew down the steps as fast as her feet could take her, her frying pan swinging. She grabbed the doorknob with her free hand and floored it outta there.

I hurried down the steps and stuck my head out the door, screaming, "You ratface! Get back here!" Her image shrank into the distance.

"What are you hollering 'Mom' for? And why are you screaming out the door?" my mom asked, a hand on her hip. She frowned down at me, and her gaze lowered to the half-wrapped sandwich in my left hand. Without notice, she snatched it. Before I could answer her questions, she flung me another.

"Where'd you get this cheeseburger?" she asked. "I thought I told you to go to your room."

"It's from Mama's Child." I was utterly and completely confused at how this day had unraveled.

My mom finished unwrapping the sandwich and took a bite. "This is pretty good," she said through a full mouth.

"Uh—" I trailed off, looking out the door once more.

"Shut that door. You're gonna let every skeeter in the county in here."

I blinked dumbly, then shut the door. As I slowly started up the steps, my mom stopped me again.

"Oh! DJ." She took another bite.

"Yeah?" I asked, one hand gripping the banister.

"Happy Birthday."

The first day of summer was boiling hot. It was so hot that all of the weather channels were repeating the same corny old joke: "How hot is it? Hot enough to fry an egg on the sidewalk!" Oh yeah? Well, I tried just that. I cracked an egg and tried to fry it on the sidewalk. It actually *worked.* But then my mom found out and told me it was an extremely disrespectful waste of perfectly good food. She made me eat that egg. Barf.

I stumbled out of bed, deciding that the germs from the sidewalk egg weren't going to kill me today. Naps could have that soothing effect, and this nap had been particularly sound. Why was it so eerily quiet? It finally dawned on me. Narks. I forgot that today my dad was taking all of us to the pool at 8:00 a.m. so my mom could have a break. He must've forgotten about me, just like I had forgotten. How could I forget? Was I stupid? It looked like it would just be Mom and I today.

I was rummaging around, trying to find a good snackie in the kitchen when the doorbell rang. Alarmed, I clutched my juice pouch to my chest and shoved a mitt into a bag of stale Cheez-Its like a thief. If my siblings were back, it was every kid for themself. My mom answered it, and I peered around the kitchen archway to see who it was. Mrs. Sanchez strolled in wearing a green dress with a thick black collar, and I gulped down my nom-noms in shock. How was she not fainting from the heat? My mom told her to have a seat, so when the two of them had sat down, I crawled across the floor and sat behind the couch, so I could listen.

"What did you want, Deniese?" asked Mrs. Sanchez.

"This had better be good." My *mom* had invited her over here?

Papers rustled.

"What is that?" asked Mrs. Sanchez.

"That's a year's worth of free workbooks is what that is."

I almost spit out my juice. My mom was trying to get all of us kids free workbooks. Sanch hated when people asked for *discounted* workbooks. But *free* workbooks? My mom must be cracked off her rocker!

"I'm very offended that you are asking for my handcrafted workbooks for free in exchange for this."

What was '*this*'? I wished I could see, but that would totally blow my cover.

"Deniese, I knew your family was full of frauds, but I cannot believe you would stoop so low as blackmail. The only way you'd get free workbooks from me would be if you were my landlord."

What?

"You need a landlord?" my mom scoffed.

"I know you have an attic to this place and an outdoor entrance."

Mom kept the attic locked. Nobody used it for anything but storage, but she said she didn't want us kids to roughhouse up there and get hurt.

"You want me to rent you my attic for *one* measly workbook?" My mom raised her voice and scoffed dramatically.

"I would give you ten workbooks per month."

"Do I get thick workbooks?"

"Deniese, you know the drill. It's a random selection, and you could get a one-pager or a twenty-pager."

I let out a snort, then covered my mouth, hoping they hadn't heard me.

My mom didn't even pause to think before blurting her answer. "Fine, deal. Come outside with me and I'll show it to you." Was my mom honestly so desperate to make ends meet that she would rent our attic for *workbooks?* They stood and went out the front door. When I was certain they were out of range, I hurried up the steps to my bedroom.

Mrs. Sanchez would be living under our roof. I knew that she wouldn't be staying in our house, and that the attic would be like her own apartment with her own entrance. But it infuriated me! I took some deep breaths and told myself, *Bottom line—she hates all of us, so she'd never dare come into the main house.*

When my mom came into my room, I tried to act normal. If I acted mad, then she would know I was eavesdropping again.

"Hey," I said casually.

"Shouldn't you be at the pool with all of the other kids?" she asked.

I could lie and tell her that I wanted to stay home with her, but she would see it for the lie it was, and then I'd be in even more trouble.

"I forgot about the pool. Everyone was gone before I realized. So I just stayed home."

She nodded, and uncomfortable silence filled the room. It was weird actually being one-on-one and talking with her.

"Did you know that Mrs. Sanchez was here?"

"I heard you talking to someone…"

Mom twisted her mouth, hesitating. "Well, Sanch is going to rent our attic."

I acted surprised. It was the only reasonable response. "You can't rent our attic to Sanch!" I gasped, then realized she already told me, so I didn't need to fake surprise. I scowled at her instead and gave her the angriest glare I could muster.

"You learn your place young lady!"

My mom raised her voice, and a stern expression crossed her face. Nobody told her what to do. She was her own boss. I needed to tone it down.

"Okay. Sorry. But won't the other kids be ticked off, too?"

"I don't care what the other kids think. This is my house, and I pay the bills. It's not like she'll be living in our house with us."

"Better not be," I muttered.

"Dennis," she warned.

"Okay." I straightened my back and pulled my knees toward my chest. Mom huffed, pushed her stomach out further than humanly possible, and waddled out of the room.

When the rest of the kids returned with my dad, they were all hee-hawing and roughhousing around, having a good old time. Then my mom dropped the bomb on them about Sanchez, and everyone started complaining. I had to cover my ears because the cacophony of overlapping voices was just too much! My dad showed his disapproval for her decision by saying he was going to go to work, then he left —just decided right on the spot he was picking up an extra shift, whether they would pay him or not.

Everyone talked about the pool being so fun. Lil' Shelbi kept telling me "green star," and Shaye finally explained that the Greens and the Stars had both been at the pool today, too, and that it was more like a party than a typical pool day. Of all the days to forget! I groaned and stormed off to my room, wondering why the universe hated me with a passion.

A few weeks later, I woke to the sound of slobbering to

find Rochelle and Lil' Shelbi eating corn dogs. Where did they get those? I wanted a corn dog. I covered my ears to block the disgusting slurping and tried to find the perfect outfit for the barbeque at the Stars today. Switching back and forth between outfits, I wondered if this would be more of a dress party or a romper party. Well, it was gonna be outside, so I slipped into a neon orange tank top and pulled my purple romper over top of it. I hated the color purple because it was my mother's favorite color. But this outfit was actually nice and cute, so I made an exception.

If I couldn't get into the popular squad through Monica, maybe I could try to get in through Haylee and Hallee. They were my cousins, after all, and BFFs with Monica. This barbeque would be the perfect chance.

When we showed up at the party, my eyes had trouble taking in the smorgasbord of food and brightly colored balloons. Naturally, I went to Dude Green's portable grill. He was the only one serving real meat. The Stars apparently didn't eat meat, but Dude Green claimed that he'd die before eating a tofu burger. I was glad he brought his grill and his own meat because I was scared of trying new foods. What even was tofu? A fish? Wasn't fish meat? Anyway, I ate a hot dog. And, boy, was it *dee-lish!*

"Hey, buddy!" Dad yelled, and Dude whipped his head around from the grill.

"Yah?" He turned a hotdog over.

"You puttin' any of them pigs in blankets?"

Pigs.

"No way man, I ain't no chef." Dude Green smirked. My dad clapped him on the back.

"Yeah, that's chick stuff. How bout some beans and wieners then?" he asked. "But make 'em spicy." Dad slapped his stomach and belched.

"I think Lucas brought the beans."

Beans.

The word gnawed at my heart before shredding it to smithereens. I ran behind a tree and crouched, bringing my knees to my chest. Glancing in each direction, I made sure no one was watching me. There was no way I wanted to be caught being a cry baby and get bullied. A fat tear skidded down my cheek and plopped straight onto my shoe.

What if Beans was being hurt? Oh my lands. What if he was dead?

It was too much for me to handle. The thought of my Beans suffering that fate. My shoulders shook, and the tears spilled out in a stream.

"Do you hear that?" Brad asked.

"What?" asked a boy's voice.

"Sounds like some freak is sobbing." He laughed, and his clodhoppers approached the tree to investigate.

I wiped my eyes and scrambled to my feet, so I could hightail it out of there.

"Dennis! I knew it was the little troll." He chuckled then mock-sobbed at me as I ran and hid in a porta potty.

After I regained my composure, I exited the porta potty, and Brad was gone. So I walked over to Haylee and Hallee, who were wearing matching pink and blue sundresses, then started telling them some knock-knock jokes that were in the newspaper the other day. They laughed a little bit but didn't act like they really thought I was being funny. So I tried a more direct socialization strategy.

"I don't know if you two know this, but you and I are cousins." I smiled because I'd seen other people make friends doing this.

"Yeah," they answered in unison, glancing at each other. So they did know. *Excellent job, DJ. You are talking with popular girls.*

"We should totally play together sometime." I crossed my fingers and my toes. I didn't care if they noticed, I needed the good luck.

"Maybe," Haylee said, "but I'm pretty busy. I like to study for school."

"It's summer." I laughed, but Haylee scowled at me. She apparently didn't think that was funny.

"Playing sounds fun," Hallee squeaked, but her sister immediately cut her off, "You have to study, too. Don't you want to be smart?"

"I want to have fun," Hallee answered, rapidly blinking her hazel-colored doe eyes.

"Oh, well I am *lots* of fun. The funnest, if you will." I fiddled with my fingers, uncomfortably self-aware.

"I want to be the best." Haylee placed her hands on her hips and stood like a superhero. "So I have to get started now. Summer or no summer."

Hallee nodded, but by her solemnly glazed eyes, I could tell she thought the whole idea sounded as boring as I did. When I caught sight of Monica's auburn braid, I excused myself from the conversation, so I could thank her for my birthday present. She jumped a little when I tapped on her shoulder but turned around.

"I just really want to tell you how much I appreciated your gift. It was the nicest birthday present I had ever gotten from anybody, ever—" Words just kept flying out of my mouth like uncontrollable vomit. She listened to me and nodded, but I needed to wrap it up. I wasn't used to conversing with kids my own age. Or any kids for that matter. Siblings didn't count, and they hated me anyways.

"You're welcome," she finally answered, when I shut up. Her eyes searched for Haylee and Hallee over my shoulder.

Monica waved at them, so I bit my tongue, faked a smile, and walked away. I wished she had invited me to play, but I was already putting myself way out there. Feeling a little proud of myself, I patted myself on the back when nobody was looking. I had just talked to three people. Popular people. All in one day.

A frisbee nearly took me out, but I ducked out of the way at the last second. That was when Bob Waltzer strolled up with Alissa, Timmy, and Tommy. Timmy caught the frisbee from who knows where, and light applause followed. Katrina skipped over to Tommy right away, and I narrowed my green-monster-of-jealousy eyes at her. I still had a crush on Tommy, and I really couldn't stand Katrina. She must've just come out of the house 'cause I ain't smelled no raccoons frying on the grill yet— Tee-hee!

Bob loudly suggested that we should all do some karaoke, and while everyone declined, the Stars did put on some music. I was starstruck, like I was at an awesome, famous party. They had music *outside*. How cool was that?

During a transition of songs, it got quiet enough that despite the chaotic ramblings of my siblings, I could make out a fight brewin'. I glanced at the empty tables besides me before stealthily ditching my spot like a panther. The tension was thick as I approached the three pregnant women under a big umbrella. Megan was expecting a girl, Marti was expecting a boy, and my mom was expecting her triplets of unknown genders. Maybe God planned for all of them to have babies at the same time, so they could become BFFs, and then their babies could all be BFFs. But they weren't acting like friends, and Mom's voice was turning too brash. My mom and Marti both had letters in their hands, and Marti insisted on seeing my mom's, setting hers down. The wind swept it up beautifully, and it flew into the grass a few feet away from me. *Perfect. Detective Dennis June is on the case once again.*

Picking up the letter, I walked briskly to an empty picnic table that was set up and unfolded it. This must be *really* juicy if it was starting a fight. Especially one in front of Megan. My mom hated her sister, but she would never risk looking bad in front of Megan. It read:

"Dear Marti,

I am in a program, and they are encouraging me to make things right with my family. So I have decided I should finally tell you something. I am sending a similar letter to Deniese and your other siblings. Two years after I had Deniese, I got arrested and met the only other friend I ever had besides Bev. She was my cellmate, and she had a daughter only a month before she went in. After she got out, she got in a fatal car crash and left her daughter to me. I know what you are thinking, that you have an adopted sibling the same age as you that I didn't tell you about. But you don't. That child is you, Marti. You are not my biological daughter. I am sorry I never told you, but you were my favorite. You have no other biological siblings because you were an only child. After everything that has happened in the past few months, I can no longer taint your name by claiming you as my child. My best friend wouldn't have wanted that. I hope you will understand.

—Beverly Hill"

I folded the letter back up, my heart doing somersaults in my chest. This meant I wasn't related to any of the Stars. None of my family was. If Haylee and Hallee weren't my cousins, they had literally no reason to be nice to me. As casually and unsuspiciously as possible, I high-tailed it back over to where the moms were all *still* arguing. I placed the letter on the ground beside them while my mom raged about how highly offensive the letters were, and it bothered me to have no idea what hers had said. But why was Megan in on this? I soon found out.

"She didn't know, Deniese. It's not Marti's fault that she was favored in your home, or that she's not blood relation."

Megan was backing Marti up, just there for support.

"Marti was my mother's *favorite*. Her princess. She got *everything,* and we all— *I* got treated like absolute *trash.* She had everything! I had rags! *I* was the one who was dealt the worst of mom's illness. What did I get for it? Nothing!"

I tiptoed away from them before they'd notice my eavesdropping. Unable to keep the secret for more than two minutes though, I began to spill the beans. It spread like a wildfire, and before I knew it, Brad was announcing to everyone that "the dating pool had just gotten bigger!" like the creeper he was. The commotion drew the eyes of the parents, and soon the moms came over to investigate.

"What's going on over here?" asked my mom, her face all rank and furiously crumpled from the letters. It seemed as if a million voices started to overlap one another, until eventually my mom placed a hand to her forehead and demanded, "Whoa, whoa, whoa. *Who* said that you guys aren't cousins?"

I shriveled up into what felt like the size of a mushroom.

"Most of us are half-siblings anyway, Mom. It's not like it's *that* big of a deal." Brad laughed.

"Hey!" my mother warned him, raising an eyebrow and shooting him a threatening glance. It felt like I was in a separate universe to see Brad get scolded by her. Brad was totally unfazed by it, though, and continued laughing.

"What's he talking about, Deniese?" asked my dad, turning away from his conversation with Dude Green.

"It's not important right now," my mom muttered, her cheeks blushing a fierce shade of crimson. "I just found out that Marti's not my real sister."

"What?" His eyes widened, and my mom trudged to where he was standing, handing him the letter. He skimmed the words quicker than I'd ever seen anyone read.

"Well, Happy Liberation Day, Marti!" my dad yelled, chuckling. My mom punched his arm hard, but my dad kept laughing and didn't take her anger seriously in the slightest. He turned to Dude G., slapped him on the back, and asked him if he wanted to play football. Could he be any more stupid? My mom could kill him for that!

"I cannot believe you are ignoring me right now to play football with your friend," my mom seethed. She shook her head, her hands balled into white-knuckled fists. And I didn't blame her for it at all. Marti's husband—Lucas— asked Marti about everything, then apologized profusely, hugging her tightly and rubbing her back. It seemed to really make her feel better, and I thought my dad should've done that to my mom instead of laughing like a heartless buffoon.

We were all going to be walking on eggshells tonight. Finally, after Lucas asked Marti if she was okay about twenty more times, he joined the Dudes to play football. Bob and Broccoli Waltzer joined in, along with the other older boys. Having nothing else to do, I watched them play for an eternity and thought nothing could be more boring than this.

Chapter 11

THUS BEGAN THE crescendo of babies.

In June, my mom cried out and weaved her car into the left lane of traffic. I clutched my seat belt and screamed as loud as my little lungs could. Was she trying to get us all killed? Wasn't it bad enough that several kids were sitting on laps because there weren't enough seats? I suddenly regretted my decision to "come along for the ride."

"What are you doing?" gasped Shaye, her eyeballs so huge they were about to pop out of her head.

"I think I'm in labor!" my mom wailed. My dad—who for unknown reasons wasn't at work, but was in the front passenger seat—reached for the wheel, but my mom slapped his hand and made a U-ie.

"Mom!" I cried. My heart felt like it was going to burst and kill me any second now.

"I gotta go to the hospital, Dennis!"

"Honey, let me drive." My dad reached for the steering wheel again, but my mother slapped his arm again and shot him an evil glare.

"No. This is *my* car. I'm the only one who can drive it."

She was such a control freak!

When we arrived at the hospital, everyone who came with her today had to go in and wait because if she wasn't going to let *Dad* drive her car, then no way would she ever let one of her *children* drive it. I groaned and dragged my feet as I followed everyone through the hospital doors. The smell of alcohol and disinfectant wipes filled the air, and it took my eyes a hot second to get adjusted to how bright and white it was in there. My mom was extremely rude to some young girl wearing a red-and-white striped dress. She demanded that a wheelchair be brought to her immediately. It reminded me that my younger sister Jillian was supposed to be getting one of those soon, but that upsetted me, and I didn't even want to think about that. The worker complied, but my mom must not have thought she was moving fast enough because she nearly ripped the chair from her hands and jerked it toward herself.

"Give me that, I'll do it myself," she gritted through her clenched teeth.

I saw an open seat and sat down. This could take a while, and I was not about to stand the whole time. Nobody would even know I was sitting. I had a feeling they'd be easy to spot if they left. That many kids was not a common sighting, and if all else failed, I'd follow the trail of the sound of my mom's screeching at the poor doctors and nurses.

Not even three hours passed, and my dad announced that the babies were born. I was surprised that they got them that fast. It took them forever to give Stacey *her* baby, and these babies were in my mom's belly. I figured it would take much longer.

"First one took some convincing, but after that they slid right out like butter." My dad was grinning ear to ear.

"Ew! Dad, that is disgusting. Nobody wants to hear that. Sick!" Ty grimaced and looked pale.

"How do they slide out like butter?" I asked.

"*Don't* answer that," Ty hissed at my dad, who just laughed. I didn't see why it was so funny or disgusting. Why wasn't I allowed to know? I prepared my protest, so I could find out what the meaning behind all that was, but my dad led us back to my mom's room before I had the chance.

"Where are the babies?" I asked, taking in the railed hospital bed she was lying in and not seeing any cribs.

"They're cleaning them up." Mom's hair was all mussed, and she was sweating profusely.

"That is rude. They got them dirty *already?*" I asked.

Shaye chuckled and tousled my hair.

"I can't wait to find out the stats." My dad rocked on his heels like he couldn't take the excitement and wait any longer.

"You make it sound like they're the score of a football game," my mom groaned, sipping out of a paper cup with a bendy straw. I wanted a bendy straw. Where did she get that?

"I know at least one of them is a boy. I heard the doctors say that." My dad looked like a kid on Christmas morning. Not last Christmas, of course. Because, well, that had just been awful.

"We got quite the surprise here," a doctor announced, walking into my mother's room.

"Oh, no. What's wrong?" Mom leaned up in bed and searched the doctor's eyes.

"Nothing's wrong. Well, not anything *too* worrisome."

"Just say what it is before I slap you silly," my mom spat. "Those are my kids you're talking about." It was strange seeing her so defensive when she hated children.

"Well, we got two premies and a whopper."

"What does that mean?" my mom asked. "Did you just

refer to one of my kids as a *Burger King sandwich?*" She frowned, and the doctor knew she was getting irritated. The whole room knew, and it was not going to be good if he pushed her one split second further.

"I think he means the weights." My dad rolled his eyes and made the crazy signal when my mom wasn't looking.

I winced, fearing she might see his gesture.

"Two of them are under six pounds. They will need monitoring, but it's nothing too serious. It's a common finding for multiple births, like this one. The more babies, the less they weigh and the earlier they come... It can be a tricky process."

"And the other?" My mom narrowed her eyes.

"You're not gonna believe this, but no wonder you struggled so horribly to birth the first one. Ten pounds and four ounces. Very unusual for a triplet delivery."

"Oh my word!" My dad grabbed his face and grinned. Then he gasped and said, "It's the boy, right? Please tell me it's the boy. He'd make such a great football player. Babe! Think of the opportunities!" He turned to my mother, who didn't share his enthusiasm.

"Err, no." The doctor paused and raised an eyebrow. "It's a girl."

"*What?*" my dad blurted.

"That's a big baby!" I laughed, but my mom looked like she wanted to murder me. Suddenly it wasn't so funny anymore.

"My guess is that she was sort of the '*alpha*,' if you will. Deprived the other two of the available nutrients and claimed them for herself. It happens." The doctor looked down at his clipboard and flipped through some papers. His pager beeped, and he left like nothing happened. He didn't even tell us bye!

You'd never guess what their names were. I honestly believed my mom was high off whatever stuff they were putting into that tube in the elbow-pit of her arm. When my parents announced the boy's name, it was totally normal. Routine, even. They called him Brandon. Then the small girl was named Deniese. Deniese the Third. I threw a fit and told them that was *my* name, but my mom said it was *her* name first and she could "do whatever the Bessie dung pat" she wanted.

The blanket they wrapped Deniese the Third in had frogs on it, and they were so adorable, so everyone started calling her "Froggy," and just like "Dennis," I had a feeling it would stick. Because all of the best and worst nicknames did.

Then came the *Burger King Whopper*—Frogster. She was the chunkiest ball of fat rolls I had ever seen in my life. She looked like that Marshmallow Man from the movie *Ghostbusters.* I knew everyone was thinking it, too. But no chance would I let my brain blurt that one out. I'd be in the grounded room for an eternity.

The two small babies never opened their eyes when I saw them. They just kept sleeping. They were so peaceful that they almost didn't look like they were real. More like those super fancy, expensive baby dolls. But *Frogster*—UGH! I needed earplugs. The entire maternity unit needed earplugs. When my siblings and I went down to the cafeteria, I *swore* I could hear her screaming even though tons of people were talking and we were two floors down.

My mom left the hospital as soon as she was cleared to do so. They wanted her to stay a little longer, but she said she was "not getting ripped up the crack with a hospital bill like that." I had no clue how my parents crammed three more cribs in that nursery, but they did. Even though the nursery wasn't near my room, I could still hear Frogster wailing all throughout the night and during the day, too. All she did was let out bloodcurdling screams.

I found it very odd that Mrs. Sanchez hadn't complained once, so one day I brought up my concerns to Mom. She told me that apparently Mrs. Sanchez had had the attic "soundproofed," but soundproof or not, I couldn't see how *anyone* could *not* hear Frogster's discontent.

A month after the babies were born, they started to babble. *I* didn't consider it talking, but my dad insisted they were going to be geniuses. My mom told him he was being an idiot. Frogster didn't babble, though. She just continued with her notorious screaming. The only time she didn't scream was when she did this low-pitched sound that was actually terrifying.

"She's laughing," Rochelle would say. Her and Lil' Shelbi just *loved* Frogster with a passion. After all, Frogster was one of Rochelle's middle names, so it was almost like she was named after her. I found the laugh monstrous and terrifying, but sometimes it was kind of funny. If you were expecting it, that was. Anytime Frogster saw me looking or trying to play with her like Rochelle and Shelbi did, she began screaming again. It was really embarrassing and made me feel terrible. What was so special about Rochelle and Shelbi? Why was I in the group of people that made her scream?

Comparing my abnormal family to normal ones, I thought back to yesterday, when my mom told us that Marti had her baby boy and named him Roger. Apparently he came out looking just like Lucas's dad. He didn't have black hair like his mom or dad, but instead the blond hair of his grandfather. My dad showed us a picture that Lucas gave him, and he was pretty cute. Almost like a little cherub angel.

My mom had groaned and declared *her* babies were always the cutest.

Hope flickered within me because I was one of her babies and that meant she thought I was cute.

Then my dad rolled his eyes and said, "Well, we *have* to say that, babe. They're our kids. Everyone says that about their kids. Even if they are uglier than dirt."

"I'm *not* saying it because they're 'our kids'," Mom snarkily remarked. Hurt flashed across her face, but the arrogant way she was acting made me question if she really thought we were cute, or if she just wanted to be better than her friends—or whatever her 'not sister' was to her now. Mom could be extremely competitive, and I didn't see a reason why this would be any different.

Drifting back out of my thoughts, I zoned back into reality and took a walk. Exercise wasn't for me, but I wanted to get away from the screaming baby. After quite some time, I passed by a shop that had beautiful patterned and sparkly gowns and dresses in the window. I stopped. A yellow paper taped to the window flapped in the wind, and I held it still so I could read it. Megan Green was apparently a sponsor to a new fashion line, and the paper mentioned that the new additions were also supported by her co-sponsor, Marti Star.

After I pressed my face and hands to the glass, a fog started to form. I squinted and looked around the store. My mom hadn't said anything, so I thought she had forgotten about banning me from the Back to School Dance. The gowns inside looked pretty enough for a princess to wear to a ball, and even the casual dresses for kids looked ritzier than anything I had ever owned. Despite knowing they were probably outrageously expensive, I picked out my favorite anyway. With a wishful-thinking sigh, I turned back around to head home.

❖

August brought forth the final baby of the summer—Megan's baby girl, Jennifer. She was the cutest little doll baby. Even cuter than Roger. When I was riding my bike and being healthy (okay, fine. I was really trying to snoop on Monica), I saw her parents bring her home from the hospital. Dude Green was cooing over her and tickling her as she lay in the car seat. Megan got on a fancy portable phone and called someone.

Before I knew it, Marti was there and so was my mom. My mom had left the two small babies and screaming Frogster at home (thank goodness), and Marti made a comment about how little Roger was asleep in the car. The women cooed all over the baby, so I put my bike down and crammed between them so I could see.

"Dennis June!" My mom gasped, clutching her monstrous chest. "You're gonna give people heart attacks, pulling that crap!"

"Sorry." I shrugged, then pushed my way up against them and up onto my tiptoes. A rosy-cheeked baby lay smiling and cooing.

"Aww." So much cuteness.

"You shouldn't have just shown up at the Greens' house like this, Dennis. And you know how I'm always telling you not to join into people's conversations and eavesdrop." My mom's cheeks reddened. I had embarrassed her, which embarrassed me in return.

"I don't mind if she wants to look!" Megan's voice was soothing as she waved a dismissive hand at my mother before handing her sleeping Jennifer. "Jenni is the most behaved baby I have ever had. She scared me with how well

147

she slept through the night!"

"Must be nice," my mom muttered, blowing hot air out of her lips and sounding like a horse. "You know, Megan. Next time you should let someone throw you a baby shower." My mom offered her a warm smile that we kids rarely got to see.

"Oh! I threw her one. It was just family and *close* friends," Marti chimed in. I could tell my mom was trying not to get upset about not being invited by the glistening tears in her watery eyes. But I didn't really know why she would want to go. I knew it was a huge deal for her to befriend and impress Megan, which in turn included befriending Marti, but she *hated* spending money. Buying gifts for babies could get expensive.

Later that night when my dad came home from work, he said he had stopped at the Greens' to see their new baby. He went on and on about how adorable she was. I wrinkled up my nose at how sweaty he smelled and struggled with whether or not it would be considered rude to ask him to take a shower. I decided that, yes, that would be rude, and didn't say anything. But then he said something that was *way ruder.*

"Deniese?" he asked my mom, who turned to look at him.

"Yeah?"

"Do you think you want to have any more kids?"

I'm pretty sure everyone within earshot was screaming internally.

"Absolutely not!"

"But, why?" he asked. *Why? WHY?*

Frogster started screaming, and my mom pointed one finger toward the ceiling and said flatly, "That's why."

Chapter 12

TOWARD THE END of summer, word on the street was that a huge truth or dare party was happening at night. Everyone from school was invited, which meant I was invited. I smirked at the thought of being included until two unfortunate things hit me. Number one: everyone hated me, and I would more than likely be embarrassed. Number two: if everyone was invited, that meant *Mama's Child* was going, too. Thinking about the last disastrous game we played, I knew for a fact I didn't want Mama's Child asking me any truths or dares.

When the day of the party arrived, more information was released. The party would be at the Stars', and Cherry was hosting it. Her fancy jungle red pants popped into my brain, and I wondered if she was disgusted that I attended her party. But I didn't think she even saw me. Not at first, that was. Everyone pushed picnic tables together and set up lawn chairs while Cherry announced the rules. This was going to be a special edition known as *"Elimination Truth or Dare,"* and that basically meant if anybody refused to do their dare or answer their truth question, they had to leave the party. It was starting to cool off, and sweating from nerves already, I was glad that I had dressed in overalls, but nice ones.

People picked their seats, the same old cliques sitting together. Cherry was right beside Derek, who for whatever reason was sitting by Lil' Shelb. I wrinkled my nose. Why was she here? It probably had to do with Mom refusing to babysit. Monica's older sister, Izzy, sat next to Chad Star, Brad's best friend. Nobody sat by me. Until…

Mama's Child. She plopped a squat right next to me and breathed, "Hey, Denny," into my ear.

"Hey, Mama's Child."

She grinned, her missing tooth gap gone, and a shiny new tooth in its place.

"Ready to play truth or dare?" she asked. I scanned her hands and pockets as unsuspiciously as possible, in case she had another one of them boxes on her. She blabbered in my ear clear up until the game started. Everyone quieted down, so the big kids took votes on who would get to ask first. They decided on Rochelle.

"Dennis June," she said, and my entire stomach nearly fell out my butt.

I hesitated, and swallowed the lump in my throat. "… truth."

"Who is your crush?" She smirked. I knew for a fact she already knew who it was and was just being mean. She was such a turd. But I didn't want to be a loser or the first person out of the game.

"Tommy Waltzer," I croaked, and flames licked my face like someone had a lit match to it.

Tommy straightened his posture and wrinkled his eyebrows like that was disgusting.

"Tommy is my boyfriend," Katrina announced. As if *everyone* didn't already know that. "He's thirteen, and you are six," she droned on. The number six sounded even more horrid coming from her lips.

I had nothing to say to that, so I kept quiet.

Mama's Child slapped my thigh and whispered, "Nice."

People got eliminated one by one as they refused to do the ridiculous dares or answer the intrusive questions. It landed on Rochelle again, and she picked Mama's Child. I let out a sigh of relief that it wasn't me and waited for Mama's Child to get embarrassed. I honestly felt a little bad for her because Rochelle was brutal. When Mama's picked *dare,* I couldn't believe my ears. Who in their right mind would pick a dare from Rochelle?

"I dare you to kick the person you think is the most awesome straight in the shin."

My pulse quickened, and I went to draw my legs up in my chair. I barely got out the word "no" before Mama's Child kicked me in the shin, and a bruise gnawed its way beneath my skin.

"What is wrong with you?" I asked Mama's Child. But she looked like she was having the time of her life. I didn't know if I should be flattered that she thought I was so awesome or feel like the unluckiest person on the planet.

"Truth or dare, Denny?" she asked. *Oh my gosh, no.*

Rolling my eyes, I told her, "Truth."

"When was the last time you took a dump and what color was it?" she asked, sticking her tongue out, her freckles dancing across her squinty eyelids.

"Ahh, gross," groaned practically every girl at the party, and even a few guys. Except for Mark Melon, who grinned and hollered, "That's what I would've asked!"

What was it with kids and "poop" jokes? That was so disgusting.

"You have to answer!" hollered Brad, and I hated his guts even more than I thought was humanly possible.

"Answer or git, Dennis!"

"Around 2:30 and it was brown," I muttered.

Everyone groaned. Except, of course, Mark Melon, who was bent over at the waist like he was going to die from laughter. The shame washed away, an opportunity of a lifetime rising in its place.

"Monica, truth or dare?" I asked.

She placed a finger to her dainty chin and twisted her tickle-me-elmo pink lips.

"Truth."

"Who is your best friend?"

"I don't have a best friend." Monica blinked, and I wanted to scream, *"I'll be your best friend!"* But then she explained it was because she had two. I crossed my fingers and my toes, hoping that one of them would be me.

"Haylee and Hallee," she answered, and the familiar wave of disappointment washed over me.

More people got eliminated. A dude who was nicknamed "Chester Cheater," for obvious reasons, was dared to stay with the same girl for a week and not cheat. He broke his dare when he turned right around and dared my oldest sister, Emma, to kiss him, so he was eliminated. My sister Ashley was livid because *she* was dating him. But I was going to take a wild guess and say she wasn't dating him now. I couldn't believe all the drama and weird stuff the older kids dared and asked. For example, Cherry dared Nicole Green to leave the party. If she refused, she'd have to leave. If she completed the dare, she'd still have to leave. I didn't think that was fair. Cherry was kind of a jerk if you asked me.

Someone dared Rochelle to kiss the father of Lil' Shelbi, and she kissed Broccoli Waltzer! I didn't understand how he could be Shelbi's dad. Rochelle wasn't married to him, and everyone thought that he was a ghost for years!

Mark Melon had dared Lil' Shelbi to ding-dong ditch my mom, and I wasn't even aware that Shelbi was playing.

"No way is my child turning down a dare!" Rochelle declared, and she proceeded to teach Shelb how it was done.

Everyone, including me stood and walked far enough down the sidewalk that we could watch Rochelle help Shelbi ding-dong ditch.

They hit the doorbell, hid, and my mom opened the door. Nobody was there, so she shut it. The second "ding dong" pierced the air, and we all snickered when Mom opened a window and hollered, "Who is *doing* that?"

She shut the window and disappeared.

Lil' Shelbi waddled to the door again, and Rochelle lifted her up. Shelbi yelled, "Ding dong!" then they trucked it behind a bush.

My mom flung the door open with a loud thud and threatened to call the cops, so that ended the ding-dong ditching. Plus, I think she saw some of us standing on the sidewalk and was getting tired of our shenanigans. She had no tolerance for that sort of thing.

When it rounded back to Mama's Child, she asked me another disturbing question.

"On a scale of one to ten, how bad are your farts?"

EW. I looked around and thought everyone was thinking the same thing, but I already answered the poop question and wasn't about to go home now. My stomach flip-flopped. I shakily answered, "Seven," because you can't lie when you're tellin' a truth!

Everyone groaned again, and Mark Melon pinched his nose, pretending to waft the air like the troll he was.

Katrina was still in the game until someone dared her to make her email account profile picture a picture of my face. She didn't even say anything, just folded up her chair and went inside her house. I was glad she left but also kind of insulted. Did she really think I was *that* ugly?

Danny Jr. (the town's biggest gossip) dared Cherry to tell him something secret that he could yell, "Hey everybody!" about. Whenever he did that, everyone knew he was about to drop someone's secret. He probably even knew the secret about my grandma before I did. I bet he was devastated when Mama's Child beat him to the punch.

"I have a secret tattoo," Cherry's hand was to her mouth in typical secret fashion.

"Hey everybody!" Danny Jr. screamed as loud as he could.

I swear my mom's head popped out of one of the windows of our house. Even though she was always scolding me for eavesdropping, she lived for gossip.

"Cherry has a tattoo!" he howled.

"*Shut up!*" everyone yelled.

"Yah, before someone makes a noise complaint." Chad laughed.

Rochelle actually left when someone asked if she was in love with Broccoli Waltzer. I couldn't believe she picked a "truth" in the first place. Did her leaving mean that she was in love with him, or did it mean that she wasn't? I was so confused. Broccoli and Lil' Shelbi left with her. Shortly before the twins were eliminated, it was revealed that Katrina had kissed both Tommy *and* Timmy Waltzer. I sat there with my mouth hanging open, wondering if she was a two-timing fish. How dare she cheat on Tommy? If she didn't want him, I'd take him! I wanted to have a boyfriend.

Believe it or not, it actually narrowed down to just me, Mama's Child, Chad, Izzy, and Derek. I couldn't believe I had made it this far. It was Chad's turn, and he picked Mama's Child.

"Mama's Child, what is the meat in your mom's diner made of?"

Everyone snickered.

"Uh, I don't know." She looked at me and shrugged before muttering, "Could be horse meat. That's what people at school say." I expected her to just lie, but maybe she was actually following the rules. Mama's Child picked me again and asked me another downright disgusting question, so I had to get her out of this game.

"Mama's Child, I dare you to stay away from me for the rest of your life."

She hesitated and stared at me, blinking rapidly. "Uh, I don't want to do that. I don't accept your dare, Dennis! I'll just leave the game." Then she began her walk home in the dark. Wherever her home was, that was, because even though I had awesome detective skills, I had no idea where *or* what that was.

When it was Derek's turn, he asked his girlfriend Cherry her "truth" question. He had leaned forward, licked his lips and said, "Will you marry me?"

"Umm, like right now?" Cherry's voice was unusually high, like a mouse. Was she going to cry? Derek pulled out a huge, shiny diamond ring. This was so crazy, and I was actually *here* for it. I wasn't just hearing about it like a left-out loser. Cherry squealed, "Yes!" The two of them were laughing giddily and oblivious to the world. It looked like it was just going to be Izzy, Chad, and I now.

"Do you even still want to play?" Chad asked.

"Not really." Izzy shrugged.

I screamed, "Woo-hoo!" Standing up on my chair, I yelled for the entire world to hear. "I won!"

The back door to the Stars' house opened, and Marti frowned. "What is all the commotion going on out here?"

"Mom!" Cherry exclaimed. "Look! Derek proposed. Isn't it wonderful?"

The conversation got quieter but much more heated.

"I don't *have* a problem with Derek. I just don't understand why you have to get married so soon. You're so *young!*" Marti's eyes widened to double their normal size. I crouched down on my chair as quietly as possible, not wanting to get kicked out before getting the scoop.

"I'm going to be eighteen soon, and Derek is nineteen," Cherry popped a hand to her hip.

"You *are* going to finish highschool, right?" Concern or disgust tainted her mom's face.

If I had a choice between getting married or going to school, I would definitely get married.

"Where will you live?" Marti's face had grown pale, and in the moonlight it looked as though she had aged before my eyes.

"We're gonna look at apartments next week."

"Next *week?*"

"Izzy thinks a fall wedding would be really pretty." Cherry's smile reached both her ears and made her eyes go all squinty.

"Have you ever even thought about a wedding before, Cherry? Do you understand that these things take planning?"

"Izzy and Chad will be the maid of honor and best man, duh. Stephanie Green and Brad Tipper will be in it, too. We can have Haylee and Hallee hold my train, Monica can be the flower girl, and Cameron can be the ring bearer."

Her mom's eyes searched her face frantically. She bit her lip. "Well at least you are including both families. If you really love him, then I'm happy for you both. Congratulations."

"Can I be in it?" I asked. I'd always wanted to attend a

wedding. They were so pretty on TV, and everyone was so happy. Plus there was always cake. And dancing. Score!

The three of them shot strange looks in my direction, and I looked around me. Not seeing Chad and Izzy, my cheeks heated.

"Dennis June, why are you even still here?" Cherry asked, frowning.

"I won the truth or dare game." I smirked.

"Okay…well it's over."

"I know." I leaned back in my chair and got all comfy.

"You can, like, leave now," Cherry said, shooing me with her ring-adorned hand.

I frowned and stood. "So is that a no?"

"Dennis, get out of here!" Her voice sounded a lot more irritated than it did a few seconds ago.

"Be nice to the poor dear," her mom told her.

But I was used to being spoken to like that, and I had already stepped off their property to make my way home.

Chapter 13

MUCH TALK WENT AROUND about the upcoming wedding. Ashley was disappointed, resorting back to her crush on Derek Green after her breakup with Chester. My mom naturally wanted one of her daughters to marry Derek, so they could be rich. I worried she would take the bad news out on us, but it actually worked in our favor.

With all of this drama, Mom had forgotten I wasn't allowed to go to the Back to School Dance, and I was triumphant, like I had won the biggest prize on a game show. With the dance only two weeks away, it seemed this was the greatest thing to happen all summer. But then it got even *better*.

My mom received a phone call that changed everything. Apparently, we were going dress shopping. *Dress shopping*! I had never been dress shopping in my entire life. The little boutique instantly popped into my mind. How in the world was my mom planning on affording a dress for each of us girls? Because, I don't know if you've noticed, but there were *a lot* of us. I may or may not have eavesdropped when we met Megan outside the dress shop.

"Every girl should have the opportunity to feel like a

princess," Megan explained. *I* wanted to feel like a princess.

"Just make sure your girls don't get the dresses too dirty, and it will be fine. We do it all the time. I call it the old *switcheroo.* They wear the dress for a night, then you return it the next day." Megan giggled as she took in the long trail of us girls.

"Do we get to pick whatever we want?" I asked, tugging on my mom's shirt tail.

"Uh, I don't know about that—" Mom smoothed her hair, and her eyes scanned the shop windows before settling on the ground.

"—of course you can pick whatever you want!" Megan exclaimed with a cheery smile. Something about her just felt so warm and inviting. Trusting her, I struggled to pull the door open then ran into the store as fast as my little (big) feet could take me!

It has to be here. I scoured the room for the dress I had seen weeks ago. *Please still be here.* And there she was. The pink and red sundress, hanging on a hanger. Snatching it off the rack, I yelled for my mother, who scolded me for "acting like a heathen."

"I want this one, Mom. I want it!" I jumped up and down.

"Well, try it on!" Megan waved a hand at me as if to say, "Go Ahead!"

The dress was a little snug but otherwise perfect. I was getting it. And I was going to that dance. I hoped Monica would like it. Holding a hand to my forehead like a pirate, I searched the crowded shop for her until I finally saw her picking out a dress that was blush pink and lacy. She would look so beautiful in that!

"I'm getting this one," Cherry told Izzy, a few steps away from me. She motioned to a mannequin that had a midnight blue gown with stars on it.

"Because my last name is Star," she explained. *Well, duh,* I thought.

"What is Chad going to wear?" Cherry asked Izzy.

"Well, he's *your* brother, you tell me."

"What *are* the boys going to wear?" I asked. They turned and frowned at me. I think they muttered the word "ew." It made me feel like a piece of dog poo on the bottom of a shoe.

"Most of the guys could care less." Izzy shrugged.

Sighing, I wondered what Marcus Delon would be wearing.

I must tell you about the beauty that is Marcus Delon. After much bullying and embarrassment over Tommy, I decided I needed to have a crush on someone my own age. So I picked Marcus. He had the most beautiful, silky blond hair with waves in it that reminded me of the ocean. Just like his eyes, which were the deepest blue I had ever seen. His clothes never had any wrinkles in them, and I liked that. And he wore his shirts tucked in. I liked that, too.

"Are you signing up for cheerleading this year?" Stephanie Green asked, sidling right up between Cherry and Izzy. Stephanie appeared malnourished—skinny as a twig, but her body was vastly out of proportion. Brad was always staring at her chest and her butt, and it made me half sick.

"*I* want to be a cheerleader," I said, and they all looked at me with the same disgusted look that everyone did.

"Who let *you* in this store?" Stephanie cackled.

"Uh, myself?" I asked, remembering the struggle of opening the door. That was a dumb question. She just smirked and rolled her eyes.

"Idiot," she muttered. I agreed with her. She *was* an idiot.

"You *are* being an idiot," I agreed out loud, and Cherry's and Izzy's jaws hit the floor. It felt like everyone in the building had stopped talking. Almost like the entire planet had stopped spinning.

"*What did you just say to me?*"

Let's just say I was *not* going to be making the cheerleading squad this year.

While I didn't make the cheerleading squad, I did manage to score a spot in the school band. I got to participate some in kindergarten and preschool, but I wanted to be a star. My instrument was the most important out of all the instruments. That's right. You heard me. I played the *tambourine*. And I was pretty darn good at it, if I did say so myself.

I also earned myself a place in the academic excellence club based on my work last year. This was described on the paper they gave us as being sort of like a study group, and it encouraged students to, well, continue being excellent. Brad told me that I rigged it and that I was the stupidest person in the world. But Brad was the one starting a club called "The Dating Advice Club." As dumb as I thought it sounded, I wanted to impress Marcus Delon and become his best friend *and* his girlfriend. So I signed up.

Pulling my dress over my shoulders the night of the dance, I squeezed every inch of pudge inside and wondered if I ate one too many Debbies. But she made 'er on. I had no idea how I would be getting out of it, but I would worry about that part later. I gave my hair a couple of quick swiper-roos and patted my nearly-white cowlick down. I pinched my cheeks super hard, because I didn't have any makeup, and I wanted it to look like I was wearing blush. It didn't work. I'm ashamed to admit that I half considered asking Rochelle to slap me across both sides of the face, but something told me that was a bad idea. That being settled, it was time to go.

"Hi," I said, standing behind two big kids waiting in line for the dance lemonade. Or was it a promenade? Either way, we had to walk around in our outfits for the adults then vote for a dance queen or something dumb. I just wanted to eat snackies and amaze everyone with my epic dance moves. But everyone was walking slower than a turtle that had been flipped on its back. Let's get this line movin'!

"Sup," the boy said to me.

"I'm Dennis June," I told him.

"I know. I'm Kevin. This is Candy." He motioned to his girlfriend whose hair was pink. It was *PINK*.

"Your hair is pink," I said, pointing at it.

"It is," she responded flatly.

"Does your mom know that your hair is pink?" My eyes widened with every word I uttered.

"Yah. She does." She snapped some bubble gum loudly. *I* wanted some bubble gum.

"My mom would kill me. Who's your mom?"

"Megan."

"You're Monica's sister?" I asked, before squealing, "She is so cool."

"She's whatever."

"You're really short. How old are you?" I asked. She looked old, but she couldn't have been more than five feet tall.

"Older than you," she muttered before murmuring to Kevin something about Paris.

"You've been to Paris? That place with the big tower?" I asked.

"I've been there several times. And I will be going back." Then she whispered to Kevin, "We should totally just ditch this place. I'm tired of Sanch's crap. She's not even certified to teach college courses. We can finish school in Paris." Were they going to run away? This was juicy!

After we finally all got squeezed into the building and the adults got to look at us like we were under a microscope, we did our voting. I naturally voted for Monica. Somebody said she liked Mark Melon one day at school, so I voted for him. When my mom read the votes, she announced that Cherry and Derek won king and queen, the prince and princess were Chad and Izzy, and Danny Jr. and Nicole were runners-up. Danny Jr.'s mother, China Lady, whooped so exuberantly that my mom whistled loudly to shut her up. China Lady was a black woman that my mom knew from way back in her school days. She always wore the most exotic clothing and earrings the size of an elephant. Her home was sort of like an orphanage: her heart had enough room for homeless and needy children even if her house didn't. It was obvious that she wasn't Danny Jr.'s biological mother by looks, but she treated him like he was. And that was what was important anyway.

When the room was quiet again, Mom read the most important part. The mini-queen and mini-king: "Monica and Mark Melon."

"Yes!" I squealed, shaking my fist in the air. I got some strange looks, but I was on top of the world. They must have won because of me.

"You're welcome," I blurted to Mark Melon, who happened to be standing beside me in a pair of jeans and a grey polo shirt.

"Go eat a fried egg." He snickered and walked away.

Why would I do that? I hated eggs. Especially after I had to eat that sidewalk one.

"I also have another announcement," my mom spoke into the microphone. Everyone kept talking and ignoring her. I gave the whole crowd the "shh!" sign, but they didn't listen like the disrespectful hooligans they all were. My mom whistled and bellowed, "AYE!"

A hush snapped over the crowd.

"I'm pregnant."

"Mom!" groaned what felt like half of the school's population.

"It's twins." Her voice was blunt, but she had a satisfied look in her eyes, now that the attention was on her.

"What is wrong with the universe?" I yelled, stomping my foot. "I don't want more babies!"

This all had to be my dad's fault. You couldn't go around crossing your fingers like that! Everyone knew that was magic and that it made your wishes come true if you did it right. Unless you were me. I even crossed my toes, but the universe apparently never appreciated my efforts.

"Dennis, shut up!" Brad spat in my direction. I think he was just in a rank mood because he didn't win the dance king. Rightfully so. He was the absolute worst.

"You shut up!" I snapped right back at him.

He rolled his eyes.

Cherry stepped up to the microphone and made some mushy dance queen speech, which was a snoozer. I think my mom's pregnancy announcement was more welcomed than that stinker! When we finally were able to start the dance, we all went into the cafeteria, which was decked out with some colorful streamers and balloons that were already deflating. Cherry approached a mic, and insisted that her and Derek's first dance would be to the song "Fly Me to the Moon" because of her last name being Star and her dress having stars on it. We got it, Cherry. We knew what your last name was. It wasn't that awesome.

Broccoli Waltzer and Rochelle actually showed up—

after all the boring stuff was over. I should have done that. They brought Lil' Shelbi with them, and they all danced together.

While sticking to the sidelines, the popular kids started forming some kind of a circle, and I couldn't see what was going on. I was praying they weren't doing some kind of a weird sacrifice. I didn't want to die. Brad was always in control of the TV at home, and that was the kind of terrifying crap he watched when he wasn't watching half-naked women in bikinis dance around on the beach. If you asked me, both of those options were just asking for nightmares.

I stood in line for some snackies, and let me just tell you, that line was *packed,* and I worried I was going to faint just waiting on some crisp potato chippies. Mom was supposed to be a chaperone tonight, but you'd never know it because she was in the food line all night claiming that she was "eating for three now." Mrs. Sanchez made her go home, and that sped the line *way* up. As I reached for a red solo cup, an older boy grabbed my wrist and said, "I wouldn't do that, kid. It's spiked." So I got bottled water instead.

Wowzers. I was not going to forget this night. Even the air smelled different. Okay, it smelled like deodorant speed sticks and nasty boy cologne, but this was the first dance I had ever been to. And now with my mom gone, it felt like I was at a *real* party. Her presence was enough to keep me from relaxing. People groaned that too many slow songs were played, and I agreed. I could only sway back and forth so much before it got boring. So when they bumped up the jams, I let it all go loose. I got down on the floor and did the worm.

I heard a girly giggle, and when I stood, Monica was behind me, giving me a thumbs up. *She must think I am an amazing dancer.*

People started to filter out. Danny Jr. and Ashley giggled and rushed to the door, solo cups in hand. Danny Jr. was Orange's boyfriend. So where was Orange? I stuffed a plate full of food and took it outside. Sitting on the sidewalk right outside the door, I crammed potato chip after potato chip into my mouth. The chaperones were inside taking down tables and chairs and cleaning up. Even my mom came back to help.

I scoffed and shook my head in disbelief when Mrs. Sanchez dumped all of that perfectly good food into the trash can propping the door open, and it was starting to reek from whatever people already dumped in there. I would have taken that food home if I knew she would do that! My mom had the same expression I did on her face, until one of the adults screamed.

"Get over here and smell this!" I recognized Marti's voice.

"Woo-ee! That is strong!" my mom hollered, waving a hand in front of her nose.

"Did they spike this punch?" Mrs. Sanchez demanded, even though she had been the main adult watching us all night.

"There's no doubting it. Do you even have to ask? That smells like straight up vodka!"

Megan and Marti shifted their gazes at each other, and Marti folded her arms. My mom shrugged and continued, "I mean, I'm guessing. It could be anything. I wouldn't know."

"The children all need to be punished," Megan decided, and it surprised me. I didn't know she *punished* her kids.

"Everyone is in the grounded room indefinitely!" my mom declared, and I chucked my plate into the trash and took off running for home. *Could my mom put other people's kids in the grounded room?*

The door was unlocked, so I whipped it open and shut it before sliding down to the floor and going kaput.

"How is the grounded room even going to hold that many people?" I thought out loud.

"What?" Shaye asked.

"Nothing," I said quickly.

Chapter 14

SHORTLY AFTER THE DANCE fiasco, my mom decided we were going to go grocery shopping. I groaned at first because—ew! Walking! But when we were at the grocery store, we ran into Megan Green who said she was going to be throwing a "smoothie mixer" party for the adults. Apparently Marti already planned on going, so my mom couldn't be left out a single second longer.

"I will be there for sure." My mom smoothed her blouse, and I took in her fancy clothes. I bet she knew Megan was going to be here. It wasn't even a Tuesday.

"You know, I thought it could be an opportunity for some of the older kids to work off their punishment. They could waitress us. Set the table, cook the food. We'll need someone to be in charge of making the smoothies, the cookies, and ordering pizzas. We might as well have some of the children do it." Megan sounded like she had a whole plan thought out and ready to go for this. It wasn't my mom's preferred form of punishment, but this was *Megan Green*, so she agreed and acted like it was a brilliant idea, even though I knew she'd rather just force us to stay in the grounded room or paddle us with a shoe and get it over with.

"Can I participate?" I asked. I wanted to be at the party. And I did *not* want to be in the grounded room. As confident as I was that the punch spiking couldn't be traced back to me, it was still my *mom* we were talking about. And she would rather punish us all then go through the pesky process of picking out each of us one by one until she found the culprit or someone who knew who it was.

"Well, that's nice of you to volunteer! Though I don't see why you would have been punished." Megan blinked but smiled down at me, then she furrowed her brows at my mom before fiddling with a box of cereal. Were the other little kids not being punished? I gave Mom a hopeful look, but she shot me a scowl when Megan wasn't looking and shook her head.

Her fake smile returned the instant Megan continued, "I'm thinking we have Stephanie help out, due to her busy cheer schedule. It's the only day she's free all week. Marti said Katrina is on the cheer team too, so she will be working it. Who else besides DJ would you like to help out?"

"Might as well do Rochelle. I can't have her missing work, and she'll be off that day. She brings Lil' Shelbi everywhere with her though…"

"Not a problem at all! I've heard lots of…uh, things about the little tot." Megan laughed, but it sounded forced.

"Marti's son Kori and your son Ty brought furniture over and set up everything real nice for the party. So make sure you check him off the list."

My mom frowned a bit, but then quickly corrected her smile. She didn't like people telling her how to parent us kids, and she probably wondered when he left the house. We were absolute heathens, but we were *her* heathens. Her *property.*

At the party, Rochelle, Katrina, and I were escorted into a ginormous, sparkling clean kitchen, then led into a walk-in pantry where Megan kept all of her smoothie ingredients and her blender. Megan explained briefly where everything was and listed about a billion devices and ingredients I'd never heard of in my life, then left us. I made my way back out to the kitchen where I was put in charge of baking cookies. I didn't know how to make cookies, but apparently there was this magic thing where you could open the package and just put it on a pan. Then you hit a few buttons, and BOOM! It made cookies. The delicious and decadent smell of chocolatey chunks melted over me, a rare but savored experience. My mom needed to buy these for us.

A knock at the door broke me out of my chocolate trance, and Katrina went to the back door and paid the delivery guy for the pizza. Lil' Shelbi was outside learning how to set the table with our parents.

Stephanie entered through another room of the house, and I was annoyed because most of the work was already done. She held a little green bottle and snickered before whispering something to Rochelle, then handed it to her. Rochelle came over to where I was admiring the beautifully golden brown, warm and gooey cookies.

"Put some powdered sugar on the cookies, Dennis." Rochelle snickered, handing me the bottle.

"But isn't there already sugar *in* the cookies? Why does it need to go *on* them?" My gaze slid to the bottle.

"The adults *love* sugar," Stephanie piped up, and I averted my eyes. "So pour a *lot* on there. But not so much you can see it."

I wrinkled my nose. Why would it matter if they could see it? The bottle was sticky, and it made me uncomfortable. Nothing was written on it. Uneasy, I did as I was told and handed it back to Rochelle.

"Okay, that should be good," I murmured, but it didn't *feel* good.

She smirked and said, "Perfect."

I watched her suspiciously as she approached Katrina and told her to put some "parmesan cheese on the pizza." She clapped Katrina on the back and proceeded to hand her the *same exact* bottle she had given me five seconds ago. Katrina giggled.

"What the dung patty?" I muttered under my breath, watching as Katrina sprinkled some on.

"A little bit more," Stephanie told her.

We went outside with the pizza and the cookies, and Stephanie asked the adults what they wanted in their smoothies.

"Everything," Megan said, waving her hand in the air with a flourish. So we went back into the kitchen.

"I'll handle the smoothies, you guys wait and then help me carry them out." Stephanie's lips curled maliciously.

"Okay," I said, standing behind her. I watched closely as she put ingredient after ingredient in the smoothies because I might want to try to make myself one someday. She picked the green bottle up off the counter and dumped the rest of its contents into the blender before pressing the button to blend it. *What is in that bottle?* Something told me it wasn't sugar *or* cheese. I took a smoothie in each shaky hand and followed the rest of them out the back door to serve the adults. Stephanie and Rochelle went back inside, and I didn't know where Katrina had run off to. I sat in the grass with my back up against a flowered tree. It was a nice day, and all the moms and dads seemed in good moods. My fingers were crossed that they would have leftover cookies, and I would get one for acting like an angel and staying out here the whole time "in case they needed me." It seemed like a smart plan to me, even though I knew leftovers were highly unlikely if my mom and dad were at the table.

I was lost in my daydreams while the adults chatted casually. That was when it all started going down.

Dude G. let one rip really loudly. Megan scolded him, and he shrugged before claiming, "I can't help it." Then my dad literally jumped a few inches off the bench when he let one three times as long as Dude G.'s rip. My mom glared at him, her face red and mortified. A belch interrupted her disapproving mutters, and she clapped a hand to her mouth before letting out a little squeaker.

"Deniese!" Marti and Megan claimed in unison.

"It must be the food. I'm eating for three now!" she flailed her arms frantically. Her face was switching colors so fast, she looked like she wanted to die.

Lucas started farting too, and my dad let out a big boom followed by a little squeak. Were they all losing control of their bodily functions right now? I wrinkled my nose when the breeze wafted the smell over toward me. The guys all laughed at my dad's "accomplishment" like he should win a prize. It reminded me of Mark Melon. Did boys ever stop thinking farts were funny? Then Marti and Megan both burped and covered their mouths. They both turned white as ghosts.

"I'm being *crop dusted!*" my mom bellowed, pinching her nose and groaning. I pinched my nose, too.

Dude Green ran across the street to where our outside bathroom was and grabbed the handle on the door. There was only one stall in there, the shower, and my mother's golden bathtub, which no one was allowed to use but her. My dad tackled him. "I gotta take a dump the size of China!"

"Oh yeah? Well, it's literally leaking out of my butthole as we speak," Dude retaliated. I laughed involuntarily. The moms all turned toward me and scowled.

"I've gotta go, too!" Lucas yelled.

Dude Green won and plowed his way into the bathroom.

"I am literally going to crap my pants!" my dad screamed, pounding on the door. When he turned, I saw that he actually *was*. A brown circle had formed on his pants. Lucas and my dad opened the bathroom door and disappeared behind it. What was going on in there? There was only one terlot, and it was separated from the shower and tub in an enclosed stall!

Katrina, Rochelle, and Stephanie appeared out of thin air, so I turned to them and tugged on Rochelle's shirt, saying, "Oh, no! They got food poisoning!"

"It's called a *laxative*," Stephanie mused.

"What?" I asked.

"They punish us, *we* punish *them*," Rochelle explained, shrugging like it was no big deal.

A faint scream came from the bathroom. *Boy, it must be really coming out now.* I made my way across the street and stopped outside the bathroom door, then plugged my nose shut and listened quietly. It sounded like the Mississippi River was flooding. Then I jumped back in alarm, seeing a suspicious brown liquid seeping out from under the bathroom door. All of the moms were pounding on the door too, now, saying that they needed in. Krissy and Dominique appeared behind the bathroom door with their noses pinched shut, stepping carefully around the brown liquid. The door slammed shut behind them like someone had kicked them out and was holding it shut. *Were they in there that whole time?* Gross!

"Dad's taking a dump in your bathtub!" Dominique

laughed, motioning a thumb over her shoulder. My jaw dropped open, but I quickly clamped it shut. I didn't want to swallow any fart fumes.

"No, he's not!" My mom gasped.

"Yes, he is. Yes, he is!" Krissy confirmed, and my mom straight up *broke* that door down.

It didn't take long for her to come back out, covering her eyes and wailing about how horrible it smelled. Standing this close to the door, I knew she wasn't lying. She couldn't have even been kidding. It was absolutely horrid.

When the moms were all done excreting their meals, those of us "working" at the party were lined up in the kitchen as Megan searched through all of the ingredient containers. The dads were still...*preoccupied.*

"Nothing has expired. We bought it all new!" Megan tossed the containers that were left on the counter away, and I remembered that nobody had actually *emptied* the garbage, where the green bottle probably was right now.

"Who did it?" Mom snapped viciously. "Who put the laxative in our food?" It was clear that none of the moms were happy, but *my mom's* expression was downright terrifying. Her face was boiling red and distorted.

Everyone was quiet until Rochelle spoke up. "Laxative?"

"Deniese found it in the trash," Megan stated. *I knew it.*

"Dennis June put it in the cookies." Rochelle pointed an accusing finger at me.

"You told me to sprinkle sugar on the cookies!" I exclaimed. I was *not* about to get blamed for this.

"Yeah, sugar. Not *laxative.*" Rochelle folded her arms and stared at me.

I waved my hands wildly and yelled, "*You handed* me the bottle!"

"We *know* that it wasn't just the cookies," Marti chimed in. Her delicate arms folded, and her small hip jutted out to one side. "We didn't all eat the same thing, but we *all* got sick."

"Katrina sprinkled it on the cheese pizza!" Stephanie blurted, pointing a finger at her.

Katrina's porcelain-pale cheeks turned a fierce shade of crimson, and she stammered, "But...but...you told me to put parmesan cheese on it and handed me the bottle!"

"Oh, *right.* I told you to put laxatives on the pizza." Stephanie rolled her eyes as if this was the most ridiculous statement anyone could have ever made. I loathed her. She was a backstabber and so was Rochelle.

"Well, what about the smoothies?" Megan asked, before lowering her voice to an accusative octave. "Marti only had a smoothie and *nothing* else because she ate earlier."

"You told me to throw *everything* in there, and that green bottle was back there." Stephanie's eyebrows rose, and she jutted her chin out sassily.

"I don't buy laxatives, Stephanie. I only use exercise as my method to stay fit." Her mother had a very stern expression on her face now. Stephanie averted her eyes.

"I only use exercise and a strict diet," Marti confided.

Marti's and Megan's gazes shifted to my mother.

"Well, why are y'all lookin' at me?" My mom stiffened and frowned. "Why would I wanna crap any more than I already do?"

I rubbed my chin and nodded. Marti and Megan mumbled to each other.

"That's true," I said.

"Good point," Megan and Marti agreed.

"Did one of you *kids* buy the laxatives?" Marti asked, motioning toward us.

"No," I said immediately. It wasn't like I had the money to do so, anyway. I would've had to steal it. And I would've had to know where to find it.

"When would *I* have time to buy laxatives?" Stephanie lied.

"Well, *I* wouldn't buy that!" Katrina scoffed. "People would think I was weird! How embarrassing would it be to buy something like that? I don't want people knowing I poop."

"Everyone poops," I informed her, and all of them—including my own mother—looked at me with disgust.

"It had to have been Rochelle or Stephanie." My mom's greedy eyes pored over all of our faces. "I know when somebody be up to that lying game. It's one of them." She wagged her finger between the two of them.

"Why not Dennis?" Rochelle asked.

"Dennis was definitely involved," my mom agreed.

"Hey!" I whined. I was always getting blamed for crap.

"But there's no way she bought them."

"Thanks, Mom." I never thought I'd be thankful to my mom for anything in my entire life, but this was one of the first times she had ever defended me.

"Stephanie, you're grounded for a week," Megan decided, and Stephanie paled. I doubted her mom had ever scolded any of her children for anything. Especially since she apparently wasn't grounded already.

"Uh, yah. Rochelle—same for you." My mom copied Megan, and I assumed it was only to fit in. If the other moms weren't here, and Rochelle gave my mom the craps like that on *purpose*, Mom's shoe would've been off quicker than you could say the word "whipped." But I was just glad it wasn't me for once. And a week without Stephanie and Rochelle? That would be pure bliss.

Well, it *was* pure bliss. Until my mom decided her golden bathtub was more important than my dad, and she would be *divorcing* him! I looked that word up in the dictionary, and I couldn't believe it. She was honestly going to end their marriage because he took a dump in her bathtub? I knew people said that pregnancy hormones made women crazy, but this? Wasn't it just *a little* extreme?

I asked my mom if she thought so and got the left shoe to my butt. She was not playing games, so I decided that if her and my dad wanted to split up, I would survive. He was barely home as it was anyway, and he was always making comments about other women. My mom was always pregnant and mad. I didn't know if it was legal to just decide you were mad at someone and end your marriage. Was that even a real thing? Even if I did think the bathtub incident was the *teensiest* bit funny, all humor surrounding it went away when my parents decided to divorce and that shoe cracked me for asking questions.

As the next couple of weeks passed, I thought maybe the whole thing was a joke. Or that it had blown over. But then my dad started taking stuff out of the house little by little. My mom cried for what seemed like one minute, then invited Bob Waltzer over, who showed up with *suitcases.* What did he think he was doing?

"What are you doing here?" I asked him.

"Um, your mom and I are going to be living together." Bob glanced at my mother, who was sitting on the couch with her back to us.

"So what you're saying is that *we* will be living together?"

He just stared at me, his brows furrowed. "Ew. Don't word it like that, kid. Your mom and I are dating now."

"No shacking up!" I screamed because that's what the

old people always said about people who lived together but weren't married.

Bob rolled his eyes and carried his luggage upstairs.

My mom rolled her eyes too and muttered, "Just go away, DJ."

What felt like only a few days later became one of the oddest days of my life. Or my mom's life. I wasn't quite sure how to put it. My dad rolled up to the curb in front of our house, and I ran to meet him, thinking he was coming home and was going to kick Bob Waltzer out. But when I knocked on the passenger window, and he rolled it down, it revealed the blond hair and makeup-clad face of Alissa Waltzer. What was he doing with *her*?

"Go get your mom, DJ." My dad didn't smile in the slightest, so I did as I was told.

My pregnant mother flung open the front door, and I trailed behind her so I could see what he wanted her for.

"Deniese! Get in the car." He motioned to the back seat, and I wondered why he had a death wish.

"Excuse me?" My mom had curlers in her hair, and they shook with the sassy swishes of her head.

"Alissa and I are eloping."

"Good for you!" she sneered, stomping a high heel against the pavement.

"Come with," he called, motioning for her.

"Did you fry up your last remaining brain cells in that factory?"

"It's a steel factory, not a science lab," Alissa scoffed.

"I *know* that, you hussy. He was *my* husband."

"Yah, and *Bob* was *mine.*"

My mom shook her head in disbelief. "Why do you need me?"

"We need a witness. For our elopement." My dad gave her praying hands and pouted.

"You left me here with *every single one of these kids,*" she hissed. "What's in it for me?"

My dad bent down and reached for something under the seat of his car. Then he chucked a pair of high heels out the window, and they hit the grass with a thud.

"What are those?" my mom asked, her eyes bugged out.

"Louis Vuitton high heels. Brand new, fresh off the market." My dad stuck his nose in the air, and I begged my mom in my thoughts not to do it. She was too good for him. *Did I really just think that?* But she couldn't resist the bait and picked up the shoes. She got in the back seat of the car, hair curlers and all.

"Mom!" I yelled. "Where are you going?"

"I'll be right back!" She shushed me.

"We'll drop her off before we head to New York for the honeymoon!" Dad let out a whoop and then honked the horn.

I stepped toward the car, but he rolled the windows up. I barely touched the glass before they sped off and faded in the distance, leaving me in the dust.

Chapter 15

I KNEW I SHOULD probably feel more about my parents' divorce. About my dad moving out. But it had honestly pretty much been the same. Bob Waltzer was around, but he usually was only in my mom's room or at the picnic table. Occasionally he hoarded the bathroom to primp for work at the Karaoke Club. From my perspective though? The house still felt as full. Mom was still loud. Dad was not really around. It felt almost…the same.

When my mom made note of a going away party for the graduating kids at Parzay Parzay, the most swanky restaurant in all of Crab Cove, I thought she would be going with Bob. But she was going with *my dad*. She made Bob watch us, saying that since Emma and Emily would be moving to Washington, Dad was responsible for buying her dinner. As I was being told the news, I also was being told things I didn't *need* to know. Like that she thought Bob was a better kisser. Or how she was going to order the lobster because my dad owed her for the havoc he wrecked on her body. Nasty. I plugged my ear holes so I couldn't hear anything worse than that.

Apparently all the Star's and Green's kids didn't go to

school because they got to go to Parzay Parzay. *I* wanted to go. Instead, I watched Bob sort through all of the groceries in our cabinets and organize things, cleaning everything in sight. He sniffed some ingredients and winced as he chucked them in the trash. It was pleasing. Much more pleasing than attending school. I didn't like that Bob was living with my mom and dating her, but I liked how he sorted our food.

❖

Ol' Sanch was mad because nobody showed up for school yesterday. Because they were partying at Parzay Parzay. I was partying internally because two of my siblings moved out. And okay, maybe Sanchez *wasn't* old, but anyone who was that mean and cranky got that nickname automatically. In her rage she assigned us a big science project, and I got paired with Haylee Star. How glorious was it that I got both a smart and *normal* partner? Well, it *was* very glorious. Until Brad decided we had to trade partners, and for some dumb reason his bullying tactics worked. Brad cornered me in class and threatened to do all kinds of gross things to me, and I gave in. I wished I had let him crop dust me instead. Because his partner?

Mama's Child.

"Denny!" she hollered when school let out, and I turned around to find her red afro flapping in the wind, her hand flapping just as eagerly. I groaned and stopped.

"We're partners," she told me.

"Uh, yah. I know."

"Let's go to my house to work on the project."

"Not tonight, Mama's Child." I didn't want to go to her house. What if it was scary? What if her mom was turning horses into hamburgers in the backyard?

"Well, have fun walking home then. 'Cause ya missed the bus."

I rubbed my forehead and took in the dark, threatening sky. *Why?*

Her snicker nauseated me as it ripped me out of my head and forced me back to reality.

"Fine, Den. We can go to your house!" MC squinted her eyes and stuck out her tongue, clapping me on the back.

Oh my gosh, did she really *just invite herself over to my house?* I started walking and nodded to myself in affirmation when she followed me. Yep. She was coming to my house. Sirens roared through the air, but I continued, unresponsive. Mama's Child kept nudging me, but I was indifferent to the chaos. My whole life was chaos. I couldn't take her nudging anymore and finally asked, "What?"

"What'd yer ma do this time, Dennis?" She stopped and slapped her knee, claiming she was going to pee herself from laughing so hard. A stick flew from a nearby yard and landed at her feet.

"Mama's, you are a heathen." I shook my head. Monica's big mansion came into view, and I jolted, feeling like a burglar caught red-handed when Monica herself opened a window and stuck her head out. What if she thought we were spying on her?

"What are you two *doing?*" she called out at us. Monica was talking to me!

"Uh, I'm walking home." I pointed to my house, which was practically across the street.

"We're under a tornado warning! Come over now!" I envied her blushed cheeks. Did she wear makeup? *I* wanted to wear makeup.

MC was rambling on about something, but I was too busy taking in Monica and her mansion, lost in my thoughts. I jerked backwards when something pulled on me.

"Den-aAH!" a guttural sound choked off. My backpack?

My BACKPACK!

I patted where it had been, and when I turned back toward my house, there was Mama's Child, flung into a *tornado,* with my backpack! It done sucked 'er right up! Losing sight of my backpack, I ran a few steps toward my house. Mama's Child was whipping around and around, and out of nowhere my backpack smacked her straight in the face! She screamed. Running toward a payphone near the sidewalk, I fished around in my overalls and found a single quarter. *How'd that get in there?* I paused as I stared down at it. Mama's Child's bloodcurdling scream pierced the air again, reminding me what I was doing in the first place. I called Stacey because she just got a job driving an ambulance yesterday.

"Yullow?" asked Stacey.

"Stacey!" I blurted, trying to hear her over the wind.

"Who dis?"

"It's Deniese."

"Who?"

"Deniese!" I blared, bringing the phone as close to my mouth as possible without touching it, because *germs!*

"Uh?"

"Dennis."

"Oh!"

"I need you to drive here in the ambulance. The nado took MC."

"Are you insane?"

"It's your job!" I yelled, though I wasn't one hundred percent sure it was.

"Kay kay," she said, and hung up.

The nado ripped behind the house, and I searched, squinting through the dust cloud until I finally caught a flash of red permed afro. Mama's. Stacey pulled up in the ambulance, and when she got out, she was ashenly pale.

"What's wrong?" I asked her.

"I've never done this before."

"Never done what?" I asked.

"Where's the tornado?"

"Uh…" I hesitated, looking around, seeing nothing but funnel clouds in the sky. Then a loud "Moooooooooooooooo!" pierced my eardrums.

"Bessie!" I yelled for what felt like a full minute. Stacey grabbed her ears.

"I see Mama's Child," she stated when my outburst had ended, pointing to where she was lying on the ground. I searched the tornado frantically. Where was Bessie? She was a cow, for crying out loud! She couldn't be that hard to spot!

I followed Stacey across the street but kept a safe distance. I didn't want that nado coming after me.

"Is Bessie gonna die?" I asked. Nobody answered me.

"Yep," Stacey said, glancing down at Mama's Child.

"She is?" I cried.

"No, what? I was talking about Mama's Child. You've definitely broken your spleen." She started pushing on Mama's Child's belly, before tapping at her elbows and knees. Then she crumpled her face and muttered under her breath, "Wait. Can you break your spleen? Where even is the spleen?"

Poor Mama's Child, I thought as Stacey loaded her into the ambulance. Poor thing never saw it coming. Monica's muffled yells reached my ears, and she waved to me, so I rushed over. I got to go inside her house, and not just the kitchen. It was spotless, and the ceilings were higher than the sky itself! I heard a familiar scream in the distance, and Monica peeked out the window before asking me, "Was that your mom?"

"She probably just ran out of Mystery Meet."

"What's that?"

"Er, nevermind." I wanted to snoop in here so bad. I bet her bedroom had tons of toys. Like a *Toys R Us* at home.

Something started beeping, like a timer or alarm clock, and I searched the room for the source of the noise.

"What's that?" I asked.

Monica pointed toward a computer. She had a *computer* in her house! "My mom's computer. Someone's doing a video call."

"What?" I asked.

She shook the mouse and said, "My mother's getting a call from...is that *your* mother?"

I squinted at the screen and nearly crapped myself when my mom's tomato-red face blew up full size on the monitor.

"Have you dumping seen Dennis June?" my mom bellowed. *Did she own a computer?*

I jumped a little, even though she wasn't even really here.

"I've been screaming my head off for her! Bessie's outside groaning. She's in pain from not being milked at four!"

"It's for you, Deniese." Monica cowered, backing away from the screen. A brown dog with white spots scurried across the floor.

"Aww! You have a dog?"

"Yes," Monica answered.

"What's its name?"

"Dennis!" My mom's voice put me in line like I had a fish slapped across my face.

My shaky legs took me to the monitor. "Where do I stand?" I asked Monica.

"I can *see* you!" My mother hissed the words like I was an idiot. How did this even work? How could she see me? How could I see her?

"What is *wrong* with you?" Her voice grew louder and louder, and Monica's mouth plopped open into a little round "o."

"You are in the grounded room for *life*. Do you hear me?" My mom huffed air out through her flaring nostrils.

"Bu-buh-but my backpack is in the nado," I stammered.

"Bessie is in pain—"

"—Bessie is also in the nado."

"*What?*" she hollered. We stared at each other in silence for a few seconds, neither of us willing to speak.

"I'mma look out the window, and if you're lying, I swear —" my mom's voice grew muffled as her huge bosom filled up the whole screen, then her pregnant stomach, then she finally was nowhere to be seen. I rushed to the window and looked out, across the street.

As odd as it sounded, I thought I saw the crash before I heard it happen. The wind was so strong it was visible. Sticks and leaves were swirling about, and trees looked like they were about to snap in half. When my mother leaned out the window, the nado pulled her out with it, the crash thunderous. The front door flew open, and Bob Waltzer rushed over to where my mother was on the ground, crying, "My love?"

My backpack! A blur of an object whizzed past, slapping Bob in the gut and sucking him straight up in the tornado with it.

"Moooooooooooooooooo!"

"Bessie!" I hollered at the top of my worn-out lungs.

"Who's Bessie?" Monica asked, walking over and placing her face up against the glass with me. "Should we help them?" she asked.

"Can ya lift a cow?" I asked.

Her eyebrows furrowed together, knitted like an ol' granny's sweater.

"I'll take that as a no," I breathed. "Do ya got a phone?"

"Yes!" she cheered, looking relieved to be able to help. I called Stacey again, who told me she would make a U-ie. It didn't take long for her to get here. *How'd she get here that fast?* But when she pulled open the ambulance doors, a small body was lying in there on a stretcher. Poor Mama's never even made it to the hospital! What was Stacey doing? She should've dropped her off first, the idiot! Monica and I watched as she struggled to load my mom and Bob onto stretchers, pushing them hard against the wind toward the ambulance. *How did she plan to fit three people in there?*

Then I saw something I would never forget in a million years if I tried. Bessie—Bessie *the cow*—plowed straight into that ambulance, and the whole thing got slurped up into the nado!

"Oh my goodness!" Monica cried, grabbing both of her cheeks.

"*That's* Bessie!" I explained, pointing at my cow, which was swirling around in the nado. Her pink rubbery udders flapped in the scribble of wind and dirt. Mama's Child's stretcher started creeping out of the ambulance, and the doors kept slapping open and shut, slamming into her cot. Until the ambulance flipped upside down, and out came Mama's Child, her IV ripped clean out of her arm!

"Ewwwwwwwwwwwwwwwwwww!" Monica gasped, covering her eyes. I took it she had a phobia of needles.

"Yowzers! That had to have hurt," I exclaimed, pressing my face as far against the glass as it could do. I was pressed up against it so hard that my bodily imprint was probably going to be left there, and they'd have to have special fancy cleaners come get rid of it. Somebody had to tell Stacey she was being ignorant. I opened the window a crack, and the wind whipped at it, threatening to force it shut.

Mama's Child's twangy voice hollered, "Why me?"

"Shut that window, Deniese!" Monica cried, peeking out from behind gaps in her fingers as she slid onto the floor. I did as I was told.

Poor Mama's Child. I was wondering why nothing bad had happened to *me* yet. Normally I would be the person in Mama's Child's position. I thought long and hard about it for about two seconds before I decided, *Welp! Oh, well.* I shrugged. *Can't be helped.* The nado was gonna dish its worst, and I was at *Monica's house.* Might as well make the most of it!

Monica put extra blankets on the extra bed in her room and said I could stay the night. She even gave me one of her teddy bears! We watched cartoons and ate ice cream until 11:00 p.m., which was two hours past my bedtime! I loved Monica's home.

Snoozing peacefully, I drifted into the most blissful sleep. Until I sat up straight in bed, sweating all over. I breathed heavily. Something wasn't sitting right. *That little rat!* I thought. It was suddenly so clear now. Mama's Child must've ran into that nado on purpose so that *I'd* have to do all the work myself! I huffed hot air out of my nostrils, boiling mad. But the sleep fairy must've thrown its magic dust over my eyes. Or maybe it was something about Monica's house. Lying back down, I drifted off once more.

Three days later in Sanch's class, realization hit me like someone had chucked a raw hamburger patty at my face.

"It's presentation day!" Mrs. Sanchez sang maliciously,

waving her stupid ruler. I stared down at my hands. Treasonous hands! What have you done? *Or what have you not done.* With the excitement from staying at Monica's house, and the horror that was the tornado, I had completely forgotten about the project! My mom and Bob had been in the hospital, and I was a wreck, worrying about Bessie. I shifted in my seat, trying to come up with a plan. Counting on my fingers and looking at the number of people who had to present, I figured that as long as I did not get called on today, I could probably squeeze out a decent C-.

I was the first group to get called on.

"But Mama's Child is still in the hospital!" I exclaimed, appalled at the demand.

"I don't care for procrastination, Dennis. Present *now.*"

If you asked me, I thought she was still hoarding a grudge over my grandma killing her mom. Like come on, lady, that was *two* summers ago!

"I have nothing to present," I finally said. What was I supposed to do?

"*Nothing?* What have you been doing the past four days?" Her voice bordered on shrill. I thought about what I had been doing the past four days, and the only thing I really did was write in this journal.

"Literally, nothing." We made uncomfortable eye contact before the death stare forced me to continue, "Otherwise, I would've had it done." I muttered, "Obviously," which was a grave mistake.

"Demerit for your sass! And you and Mama's Child fail this project. F!" she screamed, all red in the face. She slapped that stupid ruler down on my desk. *It'd serve ya right if it cracked in half.*

I swallowed hard. Mama's Child would make my life absolute crap for this. Something niggled in my mind, something MC had been saying before the tornado took her. She had been rambling, saying she almost failed kindergarten and that she needed a good grade on this science project. I really needed to stop tuning people out. Then again, she could've been lying. Mama's Child struck me as the type to lie. Mrs. Sanchez kicked me out of class, but I didn't even know it until she hollered, "Git!" *There you are doing it again, Dennis! Pay attention!*

I sat outside the classroom door, bored like no other, until the school day ended.

Chapter 16

SO YOU'LL NEVER BELIEVE it, but somebody done got pregnant again. *Ashley.* It all started when this bill came from the hospital, and it wasn't for my mom. Ashley had muttered something about needing to go to a gynecologist for her first checkup, and my mom said, "Ain't no way!" My mom didn't take us to the doctor. She told us to get over it or take one of her "magic pills" that I was convinced were just breath mints. I thought the universe must have given Ashley a baby because of Emma and Emily moving out, though it was weird it was in her stomach. Did that mean tummy babies weren't just for married people? If it was because of Emma and Emily, that meant there was still one more replacement needed. I hoped God didn't give me the baby because I was already chonky enough as it was.

Monica and Haylee had been talking about going to a party tonight, and I decided that I was going to go, too, since it was at the Star residence.

I knocked on the back door, the pop-princessy music fluttering out. After knocking, I noticed a sign I didn't see on my way here and knew I had made a grave mistake. Because apparently I had just shown up at Katrina's birthday party. Yikes. A tap on my shoulder nearly made me jump out of my skin, and I turned around, clutching my palpitating heart.

"Hey, Denny," Mama's Child said. Bruises spackled her skin—almost matching her freckles—and she was paler than a ghost.

"I'm not mad at you anymore for pushing me into that tornado."

What?

"I did *not* push you into that nado!" I screeched, ready to have a meltdown. What if someone had heard her? What if people thought I tried to kill her and I got arrested like my grandma?

"I'm just kiddin', Den." Mama's Child's Cheshire smile returned, and I knew the nado must not have rattled her brain too much. That was a few weeks ago. Bob and my mom returned from the hospital shortly after, but I had no idea when Mama's Child got out. She'd only been at school the past two days. Bessie had shown up a few yards down. Thankfully she was alive, and it wasn't Monica's yard. Or Katrina's.

"Stalker alert," a voice said from inside. The music turned down, and everyone quieted. Katrina's face appeared in the window, peeking out at us.

"Ew, it's Dennis and Mama's. Major *loser* alert!" Katrina stuck her tongue out and made a gagging motion. My cheeks reddened.

"Mama's wouldn't be a loser if she stayed away from that freak!" another girl called.

"I'm no longer friends with Denny," Mama's Child blurted. "She pushed me into that tornado."

Now my clams were *really* boiled.

"You *lie*, Mama's Child!" I bellowed.

"Let MC in," Katrina said, and Mama's Child flipped her afro and walked inside. My gut boiled.

"Just let DJ in, she's not that bad." Monica's voice echoed through my brain on a loop. I could distinguish that voice anywhere.

"It's *my* party," Katrina demanded.

"If you don't let her in, then I can just leave," Monica answered, and I couldn't believe my ears. Until Monica was shoved outside, and the door slammed shut.

"Thank you—" I began, but she had already begun walking to her house, not saying a word.

The next day at school was awful. I sat in my bedroom reflecting on how the whole morning everyone made comments about the tornado *they weren't even involved in*. What was worse? People weren't just making "moo" sounds about Bessie or making jokes about my mom and Bob. Everyone was convinced I had pushed Mama's Child into the nado. Except for Monica, because she saw it, of course. But she didn't say anything to defend me. And why would she, with what happened last time?

A knock at the door came, and it was none other than the accuser herself.

"Denny!" she called, like we were best friends. Maybe we were? I'd never had a best friend.

"Are you in the chatroom yet?" she asked.

What the dump was a chatroom?

Mama's Child convinced me to push a button on Bob Waltzer's computer. It was set up in the living room, and MC helped me make an account for this "chatroom." I made my username TomorrowIsAnotherDay, the same name I used for the title of this journal. Mama's Child told me I chose a stupid name. I told her to shut the Bessie dung patty up. Then we co-created an account together and named it TownSpy...for obvious reasons.

Rochelle's voice boomed from upstairs, "Dennis, your username is dumbo!"

"How do you know what my name is?" I hollered back up.

"Uh, it's not that hard. TheDJ is you, ya dumbturd."

"That's not my username!" I called back.

"Everyone knows that's your username," Brad said, fiddling with a phone on the couch.

"It's not my name!" I protested.

"Mama's Child, *who in the world* is 'TheDJ'?" I muttered, lowering my voice so the others wouldn't hear. She shrugged but snickered. What was her problem? Was it *her?*

Mama's Child and I roamed around town, eavesdropping and looking for secrets like detectives. We spied on everybody. And I meant *everybody*. Even random people I didn't know. Anytime we saw or heard anything juicy, we updated TownSpy. People were getting so upset, and all the beans were getting spilled! It was like a whole new world. Mama's Child called it "stirring the pot." I told her the only "pot" I knew of was the kind that made my sister Tiffany smell like poop on a stick. Then Mama's told me, "I'mma tell the cops, Denny! That's illegal!"

My sister Tiffany got sent away for a while after that. I always wondered if it had anything to do with what I told Mama's.

Logging onto the chatroom at a public library, Mama's Child and I got to work.

TownSpy has signed on.
TownSpy: Brad and Stephanie are

definitely making out behind the theater.

TownSpy: They are an item.

TownSpy: Broccoli Waltzer lies about having back problems so he only has to work one shift.

TownSpy: Ashley looks fat today…

TheDJ: Sanchez is a freaking rip-off. She gets pleasure when everybody is poor and she is rich yet dresses like she went dumpster diving for clothes.

SpicySanchez: Dennis, you get a Demerit, you hooligan!

ApplePie: I would give her two…just saying

SpicySanchez: ApplePie, that is a splendid idea.

Mama'sDiner: Buy one, get one free burgers all week!

Younggirlohyoujealous: More like buy one, get food poisoning…

ApplePie: Younggirl, you must eat a lot of them to know that, you fattie.

Younggirlohyoujealous: I'm the sexiest person on the block.

ApplePie has signed off.

TownSpy: Deniese Tipper is shacking up with Bob Waltzer.

FootballFever: Deniese is a joke.

NiteInShiningArmour: You're obviously Dude Tipper. And you are just jealous.

FootballFever: Bob Waltzer is taking a dump in the playground sandbox.

TownSpy: I was just about to say that.

NiteInShiningArmour: I'm at work.
NiteInShiningArmour has signed off.
FootballFever: Do you work in a sandbox? Buttmunch.
TheDJ: KEEP them coming Sanch!
SpicySanchez: You're going to fail this year, Dennis.
ChampionBeatdown: DJ is asking for an expulsion.
TomorrowIsAnotherDay: Quit picking on DJ!
Football Fever: Who the duff is TomorrowIsAnotherDay?
FootballFight: TRIPLE SHIFT?! TRIPLE SHIFT!
FootballFight has signed off.
FootballFever has signed off.
Factory4Ever has signed off.
EatYourVeggies;): I think I will pull a single, my back hurts.
TownSpy: Broccoli's "Back Problems"
EatYourVeggies;): I DO HAVE BACK PROBLEMS TOWNPOOP
ChampionBeatdown: First Shift Ever
BeachBoy: It isn't fun.
Hotness: Quit before you start.
Younggirlohyoujealous: Who are you hotness? ;) I am also hot.
TownSpy: If hot meant ugly.
Younggirlohyoujealous: TownSpy, when I find out who you are, I am going to tell Danny.

HeyEverybody: DO IT PLS
TheCheats: I am hot, Younggirl.
Younggirlohyoujealous: Cheat as in
cheater? Are you Chester? Or Danny Jr?
Whatever: WHAT DO YOU MEAN DANNY
JR?!
TownSpy: I know what she means... ;)
SpicySanch: TIPPER DIRT
RichHeiress: What did Danny Jr do?
TownSpy: Ask Ashley...

I looked up from the computer and turned to Mama's Child, slapping her arm.

"Mama's Child, that was a *secret!*" I hissed. The librarian shushed me, so I took deep breaths to calm myself down. I couldn't believe she was hinting at what I told her. MC wanted to know all the dirt I knew, and I told her a lot, including how Ashley and Danny Jr left the dance together and that she was having a baby. MC told me that meant Danny was the dad. But Danny was *Orange's* boyfriend.

"Secrets are meant to be spilled, Dennis!" Mama's Child snickered. She stood and made stirring motions with her arms, as if a big cauldron sat in front of her.

"What are you doing?"

"I'm stirring the pot, ding dong." She laughed. The librarian shushed us again, but more threateningly this time.

"Do you want in? Or wanna be a victim of TownSpy?" she whispered. I sighed and looked around at the poor souls who would be her victims. I didn't know them, but everyone was fair game according to MC. And I did *not* want to be one of them.

"I'm in," I decided.

Staring at the screen once more, I tried to decipher who was who. I knew that "SpicySanchez" was Sanch,

"Mama'sDiner" was Mama's Child's mom, "EatYourVeggies;)" was Broccoli Waltzer, "FootballFever" was dad, "NiteInShiningArmour" was Bob Waltzer, "Younggirlohyoujealous" was my mom (cringe), "Whatever" was Orange, and "HeyEverybody" was Danny. But who in the world was everybody else? This thing could be great. I mean, I could say whatever I wanted, and nobody would know it was me. But at the same time, it could be horrible. Someone claiming to be me was already getting me in *heaps* of trouble. Biting my lip and glancing at Mama's Child, I just prayed I had made the right choice.

Chapter 17

IT WAS NOW OCTOBER, and the only thing people had been talking about for *weeks* was the upcoming Halloween party at Bob's Karaoke Club. A $1,000 reward (that my mom said "better not be from my wallet") would be given to whoever sang the best, and Bob was the judge. I had been working on my costume for about a week and had decided to go as Betty Boop. Krissy and Dominique beat me out for the "cute factor" when they dressed up as Thing One and Thing Two from *The Cat in the Hat*. I nearly lost my Mystery Meet when my mom came downstairs in a skin-tight leopard costume. Lumps and bumps were in all the wrong places, and I cringed at the sight.

When I got to the party flooded with flashy strobe lights that made me nauseous, Katrina strutted past in a short dress with gogo boots. Did her mom let her go to *church* in that dress? Because even though Katrina and the rest of her older siblings weren't, Marti Star was a *saint* if I ever saw one. A real proper lady.

Haylee and Hallee struggled to walk through the doors in a joint costume. They looked like green balls to me, but when I asked them, they claimed they were "two peas in a pod" because they were twins. Apparently their mom still made their costumes.

Adjusting the black wig I snatched from my mom's beauty parlor, which was probably backwards by now, I searched for Monica. When I couldn't find her, I asked her mother, who was painted blue supposedly trying to be "Smurfette." She told me that Monica had gone to the bathroom, so I naturally went to the bathroom. I didn't have the urge to go, so I just lingered by the sink and got lots of dirty looks from people who definitely should've looked in their mirror twice before coming tonight. Yowza!

Monica finally exited a stall and walked to the sink to wash her hands. Her costume was perfect for her—Daphne from *Scooby Doo*. I sighed, wishing I had come as Scooby. She smiled at me, and I got scared, worried she would be embarrassed to be seen with me. So I hid in a stall and made "Ssssssssssssssssssssss" noises with my mouth so it would sound like I intentionally came in here to take a wazz. Then I wanted to punch myself because *really, Dennis?* You wanted to talk to somebody and be their best friend, but the first thing you did when you saw them was *pretend* to pee? *Smooth. REAL smooth.*

When the competition got started, a *lot* of people were eliminated in the first round, and rightfully so. Except for my mom, who somehow made it through even though she sounded like a cat getting run over. Bob was giving her special privileges because he was shacking up with her. I placed my hands on the stage and leaned forward, right in the action. Timmy Waltzer was up first in the second round, and when he got on the stage, he chose the song *Ice Ice Baby. That's a great song. Sweet.* Or it *was.* Until he screamed, "Let's kick it!" and kicked me straight in the face.

I wailed, screaming, "It's broken! It's broken!" Sticky

wet stuff plagued my face, and I was ninety-nine percent sure it wasn't snot.

"Sorry, son," Bob Waltzer told Timmy, cutting the music. "I have to disqualify you for that violence."

"It was an accident!" he defended.

"It's my *nose!*" I wailed, holding it like it'd fall clean off if I didn't.

"It's your own fault for standing that close, Dennis," my mom groaned, before adding, "Kill joy." Then she crushed her soda can with her fist. I winced as it crumpled down flat. I bet my nose was crushed just like that can.

Bob Waltzer gave me a free pass to the top four, and I had tissues stuffed up my nose. It felt good to have someone do something nice for me. People complained and were mad about it though. Not because he was being nice to me. I think the majority of the population in this town just hated me.

The final four was Dude Green, Brad, me, and surprisingly…Mama's Child. She was dressed up like a pig. It was kind of cute, actually, and it made me think of Beans. Poor Beans. My baby. I hoped he learned how to make bacon so that mean old man didn't kill him. Tears welled in my eyes, but it was go time. So I wiped my eyes and brushed it off as my nose hurting.

We had to sing the song *Endless Love*, and Brad and I failed miserably. Even with the words running across the screen, I had never heard that song before in my life, so I had no idea how to sing it. I think Brad botched it on purpose because it was a mushy love song. Dude Green was a soprano, believe it or not. His voice was higher than a little girl's. I cracked up because it sounded nothing like his talking voice, but also just because he sounded like a girl. But it was not supposed to be funny. Dude Green took his soprano singing very seriously. And he judged anyone who wasn't one.

When Dude Green won, Mama's Child looked madder than a hornet. My dad stood from his chair and made a big scene. He pretended to wipe tears from his face and cheered, "That's my *best friend!*" Why did my family have to be so embarrassing? Why did *I* have to be so embarrassing?

Lil' Shelbi got on the stage and started dancing to the song "Beverly Hills" by Weezer. But my mom shrieked and made Bob turn it off immediately. Everyone stared at her like she was drunk, but she wasn't. She swore that song "summoned my grandma." *Summoned.* I cringed, as did everyone else, and nobody cared so much about the song being turned off.

I'd admit I snuck onto Bob Waltzer's computer when I went home that night, wanting to see if any beef was going down. That was what Mama's Child and I called it. *Beef.* But nothing really was going down other than an argument between TownSpy and NiteInShiningArmour (Bob Waltzer), who had to have been using his work computer. Mama's Child was writing that the whole thing had been rigged, but she was just being petty because she lost. Tee-hee!

Chapter 18

MEGAN GREEN INVITED practically *everyone* to her house for a Thanksgiving get together. My mom was thrilled because she didn't want to have to pay for or cook anything, and she *loved* Megan Green. Probably just as much as I adored Monica! I had seen the invitation mentioned "plus ones," so naturally I invited Mama's Child. A bunch of the popular kids screeched at me, and it was possibly deserved. She brought her backpack and a little device that she said could get on TownSpy. I thought she was poorer than me, so I had no idea where she got that. Maybe since she was an only child that made a difference?

Dude Green had invited my dad, so it got real awkward, *real fast,* when he showed up with his new wife, Alissa—who used to be the wife of my mom's new boyfriend. It was one big, messed-up love square. When we all sat down at the tables set up, my dad announced, "Well, *I,* for one, am thankful. I am thankful to have three babies on the way."

"I'm pregnant with twins, not triplets. Moron," my mom muttered bitterly.

"I know." My dad snickered. I wrinkled my nose.

"I'm pregnant," Alissa announced. I wiped my forehead

and let out a "phew." *There* was the extra replacement. I wouldn't have to be the pregnant one.

My mom's jaw dropped.

"Take that, Bob Waltzer!" my dad bellowed, his arms in the air like he had made a goal in sports.

Bob Waltzer stood and went to the other side of the room, taking an empty seat between Sammi Green and Katrina.

"Well, then." Marti squirmed in her seat.

"Congratulations," Megan told her before saying to everyone, "Perhaps we should all go around and share what we are thankful for."

I watched Mama's Child type "Alissa is pregnant" on TownSpy. She snickered. A few phones dinged.

"*I* am thankful for triple shifts at the factory," Dude Green announced. My dad and Lucas Star agreed, shaking their heads and muttering, "I wish I had thought of that." Dude Green smirked like he was an angel for choosing that. The three of them all worked at the factory, and all of them were obsessed with it.

"Why do y'all love work so much?" I grimaced. All three of them shot me the stank eye.

"Is that *your* child?" Dude Green asked Dad.

He turned red for maybe the first time in his life. Embarrassed to claim me. And he claimed practically every child who was born to this world.

"I'll go next," Megan began. "I am thankful for my husband and ten beautiful children."

"Well, I'mma top you all, so hold on to your bowels and bladders," my mom snorted. "I'm thankful for Bessie the cow and Black Friday sales on Mystery Meet."

"I'm thankful that my best friend threw this lovely party." Marti smiled.

My mom scoffed and fake coughed. "Ahem AH! Suck up. Huh!"

"Well, *I'm* thankful that my doctor actually *believes* I have back pain from work. Unlike *everyone* in this room." Broccoli shot daggers around the table. Mama's Child snickered and nudged me.

I whispered, "Don't blow our cover!" She stuck her tongue out at me.

"I believe you, baby," Rochelle told him, and I snorted. I had never heard her call anyone that, ever.

"Liar!" all the guys from the factory yelled. "You're just lazy."

"I'm thankful for corn dogs." Clumps of mashed up food sloshed around Rochelle's mouth as she spoke.

"I'm thankful I dumped Brad," Nicole said nonchalantly, and I spit my punch out all over the place. Brad rolled his eyes. Marti gasped and Megan passed napkins over for me to clean it up. My cheeks turned as red as the punch, and I dabbed at the liquid fervently, hoping everyone was more focused on Brad's embarrassment than mine.

"I'm thankful for Orange," Stephanie said.

Orange—unsurprisingly—responded, "Whatever." Then they hugged.

"I'm thankful I'm not related to the girls who are actually *hot.*" Brad smirked, like the absolute slimeball that he was.

"Hey!" my mom complained. "*I'm* smoking." Then she added, "Literally," and lit a cigarette. My mom didn't smoke. Where did she even get those?

"You're pregnant with my kids, you sicko. Put that out!" my dad demanded.

"I'm not the only one."

"Get over it!" he snapped.

My mom motioned across the room and said, "Come

back over here, Bob Waltzer."

I wondered why she called him by his first *and* last name. But come to think of it, *everyone* called him by his first and last name.

He leaped up to obey her summon and tripped over Katrina's chair. It tipped backwards, and she went with it. Her dress flew up, and Mama's Child and I laughed.

"Katrina! I cannot believe you wore such a short dress. Close your legs, immediately! You are in trouble, young missy!" Marti scolded, rushing to help her up.

Krissy and Dominique said they were thankful for the storage unit in their butts, and Dominique reached down her pants, handing my mom her car keys. She grabbed them and gagged, rushing to the bathroom.

"Wait till she finds out I got her cellphone in mine!" Krissy giggled. There were plenty of grimaces and green faces at this.

It eventually came around to me and Mama's Child. I looked at her, and she went first.

"I am thankful to be alive after that tornado." She stood from her seat and acted like she was walking down a fashion runway. Everyone clapped. *She* would *get the pity clap*.

Mama's Child returned to her seat, and all eyes fell on me. I got nervous and couldn't think of anything else, so I said, "I'm thankful that Mama's Child caught my backpack in the nado. I didn't know it, but she brought it back to me." People's eyes widened, and a few even curled their lips up at me.

"Wow," somebody muttered.

"What happened?" asked my mom, flopping back onto her seat. "Did somebody die?" She shook her napkin out, and it made a loud slap against her thighs.

They told her what I had just said, but I saw nothing

wrong with it.

"Dennis, apologize to Mama's Child, right *now.*" My mom glared at me.

"Uh, why? I was *thanking* her."

"You should have said you were thankful she *lived.* Not that you were thankful you got your backpack back."

I looked around and saw people nodding. "Um, but I am particularly fond of my backpack," I scoffed.

"What six-year-old says 'particularly fond of'?" Brad laughed.

My mom gritted her teeth and made a subtle pointing gesture to her high heel. I apologized to Mama's Child. I didn't want to get smacked with a high-heeled shoe.

"It's okay, Denny." Mama's Child clasped her hands together, smiling like she was a perfect little angel.

Everyone dug into the food, even though Rochelle had started eating like a half an hour ago. I'll admit I nibbled on a roll when people weren't looking, and drinks didn't count.

After picking at her food, Mama's Child motioned under the table cloth, and we slipped under the table when nobody was watching. Then we logged onto TownSpy on her little gadget. It didn't take more than her writing "that meal was delectable" for everyone's phones to ding, and Rochelle announced to the entire room, "TownSpy is on!"

A bunch of chairs moved, and people pulled phones out of their pockets. I squinted at the little screen and read:

NiteInShiningArmour: I know TownSpy is Dude Tipper.

FootballFever: I'm Dude Tipper, my username is tattooed onto my back.

EatYourVeggies;): My back hurts.

SamIAm: From the food?

EatYourVeggies;): Nope.

TheDJ: I ate so much, I feel like Sanch.
SpicySanchez: Demerit again, DJ.
I demanded MC let me defend myself, and logged into my account. We kept switching back and forth.
TomorrowIsAnotherDay: Seriously? You are being unreasonable, Sanchez!
SpicySanchez: Don't protect Dennis.
FootballFever: Is TomorrowIsAnotherDay Mama's Child?
TomorrowIsAnotherDay: No!
Football Fever: Then why are you upset that Sanch is giving DJ a demerit?
MissPopularity: Who cares how many demerits DJ gets?
TomorrowIsAnotherDay: I do.
TownSpy: Why is Ashley looking nervously at Danny Jr.?
Whatever: What?
TownSpy: Look at her! It's like she is bloated with a food baby.
Whatever: Danny…
TownSpy: Danny went to the bathroom.
HeyEverybody: No, I didn't.
TownSpy: The other Danny.
TownSpy: Sanch is wearing an engagement ring. Who's the lowlife who wanted to marry her?
SpicySanchez: Not your business.
TheDJ: I bet it was an ogre.
Championbeatdown: I like DJ's new attitude.
TomorrowIsAnotherDay: TheDJ, please

stop.
SpicySanchez: That's three demerits, DJ.
You owe me time.
TomorrowIsAnotherDay: Quit picking on
DJ. She doesn't need a detention.
EatYourVeggies;): TomorrowIsAnotherDay
is getting on my last nerve. It's making my
back hurt.
HotGirlsHitMeUp: Can't wait for bikini
season.
RedVelvet: DJ, you are only hurting
yourself when you say things about
Sanchez.
SpicySanchez: Who is RedVelvet?
Survivor: Let's all be nice here.
TomorrowIsAnotherDay: I agree.
TownSpy: If someone doesn't share a
secret in the next four minutes, I am
sharing someone else's.
Whatever: Please share Ashley's secret.
TownSpy: The secret will be Kayla's.
TownSpy: Kayla and Lil' Shelbi put bleach
in Stacey's shampoo.
Championbeatdown: Awesome.
EatYourVeggies;): That's my girl.
That'sNotMyName: :(

Marti scolded Kayla, who yelled, "TownSpy, I hate you!"

What a Thanksgiving!

Chapter 19

THE FIRST SNOWFALL of December made me late to school. It didn't usually snow here, but today it did. My mom was in a rank mood the whole morning too because she hadn't started her car up, and it was freezing outside. She was on the rampage the whole way to school about how she would be late to work for dropping me and a few of the other kids off.

"This is the whole reason why I live in California. Are you *kidding* me!" she kept repeating.

I arrived at school, and Sanch was mad at everyone who was tardy. Which included me. I was used to her hatred by this point, so I took my seat like nothing was different. She gave us a homework assignment to write about winter. I thought it was going to be super easy and I could get it all done before school ended, but Mama's Child kept talking to me, and I couldn't focus on my work. Sanchez had made the mistake of seating us next to each other. It felt like a punishment at first, but she was actually kinda growing on me. In a weird, scum-on-a-boat type of way.

"That's it. Mama's Child, go sit in that seat by the window." Mrs. Sanchez pointed across the room, and

Mama's Child gave her a threateningly dangerous glare before she slung her backpack over her shoulder. This quickly faded and turned to laughter. She was still snickering as she took her seat.

"Denny!" She waved, calling to me anyway. I waved back. Some of the other kids rolled their eyes and groaned. I knew they hated the two of us with a passion. Mrs. Sanchez was at the top of that list, her eyes filled with fire. Sanch cradled her head in her hands before giving up and putting her head down flat on her desk.

At home, I finished my paper about winter, then Mama's Child came over. My mom actually acted *cool* about it.

"'Sup? Do you want some Mystery Meet?" she asked. She was offering to share food that *she* paid for?

"No, thanks," Mama's Child answered, wrinkling her nose. That sort of bothered me. Did she think it was below her to eat Mystery Meet? She wasn't even sure what the meat at her mom's diner was. Her and I were on the same level, whether either of us wanted to admit it.

We played Go Fish (I wasn't a sore loser, MC was a cheater) then we took things outside. The ground was barely dusted, but we made a hand-held-sized snowman and flopped around in the bristly grass to make "snow angels." We wanted the full wintery "white Christmas" experience that all the other kids in the world got to enjoy.

Mom flung open the door with a slam, and I thought I was about to get beat with a shoe. My eyes nearly fell out of my head when she bellowed, "Come in for a surprise." My stomach heaved. I used to think surprises were good things, but I didn't know what to expect.

My mom actually splurged and made *hot chocolate,* making me feel cooler than it was outside. She was being nice, and we were being real high-class now. I remembered when I spent the night at Monica's.

"Monica's dog is so cute," I told Mama's Child. "Its name is Hot Chocolate. It's brown with white spots. Just like hot chocolate with marshmallows."

Her face grew pinched, rubbed the wrong way by this, and she snapped, "I don't wanna hear 'bout Monica's dog, Den." It got awkward after that, and she went home.

"You know she likes Marcus Delon, right?" Rochelle asked me when I entered my bedroom.

"Does not," I spat. She was just trying to "stir the pot," as Mama's called it.

"Does too."

"You're lying."

"Call her and ask."

I did just that, running downstairs and grabbing the phone. The line to the diner rang for what felt like forever, and her mom was less than happy to let me talk to her.

"Do you like Marcus Delon?" I asked immediately.

"Duh, he's cute."

"Uh, yah. I know. You know I've had a crush on him for like forever." It may not have been that long, but being that I was only six years old (Cringe. I hate the number six. Major eye roll!) it felt like it had been practically my whole life.

"Well, I got a crush on him too."

"Well, ya gotta back off, Mama's!" I panicked. "If you don't like him, then he will like me more."

"I like him a lot more than you do!" Her voice sounded downright angry now.

"Well, I liked him first! So I got dibs."

"Dibs don't count unless you call them *first*."

I groaned. "I liked him first!"

"I don't care!"

"We ain't friends no more." Tears welled in my eyes

with a watery sting.

Mama's Child just laughed."Ha! You'll come back, Den. They *always* come back."

What did that even mean? She didn't even *have* any friends! Wait a second... Neither did I! Maybe I should apologize.

The line went dead as she hung up the phone.

My dad and Alissa were throwing a Christmas party Christmas Eve, and everyone was invited. I was super excited. My mom said that he told her there would be singing, dancing, food, and a game called Secret Santa. It was when people drew a name and bought whoever they got a present, which sounded *great*...until I drew Mama's Child. *Just my luck,* since we weren't friends now. I didn't know what she'd want, and my mom wasn't giving us a ton of money to spend on gifts. So I got her a clown doll. It was creepy. Just like her.

I got my winter paper back on the last day before break, and earned an A+! Mrs. Sanchez even wrote "Good job!" on it. Mama's Child frowned at her paper, but I couldn't read what her grade was from where I was sitting. Mrs. Sanchez still had us on "proximity probation" and wouldn't let us sit next to each other. Which worked out kinda perfectly at the moment. Since we were fighting. Or whatever.

At lunch, I sat down in my casual, usual seat at my casual, usual lunch table. I had been sitting at this lunch table since preschool and always in the same exact seat. Just recently, Mama's Child had taken to eating at *my* table. I was surprised she had given in to it, considering how persistent she was last year about staying at her own. She must have assumed I would never move from this spot, and rightfully so. This was *my* seat. If I couldn't sit here, then horrible things would happen, and my life would be derailed instantly. MC apparently claimed this as her new turf, because she never went back to her old table.

We sat in silence, eating. The same thing we'd been doing since our fight. She sat across from me, we both ate, but we *never* talked. I glanced across the cafeteria toward Monica's table. She was sitting with Haylee and Hallee, and Mark and Marcus were there, too. You could say I was a *teensy* bit jealous. When I turned back around, Mama's Child was looking over there like she longed to sit there instead, too.

Maybe we wanted to be over there, but we had each other, and that was good enough for now. I couldn't finish my yogurt, so I slid it across the table. She eyed it hesitantly before picking it up and eating a spoonful. She slid a granola bar with berries and chocolate drizzle toward me, and I took it. I muttered, "Thanks," but she didn't answer. At least this felt like a start.

Christmas Eve had arrived! I was almost done getting ready for my dad and Alissa's party when my mom came into my bedroom, rushing this way and that, shoving earrings through her ear lobes and having to adjust her bra over and over again.

"Dress nice, Dennis. Nice enough to where they think I take care of you, but not so nice it looks like you care about what your dad or her thinks."

I blinked dumbly, then took off my white sweater and jeans, settling on a hand-me-down dress. It was sparkly green, so it was fitting for Christmas. But it had a huge rip in it (thanks to Little Debbies), and my mom had promised to sew it back up but never did. That might classify as "not being cared for," but a dress looked nicer than pants, right?

Famous rich ladies always wore dresses. *I* wanted to be a famous rich lady.

Once outside, something pink caught the corner of my eye. *It couldn't be.* But upon doing a double take, I knew it was not just my imagination. I took off running toward the pen that had long been empty and gripped the fencing. My knuckles turned white, and I squealed. He squealed.

I knew those eyes. My heart raced like a drum in my chest.

Beans.

My Beans.

"What's all this commotion going on?" my mom hollered, and I turned to find her nonchalantly staggering toward me, careful not to sink in her high heels.

"It's *Beans!*" I squealed, then squinted at something glinting in the sun. Shiny.

"Mom sold the pig," Brad muttered.

"It ain't him," another voice said, but I didn't bother to see who it was coming from. I *knew* those eyes, that chip in the left ear and dark patch around his right eye.

The pig snorted and approached me, rubbing his wet nose against my fingers. He was fatter than he had been when I'd last seen him, but it was *him.* I squinted at the shiny metal, a tag around a collar, and it read:

BEANS

"But you *sold* him! And now he's back?" I whirled around, facing my mom.

What appeared to be a whisper of a smile vanished from her face, and her frown looked forced. "And I *paid* for it, too," I thought she muttered.

"What?" I asked, patting Beans on the head.

"Nothing. Santa must have had other plans. Must've dropped him off when I wasn't here." The same whisper of a smile appeared again, but she cleared her throat and turned abruptly.

"Let's go," she grunted. It was hard for me to leave him.

I rode in my mom's car to get to my dad and Alissa's other house. She still had her one next door to us, but I guess she was so rich that she had multiple houses. I didn't know why she needed multiple houses. What if you really wanted to wear a certain outfit, but it was at the other house? Or if you went to sit down, but oops! The chair was at my *other* house. Rich people. I shook my head just thinking about it. With as many kids as we had, us poor people were the ones who needed multiple homes.

The driveway was beyond packed when we got there. It was starting to get dark outside, so I couldn't make out much besides a big hunk of a house with loads of cars littering one of those fancy wrap-around U-shaped driveways. My mom was about to get out of the car when about half of us told her we forgot our Secret Santa gifts. She groaned and slapped her wheel so hard the horn went off. Tee-hee!

"Are you kids for real? I literally *hate* you all." She huffed and stretched the seatbelt back over her pregnant stomach.

"We don't have to have them. It's fine." Shaye cowered in her seat.

"Um, I *have* to have mine. Mama's Child isn't speaking to me, and I drew her name. If I don't bring her a gift, she will think I hate her and it's a declaration of war." *Speak for yourself, Shaye. My life might very well depend on that creepy clown doll.*

"Did any of you draw one of the Green children?" my mom asked, turning around and searching all of our faces.

Ty nodded.

"Ugh!" Mom groaned, throwing her head back against the headrest. "I guess we gotta go home. I can't have you guys looking uncivilized. You make me look bad."

"Whatever," Orange muttered.

The second time we pulled up to the house, it was even more packed than the first time. And being that our family wasn't exactly small, we made the whole situation worse. My dad greeted us as we walked in a long line.

"I'm so glad all of you kids were able to come. Daddy has missed you all so very much." Most of us just nodded, Orange said, "Whatever," and I stopped, waiting for a hug that never came. I couldn't help but think, *If you miss us, then why haven't you come to visit?* Deflated, I stepped to the side as he greeted my mom. She eyed him very cooly, and I wasn't sure if she would even speak to him.

"Deniese."

"Dude."

Then he bowed. Like he actually *bowed*, like people do after a performance. Why would he even do that? They screeched at each other and bantered for years. They may not have acted "in love," but they definitely spoke their mind about anything. So why were they not talking now? Why the formality?

I got so in my head about it that I tripped over the rug in the entryway and nearly face-planted onto the floor. Looking around to see if anyone saw, I kept walking like nothing happened. Why was I so *awkward?* I was always the odd man out. Hating myself, I threw a little pity party in my head about how I didn't even have Mama's Child to lean on now. How had she gone from my enemy to the only person who made me feel okay? Everyone kind of hated her too. Except Mama's Child didn't care. She got me.

"Denny!"

My heart leaped. I turned around, and Mama's Child's grin quickly deflated into a frown.

She muttered, "I mean, ew. It's Dennis June."

My heart sank to the deepest depths of the ocean. Why couldn't she just apologize? Or at least *try* to talk to me?

When everyone had finally found places to sit, I was more than ready to eat. But apparently my dad decided to be all classy-like, and he said he wanted everyone to wait until we prayed for the food. I'd never been to church in my life. Marti's family did, and I wanted to, but it was just not something my parents did. And the only church in Crab Cove was a *long, long* ways away.

Marti clasped her hands, her eyes bright at this idea, and we waited for my dad to pray. He didn't.

"Are we ready to pray?" Marti asked, looking around the table

I was looking at the warm, steamy rolls. My mouth watered like a sieve.

"Oh, I'm not praying," my dad said, wide-eyed.

"Then who is?" I asked.

"Who wants to pray?" Marti asked gently, smiling at everyone.

"I think that red afro kid should do it," my dad said. *Of all people, really?*

"I'd be happy to," Mama's twanged. She folded her hands and bowed her head. Everyone else copied, so I did too. I'd be lying if I said I didn't keep glancing up and sneaking peeks at the rolls. You know, just to make sure they were still there.

"Blez dis food, which smells heavenly," Mama's slurred. Then she looked up and paused. "Which is a Christmas word, by the way." She stopped again, as if she was expecting applause or something. She continued.

"Blez deez peeps who chose to spend their evenin' with me. Blez dis holiday. Mah favorite. Da season of givin', but more importantly da season of receivin'."

A few people coughed, and when I opened an eye, most people's eyebrows were furrowed. My stomach growled. She needed to wrap this up.

"Blez my Secret Santa, who I'm sure got me da best gift of all."

My nerves tangled into a big old bundle.

"Blez my favorite hat, which I am wearin'. Nothin' compares. Blez horse meat. Blez my mama's diner, that she'll get plenty of business dis holiday season, so we won't be poor." She paused again and opened her eyes. She glared at us as if she was threatening everyone to make this happen. I avoided eye contact with her, as did most everybody. Most people were looking around, probably wondering the same thing I was—*when is this blessing ever going to end?*

My dad was nibbling on a chicken leg and trying so hard to be quiet and not let anyone notice. But I noticed. Because I always do.

"Blez social networkin'. 'Cept for that TownSpy, who oughta be ashamed of themself." I glared at her, and she glared at me. Then she pulled her gadget out of her pocket and typed under the table.

Several phones dinged, and Rochelle snickered, "TownSpy says, 'Blez dis, and blez dat, who is this hillbilly?'!"

Mama's Child pretended to cry and whine, "TownSpy is so mean!" even though she wrote that *herself.* I gave her the side eye as she went on sniffling for a few seconds.

People opened their eyes, assuming the prayer was over, and Mama's Child bore holes through all of us. Then she turned off her crocodile tears and hollered, "Ayyyyy-man!" *Why couldn't she just say "Amen" like a normal person?*

"Lez eat!" she finished, and everyone grabbed at the food like they were starving. I grabbed a roll like my life depended on it and hefted my belly up onto the table so I could steal the entire stick of butter. I had plans on eating it all.

My dad belched for what felt like forever before agreeing *way* too late, "Amen!"

Every eye at the table shifted from one person to the next, and murmurings fluttered about TownSpy. I think people were worried that they were going to start spilling secrets again. I didn't have a phone, so I could guarantee that *I* would not be posting to TownSpy. Mama's Child, however, was a completely different story.

I focused on the food, because it was delectable, and I had already eaten half the rolls in front of me. And that entire stick of butter. Alissa actually stood up at one point, for one of her many trips to the kitchen, and complained, "Where in the world is all of our *butter* disappearing to? I've had to get up three times now and I've used all the sticks in my fridge!"

...

Tee-Hee!

When everyone got up to dance and sing, my dad decided he wanted it to be what he called, "an authentic experience." He told all of us to grab a dance partner and that it didn't have to be romantic, but we had to dance. Everyone stole all of the good people, including *Marcus Delon*. I wasn't entirely sure why he was here, but I was happy he was. Because he was wearing a light blue sweater that made his eyes gorgeous. It wasn't like I would've asked him to dance anyway, though. I'd be too chicken.

The only person who didn't have a partner now, besides me?

Mama's Child.

We made awkward eye contact and crumpled our faces up at each other. But then she shrugged, and I did too. We took a few steps toward each other, agreeing we'd dance. The next song that came on was unfortunately, "Baby, It's Cold Outside," and we swayed back and forth to the music. Rochelle made a barf face at us, and Mama's and I stuck our tongues out at her.

Whenever the song changed, people were supposed to change partners, but nobody would swap with me or Mama's Child. And this "brilliant idea" didn't really pan out because people eventually got paired with their enemies. That's when all the TownSpy talk got going again.

"I know you're TownSpy!" People raised their voices, to which the obvious, "No, *you're* TownSpy!" was replied even louder.

People were getting in screaming matches. A few people were shoving. Stabbing fingers into chests. Marti and Dude Green were singing, "All I Want for Christmas is You," and they totally just droned everyone out. They kept singing as if nothing was happening.

When I faced my "dance partner," I didn't even have a chance to prepare myself before her fist came at me and she screamed, "I *know* you're TownSpy!"

I grabbed my arm upon the impact, my mouth gaping open.

"You are such a drama queen!" I hollered. There was no call for that whatsoever! *She* was the one posting as TownSpy, for crying out loud!

"Aye!" my mom bellowed, but people kept fighting. Now *more* people were throwing punches, too. Objects clattered, and utensils dropped, my mom's shoe came off, and then a table got flipped.

"Stop this madness!" my dad yelled, and everyone got real quiet. "It's *Christmas*. What is wrong with everybody?"

I nodded. So did a few other people. My mom still had her shoe raised.

"We really should just move on," my dad said.

"You started it…" some people muttered.

"I can't believe you *punched* me," I murmured to Mama's Child, who shrugged and said, "I got caught up in the moment, Den."

"Let's just exchange the gifts. Maybe it will make us feel better," Marti said, making calming motions with her hands.

"This is absurd," a blond woman in panty hose and a pencil skirt stated. "We are going home."

Marcus Delon left with her, and I had never felt more embarrassed of my family in my life. Even with the murder trial and *everything*.

People began to exchange their gifts, and I approached Mama's Child warily. She raised a suspicious eyebrow but stepped toward me, too.

"I was your Secret Santa," I told her, handing her the gift. She unwrapped the clown doll, and grinned, creepily. She told me that she loved it, then she handed me a gift because, ironically, she had been my Secret Santa, as well. I unwrapped a couple packs of orange jello (the best kind) and a keychain. I smiled.

She raised her hand, and I slapped it.

"We cool?" she asked.

"We're cool."

I tried not to act as happy as I actually was because she hadn't *really* apologized to me. But then again, I never *really* apologized to *her* either. Fighting over boys was stupid—especially if it cost you a friend. Unless it was Marcus Delon, because, well. It was Marcus Delon.

As my mother drove us home, I ate one of my jello packs. In between bites, I reflected on the weirdness of the night. Why couldn't we just have a normal Christmas? One where I didn't lose my pig or people broke out in fist fights? My family was anything *but* normal, so I should be used to it by now. I turned my focus back to Beans. My precious little Beanie, all home for the holidays!

My mom's shriek broke me out of my thoughts. She cut the ignition.

"Did anyone else see that?" she asked, flipping around and looking at us all.

I widened my eyes and looked around, trying to figure out what she was referring to.

"See what?" Ty asked.

"In DJ's bedroom window." My mom pointed, and everyone drew their attention to my window.

My heartbeat was going about a billion beats per minute, and I dropped my spoon onto the floor. I gagged when I picked it up and it was covered in dirt and suspicious hairs.

"What was it?" Dominique asked, trying to peek out the window.

"Yeah, what was it?" Krissy repeated.

"Uh, a lady with curly brown hair, dressed in dark red… Who does *that* sound like? Are you guys messing with me? You really didn't see that?" she asked, giving us all the shifty eyes.

We all confirmed we hadn't.

"Well, be careful. I'm almost positive. That looked just like my mother," she stated, opening her door and stepping out.

The jello in my stomach had gone sour, and I no longer

felt like eating. Which was *big* for me.

"Mom," my voice shook. I tugged on her sweater. "That was *my* room. Shouldn't you check it?" *What if she was coming for me to get her revenge?*

"Uh, no?" She wrinkled her eyebrows like she was confused I would even suggest such a thing.

"But—"

"—you're not the only person who stays in your room, Dennis. Rochelle can kick butt if she needs to."

"Rochelle is gonna fight your mom?" My eyes widened.

"Of course not, she'd never win."

"Mom!"

"DJ!" she mocked back in a whiny voice. I frowned, and she gently shoved me out of her way and reached into the trunk to get the gifts and the leftovers she stole out.

Chapter 20

IT WAS NEW YEAR'S EVE, and things had settled down since the Christmas party. Mama's Child and I still weren't close friends, but we were getting there. She called me on the phone once or twice, but she hadn't come over. Though I lived in extreme fear for a few days over my mom seeing my grandma in my room, I finally was allowing myself to breathe. Not a whisper of her had been seen ever since. Maybe my mom was going crazy!

Marcus and Mark were playing with snowballs outside yesterday, and they said "hi" to me. They actually said "hi." I was so shocked that I just stood there waving like an idiot until they went back to their game. So embarrassing! I'd been reliving the experience all last night and all of this morning, too. Until Mama's Child called me to say she wasn't coming over tonight and that she was spending the holiday with her mom. Apparently her mom didn't want her to visit me anymore. Something to do with her hating my mother, and my mother hating her. Why did our moms have to be such angry people and our dads practically non-existent?

Mama's Child had told me before that *her* parents were

also divorced. But I'd never met her dad. She didn't talk about him much, other than saying that he was "a cool guy." That was pretty much all I could say about my dad, too. My heart went to putty recalling how he didn't even hug me on Christmas. I rolled my eyes to the ceiling so the tears couldn't fall.

Before Mama's Child hung up the phone, she told me, "I hear word on the block is that Stephanie has been flirting with Princeton."

Princeton was Shaye's long-term boyfriend. I rolled my eyes. That would never happen in a billion years. I told Mama's Child as much. Princeton was super smart, like Shaye, and he was very nice and shy. Stephanie was a walking nightmare in high heels and a pink sparkly mini skirt.

"If you say so," she had told me, hanging up the phone.

It was New Year's Eve, and my mom's hands shook as she made the food for our party. I think she was actually afraid that Beverly Hill was really back.

We hardly invited anyone over. Lots of people were too busy or didn't want to get together because of the huge fight that broke out at Christmas. My mom didn't want my dad to come because she knew he would bring Alissa with him, but he insisted on coming anyway, and she finally agreed.

The guests showed up, and the party was pretty calm. Not much happened surprisingly. People got along a lot better, and my dad didn't even bring Alissa. I sat on the floor and watched the show with the ball drop at midnight. This was my favorite part of New Years.

"Hey, Mom!" I hollered, pointing at the screen. "Can we set off fireworks?"

"Absolutely not, Dennis! What is *wrong* with you? Those

are expensive, and who in their right mind would want a six-year-old like you playing with explosives?"

Well, when she put it that *way.*

My mind kept reminding me of that number, and I winced.

"Please don't refer to me as being anything associated with the number six. I don't want to hear it in the same sentences that contain my name."

She stared at me quizzically, and my dad murmured to her, "Where does she get this crap?"

"Why are you asking me? Do *I* look like a weirdo?"

Was she implying that *I* was a weirdo?

"She's implying that you are a weirdo," Brad muttered, without even looking away from the television set. How did he know what I was thinking? I couldn't stand him. I hoped he'd fall off the couch or roll over on a crispy potato chip.

Out the window, an eruption of bangs sounded, and it wasn't hard to see the bright flashes of color coming from the sky above Monica's house. Mama's Child popped into my thoughts, but the fireworks pushed her out and brought me back to Monica and the fact that the Stars were probably there at her house. *I* wanted to go to Monica's house. The noise paused, and the fireworks stopped. And for a few seconds, it was quiet. Until my mom started screaming that she was in labor.

"On New Years?" I asked, clearly annoyed by her outburst.

"Well, it appears to be that way, now doesn't it, *Dennis*?" my mom snapped.

"But the ball just dropped. I wanna watch the rest of the show!"

The older kids just sat there, paying her no attention. They must've been more used to this than even *I* was.

"No. We gotta go to the hospital."

"We just *went* there!" I groaned, slamming my head back against the seat of the couch. I got demoted to a floor seat when Brad decided he wanted to stretch out. I rolled my eyes just thinking about it. *What a turd.*

"Dennis, seriously?" my mom sassed, placing a hand on her hip and giving me the angry eyebrows.

"We just gotta sit in the waitin' room, and it doesn't help you any." My eyes remained peeled to the show.

"Dennis, get in the car. *Now.* "

"But, Mom!"

"Don't give me sass!"

I listened to her. For the most part, anyway. She grabbed my hand and made me and the younger kids get in the cars with her and my dad. She insisted on driving herself, of course. Because *nobody touches her car.*

"Why can't we stay with the teenagers?" I asked.

"They got invited over to the Greens' last minute."

"I wanna go!" I retaliated. Like I'd choose the hospital waiting room over *fireworks* at *Monica's Mansion.*

"It's just for the teenagers, DJ. Her little ones already went to bed."

"I'm not little." I crossed my arms.

"You're six."

"Stop saying that!" I demanded, covering my ears.

She gave me the look that told me not to say one more word, or I'd be in for it.

My mom was in labor for five hours. A small TV hung in the waiting room, so I at least got to watch the rest of the show. But it was just crowded and hot, and it made me very uncomfortable. The whole place reeked of beer, and I kept trying to keep my nose plugged and my eyes from watering at the stench. Why couldn't we wait on the maternity floor?

Why'd we have to sit with all the drunks who kept coming into the ER? It was nasty. The dude sitting next to me for the past two hours smelled like he hopped straight outta a dumpster, and he kept asking me, "Hey, kid. Do you got any money?"

I begged my dad to trade me spots, but he kept hushing me and saying, "You're not being nice." I didn't care if I wasn't being nice! The dude was giving me the creeps, and he needed to stay out of my personal space.

When we finally were able to go in and see my mom and the babies, Katy and Maria, my dad insisted on staying at her side at all times. He was so proud of the new babies, like he always was. I didn't know why. He wasn't even living with us anymore. He made a comment about staying the night with us, and I wondered where Bob Waltzer would be staying. Then my dad made *another* comment about staying the *whole first week.* When we did go home that night, Bob was nowhere to be found. Maybe my mom or dad had called him and told him to leave. I didn't really like Bob being with my mom, but I still pitied him getting kicked out. I also mourned for our cabinets because they had looked so much nicer when everything wasn't just flung in them. Now they would have spilled food all over the place because nobody shut the lids or rolled the bags down.

A couple days later, I was so tired from being up late on New Years Eve, going to the hospital, and doing chores that I had fallen asleep, trying to catch up on some Z's when Mama's Child called, and a phone slammed into my chest.

"It's for you," Rochelle said, storming off.

I rubbed my chest. *That's gonna hurt later.* Then I lifted the phone to my ear. "Hey, Mama's!"

"Hey, Denny! What was that sound?"

"Rochelle hit me with the phone," I said, as if it was a

normal event. Because it was.

"You probably deserved it," she snickered.

I frowned, even though she couldn't see me.

"Don't frown like that, you'll look like Sanch!" She laughed.

"How'd you know I was frowning?"

"I know everything."

"Nevermind. What'd ya want?" I asked, curling my legs up into a cozy ball and yawning.

"Just wanted to let ya know that I updated TownSpy. It says that Princeton broke up with Shaye."

"Are you making that up?" I asked, suddenly gaining a burst of energy I didn't know I had.

"No, Denny! Of course not!" Mama's Child sounded offended that I had asked such a thing.

"Why'd he break up with her?"

"To date Stephanie!"

I groaned. "Stephanie will just break up with him in a week—tops!"

"I know, but he doesn't seem to notice. He thinks she likes him. The idiot!" Mama's Child snickered. She lived for this kind of pot stirring.

"Maybe she does like him," I offered, even though I wasn't very convinced myself.

"Ha! Very funny, Den."

"She's the worst. Shaye is so nice and doesn't deserve that."

"Do you want me to rip her apart on TownSpy?"

"No!" I raised my voice, getting the word out as quick as possible.

"Okay. But say the word and I'll destroy her like a pizza."

I laughed. That was actually a good one. *Mmmmm,* I

thought, and my stomach growled. *Pizza.*

"Den, I can hear your stomach growling clear from here."

"Are you a superhuman?" I gasped.

"Basically."

I smiled. We said goodbye and hung up the phone. So much had happened over this winter break that I was almost positive I'd get an A+ if Sanch had us write about it. She lived for the drama almost as much as Mama's Child did. I stared up toward the ceiling and couldn't help but wonder…

What was *she* doing all break long?

To my disappointment, Mrs. Sanchez never assigned a paper over our Christmas break, because she said, "No more cushion grades for you!" and told us in a strict voice, "We need to really crack down on learning the important stuff."

If it's so important, then shouldn't you refer to it as something other than "stuff"?

We studied and studied for weeks to get through *huge* chunks of the textbooks Sanch passed out. *It's a good thing these were free, considering she rips us up the crack for those workbooks!* Totally not worth her living in our attic, if you asked me. She didn't do anything, and we didn't really see her or hear her (thanks to the soundproofing!). But I *knew* that she was there. And that was enough to make me feel like someone was watching me at all times.

Then after a week or so of grueling labor, she just flipped all polar opposites on us, and said that we would get a couple of free days at school. She claimed it was for "relaxing from our hard work." I was suspicious as to why she was being so nice all of a sudden, but then she lowered her voice and smirked maliciously.

"Two more chapters until we get to learn about the most important event ever."

"What is it?" a few kids asked.

The sound of pages flipping in the textbooks filled the air until finally Brad yelled, "This is pure crap!"

Everyone turned toward him.

"You'd better watch your words, boy!" Sanch warned.

"It's the freaking French Revolution. *Again!*" Brad slammed his fist down on his desk.

"Every year!" groaned Tearston.

"Come on, really?" Izzy rolled her eyes and continued filing her nails. Then she started whispering with Cherry.

Mrs. Sanchez stood and yelled, "Silence! The French Revolution is a very important part of our history."

"But…we don't even live in France," I stated, wrinkling my nose and looking down at the textbook.

"Some of *my* ancestors are from France!" Mrs. Sanchez gasped, and I knew I had clearly struck a nerve.

Mama's Child snickered from across the room and mouthed, "Nice one, Denny!"

"And it is in the criteria to learn about *world* events. Not just the US or our specific state."

"But we learn about the French Revolution *every year!*" Rochelle groaned, shoving her textbook to the floor.

"Do you want free days or not?" Sanchez asked.

"Do we have to come to school if they are 'free days'?" asked Stephanie, scoffing loudly.

"Will you kids appreciate the French Revolution more if you don't have to?"

"Yes!" we all yelled. Me included, because I hated school.

"Then no, you don't have to come."

My eyes bulged out of my head.

"In fact, don't. I'm not going to come either. I need to prepare new lesson plans on the French Revolution." Mrs.

Sanchez stuck her nose in the air and gave us a satisfied grin.

Mama's Child had asked me on the bus ride home if I wanted to hang out on our three days off. I told her "sure," so that's exactly what we did. During our three days off, many people went shopping. But Mama's Child came over (with or without her mom's permission, I have no idea) and stayed the second night. I revelled in it. It was my first time throwing a sleepover. She told me that when she was spying on people she found out that Cherry had been adding the finishing touches to her wedding plans. According to Mama's Child, she picked out pink, red, and white attire since she was getting married on Valentine's Day, not last fall, obviously. I thought that was so romantic.

We spent our third day eavesdropping, and Cherry and Izzy were throwing their eighteenth birthday parties. They weren't born on the same day; they just wanted to celebrate their birthdays together. It was a blast for everyone invited, we heard. *We* spent their birthday party looking through their window at the cakes, the party games, and quietly singing "Happy Birthday" while dancing outside to the music.

At school the next day, we took a review quiz over what we had crammed before. Mrs. Sanchez made it different difficulty levels according to our grades. I got a 7/10, and Mama's Child got a 4/10. I told her after school that she had to do better because she might fail, and then we wouldn't be in the same grade. Of course we'd still be in the same school, but we wouldn't be able to graduate together in the future! Mama's Child said she didn't even know what graduation was, but she would study from now on if I helped her.

It dawned on me how crazy it was that somebody could

go from being your absolute *enemy* to being your *best friend.* Back in the day, I couldn't stand her. Sometimes I still couldn't. *Most* of the time I couldn't. But I cared a lot about her. And as someone who'd never had a friend before, that spoke volumes.

Chapter 21

I WAS SO EXCITED to go to Cherry and Derek's wedding, because I had always wanted to go to one. Unfortunately, since it was on Valentine's Day, I had a nagging sensation of disappointment. A Valentine's Day kids' party was taking place at the playground, and I bet Marcus Delon would be there. I loved Marcus Delon.

We arrived early at the wedding, and I think it was the first time we had been early to anything, *ever*. Except for me on the first day of school last year. That was the worst. Everything was decorated so pretty, with little pink and white roses and pink silky fabric elaborately draped around the room. I kept getting bumped into for stopping and staring at it. My mom leaned over to a random person sitting near us, muttered, "Must be nice to be rich, huh?" and started laughing. The person got up and moved, pretending it wasn't because of my mom, but I bet it was. I bet they were rich.

"Mrs. Sanchez?" I asked, when she walked in, wearing her favorite bright green dress with the black fur collar. The same one she wore to my house in the summertime. And all the time.

"I'm here for the food, and the food only. I do not support people getting married so young. It's obscene."

"Sanch, are *you* going to get married?" I asked. "I mean, we call you 'Mrs.' but I ain't ever seen your husband."

"You kids rarely call me anything other than that butchered syllable. And that's none of your business, now is it, Dennis?"

I blushed. "Guess not." I sat back down, feeling antsy. I jiggled my leg. The wedding music played, and it distracted me from my anxious thoughts.

The bridal party began doing that thing they do on TV where they come down the aisle. The flower girl, Monica, walked past, and the flowers made me sneeze. I didn't think it was that loud, but I guess it was because the musician lost his place for a couple seconds. He scanned his sheet music frantically, his cheeks turning red. A few people rolled their eyes at me, but I mean, *I can't help it if I got to sneeze, people!*

They said their vows, and it was really nice until Ashley started to cry. I didn't know if it was from all the hormones or because she used to have a crush on Derek. My mom was crying too, but she probably was either trying to get attention or sad that it wasn't one of *her* daughters marrying Derek.

I got to try their wedding cake, and it was absolutely delicious! Never in my life had I heard of a "pink velvet cake"! It had tiny hearts on the lacey white icing, and Mama's Child and I fought over who got the piece with the most. She won, but in return I told her she had to give me a bite of her cake to make it even.

"No, I want it all," she said with puppy dog eyes. "Just think of it as I owe you one."

"But what do I get to make it even?" I asked.

"How 'bout a quarter?"

"A quarter?" I frowned. That was so not equivalent to cake. Cake was *cake*.

"Yeah."

"Fine," I said, shrugging, not wanting to cause a scene. But then she handed me a nickel.

"Mama's Child, this is a nickel, not a quarter."

"It's all I got on me. I don't have any more money than that."

She probably just forgot to bring any more with her. "It's okay. You don't have to give me the rest now. Do you have a piggy bank at home?"

"Nope."

It hit me then. She was *poor*. It must be hard for her mom to keep that diner going with everyone believing she served toe jam gravy and horse meat.

"Here's your nickel back." I tried to hand it over.

"I don't want it, I owe it to you."

"No, you don't. I want you to have it back."

"Okay." She grabbed the nickel and hid it in her pocket.

The dancing, the food, everything went just how Cherry had planned it. Except for me sneezing, of course. She gave a long speech that was all mushy. It was almost as bad as her speech at the Back to School Dance. Yawning, I turned to MC and asked when she thought we could leave.

I didn't get a chance to talk to Monica at the wedding, and I hoped she didn't think I was rude. So a few days later, I studied her from my seat in class, but she didn't seem any different. Still smiling as always. *She probably didn't even know you were there,* my brain told me. I told it to shut up, and that it was wrong, to which it made me think, *Okay, fine. She knew you were there. But only because you* sneezed *and totally ruined her brother's wedding.* I placed a hand to my forehead to try and cope with the stress.

We were learning more about the French Revolution. People complained about how it was really dragging on, so Sanchez threatened, "If you don't keep it down, you are all getting demerits!"

"Please be quiet!" I groaned, turning around and making eye-contact with the loudmouths. I didn't want to get in trouble because of them. I had a growing collection of demerits as it was. People refused to listen, though, and kept talking louder. Mrs. Sanchez scolded *me*, of all people, even though I was just telling everyone to shut their holes!

"One more word from you today, and you are going to get a demerit, Dennis. I mean it." She straightened her back to appear taller and waved her ruler around in the air. I didn't understand why she always had a ruler. She wasn't even teaching math right now.

"Sorry," I muttered, even though I didn't want to.

After a few minutes passed, Mama's Child made "psst" sounds, and it drew my eyes in her direction. She was waving. "Denny!"

I waved back but said nothing. I didn't want a demerit!

Two weeks later, my mom and Bob Waltzer eloped without telling anybody. When they spilled the beans, I told them that I was glad they finally decided to get married. If her and my dad were not going to get back together, and he was going to live here, then they needed to just get married. Shaye immediately claimed that she was going to go buy a mini cake for them to celebrate, and I wasn't going to complain. I mean—*cake!* And being in the know increased my chances of getting a slice!

I just really hoped my mom and Bob Waltzer didn't have

any kids. My dad and Alissa would be having their baby soon, and so would Ashley. This house was packed enough as it was. I knew for a fact that my mom didn't want more kids and neither did Bob. So fingers crossed we were in the clear there.

The next day, my dad came over and said that him and Alissa were "on a break," and he needed to move back in. Mom was hesitant, and Bob didn't want him to. But it ultimately was my mom's house, and my mom's decision. And she agreed. She made a point of mentioning that he worked all the time anyway, and most of the kids wanted him to stay. He ended up in Brad's room, for obvious reasons.

Mama's Child called me later that night, and I told her all the grease about how my dad moved back in.

"I bet your mom flirted with him, Den! That's why he broke up with Alissa."

"That's not why, and they are on a *break*. They did not break up."

"Same thing. I heard she's moving to Mexico and is going to raise her baby there."

Flopping down on the couch, I asked, "Mama's, where do you even hear this crap?"

"Denny, I'm tellin' you. I'm gonna get your parents back together."

"You are?" I crinkled my face up. "How?"

"One word, Den. TownSpy."

"Mama's Child, how's *that* going to help? And I never said that I *wanted* them back together."

"Dennis, who the dump are you talkin' to?" my mom hollered from the kitchen.

"Uh, nobody!" I lied, panicking.

"DJ, my parents are divorced. Trust me. You want them

back together."

"I know you're lying!" My mom's footsteps were coming.

"I gotta go," I blurted hastily.

"Make sure ya check TownSpy for updates later tonight."

"Got it." I hung up the phone and placed it on the coffee table before my mom came in. I tried to act casual.

She just gave me the stank eye, placed a hand on her curvy hip, and muttered, "Mmmmhmmm. That's what I *thought*."

When she disappeared up the stairs, I got on the computer. Well, Bob's computer. Because he was at work right now and would never know.

TomorrowIsAnotherDay has signed on.
TownSpy: Dude T. and Alissa broke up.
TownSpy: It sounds like it's for good this time.
Footballfever: No, it's just a break, and it's none of your business anyway.
TownSpy: Are you sure?
Footballfever: Duh.
Looksb4books: Why do you care?
TownSpy: Everyone knows that Dude and Deniese will always end up back together.
Footballfever: Deniese is married.
Townspy: Not for long.
NiteInShiningArmour: Townspy needs to lay off.
TownSpy: They flirt all the time.
NiteInShiningArmour: No, they don't.
TownSpy: Yeah, they do. They love each other.

SpicySanch: Ugh.
TheDJ: I really hope they get back
together.

I groaned. Mama's Child was going to cause a fight, and who was this "TheDJ" who was *still* pretending to be me? I logged out and picked up the phone to call Mama's Child back. I told her to tone it down, but she reassured me, "It's working well, Denny!" For everyone's sake, I prayed she was right. I wasn't sure if I wanted my parents back together, but I didn't want this to backfire and make things *worse.*

My mom caught me on the phone and made me get off, claiming it would run up our bills or something dumb. Then she saw the chatroom's login page was pulled up on Bob's computer. I studied her from a few feet away as she typed in her login info then scanned all the recent comments. Afterward, she faced me and frowned. "DJ, quit meddling."

I was about to give her an answer before realizing she wasn't asking for one.

"Wait," she murmured, catching my attention. "Did Alissa break up with Dude because she's jealous of me?"

"Uh, I don't know—"

"—I wasn't talkin' to *you,*" she snapped, even though we were the only two people in the living room right now. I didn't ask any questions, or say anything else to her. But as she walked away, she smiled.

And I wondered if Mama's Child had been successful after all.

Chapter 22

WHEN MARCH ROLLED around, everyone got pumped for spring break and Easter. Believe it or not, we were *still* learning about the French Revolution. Sanchez even told us that we would be writing a five page essay on it. I told Mama's Child she'd better not fail and that it would count for a lot of our grade. She said she would study for it, but part of me wanted to search her all over to make sure she wasn't crossing her fingers or toes. I wouldn't put it past her.

Within the next week, we received the rubric for it. It was different based on your age and grade level, but everyone, including myself, was freaked out. The academic excellence study club was filled to the brim! People were murmuring questions to one another, trying to get whatever ideas they could, and those who had written essays like this in past years reviewed their old ones to reword them. Shaye told them not to do that because Sanch kept a big ol' stack of old essay copies to make sure nobody turned in one they already had.

I was majorly stressed because I wasn't just writing my own, I was also helping Mama's Child. She had to pass so we could be best friends and graduate together. She was constantly telling me I worry too much, but the poor thing had letters all backwards and didn't capitalize anything. How was she so good with typing on TownSpy when she clearly struggled with school work?

"How do you type on TownSpy?"

"What?" she slurred, taking a break from her dum dum sucker. *I* wanted a dum dum sucker.

"You type things mostly okay on there."

"There ain't no pressure with TownSpy! Nobody's gonna grade 'er, Den."

I nodded, kind of understanding.

After the study club, my mom announced to us kids that she had run into Marti and Megan while grocery shopping, and both of them had made arrangements to get family portraits done. Naturally, my mom said we had to do that too.

"Isn't that expensive?" Ashley asked.

"Isn't having a baby expensive?" my mom sneered back.

Ashley's cheeks reddened, and she stared at her feet.

"Do I get to be in this portrait?" Bob asked, glancing away from his computer.

"Um, no." My mom stiffened, and even *I* could tell she was uncomfortable. So I knew Bob noticed, too.

"Oh," he stammered, going pale and fiddling with his wedding band.

"Dude wants to be in it."

"Deniese," Bob gasped, "he's not your husband anymore. I am."

"He says that it's his children."

"How does he even know about this *at all?*" Bob pinned a suspicious eye on her.

My eyes flickered back and forth between them like I was watching a tennis match. I leaned against the back of the couch.

"Because I told him."

"You talk to him? Like, *on purpose*?"

My mom took in who all heard this, then gave him an ice cold stare. "I am not discussing this with you now." Her heels sounded deathly loud as she walked away, the rest of the room completely silent and still.

Even a few days after the photoshoot, I was still exhausted. So much so that I nearly fell asleep in class. It had been so crowded, and hot, and it smelled like B.O. in there. The photographer kept saying, "The towhead in the front keeps giving me a cheesy smile."

"That's just Dennis's face. Like moldy cheese," Brad remarked, and everyone laughed with him. My cheeks flared red, but I hoped it would look like a natural blush. I had no idea how this lady was going to get all of us to fit inside one little picture. My mom kept complaining for Orange to "fix her hair for crying out loud," because "she's a beautician and doesn't want her kid's greasy bangs hanging over one eye."

I was actually thankful when Mrs. Sanchez snapped me out of my thoughts. She handed back the essays we turned in on the French Revolution. As quick as she got them done, she either had a ridiculous amount of free time or really loved the French Revolution. In all honesty, it was probably a mixture of both.

Mama's Child and I talked after school, and I asked her what she had gotten on the paper. I had been incredibly disappointed in myself because I only got a B, but Mama's Child told me that thanks to my help, she earned a C. I gave her a high five.

"That's passing, Mama's!" I nearly jumped from

excitement.

"Look, Sanch even wrote a note and stuck it on. I think it's a post-it. I love those things." Mama's Child smiled at her paper. I peeked over her shoulder to read it.

"It says that if you keep it up, you'll pass!" We both jumped up and down, waving our papers in the air. Even though I was mad at myself over *my* grade, I tried to remind myself that I had the extra task of doing *two* papers. Before Mama's Child and I split ways, I invited her over to my house instead.

Later that night, Mom and Bob dropped the bomb.

"We're getting an annulment."

"What's that?" I asked, looking around at my siblings.

"What?" Shaye asked.

"Why?" Tearston added.

"There's been some…issues," Bob muttered, looking very deflated.

"We just fight a lot over money." My mom shrugged like that wasn't a big deal.

"And some…other people," Bob added, looking at my mother as if hoping she would explain. She didn't.

"You mean Dude and Alissa!" Mama's blurted. My mom searched for who the voice belonged to, and if it hadn't been Mama's, I guarantee you—that left shoe would've been *off*.

"What are you even doing here? You don't live here."

"She doesn't?" Bob asked. "All this time I thought she was one of your kids."

Mama's Child snickered and nudged me.

"You should thank me," she whispered in my ear.

"Thank you," I told her. But just because Bob and my mom were breaking up didn't mean that her and dad were going to get remarried. So I had to check. "Are you and dad getting remarried?"

Bob reddened like he had been slapped across the face with a fish.

"Dennis, go to your room." My mom flicked a hand toward the steps.

I motioned for Mama's Child to come with, and we walked up the stairs side by side. She wrapped an arm around my shoulder and swayed us back and forth.

"I bet Bob Waltz will be packing them bags before ya know it!" she cheered. She patted me on the back like my dad used to do to the boys. When he'd call them "champ."

And you know what? Mama's Child was *right*. Bob packed his bags that very night, and my dad had moved in *permanently* within the next day. I had no idea how he was going to raise Alissa's baby when he was living here. My mom didn't even like her own kids being in her presence, let alone someone else's. When I called Mama's Child, she just kept saying, "One word, Den. Mexico."

"What?"

"She's gonna go to Mexico! Taking the baby with her."

"Mama's Child, you're full of donkey dung."

"Dennis! Get off that phone now!" my mom hollered.

"I gotta go!" I spoke at rapid fire speed before hanging up and running up the steps to my bedroom.

Apparently my dad had changed a bit since he moved out. Especially in the music department. He became a major fan of Michael Jackson all of the sudden, and if you were waiting on him to get out of the bathroom, he'd be in there yelling, "Hee-hee!" in a Michael Jackson voice as he took a dump. It was pretty disturbing. He went around the house dancing to the song "Thriller," and every time he and the guys carpooled to work they played Michael Jackson songs so loud I could hear them from inside my room. I was getting tired of waking up to "Billy Jean" being belted at five a.m.

Shortly before spring break, a lot of things went down at both home and school. Katrina was whining all day every day in class about getting cut from the cheer team and how it was going to "destroy her popularity." That girl shouldn't have any anyway because she was meaner than a constipated rhino. She unusually was sidling up with the dumbest girl in school, Sammi Green. Mama's Child told me ,"That girl is the key to popularity," and I thought she was lying like she usually was. But Katrina's popularity skyrocketed as soon as people saw her with Sammi. I didn't get it.

Alissa went into labor a few days prior to our last school day. My dad had somehow convinced her to give *him* full custody of the baby. Apparently Alissa "wasn't about the mom life" and had big traveling plans anyway, so she didn't care. And you'll never guess where she was planning to go. Yep! Mexico. *Mexico!* I was beginning to think Mama's Child really *did* have superpowers.

She wasn't going to take Tommy and Timmy with her, either. No siree. I overheard Mom and Dad talking about how Alissa ditched Bob with the twins, wanting to live the bachelorette life. Dad went on about how Bob deserved it, but Mom used it to brag about how she was a better mother than Alissa.

"I may hate my kids," my mom had clucked her tongue, "but at least I didn't abandon the little gremlins."

When dad brought the baby home, my mom was *less than thrilled*, to put it nicely. To put it *very* nicely. My dad told us all that her name was Annie, and then he was absolutely outraged when nobody understood the reference.

"Are you kidding me?" he had asked.

"What?" we all asked, including me.

"I said her name is *Annie.*"

"So? Nobody cares what your kid's name is," my mom spat, her heels clicking away bitterly.

"From the *song?* 'Smooth Criminal'?"

"I don't know what you're talking about," I said, shrugging.

My dad scoffed then sang, while swinging the baby in his arms, "*Annie, are you okay? Are you okay? Annie, are you okay? Are you okay, Annie?*"

I rolled my eyes. *Of course.* A Michael Jackson song.

The day before spring break, Sanchez announced during class that she would be getting married toward the end of this school year. Confusion struck me, and I frowned. Did she *not* freak out on me for asking her about marriage like a month or so ago? Would she be changing her name? That would be weird. I was so used to calling her Sanch. How could we call her that if her name wasn't Sanchez? It would make no sense.

My mom told us we could do an Easter egg hunt this year, but we would have to go to a public one at the playground. I was surprised she was letting us do one but not surprised it wouldn't be at our house. Could you imagine my mom buying enough eggs for everyone? And paying for candy or little toys to stuff them? I wondered why the Easter Bunny didn't pay for the eggs. That seemed like his job, if you asked me.

On Easter morning, we each got a little basket with jellybeans and a pack of gum. This must've been the same deal as it was with Santa. My stomach would be rumbling for sure when all of the kids from good families told me about eating their chocolate Easter bunnies! Um, yum! *I* wanted one, and I pouted just thinking about it. Why'd my grandma have to kill someone and ruin everything?

When we arrived at the playground with Mom and Dad, I got excited and tried to keep my eyes out for any easy eggs. But guilt coursed through me like I was cheating, so I tried to keep my lusty eyes off of them. None of the older kids wanted to come. I think they thought they were too cool for it, or something. What idiots! It was *free* gifts in little brightly patterned eggs!

Mama's Child was there, so I ran over to her side immediately. She started talking all kinds of smack—telling me that she was going to beat me to all the best and biggest Easter eggs. So I told her we would make it a little competition, and whoever got the most eggs would win a quarter and a handful of jellybeans from the loser. She agreed, and we shook our linked pinky fingers on it.

Most of the Easter eggs were filled with jellybeans, tootsie rolls, or quarters. I ran to pick up as many as I could find. Tripping over a tree branch, I stumbled and muttered insults at myself for getting distracted. Mama's Child's bag was filled to the brim. I stumbled upon a really big egg, but it wasn't the golden one. None of the adults organizing the event said anything about it in the rules, but lots of kids were whispering about the *Legend of the Golden Egg*! Guilt took the place of my joy, and thoughts poured into my brain about how Mama's Child was poorer than me. So I put the big egg back, but remained in the area close to it to make sure no one else got it.

Mama's Child eventually came running past and picked up the big egg. She snatched it right out of the bush that was cradling it.

"Wow, Denny! That one was right in front of ya, ya ding dong!"

I slapped my forehead, pretending it totally slipped my

view and I was an idiot. Mama's Child snickered and ran off to find more eggs.

When the egg hunt was over, Mama's Child and I sat down crisscross applesauce in the grass, underneath a shady oak tree. We added up our eggs, and Mama's Child beat me. *Yes,* I thought, hoping she wouldn't figure out that I rigged it a little for her favor. I acted deflated as I handed her three of my jellybean-filled eggs and a quarter. I still ended up having a good bit left over, and I did make about five dollars in change. Mama's Child had seven and a half dollars (counting the quarter I gave her) and an enormous collection of jellybeans. It made my teeth hurt a little looking at it. I liked jellybeans, but even *I* couldn't eat that many. I was more of a chocolate girl.

Mom said it was time to go home, so we piled into her and Dad's cars. I rode with mom, and it dawned on me that I rarely rode in my dad's car. Why did I always choose her when she was the mean one? Or *was* she the mean one? My eyes welled up as I once again recalled that Christmas party and how he didn't even hug me. Like I didn't exist. I pushed the thought back down in my brain and focused on my treasures instead. I had a pretty good number of jellybeans and five dollars that was *all mine.* And it was rewarding to know I had helped Mama's Child not be so poor.

Chapter 23

A *LOUD CRASH* erupted outside the house this morning. I almost couldn't keep from laughing when I saw it was Megan Green in her big bright purple van with Marti in the passenger seat. Marti's eyes bugged out like a stress relief doll's. Megan had bumped into my dad's car. It really wasn't funny, but it was. Mama's Child had been writing in the chatroom over break about whether or not Megan even knew *how* to drive.

My dad, adoring Megan like he did, didn't do a thing. He, Dude Green, and Lucas were carpooling today, and they had all seen it happen. Megan apologized profusely, and I eavesdropped behind a bush while I waited for the bus. Mama's Child would've *lived* for this.

"I can get your car fixed now," Megan told him.

"I'll get my car fixed; don't worry about a thing." My dad smiled at her, and it made my stomach go a little sour. If it hadn't been Megan, my dad would be getting the shoe tonight.

Dad glanced at his watch before shrieking to the other guys that they were going to be late for their triple shift at the factory.

At school we took an exam over everything from the whole school year. Lucky for us, half the questions were about the French Revolution. Mrs. Sanchez told us we'd get our results back next week and add them to our grades. I hoped Mama's Child had been paying attention because I couldn't help her with this one.

Before recess, I sat at my usual lunch table casually and traded food with Mama's Child. I asked her about her mom's diner, and she told me it was really slow but okay. If my mom didn't hate her mom so much, and her mom didn't hate *my* mom so much, then I would be trying to get my mom to buy food there so Mama's Child wouldn't have to be poor.

"Do you wanna play tag at recess?" she asked. The thought made me nervous, but I agreed.

Pretty soon, tag developed into a tournament, and even some of the big kids joined in. Mama's Child kept bragging to everybody that it had been her idea. It was beginning to annoy me a little bit, but I just went along with it and tried to have fun. Running out of breath, I came to a halt, and Marcus Delon ran straight into me. Blinding white pain seared through my jaw, and when I fished around with my tongue, I found that one of my teeth was loose. Raising a hand to my lip, I found a sticky wetness and tasted the metallic tang of blood.

"I'm sorry, DJ," he said, then ran away to keep playing.

Most people would probably be upset about having a tooth knocked out. But I smiled, or at least *tried* to, because Marcus Delon actually talked to me again. Plus he called me DJ, not Dennis. That was totally a sign that we should be together.

My smile faded when the pain in my mouth sunk in, and I asked if I could go to the nurse. She sent me to the dentist, which my mom totally flipped out about. All I remembered was her yelling at the desk lady about money. They gave me some stuff through a mask that smelled like bubblegum. They told me it would stop it from hurting, and it *did* feel a lot better. But I was all wonky and tingly. They pulled my tooth out, but I couldn't feel it. The bubblegum scent was really strong, and I savored it, thinking this was an amazing invention. That dude straight up ripped my tooth out, and I couldn't have cared less! Even if my head floated like a balloon and I thought I was going to drift off into the open sky. I was flying high as a bird.

We got our test grades back, and I got a ninety percent. Mama's Child got a sixty. I frowned but tried not to act disappointed in her. She probably really *was* trying. Rochelle, on the other hand, was not. But that didn't stop her from complaining about receiving an F.

"I'm telling you, Sanch! I *know* I did better than that." Rochelle was up at her desk, slamming the paper down and stabbing it with her pointer finger.

"Well, did you study, Rochelle?" Mrs. Sanchez folded her hands and raised an eyebrow.

"Uh, no. Duh. That's stupid."

Sanch's eyes rolled so far back in her head, I could only see white. "That's probably why you got an F."

It started to pour outside, drawing all of our attention to the windows. I hoped it would stop because I did *not* want to get splashed by another semi again. Like, *ever.*

I told my mom about my test score, and she just grunted. Did she not see it? Did she not see the *A-* written on top? I followed her around the kitchen for a little bit before she sighed and faced me. "Your dad is taking me on another date, so if you want something from me, make it fast."

I lowered my paper and eyes and left the kitchen. I never knew they went on a *first* date.

Ashley was babysitting us tonight. Her stomach was getting huge, and she said she was due in June. I hoped the baby stayed in there and didn't come out on my birthday. It was bad enough everyone practically forgot it last year. I didn't need to compete with a cute baby. Nobody would choose *me* over that.

I was sitting on the floor of the living room, eating a bowl of cereal. Ashley had put some movie on for us and gave us all bowls of cereal as dinner, but I wasn't in the mood to watch the *Land Before Time* tonight. So I was more than happy when Mama's Child called and told me she was going to get on TownSpy. Bob had left his computer here, and I think he might have actually left it on purpose. My mom *had* said they fought over money, so maybe this was his way of paying her back. I powered it up while all the little kids focused on the TV. The older kids were off doing who knew what. I scrolled through the updates.

TomorrowIsAnotherDay has signed on.
TownSpy: Sanchez is getting married to Officer Pete on April 30th.
SpicySanch: People aren't invited to the wedding, but there will be no school, and I will have a bridal shower the week before. I expect everyone to bring good gifts.
Younggirlohyoujealous: Nobody is going to go to that. Ain't nobody got that kinda money.
Townspy: Salty.
SpicySanch: I'll give one free workbook to anyone who brings a gift worth more than five dollars.

Younggirlohyoujealous: That might be a good deal, actually.

Mama'sDiner: Buy one, get one free cheeseburger at the diner through next week.

SpicySanch: You can't have your special during my bridal shower week! People won't come to my shower.

Younggirlohyoujealous: I don't think you have to worry about people going to the diner instead of your shower.

Mama'sDiner: I can and I will have my buy one, get one special that week.

ApplePie: Sounds good to me.

Footballfever: ApplePie, do you perhaps make or sell apple pies? Every time you are in the chatroom, it makes me want apple pie.

Footballfight: My break is over. Gotta get back to that triple shift.

Footballfight has signed off.

TownSpy: I'm coming to your wedding and bridal shower, Sanch!

SpicySanch: You're not invited to the wedding, but you are invited to the shower.

HateSanch: Sanchez is getting married?

HatesSanchez: Is Sanchez pregnant?

SpicySanch: No.

HateSanch has signed off.
HateSanchez has signed off.

I called Mama's Child immediately to discuss what was going on in the chat. My mom wasn't home, so she couldn't yell at me for racking up the phone bill. Or for being on Bob's computer. Ashley would never get me in trouble, and she wasn't out here either, anyway.

"I am so happy we won't have school on Sanchez's wedding day."

"Why do you think those people are asking if she's pregnant?" Mama's Child asked and followed up with: "Who are they?"

"I have no idea," I told her and paused, trying to think who it could possibly be.

"They're acting like *they* are TownSpy. It ain't you, is it Den?"

"Of course not!" I couldn't believe she even had to ask that. Why would I make another account named "HateSanch" or "HatesSanchez"? I already had whoever "TheDJ" was getting me in trouble with Mrs. Sanchez. The sound of tires crumpling up the dirt path outside made me hurry up my goodbyes, and I hung up the phone, rushed over to the computer sitting on the little desk Bob had set up in our living room and turned it off. I picked my cereal bowl up off the floor and placed it in the sink. Then I ran upstairs to my room.

My mom ended up buying Mrs. Sanchez a gift that was *slightly* over the five dollar mark Sanchez demanded. She told us she had chucked the unwrapped gift onto the gift table and demanded a workbook before she left. But Sanch had given my mom one with only a few pages, so it put my mom in a rank mood for the whole week!

I heard that Mrs. Sanchez's wedding was good, but that was just from her and her new husband's viewpoint. They were the only people there, so everyone just had to take their word for it. I will admit she *did* seem in a better mood when school returned, and she gave us a project that was super easy as a "cushion grade." Brad and Rochelle had both sighed in relief, and I knew it was because they hadn't studied worth a cent all year, and they *really* needed this grade boost. Mama's Child told me Mrs. Sanchez said she was borderline passing, and that gave me my own sigh of relief.

When Mrs. Sanchez began discussing end of the year plans a week later, she told us *everyone* was passing this year! I hugged Mama's Child after school, and we did our own little happy dances. I resisted the urge to do the worm because I didn't want to scrape my knees all up on the sidewalk.

End of school meant my birthday was coming up, and I knew for sure that Mama's Child wouldn't forget it. I still treasured the *NSYNC mini stereo and CD that Monica got me, and Mama's Child and I played that thing so much it was starting to sound all distorted and almost broken. When it needed a good rest, because I didn't want to break it, Mama's Child would sing the song "Bye Bye Bye," and I would shake my tambourine to the beat.

My seventh birthday actually went much better than my sixth. I shouldn't have been surprised, though, because seven was my favorite number and...well. We do not speak of the number six. Ashley, Shaye, Mama's Child, *and* Monica remembered and told me "Happy Birthday." Mama's Child even gave me a granola bar from her lunch and a baby blue flower that she picked outside at recess. I know she didn't have much to give me, but I appreciated that she remembered how much I loved food and that baby blue was my favorite color.

Mrs. Sanchez (she didn't change her name) had agreed to

let Mama's sit next to me today. I thought deep down she was doing it for my birthday, but she claimed it was due to it being the last day of school, so she was feeling particularly nice. She let us do arts and crafts freetime for the rest of the day since it was the last day of school, and Monica surprised me with a birthday card that had lots of pink glitter on it. It made me feel like a million bucks.

"Thank you, Monica! I love it!"

Mama's Child frowned, and her face turned red.

"I'm making you something, *too,* Denny!" Mama's Child exclaimed, scribbling furiously with a pale yellow crayon.

"What are you making?" I asked.

"A paper airplane. And this one is a paper doll that's supposed to be you. I'm gonna cut it out, then it can ride the plane. I call 'er 'Captain DJ'." She smiled, but it was tainted with pain.

"Thank you, Mama's Child. That's nice of you."

Mama's Child frowned. *What did I say?*

"But, you don't '*love*' it?" she asked. A heavy mixture of sadness and anger tinted her voice. I instantly regretted what I had said because I had told Monica I *loved* hers.

"Of course I love it!" I placed a hand on her shoulder and grinned so hard my ears rumbled. Smiling until it started to hurt.

"Good," she finally reassured me. "I would've been sad if you didn't like my gift, Den."

"How could I not like it? It's so cool!" I tried to lay the compliments on thick. It really *was* cool. Part of me just got a little caught up in being noticed by a popular girl. By a girl that I had dreamed of being best friends with for like two years! But I could tell I had hurt Mama's Child, even if I hadn't meant to. So to make up for it, I played with that plane and the poorly cut out paper doll for the rest of the school day. Even though she did make my doll fat.

Chapter 24

THIS SUMMER WAS GOING to be the best summer ever, and it was going to start with a graduation ceremony tonight. Shortly before we had to leave for the ceremony, I called Mama's Child to tell her about the bestest summer ever, and she said that we could *totally* arrange the summer of a lifetime—including TownSpy, of course.

"As long as you ain't causing any fights," I told her.

Her laugh cackled through the receiver. "When would I *ever* do such a thing?"

I paused for a second and listened really hard. "You're pretending to stir the pot right now, aren't you?" I asked, suspiciously.

Once again, her laughter flooded my ear, and she said, "Now, I thought *I* was the one who knew everything?"

"I got to go," I said quickly, hearing my mom's heels clicking in the kitchen. "Gotta get to the graduation ceremony."

"Boooooring!" she droned.

"I know, I know. But it's a big deal. Even that dumbturd Brad pulled it off."

"I bet Sanchez passed him just to get rid of him. Just like

a kidney stone."

I snorted. Even though I had never had a kidney stone, whatever it was didn't sound good. And I knew if Mama's was saying it, it was probably a wicked insult! Tee-hee!

The ceremony began at seven p.m., and the graduates started to walk across the stage to receive their diplomas. Since we were a small school, Old Mcloofin was allowing everyone to share what they were going to do with their lives. I couldn't wait to hear what crap Brad made up on the spot. The lazy potato probably didn't have any plans of leaving our couch.

Some girl I didn't remember seeing once in my life said that she was going to Harvard and wanted to be an artist. Danny Jr. had plans to become a detective, and I didn't think anyone was surprised by that. He could definitely get all of the inside scoops; the real question was how in the world would he ever keep it all confidential? That meant *secret*.

My heart sank when Ashley announced she would be doing work in daycare services because she had already spent half her life babysitting us heathens, and she was due for her baby any day now. Boop Dawson was going to be a mechanic, and Stacey just shrugged and said she was "sticking with the ambulance driving career." Not an EMT or a nurse, she literally phrased it like that. *The poor souls who found themselves in her care,* I thought, remembering how she "cared" for Mama's Child, Bob, and my mom after that tornado. Yikes!

"I'm totally going to become a famous movie director," Brad announced, and I nearly choked on my bottled water. Well, I honestly didn't care what he did, as long as he got out of my house. I knew it wasn't *my* house, but he was the literal worst! Cherry and Izzy discussed their plans of becoming a nurse and a doctor. I zoned out because it was getting way too long and boring.

When the graduates finally tossed their hats, Brad's voice echoed throughout the whole football field, screaming the word, "Freedom!"

I cringed, thinking about how nobody was going to know whose hat was whose. Any of them could have lice or some other disease and place it on their head...and well. It just was not a pretty picture.

Lots of rumors bounced around that Chad had proposed to Izzy and they were going to move in with Derek and Cherry. *Cliques never end.* These people needed to grow up and move on! Boop and Stacey came over to where my family and I had been standing, and my mom practically shoved Ambrosia at her like she was a dirty diaper. Maybe she was. I didn't know. It did smell like poop up in here. Stacey said they would be going on a little vacation, and my mom honestly couldn't have cared less. She was more than happy to let them go. So was I. The fewer people at home, the better. It would certainly make my summer more pleasant.

We went to several graduation parties, and my dad was being annoying, loudly bragging to everyone he saw about how Brad was going to be famous and, more importantly, that he got some football scholarship. Because football and sons seemed to be what my dad cared about the most. He didn't even notice, and neither did my mom, when I tried a piece of cake at *every* party we went to. Vanilla, chocolate, *and* marble! It was all delectable. And when we were on our way home, my mom stopped at the store and actually *bought* a cake to celebrate her kids that graduated. By this time, I was getting so full of cake that I worried I might get sick. But it was yellow, and I hadn't had that flavor yet. Besides, it was *cake.* Who was I kidding? I ate another piece anyways, savoring the rich buttery creaminess.

Even *more* cake filled next Saturday because it was Krissy and Dominique's sixth birthday. Apparently my parents, or I guess I should say my *dad*, remembered *their* birthday. So much so that they actually got cake for it. I tried not to be a bitter little green monster and told them both Happy Birthday. They told me thanks, but then they proceeded to talk about how they had fun plans and were so excited. Being the curious cat that I was, I naturally had to inquire.

"What plans?"

They kept walking toward the front door, and I slipped into my beat-up sneakers, the door banging behind me as I followed them outside.

"Wait up!" I called, waving my hand wildly.

They stopped and turned around.

"What are you guys doing today?" Taking deep breaths, I tried to control my breathing so I didn't sound overly excited, nervous, or out of shape. I was all three.

"Um, we're going to a friend's house." Dominique snickered, and Krissy followed suit.

"Can I join in?" Biting on my lip and curling my toes, I hoped they would say yes. Even though I had no idea who their friend was.

"We don't have much room, Dennis." Dom smirked.

"No, we don't. No, we don't," Krissy concurred.

"What do you mean?" I wrinkled my nose. How did their friend's house not "have enough room"? I wasn't *that* fat.

"What we really wanted to do for our birthday was ride in Monica's pink car." Dominique placed her hands on her hips and kept that sickening smirk plastered across her face. Krissy snickered.

"Oh." My hands shook, so I shoved them in my pockets.

"We only had one last spot."

"Oh, yeah?" I asked, raising my eyebrows hopefully.

"I said '*had*'," Dominique snapped.

"Uh-huh." Krissy always backed Dominique up on whatever she said.

"Well, who took it?" If it was the twins, Haylee and Hallee, that didn't make sense, because there were *two* of them.

"Mama's Child," they chimed in unison.

My heart sank. "*What?*"

They just stared at me, and Dominique clucked her tongue in a way that really embarrassed me.

"I thought you weren't friends with Mama's."

"Well, she wanted to come, and we had an extra seat."

"Well, can I at least come over later?" I asked, even though my cheeks were flaming fire truck red and I was growing more humiliated with every passing second.

They didn't answer me.

Feeling excluded, I sat outside of our house and waited. Beans kept snorting obnoxiously, demanding my attention.

"At least I got you, Beans." I gave him a sad smile, and he oinked before diving into a mud puddle.

Laughter pierced the air, and I faced Monica's house again. They drove around in the car, coming into my view every few minutes, and I bit my tongue, swallowing the lump in my throat. Everyone was laughing and carrying on about how much fun they were having. Anyone could have seen that. Even me. Even from the outside looking in.

When the car stopped in front of the Greens' house, and they climbed out, I took a shaky deep breath. I brushed my dusty palms off on the knees of my overalls and stood. Building up courage, and maybe a little bit of resentment, I approached them.

"Mama's Child," I muttered, and she didn't answer. So I raised my voice a little. "Mama's Child," I repeated.

Her laughter stopped, and she turned around, her smile fading as soon as she saw me. "Yeah? What's up?"

"I really wanted to go with them for that car ride. You took the last seat," I whispered. The other girls were giggling and glancing in our direction.

Mama's Child frowned, and snipped, "So what?"

"I really should have gotten to go."

"Why?"

"They're my sisters."

"You don't even like them." She shook her head at me.

"Shh, they'll hear. I deserved to go," I lowered my voice.

"What makes you better than me?" she sneered. "It's *not* a popularity contest."

"Well, if it was, I would've gotten to ride in the car with them, not *you.*" I regretted the words as soon as they left my lips.

She blinked at me as if I'd slapped her across the face.

"I'm really sorry, I didn't mean that." I reached out to touch her, but she jerked backward like I had cooties.

"I'll show *you* who's more popular, *Dennis,*" she hissed the last word, and it struck me deeply that she had called me Dennis rather than Denny or one of her other nicknames for me. I had hated them at first, but they were growing on me. Hearing "Dennis" from her just sounded so foreign, so unnatural. Almost like we were strangers.

"I'm really sorry, Mama's."

She turned on her heel and walked away. Oblivious to our conversation, Monica announced that they should "go tanning like the grown ups do."

"I want to come, too." I couldn't believe I was putting

myself out there like that.

"Okay, c'mon, DJ!" Monica cheered, like a happy little song bird. A million butterflies flapped their wings inside my heart.

We all laid lined up in a row in her backyard, and I was at the end of the line. Some other girls had come over to join us, so I ended up right beside Kayla. She was one of Haylee and Hallee's younger siblings and was *bad* news. I tried to talk to Dominique and Krissy, even though they were further away, but everyone ignored everything I said because *Mama's Child* was already talking. They did each other's hair, Monica and Haylee showing the other girls how to separate their hair into pigtails, and Monica even knew how to braid.

"Do you bleach your hair, DJ?" Hallee asked me.

"Um, no. It's just like this."

"It's…almost *white.*"

"Yeah, I know," I told her. Hallee shrugged, and her brows were still wrinkled. I self-consciously tucked my hair behind my ears. Here they were, gorgeous and tiny, with beautiful hair. Here *I* was, with freakish white hair and a big tum tum. I sucked my stomach in, suddenly feeling self-conscious.

Mama's Child said that she could do her hair fancy too, then piled it up into a giant fluffed-up bun. Everyone complimented her on it. I looked away.

"Can you put *your* hair in a bun, *Dennis*?" Mama's Child snarkily remarked.

I frowned and picked at the blades of grass. "No."

"But your mom is a *hair stylist.* I figured you'd know how to put your hair in a bun. It's so easy." Mama's patted her bun with a smirk. The popular girls all flocked toward her. Kayla flopped onto her belly and kicked a flip flop off.

It smacked my leg.

"My mom doesn't do that stuff with me." My eyes returned to the ground.

"Well, I'd show ya how. But *Krissy and Dom* already asked me." Mama's Child raised her nose up in the air snootily.

"Hey! Since it's you guys' birthday, we should go to the donut shop!" Monica turned and offered every one of us a friendly smile. My heartbeat quickened, and I wondered if I was included in "we."

"Disney Donut Shop!" Lil' Shelbi grunted, before gripping Kayla's arm.

"We're goin', Shelb! Hold yer horses!" Kayla huffed. Shelbi and her started to rough-house and play slap each other. Rochelle let Shelb run around with Kayla a lot, and the two of them were two rotten apple seeds. Rotten to the *core*. Blacker than black. I'd never known four-year-olds could be so violent.

We walked to the Disney Donut Shop, and it was a much longer walk than I had thought. It was embarrassing because I was huffing and puffing, and the other girls weren't. But I wanted to be included. And I wanted donuts.

We sat in one of those big, wrap-around party booths. I was on one of the end seats next to Kayla again, and she kept trying to shove me off. There weren't enough menus, and some of the girls couldn't read well, so Mama's Child read the menu aloud.

"Hmm," she pondered. "There's a giant cake we could share for ten dollars."

Everyone agreed it was a good idea. It bothered me that we were at a donut shop and *not* getting donuts, but I wanted to fit in, so I said nothing even though my brain kept reminding me about it every two seconds. We all dug in greedily: lips smacking, crumbs falling, icing on cheeks, and forks clanking against empty plates. Then the waitress placed a slip of paper on the table, upside down. Monica assumed it was the bill, so everyone asked around for spare dollars. I had three dollars with me, Monica had five, and Haylee and Hallee had a dollar a piece. We searched under some tables and found two quarters on the floor to use for the tip. But when the waitress came for the bill, she said, "This is not enough," and frowned down at the money we had shoved toward her. Some of the girls were shaking or scratching their heads. Monica frowned, and I blinked dumbfoundedly at the waitress.

"That was quite an elaborate cake, and this isn't exactly a cheap restaurant." The waitress cleared her throat.

"We ain't got that much dough!" Shelbi blurted, her chubby palms facing upward and her mouth in a little round "o."

"Well, I recognized Megan Green's daughter and thought she'd given her money for you kids." The waitress motioned toward Monica, and all our eyes followed. Her cheeks blushed a feminine shade of pink. *She even looked lovely when she was embarrassed.* I wished *I* looked like that, instead of like a chunky tomato.

"The amount owed is one hundred dollars, not ten. And that's without tax."

"What?" My jaw dropped. I turned toward Mama's Child.

She shrugged and said, "Oops. I must've messed up. I'm not good at math. Sorry."

Practically all of them told her *it was okay.*

"Oh, that's fine, MC. One hundred isn't a lot," Hallee smiled.

"Yeah! My mom has a scarf worth more than that. She

bought it yesterday for one hundred and seventy dollars!" Monica giggled, and Mama's Child pretended to wipe sweat from her brow.

"My mom says all of us kids have over a thousand dollars a piece in the bank!" Hallee chirped, swinging her legs in delight.

"That's for college, Hallee! And don't tell people how much money we have. We'll get robbed!" Haylee wagged a scolding finger at her.

I was frozen to this booth and could hear all of their jokes fluttering around me. But all I could think was: *Oh dear...*

"I'll have my mom pay your share MC, don't worry. My mom *never* gets mad." Monica patted Mama's Child's shoulder empathetically.

I gulped down the ginormous lump in my throat.

The waitress called our mothers, and when the sound of a car ripped into the parking lot, I knew it was *my* mother. She arrived first and stood at the cash register, shooting me the death glare. When the other mothers arrived, Mom split the bill with them, except for Rochelle, who was at work and didn't show up.

"Hi, Graham Cracker!" Shelb hollered at my mom. All the blood drained from my face, thinking she was gonna get the shoe in the middle of this donut shop.

"Hi Shelb," Mom responded with a forced smile, before hissing something about Rochelle under her breath. Then she waited until the other moms were out the door before whipping around to face me and the twins.

"You are so going to be in the grounded room," my mom growled at Dom, Krissy, and me, and we followed her out of the diner like dogs with tails between our legs.

Part of me wondered if Mama's Child had done this on purpose to get back at me or if she really *did* misread the menu.

❖

Only a few days after I got out of the grounded room, I got put right back in. Here's the story of how it all went down.

The day started out normal, Ashley was going on a date with Danny Jr., Shaye was still upset about Princeton, and I was surprised that Stephanie hadn't broken up with him yet. I fired up the computer that morning and noticed Mama's Child had been doing some *major* pot stirring in the midst of my grounded room "vacation." Whoever my impersonator was had been doing the same. They started saying stuff as "TheDJ," and things were going a little too far. So of course I had to put in my two cents:

TomorrowIsAnotherDay has signed on.
TownSpy: Did Nicole get a boob job?
TownSpy: Is Mama's Child's hair a weave?
Younggirlohyoujealous: Probably not.
TomorrowIsAnotherDay: TownSpy is rude.
Footballfever: Who the dung is
TomorrowIsAnotherDay?
TheDJ: Can't tell if Sanch ate a big burrito
or if that's a baby bump. Preggers or not?
TomorrowIsAnotherDay: Who is TheDJ?
RichHeiress: It's oviously Dennis June.
SpicySanch: I smell Dennis's first strike of
the year!
TomorrowIsAnotherDay: Don't pick on DJ.
Fit4life: Who is TomorrowIsAnotherDay?
TownSpy: Who bets Broccoli is working a
single shift?
TownSpy: Does Megan even know how to

drive?
TownSpy: Is Rochelle missing work?

As mad and annoyed as I was about the troll who was pretending to be me and about Mama's Child's snarky remarks, Rochelle actually *was* missing work. And that message saved her hide.

"Crap!" Rochelle frantically gasped from far off, rushing down the stairs so fast it 'bout gave me a heart attack.

"I gotta be at work in ten minutes. Mom! I'm borrowing your car!"

"Mom's not home. She went with Megan somewhere," I told her.

Rochelle ignored the fact I was on Bob's computer, or she just thought the issue was too beneath her to meddle with.

"Even better!" Rochelle exclaimed, grabbing the keys off the coffee table and trucking it outside, slamming the door behind her. I logged out of the chatroom while she tore out of our driveway. Or dirt path, I should say.

Here's where *me* getting in trouble comes into play. My younger siblings and I went out into the yard, and we got into a big circle to play. The Greens and the Stars saw us, so they came over to play, too. Even the big kids joined in, and I got a little nervous when they started doing dares and challenges. This time the dare was to sing Weezer's "Beverly Hills" song because it was practically my grandma's anthem, and legend had it that she showed up if you sang it.

We all were singing it, and the deal was you had to leave the circle when you didn't want to anymore. Now remember, my mom had *banned* this, and after her explanation at the karaoke club that Halloween night, the other moms didn't question it. So *they* banned it too. Maybe to patronize my mother, or maybe out of downright fear of my grandmother. Either way it was banned.

My mom arrived home sooner than expected, and she yelled at us for singing the song. She went off the handle, so outrageously mad that she called the other moms, and *they* were upset, too. Rochelle had come home for her lunch break and got the singing all stirred up again. So the ones who wanted to live life on the edge started joining in again. I did because I didn't want to be seen as a loser or be the odd man out. Mom heard it, and once again she told us to stop.

But we didn't.

It was down to just Mama's Child (I honestly had no idea where she even came from, as usual), Kayla, Lil' Shelbi, Ambrosia, and I. The triplets were in the play pen outside, and soon we heard Frogster trying to grumble some of the words in a creepy man voice.

This made my mom *livid,* and she demanded I go to the grounded room for *five days.* Five days, in that stupid empty room, with nothing but a bed. It always bored me out of my mind! I was so upset because I was the only one who got punished, but my mom claimed she couldn't punish the other kids because they weren't hers. *Technicalities.* It was totally unfair, and as I made my way to the crummy, single-bedded room, with *no* other furniture or source of entertainment, I knew I would have to stew over how this was totally *not* turning out to be the best summer ever.

Chapter 25

ASHLEY AND DANNY JR. had been dating for about two weeks when Orange and that nasty Stephanie started trying to break them up. I guess Orange still had a thing for him because why else would she break them up? But I also thought she hated his guts since he was Ashley's baby's dad or whatever. Stephanie just was in it for the drama. She had broken up with Princeton a week ago because she told Orange that this "project" was more important. They were freaks who just sat around watching people suck faces on TV while Stephanie texted and Orange just replied with "whatever" every few minutes.

It was pleasant having a break from Brad, and Stacey, and Ambrosia who were on vacation. While Ambrosia had shown up a few weeks ago for the "Beverly Hills" Fiasco, Stacey and Boop hadn't come over until last night. The two of them announced they had eloped while they were on vacation.

"Your dad and I eloped too," Mom quipped, like it was a competition.

"What?" Stacey asked.

"Look, I got the ring back and everything," she stretched

her hand forward with a flourish. I tiptoed over so I could see the proof.

"How did I not know this?" I whined. This was something I should have known!

"I don't have to tell you everything about my life!" Mom shot me an annoyed look. "Man. You have kids, and people think you lose your right to any privacy."

"It's private to know my mom is married to my dad?" I asked.

"Shut up, Dennis." She rolled her eyes and held her ring to the light, admiring the teeny tiny stone.

Stacey cleared her throat before remarking glumly, "Well, I just wanted to give you the news and say that we purchased a trailer down the street." She was probably upset that Mom stole her thunder.

"Good riddance!" my mom had cheered, and I'd be lying if I said I didn't feel the same way. But on the other hand, I would have *much* rather had Stacey and Ambrosia than Brad, who *swore* he was "only back for a break from college." I wasn't buying it. That remote had already been in his hand all day, and potato chip crumbs covered his boxer shorts. That was right, he just lay on the couch with no shirt or pants on *all day every day.* And my mom just *let* him.

Ashley went into labor a few days after Brad's homecoming, and baby Asher was born at one a.m. on June sixteenth. I now had a nephew, and I was so happy because this one would actually be taken care of, and I wouldn't have to listen to it scream twenty-four seven. I asked if I could hold him, but she said I was too little to hold him while standing (um, I was like seven years old, thank you very much). So I had to sit down and be super, super careful while she monitored me like a hawk. My brain kept reminding me of everything that could go wrong, and I think

I was actually sweating when she took a picture of us together. Having held my other siblings, I didn't get why she was so worried I would drop him. But then again, she was a first-time mom, and my mom probably wouldn't have even noticed if I had dropped one of *her* babies. Mom got so mean every time she was in here with her babies that I think they pumped her full of stuff to make her all loopy and whatnot. Ashley seemed to be her same old self. Just more worried. The fact she even *wanted* a photo with me made me happy.

Danny Jr. was being a troll and didn't come to see her or his son until the next day. I was so mad at him, but part of me couldn't help but wonder if it had something to do with the big *S and O*—Stephanie and Orange, mean girls of the year. Even Danny's *dad*, Danny the first, came to see her. And he yelled out the hospital window, "Hey, everybody!"

Must be where that idiot got the saying from.

My mom whipped her head around, dripping with anticipation for the latest gossip.

"I'm a grandpa!" Danny hollered.

"Well, I'm a grandma, too!" my mom yelled, before frowning and muttering, "Oh wait. I've been one. And I don't even like kids. *And* I am too young and hot to be a grandma."

I rolled my eyes as my mom patted her hair all over, then went to the little mirror above the sink to check her makeup.

My dad acted like it was the greatest day of his life because he finally had a grandchild who was a *boy*. That was discrimination if you asked me. Girls were just as good as boys, but he acted that way with us kids, too. I thought I should be just as loved as my brothers. He went all googly-eyed and started asking the baby if he was going to be a football player. That was a dumb thing to do. It wasn't like the baby could talk, and even if he could, why would he know something like that? He couldn't even crawl or walk yet. Girls could play football too, Dad.

I wanted to gag when my dad was holding him in the air and repeatedly asking in an annoying baby voice, "Do you love football? Do you *love* it?"

Sick.

Well, Orange and Stephanie were succeeding because Danny Jr. and Ashley have been fighting *a lot* lately, primarily over the phone and not in person. I had taken it upon myself to be the person to answer the phone if at all possible, so I was almost always in the middle of it. But Mama's Child might call so we could make up, and besides, who was I kidding? I could get all of the details and grease that way.

Stephanie and Orange had taken it upon *themselves* to spend any days they could with Danny Jr. I knew it was because they didn't want Ashley spending time with him, but I didn't understand why. Every time he called, I knew he was about to cancel a date or plans to visit. I hated having to be the one to break the news to Ashley. He was such a turd. He had only come to see Asher one time since he'd been home from the hospital. When he called tonight, I knew it would be a similar story.

"Are you calling to cancel on Ashley again?" I asked.

"Just put her on the phone, Dennis." So I did. But I stayed close so I could hear everything.

"A pool party?" Ashley scoffed. "Right. I'm sure they *did* invite you."

I knew "they" was Stephanie and Orange immediately, based on the way she said it.

"Well, great. I'm glad I can come too. Except for the fact

that I am at home, raising *our* baby. Not to mention that I literally have zero swimsuits that fit me anymore."

He raised his voice at her, and she raised hers back. But she took the phone out into the kitchen so that I couldn't hear. When she came back into the living room, she was off the phone, and her eyes were all watery. My mom walked downstairs with Asher in her arms, a small bundle with rosy cheeks and sand-colored hair.

"I'm changing into my pajamas." Ashley brushed a tear from her cheek and avoided eye contact.

"Why?" my mom and I asked at the same time.

"I thought you had a date? I was gonna babysit." My mom raised an eyebrow and scanned Ashley's face.

Since when did my mom ever *volunteer* to babysit? She must've really wanted them together.

"Not anymore," Ashley's voice wobbled.

I said nothing, and my mom hesitated before gently asking, "Is he coming here then? I can warm up some Mystery Meet in like twenty seconds."

My stomach gurgled, and *not* because I was hungry. I had a feeling Danny Jr. wouldn't find the offer any more appetizing than I did.

"No. And if he doesn't start spending more time with me, then I don't think I want to keep seeing him." Ashley lifted Asher from my mom's arms and stomped up the steps. I coughed awkwardly so my mom wouldn't think I was trying to hide my presence.

"I know you were eavesdropping, Dennis. I'm not stupid," she spat, before folding her arms and storming off to the kitchen. Danny Jr. was putting every girl in my family in a rank mood, and I was getting sick of it.

"I'm gonna hit up that pool party," said Brad, and I jumped, forgetting that the leech was still here. He peeled his sweaty bare back off the couch then belched.

"You are disgusting," I told him.

"If I'm disgusting, then you are absolutely *putrid.*"

"I'mma tell Mom." Even *I* felt like a nark for not having a better comeback than that.

Brad just laughed. "Do it. News flash! I'm her favorite child."

I gritted my teeth.

"I'll be back later, Ma," he called.

My mom came clicking her way out to the living room and smiled. "Okay! When will you be back?"

"Uh, I don't know. I don't have to give you a time," he sassed, but my mom didn't even say anything. I'd get the shoe if I spoke to her like that.

"How long are you gonna be here?" I grumbled, folding my arms.

"I'll be here the whole week."

"Oh, good!" Mom grinned. "Well, have fun at the Greens' party."

Brad didn't even respond as he slid on a pair of sandals even though he was wearing socks—*cringe.* I despised him. He was handed everything we could afford on a silver platter, and *both* our parents adored him while he just abused their attention and gifts like they were nothing. Ungrateful slimeball.

According to TownSpy, Brad and Stephanie went out on a date toward the end of his stay with us, and I was worried it would keep him longer. I wanted him out. He was stinking up the place and eating all the good snackies. He always had the remote, never wore pants, and just took up our whole entire couch. But thankfully, he went back to college when he said he would. I was actually a little proud of him for it.

My dad wanted to have the best birthday party ever and was sad that Brad wouldn't be here for it. My mom did not want to spend a ton of money on him though, so she said that if he wanted to have a party, he would have to share with the baby triplets. He groaned, but he didn't want his kids to suffer not having a party, so he compromised. I wished he cared that much about *my* birthday.

My dad had a giant football-shaped cake, and the babies each got an individual cupcake. They were supposed to be "smash cakes," since they were turning one. Brandon wouldn't eat his, and I was excruciatingly tempted to ask if *I* could have it. You know, since I didn't get any cake on *my* birthday. Froggy only ate the bright neon yellow icing off hers, but Frogster went all in. I laughed so hard it hurt when she grumbled loudly, almost like Cookie Monster, then slammed her whole face into the cupcake. She ate every single crumb. Well, the ones that weren't glued to her face and clothing, that was.

Dad started to get petty because everyone was paying attention to the babies and not him. I kind of wanted to say, "*Yeah, it hurts, right?*" but I didn't. Dude Green came over and slapped him on the back before immediately asking when he would be returning to work even though my dad had only taken two days off—yesterday and today, his birthday.

"Um, I'm coming back tomorrow, obviously." Him and all the guys he invited over from the factory started chuckling, as if they expected nothing less.

"What a dumb question," Dad laughed. Then he got serious again and asked, "Football?"

I groaned, and I didn't care who heard. I *hated* football. It was all my dad cared about. Besides every other child on this planet but me, that was.

All the older guys and Rochelle played a long, drawn-out, boring game of football. My dad made Broccoli be the referee because no one wanted him on their team. Not even Rochelle, his girlfriend. Each team yelled at Broccoli nearly every time the opposing team got a point. I sat up occasionally, but kept flopping myself back down on the grass, exhausted from the horrible boringness. I just wanted cake!

Dude Green was on the same team as my dad because they claimed they didn't want it to come between their friendship. To me, the whole thing was stupid, and boys were stupid. Broccoli must've agreed, because he got tired of being the referee and quit.

"Why are you quitting?" the guys demanded.

"My back is acting up."

They all groaned.

"Oh, it's his *'back'* again," they joked, placing air quotes around the word "back." My mom got called to be the referee, and she was living for it. She got to boss everyone around, only one of her absolute favorite pastimes. The team that didn't have my dad on it yelled at her for a "foul call" shortly into the game.

"I know what I saw, and he made a foul!" yelled Bob Waltzer. I was actually incredibly surprised Bob was here. And that my dad *allowed* him to be.

"I don't give a *dump* what you thought you done seen, Bob! I am the ref, not you!" My mom chucked her can of soda to the ground and stomped it flat with her heeled shoe. I winced just thinking about how easily she had done it. I swear she had superhuman strength.

"That's my girl!" my dad cheered. His team ended up winning by a long shot, and I honestly thought my mom had cheated at playing ref.

After they finished their excruciatingly dumb football game, Dad got out fireworks, and I was so pumped. I didn't realize we even had any after how my mom freaked out on New Year's Eve when I asked her about them. She told him that they were for the Fourth of July, so my dad went inside the house to watch football with Dude G. and Lucas. I followed them inside, but not to watch football, because ew. I sat on the bottom of the steps and doodled, trying not to fall asleep as I had a habit of doing here. The three of them ordered a bucket of fried chicken, and it smelled absolutely heavenly. But none of them shared any with me. So, despite my best efforts, I drifted off to sleep, my mouth watering and my dreams filled with dancing fried chicken drumsticks.

The Fourth of July was upon us before I even knew it, and Dad had decided to have a barbeque party. We busted out all of our picnic tables, and Dad got out the grill and fired up lots of hamburgers and hotdogs. The scent drifted through the air, and everyone passing by seemed to be as hungry as I was. The Greens and the Stars came, the Stars bringing their own veggie burgers, and for whatever reason, my mom invited Mrs. Sanchez and Officer Pete.

"Mom, no!" I demanded. This was turning out to be one of the *worst* summers ever, and I didn't want Sanchez making it worse. This was summer. I did not want to be around the teacher I never got to escape from because she was my teacher *every year,* and probably would be until the day I graduated.

"She lives in our attic; they're going to know we are having a party."

"That's so not the reason. You hate her, and you hate paying for other people's food. You're just trying to get brownie points."

My mom shot me a warning look and muttered, "Watch your mouth," so I backed away but lingered in the general area. I wanted to be one of the first people to get my food before all the good stuff got taken. Trying new foods made me nervous, and I didn't wanna get stuck with a veggie burger. Not to mention everyone knew everyone stole the cheese like greedy little gremlins, and a *cheeseburger* was just not the same as a *hamburger,* no matter how ya tried to slice it!

"Want a hamburger for your pig?" asked Dude Green, who was helping Dad grill the meat.

I wrinkled my nose. "Beans doesn't eat those. And if he did, he would want *cheese* on it."

Dude Green exchanged a smirk with my dad.

"Who the poop-scooping boogie is *Beans?* " Dad hocked a loogie onto the ground.

"Um, my pig. You should know this," I told him.

"It ain't your pig, and it doesn't have a name."

"Beans is a 'he,' not an 'it.' And *Mom* knows his name."

"I *ain't* givin' no pig a slice of this cheese!" Dad scoffed. "Your *mom* would kill me."

"Over cheese?" asked Dude G, trying not to laugh.

"Maybe over the meat, and definitely over the cheese." A burger hissed as Dad flipped it.

"Seems a bit harsh." Dude G.'s smirk vanished, and he scanned the area like he was afraid of my mom.

"Well she divorced me over the tub, now didn't she?"

Dude Green and him laughed, and they got so carried away that I had to tell them one of the hot dogs was blacker than coal.

As soon as Sanchez showed up, she said, "I hope you know this doesn't get you any brownie points, Deniese." My mom just gave her a half smile, but when she turned around, she muttered, "darn," probably hating herself for inviting her.

Everyone sat at the picnic tables we'd brought out and munched their food. It was delicious. Then Mama's Child and Mama from the diner came, and I knew it wasn't me who invited them.

Mama's Child played with all the popular kids instead of with me, and it ate at me that we still hadn't made up yet. Especially when we had planned on having the best summer ever together.

A whistle went through the air, followed by a snapping crackle. It sounded like a firework, but it wasn't even dark yet. We wouldn't be starting *our* fireworks for several hours. My mom's car alarm went off, so I ran around the house to investigate. Detective DJ was on the mission! I hummed my own little theme song as I approached the car, where Rochelle stood looking down at its hood.

"I'm sorry, Mom. I didn't mean for it to hit your car!" Rochelle clasped her hands together like she was *genuinely* sorry. I think it may have been the only time in her whole life she had said those words and meant them. By this point, some of the other adults and a few kids were coming around the side to check things out too.

"This is my *favorite car!*" my mom cried, rubbing her pink bug like it was a baby or a small animal. Only some chipped paint and a little dent marred it.

"I said I was sorry—"

My mom's sadness turned to anger, and she immediately hardened her expression and grumbled, "Rochelle. You are going to pay to have this fixed!"

"What?" Rochelle exclaimed. "But it was an *accident*, and I actually apologized. I'm just now starting to save up money for myself."

"Fix it." My mom's words and expressions were cold and flat.

"I don't want to fix it."

"Well, do you want to be grounded?"

"No."

"Then fix it!" my mom shrieked with a red face, despite Megan being present.

"I can teach you how to pull a triple shift at the factory," my dad, Dude Green, and Lucas all said at the same time. What was their obsession with triple shifts?

Mrs. Sanchez came around the building and walked toward the car, her stomach sticking out a bit. Mama's Child was noticing it too, from what I could tell, because she kept staring at her then began to type on her little gadget. I pretended I had to go to the bathroom, but I actually went inside and logged into the chatroom. It was killing me not knowing what Mama's Child was writing on there.

TomorrowIsAnotherDay has signed on.
TownSpy: Sanchez looks preggo.
SpicySanch: Excuse me?
TownSpy: Are you pregnant?
SpicySanch: It's none of your business.
TownSpy: That's not a no.
HateSanch: Sanchez is pregnant.
HatesSanchez: Indeed, she is.
HateSanch has signed off.
HateSanchez has signed off.

Something moved out the corner of my eye, so I quickly signed off, uneasy. Then I actually *did* go to the outhouse before making my way back to the party. I approached a picnic table with an empty seat and sat casually. Mrs. Sanchez wore a pinched expression, sitting at a picnic table a few down from me. Was she *really* pregnant? People needed to stop doing that. It was getting a little ridiculous if you asked me.

I nearly had a heart attack when a flash of orange and yellow sparks crashed into the picnic table Mrs. Sanchez was at, and a small fire ignited. My dad hopped up and ran to one of the grills, grabbing a fire extinguisher. He sprayed the flames, and they dwindled. Mama's Child ran over and was throwing the foam from the extinguisher at Lil' Shelbi and Kayla, all of them chuckling. My heart raced, and I squirmed in my seat, glancing around to try to figure out where the dump that thing had even come from. What was it?

Following some of the adults and a few curious kids over to that picnic table, I searched for the thing that fell out of the sky. Maybe it was a meteor or a shooting star! I finally stumbled upon a stick-like firework in the grass, black as char and still smoking a bit. A bright red piece of paper was tied to the stick, and I flipped it over to find slightly burned, black writing. It read:

"Oops. Looks like I 'missed'. But I won't miss the next time, Sanchez."

Just reading it sent chills through my skin, and the hair on my arms and neck stood up all prickly like. I took the note over to my mom, who turned pale. She showed it to Mrs. Sanchez, who stared at the paper, reading it over and over again.

"What is this?" I asked, holding up the stick.

"A bottle rocket," my mom answered, refusing to make eye contact with me.

I thought that bottle rockets went *up,* not *down.* I shifted my attention toward the sky and placed a hand to my brow to shield my eyes from the setting sun.

That's when I saw the back of a woman, dressed in all

black. Her brown curly ponytail swished as she crouched. She was on our roof. *Our roof!* I blinked a few times, and could no longer see her. But I knew she had been up there and hadn't come down. She had to still be there.

I was wondering who the dung patty was up on our roof when Sanchez fainted—*another* sign of pregnancy according to Mama's Child, who shared this with everyone when Sanch hit the ground. How the dump did she even know *anything* about pregnancy? She was an only child, and I had almost twenty siblings. But she knew more than me. Totally not fair.

"Crap!" my mother yelled, staring up at our roof, before stringing along a strew of a bunch of *other* explicit words that I wasn't allowed to say. Officer Pete munched on his corn dogs with shifty eyes and visibly chattering teeth.

"Uh… I think I'm going to…" my dad stammered, slowly rising to his feet. "I think I'm gonna go pick up an extra shift. Right now." The other guys agreed, and they all *ran* out. What wimps!

I placed my hands on my hips incredulously. "Is *anybody* gonna address the ding-a-ling standing on our roof? And Officer Pete you're a *cop.* Why aren't you arresting her or something for trespassin'?"

Everyone stared at me. I stared right on back before sighing.

"I have to do everything around here." My eyes rolled so hard even *I* thought it was a bit much. I directed my attention to the roof and cupped my hands around my mouth. "Hey, you!" I screamed. "Get off my dumping roof 'fore I hit chu with my fly swatter!"

My mom was awfully pale, and sweat glistened against her forehead. Was it sickness? Food poisoning? It was strange. I continued on with my spiel.

"It's handmade! And it's got *lots* of nasty ol' bug guts on it!"

"Shut *up,* Dennis!" people around me gritted through their teeth.

Mama's Child sidled up next to me, and it struck me by surprise because I thought we weren't even talking.

"She's not moving. You got to let her really have it," Mama's Child whispered, urging me on. Nobody else was saying anything to help me. I groaned.

"My sister Rochelle is gonna *beat your duff!*" I bellowed. Rochelle came over immediately with clenched fists and punched me in the gut, knocking the wind straight outta me. I clutched my stomach.

"Keep goin', Den. You got this." MC nodded her head in affirmation. I didn't know why she was suddenly my friend again, but I didn't want to disappoint her.

I clutched my stomach and kept going. I yelled at the person to get off my roof again, and this time I got a response. The black-clad woman flipped me off, and my jaw dropped.

Marti gasped, "How vulgar!"

Then to *everyone's* surprise, the woman chucked a toilet over the side of the roof and ran. A *toilet!* The porcelain busted into a million pieces when it hit the ground, liquid flooding out of it. And, boy, I tell you what! That lady must've been living up there for a *week* from the smell of that stuff. Wooooo-eee! I waved a hand in front of my nose, and Mama's Child snickered, her eyes the size of grapefruits.

"What did you *do?*" my mom bellowed in my direction, the color returning to her face at an alarming speed. I was stunned. Completely speechless. But so was she, so I assumed she was waiting for me to answer.

"What did *I* do? That person is the one who flipped me off! That is a *big* no no!"

"Dennis!" she hissed.

"Why aren't *you* standing up for yourself? You never let *anyone* walk all over you! Suddenly you don't wanna show your bad side. Is it 'cause the Greens are here? And you want to look like a perfect mother?" I dug my nails into my palms and gritted my teeth. I had no intention of censoring my thoughts before I spoke them out loud this time.

If my mom could've breathed fire, I swear she would have. "Dennis! You are *way* out of line! You have an anger problem, and you need counseling!"

I needed counseling? *I* needed *counseling?*

"You're giving me an oolzer!" I whined.

"First of all, it's called an *ulcer,* you idiot! Secondly, that was *my mother!*" My mom stomped her foot like a toddler throwing a tantrum.

"Where's your mother?" I asked, trying to ignore the fact she just called me an idiot in front of half the town.

"On the *roof!*" My mom's lips made the noise of a horse as she huffed hot air. "Well, at least she *was* before you *screamed at her*!" The shrillness of her voice overwhelmed me, and I started to cry.

"No!" I said, clutching my ears.

"DJ!" my mom grabbed my wrists and forced my hands down away from my face. "Listen to me! Why else would I not get mad about someone being on my roof? Are you insane!"

"Wait," I paused, trying to untangle my ginormous knitting ball of thoughts. "Why is she living on our roof? If she's been here all along, why hasn't she visited?"

"She's probably off her meds and thinks she's that other persona of hers." My mom slapped her hands against her spandex-clad thighs. They jiggled from the motion.

"Uh…" Megan began, "I don't mean any offense, but *why* is she not in prison…or Mexico?"

Everyone turned and looked at each other in confusion, murmuring among themselves. The smell from the toilet had totally overpowered all of the barbequed meat by this point, and a wave of nausea flushed through me.

"DJ," my mom began, refusing to answer Megan's question or the murmurs, "do you have to dump off *everyone* you shouldn't?"

Officer Pete was trying to wake Sanchez with a smelling salt. I tried to focus on that instead of my mom yelling at me. I remembered when I had to have one of those used on me before. It was deep in my memory bank, back when I was younger and Rochelle "accidentally" punched me in the face while claiming to practice her boxing skills…as usual.

"DJ!" my mom's voice broke through the flashback.

"Yeah?" I asked, fiddling with my fingers and still caught in the confusion between reality and my daydreams.

"Are you even *listening* to me?"

"…yeah."

"She's probably going to have it out for all of us now. DJ, do you realize that you did an *entire* assignment on her, that *you* got her thrown into prison, and now you just yelled at her?"

"I'm sorry for making your mom mad," I told her, not knowing what else to say.

My mom groaned. "Ugh. Why do people have to be *bad moms?*" My mom brought her hands to her temples, scrubbing her face. I almost choked on the irony of that statement. But I had already pushed it way past my limits. And even I knew better than to say something snarky to that.

"Let's just hope she doesn't show back up." Shrugging, I

tried to act like it wasn't a big deal.

And with everything my mom reminded me of, I hoped for everyone, but especially *my* sake, that that was true.

It had been about a week with no sightings of Beverly. I had wished on a shooting star like they do in the movies that she wouldn't be mad at us. Rochelle had caught me doing it outside, and said that I was dumb.

"First of all," she had told me, hiking a bag of trash up over her shoulder, "that's an airplane, *not* a shooting star, you moron. Second—she's probably not showing up because she's planning her *revenge.*"

The hair on my neck turned all prickly, like a porcupine drenched in sweat.

"No, sir," I murmured. My denial was so weak that *I* didn't even believe the words.

"Whatever you say, Dennis." Rochelle let out a slow, descending whistle then tossed the garbage into the trash can.

Meanwhile, my mom hadn't talked to me *once* since we had seen her mom on the roof. I had apologized at least ten times by now, thinking she must really be mad at me over my little meltdown on the Fourth. But she wasn't really talking to anybody. Except for her clients, that was. She had been hanging out in her room, giving herself manicures and pedicures, and watching Chinese soap operas. Why did they even call them that? What did they have to do with cleaning *or* singing? Nothing. Absolutely nothing.

I knocked on her door.

She didn't talk directly to me when I poked my head in. Well, I mean she did. But all she said was, "Go milk Ol' Bessie."

I didn't even know if she knew it was me standing there,

but something deep down told me that she did. She told us countless times in the past that cliché, "I have eyes in the back of my head." I didn't think anybody ever *really* believed that. Moms just had this built in instinct or something.

I went outside in my mud boots, carrying the same old rusty pail. Bessie was standing near Beans' pen, chewing her cud anxiously. Poor soul was probably traumatized, what with the tornado and all the firework conundrums. *I'm so glad Beans missed that tornado.*

I knelt and began milking Bessie, because my mom told me to. But also because no one else did, and they would claim it was my turn anyway.

The next week *still* brought no sign of Beverly, and my mom may or may not have actually forgotten about it. I think since she was calmer, everyone else was more relaxed, too. I'd heard the saying, "If Mommy ain't happy, ain't *nobody* happy." And boy if that ain't truer than true. I clucked my tongue and shook my head just thinking about it.

A few days later, when I played beach volleyball in a sandbox area of the playground with Mama's Child, she said nothing about what had happened with our fight *or* with Beverly. I was a little annoyed. Not to dwell on things, but when I got to thinking about all that went down, I really started to wonder about whether or not she knew it was my grandma on the roof. What if instead of making up with me, she was just trying to get me in more trouble? She was very sly.

I thought she could tell I was becoming uneasy, and she may have even known it was because of her. Because she didn't even dive for the ball, and let it drop straight into the sand.

"Want to go to my mom's diner? I'll pay!" Her freckles

danced across her cheeks and eyelids as she talked, and I shrugged.

"Okay."

I didn't want to be rude, even though I hated that place. I'd never *really* eaten there or tried to enjoy it. All I could think about was the questionable meat and the whole toe jam gravy conspiracy. But I got to thinking about the diner and how Mama's Child was poor. Me eating there on her money wouldn't be helping her *or* her mom at all.

"I got a couple bucks. I can pay for my food," I offered, as we stood in the sandbox.

Mama's Child didn't have to think twice about it and agreed. She was my best friend *and* my worst enemy all in one. See, Mama's Child was like a deadly disease that you knew was going to kill you. So you lived it up while you could. It was terrible and wonderful all in its own oddly unique way.

We walked to the diner, and after hee-hawing around at a table with squeaky chairs, her mom brought us out two cheeseburgers.

Probably horse meat, I couldn't help but think. Then again…what even was Mystery Meet? Did I have a right to judge? I didn't want to eat the cheeseburger, but I didn't want to insult her. She knew I was a big eater, and she would definitely be insulted if I didn't eat at least *half* of it. Mama's Child had that sly smirk on her face, and I just eyed her suspiciously.

"What's wrong, DJ?" she asked, sounding a bit offended.

I picked up my cheeseburger and took a bite. It actually wasn't *terrible.* "Oh, I'm just thinking about something else." I waved a dismissive hand before reaching for a napkin to dab at the ketchup on my chin.

"What are you thinking about that's annoying you so

much?" she snapped.

I straightened in my seat. *What had my face done?* Or what had it revealed? "Oh, just that crazy lady walking down the street," I lied, pointing at Crazy Lady. She was almost a tourist site for this town. Nobody knew her, but she always walked around the streets, acting crazy. Hence the name.

"Hmm." Mama's Child grunted, sipping on her soda.

Something told me she didn't believe me.

Chapter 26

IT WAS THE MOST beautiful day of the summer. July thirtieth. The sun was shining, birds were chirping, and best of all—a family day trip to the beach! It didn't get any better than that, folks. I hadn't been to the beach before, but I knew it had to be awesome. I put a T-shirt and a pair of shorts over my one-piece swimsuit and packed a sand shovel and beach ball in a bag. The bag also had a bottle of water and some sunscreen in it, because you couldn't be too careful! I gots to plan for these things! Or bad stuff might happen.

My mom saw me carrying my huge bag and said we had to share bags because they would take up too much space in the cars. So I had to share with Krissy and Dominique.

"Don't pack a lot," I told them. *This shouldn't be too hard,* I thought. *After all, they store everything in their underpants.*

"Okay!" they affirmed in unison.

When we got to the beach, I tried to find my bag in the car. But I couldn't beneath the others. They were all packed to the brim and spilling over. I knew that the bags left couldn't be *my* bag because I had told them to pack light. The other kids and my mom grabbed for their bags like they were free donuts.

"What are you waiting for?" Kriss and Dom asked while I just stood out of the way, trying to avoid being trampled by the stampede that was my family.

"Must not have brought our bag." I bit my lip and went over all the things that could go wrong in my head.

Hot sun equaled sunburn. Sunburn equaled skin cancer. Skin cancer equaled death.

"That's our bag." They pointed at the remaining overflowing bag. I yelled at them for packing so much, and then they did the *unspeakable* and dumped everything out onto the ground. Our belongings were getting all sandy. There would be sand everywhere. My nerves tangled into one big bundle, and I wrung my fingers, blinking rapidly to try to calm down.

Sand in your clothes. Sand in your water. You could drink that and die.

I shook my head.

You will never be able to get rid of all the sand. You will be cleaning it out for days, and it will never go away.

"Aghh!!!" I groaned, even though I didn't mean to. I grabbed my head and tried to control my raging thoughts. My brain was like an overloaded circuit board.

Krissy and Dominique frowned at me and muttered, "Freak."

"And she thought *I* was the loser," Krissy told Dominique.

"Yes, she did. Yes, she did," Dominique answered, speaking in typical *Krissy* formation.

"Dennis June, are you seriously throwing a tantrum already?" my mom hissed. "You are too old for this crap. It's embarrassing. Let's go."

I stood there trying to take deep breaths and stared down

at the bag with its spilled contents. Everything was touching the sand, and the sand was touching everything. *It was touching everything.* Whatever was happening to me, it wasn't a *tantrum.*

Krissy picked up my sunscreen, and Dominique picked up theirs, then they took off the cap of mine, and squirted a big glop into both of their mouths. My stomach heaved, and I tasted bile sludging up my throat.

"No!" I shrieked. "You are both going to get toxic poisoning!"

They were going to die.

Their laughter flooded my eardrums, and the world swirled. I was lightheaded.

They were going to die, and here they were mocking me about it.

Squirting more sunscreen into their mouths, they took one gulp after another.

"You're stupid, Dennis!" Dom snickered. Then they ran. They took my sunscreen with them, and they left me to pick up all of their crap. All of their crap that was covered in *sand,* all of their crap that *I didn't even pack.*

My skin was starting to get tingly from the sun, and I was white as a sheet. I tried to shove everything back into the bag, but got even *more* sand everywhere.

Someone had tripped over me, and my temper was about to go off.

"Ow!" I whimpered more obnoxiously than I needed to.

I turned around to give them a piece of my mind, thinking it was some dumbturd, but it was Marcus Delon. I gasped in disbelief. Embarrassment flooded every fiber of my being, and I instantly regretted my nasally, snarky "ow" and my childish outburst.

"Oh, I'm sorry." Marcus's eyes shifted uncomfortably. "I

didn't see you there, DJ. I didn't know you were coming to the beach today."

I stood, brushing the sand off me, but it just stuck like glue to my unfortunately sweaty skin. While I was trying to think of something to say, purple fingernail-clad hands shoved into me. And for once, they didn't belong to my mother.

"You *hear* that?" Katrina snickered. "He didn't even *see you.*"

What the dump was she even doing here?

I snapped and screeched at my mom, who was practically a beached whale on the sand. I called her by her first name, and her head whipped around one hundred and eighty degrees like an owl waking from a disrupted slumber. Stumbling to her feet and sand flying everywhere, she charged up the hill. I shrieked and tried to make a run for it, abandoning Marcus Delon, that terrible Katrina, *and* the sandy bag. But I was too slow. She spanked me right there in front of everyone. Including Marcus Delon.

Both sets of my cheeks were burning red. Actually, pretty much every part of me was burning red, from the *sun.* I was still tingling, and all the fears of developing skin cancer flooded through my brain. But seeing Katrina covering her mouth and laughing, looking like the perfect model in her pink bikini, I remembered I had never told my mom why I was mad at her in the first place.

Despite the spanking, I held my ground.

"What the dump did you do?" I demanded. "Did you invite their dumps? You know how much I hate that *raccoon eater!*"

Marcus Delon stayed right where he was, totally astounded. My mom placed her hand over my mouth and leaned down to my level. I groaned and turned away from her giant chest, wondering why on *earth* she had worn a purple, zebra-striped bikini.

"I invited them to *impress* them," she gritted into my ear.

I jerked away. "Well, ya better have invited the Greens too! I can't deal with that raccoon eater without my best friend, Monica!"

My mom rolled her eyes. "Monica isn't your friend," she gritted through her clenched teeth. "You don't *have* any friends. Nobody would want to be your friend." She shoved me away from her.

Just then, Mama's Child ran up the beach in her black and white striped onesie that was probably a million years old. I pinched myself for judging because she was poor, and I wasn't any better off than she was. My mom was already storming off, discarding me like I was trash. Feeling absolutely humiliated, I approached Mama's Child and asked her to go to the bathroom with me.

"Didn't you just get here?" she asked, clearly oblivious to what had just happened.

"I had three jumbo iced teas in the car on the way over," I muttered under my breath.

"Huh?" She wrinkled up her nose, which was completely littered with freckles by this point. So much so, they were overlapping each other.

"Mom insists nothing goes to waste."

"Fine," she finally agreed. I let myself do a quick and silent cry in the stall, then took a wazz. Because, well, I was already in there, and I'd never pee in the ocean. What if something would swim up inside me? I shuddered just thinking about it. The beach was nothing like I expected.

We walked out of the bathroom (after I washed my hands, obviously) and went down with everyone by the ocean. Krissy and Dominique were throwing away my sunscreen bottle. That thing had been completely full.

"You guys are going to be poisoned!" I hollered at them again.

They laughed.

"What is *wrong* with you guys? Don't you know that could kill you?"

"Quit being a poophead, DJ." Dom laughed.

"Yeah, DJ." Krissy backed up Dom, rarely having anything original to say. "It's *vanilla pudding.*"

"It most certainly was not!" I scolded them. I didn't care that I wasn't their boss. Or their mom. Or even their real sister, for that matter.

"We dumped out your sunscreen," Dom said.

"Dom filled it with pudding!" Krissy added, rubbing her stomach and closing her eyes.

"Mmmm," they both sighed.

"Mom!" I yelled.

"She's telling!" Dom announced.

"Tattle tale." Krissy rolled her eyes.

"Am not." I scoffed. "Mom! Can I borrow your sunscreen?"

"Everyone else used it. Ain't none left." She groaned, not even bothering to roll over. I just had to stand there and stare at her big booty that was in a swimsuit two sizes too small. It was getting all tanned and leathery.

"Looks like I'm gonna roast today!" I raised my hands up in the air and slapped them back down dramatically.

A few hours later, the Greens showed up at the beach, and Monica came over to inform me of what I already knew —that I was *badly* sunburnt. I didn't need the reminder; my brain was already reminding me enough.

Katrina put in her unneeded and unasked-for two cents. "You should've put on sunscreen, like our family.

Especially with your fair complexion."

I mocked her words over and over again in my head and didn't answer her. I'd probably just embarrass myself again.

Monica played in the ocean with all the other kids while Mama's Child and I built a sandcastle. Well, more accurately a sand *trailer*. But that was okay. A wet slap of sludge hit me, and I whipped around. It stung in a salty way, and I knew it was moist. Frogster was picking up sand and chucking it at things. I held in my rage. But then she hit me with another drenched clump, and it landed right in my hair.

"A good dip in the ocean will wash 'er right off!" Mama's Child said, trying to calm me down.

So we ran out into the ocean. Mama's Child and I kept going in deeper and deeper, yelling and laughing.

"Let's play shark attack, Denny! Let's see who can swim farther! If anyone yells, it's just 'cause they're *cheering you on*."

Mama's Child gave me her Cheshire Cat grin, and the water *was* pulling me. So I went along with it. I kept swimming until uneasiness flooded me, and when I turned around, I didn't see Mama's Child. I flapped wildly, trying to find her, fearing she had drowned. But then my eyes caught sight of a flash of red perm. Her kinky curls were sticking up in all directions, and that stinker was standing on *the beach*. She wasn't even in the water! What the dung?

"Shark!" Mama's Child yelled, and an adrenaline rush coursed through my veins. I paddled and paddled, swimming back for my life. Out of breath, I crawled onto the shore and made my way over to Mama's Child. I rose to my feet, feeling on the verge of collapsing.

"Just kidding!" Mama's Child chuckled. "Ya should've seen how fast you swam!"

I stared at her in silence for a second, and her grin

disappeared.

I punched her right in the face, and blood trickled out of her nose. Maybe I *do* need therapy.

"I'm sorry!" I cried, reeling back. I blinked a million times in the few seconds it took her to respond, panicking.

"I forgive you, Den." Mama's Child grabbed her nose, blood dripping onto the sand.

"That's it!" my mom screeched, sand flying everywhere as she stomped toward us, her flip flops going all *clickety clack, wet slap!*

"You two are staying out of the ocean."

Sitting beside my mom, feeling like her prisoner, I panted in the hot sun. The salt on my skin made the sun burn me even more, and I begged my mom to let us go home.

"We are still trying to impress people, DJ." She just tossed an umbrella at me.

"It ain't raining," I blurted.

She whipped her head back around and rolled her eyes up into her skull, then placed her hands on her temples and said, "You sit under it. It gives you *shade.*"

"Oh."

"Sometimes you are the stupidest thing I ever did see," she groaned, flopping back down onto her beach towel.

Mama's Child opened the umbrella, and it hit me right in the gut. I figured that made us even.

"Sorry about your nose," I told her.

"Sorry about your pot belly."

"Hey!" I whined, slapping her on the shoulder.

"Don't *do* that," she hissed. "I've got the sunburn."

"Well, so do I!" I grunted. The two of us busted out laughing then, even though nothing we joked about was really that funny.

I think the sun was finally starting to work its damages

on us.

Chapter 27

MY MOM SIGNED ME up for therapy. She was dumped because she had to pay for it, and she said that she was actually going to keep a tab of how much my therapy cost. Said it was a hundred dollars a session that she didn't have. Well, uh, neither did I?

My mom had never signed any of us up for therapy before. She only agreed because Mama's Child's mom said that she wouldn't press charges if I went to therapy. Her mom had really flown off the handle about her nose, despite Mama's Child's forgiveness *and* my apology.

You can't tell them anything about home, I remembered my mom telling me. How the dump was therapy going to help me if I couldn't talk about anything? I didn't wanna go in the first place.

I walked into the Better Future Therapeutics building, chewing on my lip and pulling at loose strings on my overalls. It smelled like fresh paint in here, and I worried that maybe I would hallucinate or get a toxicity from breathing in the fumes. Part of me wanted to ask them when they had it painted and if there was lead in it. Something was on the news about that, once. It killed people. They died. I didn't want to die.

A tall man with curly red hair exited a room and motioned for me to come to him. I didn't know him. Stranger danger. I knew I was as curious as a cat, and a little bad at socializing, but I knew not to go somewhere alone with a man I didn't know.

"You look like my friend Mama's Child," I told him, and he blinked awkwardly before looking away.

"This is Dennis," my mother told him.

"Of course, I'm your therapist. Your doctor, kid." He smiled at me.

My mom's pupils dilated, and the corners of her mouth curled up.

"Stop," I whispered to my mom.

"Excuse me?" she muttered through her smile, giving me the side eye. She looked like one of them puppet talking people. What were they called? A ventriloquist? Yikes. What a mouthful.

"Don't," I gritted through my own fake smile.

"Don't what?" she asked.

I didn't know how all of this worked, but I was starting to get a few ideas and putting two and two together. "We don't need any more babies," I muttered.

She made a choking noise, and Anthony grabbed her a paper cup full of water from the dispenser beside the reception desk.

We went into his office, and it smelled delectable in there.

"Are you eating Chinese food?" I asked, sniffing the air. "Isn't this supposed to be a *therapy* session?" I wrinkled my nose at him.

"I love Chinese food and Asian history." He motioned with a thumb at the take out container on his desk.

"I'm Deniese, and I'm Chinese," my mom said, reaching her hand out to him and jutting a hip. She batted her eyelashes and said in a fake accent, "Ni hao."

He blushed. I yelled for her to stop it, and Anthony's eyes shifted between us. My mom acted like she was rubbing my back, but she reached down and gave me a slight wedgie before collecting herself and calmly saying, "Dennis is ashamed of her heritage because she is blond, like her father."

"My dad has red hair," I piped up.

"Your dad is Bob Waltzer, and he left me for Alissa while I was pregnant with my triplets," she murmured sadly, lying straight through her teeth. Bob Waltzer was not my dad. She was totally stringing along a line of donkey dung.

"It's just you, and Dennis, and the triplets?" Anthony asked, his brows inching together in concern.

My mom pouted her bottom lip and said, "Yes. We struggle for income. Where are all the *single doctors* these days?"

She slid the wedding ring my dad gave her off and put it into her pocket. I whispered to her that she was faker than her breast implants, and she muttered in my ear a threatening, "*Be good.*"

"I see you haven't remarried," he said, motioning toward her (just now) ringless hand.

"Nope. I'm bringing Dennis here because she has poor anger management and a *lying problem.* She's constantly getting in trouble at school and claiming that it 'wasn't her', when there are witnesses claiming it was."

I scoffed in disbelief and widened my eyeballs. I couldn't believe what I was hearing!

"In our family, we believe that *therapy* is the true key." Boy, was she ever laying it on thick!

"What's your last name, Deniese?" he asked.

"Chan," my mom lied. "My family moved here a while ago, and I switched back to using my maiden name. It probably still has my *married* name under my accounts."

"I understand," he told her, before looking at me in that sickening way adults patronized children and animals.

"Hey, Dennis," he spoke, like I was a *dog* that might bite him. If I wasn't so concerned about getting a disease, then I would have. "We're not gonna lie to each other. Now are we?"

I glared at him. I supposed he was attractive in a weird old man type of way. Marcus Delon was still my pick of the litter. This guy was at least thirty and looked like the type of dude my mom might be interested in. But then again, what guy *wasn't* my mom interested in? Mama's Child had just gotten my parents back together. This wasn't going to happen. My mom wasn't even Chinese, but I'd be lying if I said this was the first time she pretended to be. She actually *was* obsessed with their culture. In fact, she dyed her hair black last week, hoping to "appear more Asian." I told her to leave, so I could do my therapy.

"I think that *I* might need therapy," my mom crooned.

I glared at her.

"Oh, well I could refer you to a friend. I don't treat adults." Anthony rubbed his chin, empathizing like he was genuinely concerned.

"Oh, bummer. I feel like you could solve *a lot* of problems in my life." She began to leave, but then she turned around and pulled a piece of paper out of her bra. She wrote something with her glittery purple pen, then handed it to him.

"This is my personal cell phone number," she told him, and my jaw dropped open. "You know. In case Dennis acts up."

He took it willingly.

"Stop being a butthole," I snapped at her.

"We don't use those kinds of words, DJ," Anthony scolded me.

"You don't know *what* kind of words I use," I sneered back at him.

"Well, I can see why she's always getting herself in trouble."

My mom nodded in agreement.

I slapped the desk, then shrieked because my hand was burning. He gave her his card and said his name and number were on there.

"Oh, Anthony," my mom said, reading the card. "What an exotic name."

Exotic? I nearly gagged. Anthony was about as run-of-the-mill as Dennis was.

"Can I call you Tony?" my mom asked.

I frowned at her.

"You can call me anything you please." He smiled and placed his hand on her back as he escorted her to the door and held it open. Then he shut it to begin our session.

Well, let me just tell ya something, I *didn't like Anthony!*

Because Anthony? More like *An-phony.*

My third session with Anthony would be this Friday. My first session didn't go well at all. I had been so shook up by my mom's flirting, and not being sure of what exactly I *was* allowed to talk about that I couldn't. So I barely spoke five sentences, seven at most. But I still paid very close attention to details, and I used that session to ground myself. The walls were painted two entirely different colors, and the inconsistency bothered me. A paper weight shaped like an elephant rested on his desk. A cheesy couch that I had to lay on stood against one wall. You know, the kind you think are made up and surely don't exist in the real world. But they do. And he had one.

A poster on the wall with a cat on it stated, *"Hang in there, baby!"* and I found it patronizing. But the cat was cute, so naturally my eyes kept drifting to it. He didn't like that I avoided most of his questions and responded with entirely brief answers. Anthony hadn't *said* he was upset, but I could tell. He was judging me with his glasses-clad eyes.

When my mom picked me up, they flirted again. It really irritated me, but they both toned it down a little at my second session. During that one, I had spent the entire time complaining about school starting soon and how I was not having the best summer ever, like I had planned. I was big on planning. I had to have plans. Anthony listened and didn't say much. It was kind of like we switched roles, except that I wasn't asking him intrusive questions. He did seem to be glad I was talking with him though.

A few days after that session, Mama's Child showed up at my door, knocking wildly and yelling, "Denny!"

I answered the door, and it turned out she just wanted to play. So we did. We walked to the playground, and she told me that we hadn't updated TownSpy in a while.

"Well, what do you wanna write about?" I asked, looking around. It was pretty sad for it to be a summer day. Nobody was even outside but us.

"How about Beverly Hill? It would stir the pot!"

"Mama's Child!" I hissed, stopping in my tracks. She stopped too. I made a shush face at her, but she pulled my finger down.

"You know I hate bein' shushed, Den!" she twanged.

"My grandma hasn't made a single squeak since the Fourth of July, and I'd like to keep it that way." I sighed deeply, worry settling in.

"It's *just* TownSpy, Denny." Mama's Child clucked her tongue like I was being dramatic. But her playing around, meddling as "*just TownSpy*," was enough to break up two marriages and get my parents back together. Unless, of course, something happened with this Anthony guy. I crossed my fingers and muttered a silent prayer that nothing would come of it.

When we returned home from the park, Mama's Child asked if she could stay the night, and my mom actually *let* her. We stayed up into the a.m. hours watching TV on Disney Channel and singing along to the songs in the movie (even though we didn't know the words very well because we rarely got to watch what *we* wanted to). I had no idea if she even had a television at home. I'd never been to her house. We were laughing about something that happened on the show when Mama's Child got quiet all of a sudden.

"Hey, Den?"

"Yeah?" I asked, taking a bite of cereal. Mama's had finished her bowl about ten minutes ago, and mine was starting to get soggy. I needed to eat faster.

"'Member that time you got kicked in the face?" Then she started laughing again, but I didn't. She stopped and hesitated, probably thinking I was offended. But then we both bursted into a full fit of giggles because it actually *was* a teeny bit funny now.

The next day was boring because Mama's Child went home really early, and my family just sat around all day. Or at least I did. I wondered why the dump she had abandoned me to boredom. It was a sleepover! You were supposed to stay late into the evening the next day. That was the way it was supposed to work, right? I didn't know why I was even pretending I knew what I was talking about. Mama's Child was the only friend I'd ever had!

Today was the day of my therapy session. Walking into the office and into the counseling room, I was glad that my mom was busy and had to just do a drive by drop off. Practically started driving off before I was half out the car door.

"How are you, DJ?" Anthony asked, leaning back in his chair.

I flopped down on the couch. "Uh, not very good."

"Why?"

I rolled my eyes. Why did he always want to know "*why*"? He was worse than Krissy and Dom. "I have to go back to school soon, and the last couple of days were pretty boring."

"And that upsets you *that* much?"

I didn't like his tone.

"Yes. I hate school!" I rolled my eyes again. Who actually *liked* school?

"DJ. Why so much hatred toward school?"

"'Cause it's dumb!" I complained.

"Why?"

I was about to go off on him, but he continued, "You're actually pretty smart, looking at your transcript. That makes me think you would like school. Why do you think it's '*dumb*'?" He rubbed his chin like he always did when he was trying to figure out my entire life story in one session.

"Uh, because. Sanchez hates me. I have a couple of friends, *if* you could even call them that. That's about it. The boy I like doesn't like me, and then there's Katrina. Ugh!" I groaned and slapped my hands down on the leather seat with a *slap.*

"Okay. Well, um, that doesn't sound very fun."

Okay, well, um, that didn't sound like a legit medical professional *response.*

"How do you know that the teacher hates you and that this boy doesn't like you?"

"Everyone says so."

"Okay—"

I cut him off. It was my turn to talk. "—I'm not finished! Sanchez always gives me a cheap, crappy workbook. Then she blames me for stuff that other people do—"

He cut me off. "DJ."

"...yeah?"

"Your mom says that you *say* others blame you, but that's not necessarily what happens."

That really boiled my clams. How was I supposed to get any help out of this if he wasn't going to believe a word I said?

"Whose session is this anyway?" I snapped. "Last time I checked I thought it was mine, and—"

"—hey, watch the anger please. Calm down."

I took in a deep breath, still feeling the fury.

He completely ignored this and glanced at his clock. "Well, it looks like our session is about up."

"Good." I sat up on the couch.

"DJ, do you not *like* these sessions?" He raised a judgy eyebrow at me and folded his hands.

"No. I'd like to spend my time doing stuff that is fun because summer is almost over." *Not to mention that you are convinced I am a liar, and that everything is my fault. You are no different from any other person I've dealt with. Why would I want to talk to* you?

"Okay. Well, you can leave now." He shook his head and

scribbled some stuff down on his clipboard. Probably a bunch of lies saying that *I* was evil, and a liar, and overly moody. Oh, and that my mom was actually an angel, and Mrs. Sanchez was a saint.

"Bye," I said, not even looking back as I stood and exited his office.

I walked home and was nearly out of breath from it when I called Mama's Child. She answered instead of her mom, and that made me feel at least a little better.

"MC!" I yelled.

"Yah?" she blurted rudely.

"It's me, DJ," I clarified.

Her voice brightened instantly. "Denny! How was therapy, bud?"

"Crappy, but not too bad, I guess."

"Well, what's up?"

"I'm bored," I droned in a monotone. "Can you come over?"

She didn't answer immediately, so I pretended to be sobbing.

"Okur," she slurred. "Be there in five."

I turned off the crocodile tears and bared my teeth in an awkward smile.

She came over, and we ate some potato chips. Then we went to the park again and played on the slides and then the swings. As we were swinging, we were quiet. I reached out and grabbed her hand. She scrunched her nose. Mama's Child had a thing about physical affection. It had to be her idea, or it was a no-go. But she could tell I was sad, so she let me, and we swung slowly, just holding hands. Then I broke the silence.

"Hey, Mama's Child?" I squeaked, my voice cracking as it threatened to break.

"Yah?" she blurted in her accent.

I focused on the ground, avoiding eye contact. "Do you think I'm a bad person?"

She slowed her swing by placing her feet in the dirt, and it made us both come to a swinging stop. She looked at me. "Sometimes."

I winced at the hurtful remark, and Mama's Child registered it.

"Bein' honest, Den."

"Thanks," I told her, giving her a half smile. Even if it hurt, at least she wasn't being fake. Then I continued, "Do you think I'm a liar?"

"I did at first, but not anymore." She shrugged, her eyes returning to the ground.

This made my hopes build up a little higher. "I'm so glad you passed and we're in the same grade," I told her.

"Me too." She kicked off the ground, and I followed her lead. We both started to slowly swing again. It was quiet for a while before either of us spoke, and the sun was starting to set in front of us. I glanced over in Mama's Child's direction and studied her as she closed her eyes, basking in the dying rays. She was so peaceful and carefree, and the breeze was blowing her curly 'fro.

"Hey, Mama's?" I whispered.

"Yeah?" She hadn't even opened her eyes.

"You're my best friend."

"Mine too, Den. Mine too."

Chapter 28

THE FIRST DAY OF SCHOOL was the worst. Somehow my dad had spilled lasagna sauce inside my mother's purse. It put her into a totally horrid mood, which wasn't good for anybody. I knew I should've been triggered about the fact she was in a bad mood, but I was more focused on the fact lasagna was in this house, and I didn't know about it. And secondly—who the *dump* in their right mind ate lasagna for *breakfast?* My stomach lurched just thinking about it. That was just unnatural. Breakfast was reserved for strictly breakfast foods, with the single exception of cold pizza. And even *that* was iffy.

My mom stormed past me, looking madder than a hornet.

"Is that sauce stain gonna come out?" I asked.

"Shut up. I have to take a wazz," she grumbled, peering at me through mascara-goopy eyes. It was clear she hadn't taken it off before bed, and her normally perfect hair was standing up in all directions. As she walked past where I was pouring a bowl of cereal, she slapped me across the face with her greasy breakfast burrito.

"Now git!" she shooed, waving the burrito at me. "Y'all are ruining my favorite day of the year."

I wiped some mushy beans off my cheek and gave her the stank face.

At school, a huge cluster of people swarmed into the one room classroom. Mrs. Sanchez was dumped off the minute she walked in. She immediately told us to shut up and sit down, then she went on a rant about how we needed to have a better understanding of the French Revolution. Mrs. Sanchez had not been impressed with our essays last year and was apparently still mad about it. I was just as ticked off as everyone else. There was literally *no* call for learning about this every single year.

"Hey, guess what?" Rochelle yelled from the back, cupping her hands around her mouth.

"What?" Sanch snapped.

"Let them eat cake!" Rochelle screeched.

Sanch didn't even turn around to snarl, "DJ! Demerit!"

It really boiled my clams that she didn't even think *once* before yelling at me. My first demerit, on the first day of school. Plus everyone knew Marie Antoinette had not said that. It was a misunderstood quote that never happened and Mrs. Sanchez's most annoying pet peeve. She discussed that with us every year.

"This classroom is too hot. I'm due to have this baby in a month. This is ridiculous."

"You're pregnant?" asked Stephanie.

"I'm surprised you didn't figure it out a long time ago." Mrs. Sanchez rolled her eyes.

I wiggled my eyebrows at Mama's sitting across the room. Ol' Sanch had chosen to keep us drastically separated this year.

"I did!" Mama's hollered. A couple of people told her she was lying or scoffed. But I knew the truth, and *she did call it.*

"We just thought you were getting fatter." Rochelle laughed.

Mrs. Sanchez gave *me* another demerit for "saying" that, when I hadn't. I fidgeted in my seat and wanted to throw a temper tantrum, but resisted. My rage was fuming, and I didn't know what would bother me more—if I honestly *sounded* like Rochelle, or if Sanchez just didn't care and blamed me anyways. It was a good thing I'd be seeing Anthony tonight because this needed to be addressed. I rolled my eyes and shook my head bitterly in Rochelle's direction.

At lunch we were having brunch for lunch. Mama's Child and I had counted on our fingers to make sure we'd get the same lunch table I sat at all the previous years, in hopes of good luck for this year. It warmed my heart that she hadn't questioned my theories in the slightest and agreed to sit at the exact same table. Something bad might happen if I didn't. So I sat down in my casual, usual seat at my casual, usual lunch table. All was well until I spilled my food on my outfit and asked Mama's Child to help me clean it up. When she leaned over though, she knocked over her maple syrup, and it splashed into my hair.

"This is the worst first day of school *ever!*" I yelled, slamming my tray down and groaning.

"I told ya, Denny." Mama's Child shook her head at me and slurred, "You should really think of gettin' a hat like mine to protect yer hair."

My eyes immediately rose to her annoying pink munchkin hat that she had found last year. The one that she blessed at my Dad's Christmas dinner. I dismissed the immediate urge to yell at her and cooled down. She was one of my only friends, so I had to keep her close. Nevertheless, smoke threatened to come out of my nostrils. Anthony told me that I had to learn to control my temper, but how was I supposed to do that when ignoramuses flourished in *every* corner? I turned my thoughts elsewhere.

The bell rang while I was in the bathroom, washing the maple syrup out of my hair, so I was late to class. Sanchez was literally going to murder me, and it was going to be as bloody as Marie Antoinette's beheading.

The class was surprisingly in the middle of arts and crafts, and Sanch told us we could draw whatever we wanted, so I drew a picture for Anthony that clearly demonstrated the anger of this day. I told Mrs. Sanchez I was taking the picture home for my anger management therapist, and she said that she approved.

"Thanks," I told her, but then she sniffed the air.

"I meant I approve of you being in *therapy*. I think all of you Tippers should be institutionalized."

I almost lost it, but I breathed in and held it for ten seconds before letting it out like Anthony had taught me to. It soothed me a little. Personally, I believed it was the placebo effect. I told him so, and he had asked me how I even knew that word, to which I responded, "Don't worry about it, *dump hole*."

Remembering that day, I reflected on how he had warned me to watch it and I remembered to be nice. So I had apologized, and he just said, "A nice Dennis makes a happy Dennis." That was about the stupidest thing I'd ever done heard. It should be: "A *happy* Dennis makes a *nice* Dennis."

When I went to my session, I told Anthony about all of the dump that ticked me off today at school. He asked me, "How bad was it?"

"Don't even ask me about it." I groaned dramatically, taking a seat at an old rickety school desk. I hadn't noticed it before and considered asking if the old thing was new. It seemed slightly more normal than lying on the couch.

"Okay. We don't have to talk about it."

I widened my eyes. Excuse me? "Oh, we are *going* to dumping talk about it," I snapped.

"Language," he said flatly, looking back down at his clipboard and writing.

I just nodded and told him about all the dumb crap that made me mad.

Several minutes later, when I had finished, he got up, stretched, and claimed that my session was over.

Ahem! It was *not* over. "I think you've been jipping me on time, Anthony."

"I'm sorry?" He braced his hands on his desk and leaned toward me.

"I'm smart. I have an A+ in English." Before I could finish, he reached for a piece of paper that I assumed was my transcript, a need to prove I wasn't lying. "And before you even start on me, I only have a C- in math because Mrs. Sanchez hates me. I can tell time, though, Anthony. I'm not dumb." I stood and slapped my desk.

"DJ, people that can't tell time are not dumb. That is offensive."

I sighed. "I didn't mean it like *that*. I meant in general. And you are wasting my time for clarification purposes." I rolled my eyes.

"I'm sorry. I'll give you your full session time from now on."

I don't know why it was so important to me, but it was. I liked having a schedule and sticking to it.

"Promise?" I murmured weakly, suddenly self-conscious of my insecurities.

"Scout's honor." He raised a hand to his heart, and the

other in the air. I thought that was a dumb thing to say, but I kept talking. I told him how Mama's Child made me mad at school by spilling maple syrup in my hair, which made me tardy. He gave me a funny look.

"You need to be *nice* to her, DJ." His disapproving scowl made me sink down in my seat.

"Look, I didn't yell at her. I held in my rage because she is one of my only friends."

"Good for you."

"She is my *best* friend."

"Good for you," he said again, and I was beginning to get the impression he didn't like me and that his comment was purposely meant to sound snarky. I told myself it was probably just in my head and brushed it to the backburner of my brain.

"Oh!" I exclaimed, trying to change the subject. I had seen other people use that communication tactic, and I thought maybe it was the normal way to socialize. By changing the subject. "I drew you a picture today!" Unfolding the piece of paper I had crammed in my shorts pocket (which was still stained from my brunch for lunch mishap), I shoved it toward him.

"Oh. Why, you look very mad in this drawing." He frowned at the paper, which was of me. I had colored flames in my eyes and steam coming out of my ears. His judgment caused my heart to sink.

"Well, that's cause I *was* mad, but I let out my anger through drawing."

He yawned. "That sounds beneficial."

"It was, until someone else made me mad again."

He furrowed his eyebrows, his eyes judging me. "What? Who made you mad?"

"Katrina. She told me that I need to improve my drawing

skills, and that the drawing made me look like I was constipated. And that my person was wearing too much blush." I stewed over the memory again, and it irritated me.

"And Katrina is…?" I gasped. How *dare* he?

"The girl I *loathe!* I've told you this. Come on! Keep up please!" I clapped my hands in his face.

"Well, at least you said please."

"Sorry."

"That's okay."

We were both quiet for a few seconds, before my second wave of anger came on.

"She annoys me! She always outdoes me at everything. Literally! The only thing that *I* got going for me is that I'm smarter than she is, and I can play the tambourine." I pouted.

"You play the tambourine? That's nice." He glanced at his clock.

"Yeah." I shrugged.

"That's something."

I gave him a half smile. "Well, not to brag, but I'm pretty freaking good at it too," I murmured.

"Good, sounds like something you can enjoy and be happy doing."

"Yeah. I'm glad Katrina quit the band."

"She was in the band?"

"She was last year. Until she decided there were no cool kids in it."

"Oh." Anthony tapped his pen on his clipboard.

"Yep."

"What do you want to talk about now? There are five minutes left in your session."

I put my chin in my hand and twisted my mouth around, thinking about it. "The demerits."

"Okay."

"Do you believe me when I say I didn't get them *myself?*"

"Well…" He covered up a smirk, and it really rubbed me the wrong way.

"You don't?" I asked, glaring at him.

"Well, it's just that—"

"—you don't!" I stood, and I knew I shouldn't have, but I flipped the small desk over. "You're my dumping *therapist.* You're supposed to believe everything *I* say!" I stabbed at my chest with my finger. Then I started crying because he yelled at me for flipping the desk.

"I, I'm sorry I upset you," he stammered, walking around his desk and placing a hand on my shoulder. I slapped his arm and told him I did *not* accept his apology.

Anthony gave me a packaged cookie and apologized again. It felt like he just did it so I'd stop crying before my mom got here. I accepted the cookie, though, and placed it in my pocket for safe-keeping. He was at least on the right track.

"Adults don't always tell the truth either, you know. I honestly didn't get those demerits."

"Okay, DJ. I believe you." Anthony's mouth wobbled, possibly fighting a smile.

"Good." I scoffed. It was about darn time, even if I wasn't totally convinced I believed *him.*

Feeling embarrassed, I slowly picked the desk back up and set it upright. Tucking a stray piece of hair behind my ear, I apologized again.

"No need, it happens all the time." Anthony showed me the dents in the desk, so I could believe him on at least *this.*

After therapy, I went home and took a nice nap. But I had weird dreams at first. Like Mama's Child's hat becoming super popular. Everyone had one but me, and I was so depressed over it. I woke and reached for the packaged cookie. Downing it in just a few bites, I rubbed my stomach and murmured, "Mmmmmmmm," to myself. Not caring if I got yelled at, I resorted to my favorite napping place—the base of the stairs. I curled up into a ball and snoozed away. Happy dreams this time. Dreams of a big, chunky, warm, and gooey chocolate chip cookie.

Dumb, dumber, and dumbest was what ran through my brain when I was sitting in Sanchez's class. The stuff we were learning was *way* beneath my intelligence. *Poor Mama's Child,* I thought, as she sat there looking all confuzzled.

We were going to have to act out a scene of the French Revolution. Normally, we learned this at the end of the year. But Sanch thought we were dumb, and it was for a theater class Mama's Child and I signed up for after school. Mama's Child sat next to me, told me to ignore *"Les Mis,"* and think outside the box. I didn't even know what that was, but the older kids were talking about it and how they were going to act out scenes from it.

MC wanted us to do a guillotine scene. I told her under no circumstances would I act out the part of the person that had to go in it. It wasn't like I trusted her to know how to work it properly. And besides, no one who grinned and said, "I want to do the *hacking*," should be in control of one of those things.

"I just *really* wanna chop someone's head off!" said Mama's Child. She laughed before reddening and saying, "I'm just kidding, Denny."

I wasn't so sure if she *was* "just kidding."

That girl really gave me the creeps sometimes.

Sanch droned on about the assignment and had her eyes

peeled to me and MC. She didn't even want to let us in the theater club in the first place, and she was always making it a point to tell us how lucky we were to be here *every day.*

"You know, you two are really lucky to be in here." Sanch grimaced, as if on cue.

I ignored her rude comment, used to them by now. Wanting to be theater president this semester, even though it was my first being in here, I scoped out the competition and discovered that Monica was in here too. Everyone was mumbling about what a change this assignment was from the *Nutcracker* productions and scenes they performed and practiced each year. Some kid I didn't know called Monica "Mon-ick-a," and she told them it was pronounced "Monique-ah." I rolled my eyes. The *audacity.* Some people! Mrs. Sanchez nodded at Monica in approval and gave her a gold star, because apparently her name was french. Weird.

Mama's and I discussed and prepared our act before deciding on using a mannequin head from my mom's beauty parlor. Mama's Child would have me lie down and tuck my head into my shirt, placing the mannequin's head first into the guillotine. This would make it look like my head was getting chopped without either of us getting harmed. Then we could return the mannequin head without it being damaged.

We would have to present this skit in two weeks, and I was so nervous! Mama's Child claimed since I would have my head tucked in my shirt, my nerves would go away. She had a bigger part than me, but I didn't mind. It wasn't really one of those things where one part was bigger and better than the other, if you asked me. I had double the anxiety as it was. It would be at least a week before I found out if I made theater president, and I couldn't stop wondering if anyone voted for me. Sanchez probably just took a long time to count the votes on purpose to freak everyone out. That was plain mean.

❖

Tomorrow we would find out who won theater president. Mama's Child and I had been practicing our act all week long. She was *really* getting into her part. Last night, we built our guillotine out of cardboard with the help of my sister Ashley. But so many people in my family said we had to keep it at Mama's Child's house because it creeped them out. Mama's Child's mom said she'd drop it off at the school for us. I didn't understand why I couldn't just go over to her house. In fact, I didn't even *know* where she lived.

Today, school was dumb again. Our band practice got canceled! I wanted to ask if I could have a tambourine solo, but now that practice wouldn't be held, I didn't know if I'd have enough time to ask the instructor before our concert. The thought of missing out on another solo made me sad and mad at the same time. So I did my deep breathing exercises. Despite my concerns, I was taking a *mandatory* break from my therapy sessions for a week or so. Anthony gave me some intellectual spiel about how he "wanted to see if I had any improvement on my own with a break from sessions." I thought he just wanted to get rid of me. *Just like everyone else who didn't like you.*

I had told him I still needed therapy, because that deep breathing mumbo jumbo didn't always help me. But he just told me to keep working on it, and if it didn't help, to come back for more sessions in addition to the follow up. As you could imagine, this made my mother both happy *and* mad. She was upset I felt I needed it because it was embarrassing to her, and she had to spend a lot of money on it. But she didn't seem mad in the slightest about seeing Anthony more.

324

I thought she finally lost interest in dating him now, but she certainly *did* enjoy flirting with him. It was like some twisted game of cat and mouse. Yuck.

At lunch, I had the wrong sandwich in my lunch box, and I took it as a bad omen. This was totally going to throw off the entire rest of my day. To my horror, my sandwich was not my favorite—PB&J. Instead, my eyes met a cold ham and swiss, and I gagged. I did *not* like swiss cheese and was not in the mood for meat. I wanted my sweet jelly goodness.

When my juice spilled on the table, I took it as confirmation that everything had been thrown off. Mama's Child tried to quote the ol' "no use crying over spilled milk" saying, and I wanted to tell her *UM, it is* juice. *Not milk.* But instead I said, "Yeah," and just nodded.

After school, I didn't invite Mama's Child over. I wanted to take a break from everyone and everything in case anything else bad happened. What if we had a major fight and became enemies again? What if my grandma showed up and exploded our house? What if I *died?* None of that would happen or be a concern if I had just had my peanut butter and jelly sandwich. I sobbed internally and shook my head at the tragedy.

This could ruin everything. This could ruin my chance at winning theater president. Just thinking about it fried my nerves like I had stuck a fork in an electrical socket. The only person I wouldn't be upset with winning over me would be Monica, because she was such a good actress. And well, she was *Monica.* How could anyone ever be mad at *her?*

Mama's Child, my other BFF, didn't even run. She ran for pretty much anything and everything, claiming it was "because she could" and "the people *loved* her." Besides Sammi, this was the only other "key" to popularity that

Mama's Child had informed me of. But she said I'd have a better chance of winning if she didn't run against me. She was such a good friend.

The next day after school, I walked into theater class. I was excited and nervous all at the same time. Mrs. Sanchez stood at the podium and was getting ready to read the votes when I took a seat beside Mama's Child.

"Hey," she whispered.

"Hey."

"And the winner of theater president is…"

I crossed my fingers. And my arms. And my legs, feet, and oh yeah—my toes. Just for extra luck.

"Orange!" yelled Sanch, clapping her hands.

My heart sank. *One time.* I just wanted to win something *one time.* People told me I had opportunities galore since I was so young, but I ain't buying it. How was I ever supposed to achieve any of my dreams if everyone hated me, thought I was invisible, or overshadowed me? At least give me a fighting chance!

"Sorry, Denny." Mama's Child leaned over and patted my arm, giving me a pathetic and pity-filled smile.

"I should've expected not to win," I whispered to her.

"True."

"But I didn't expect *Orange* to. All she ever says is 'whatever'."

"Yes, but she's very dramatic!"

"That's true." Sanchez shushed both of us.

Orange got on the little fake stage that the podium was on and acted like she was going to cry from enjoyment. I mean she really acted like she couldn't believe she won. She was so popular that I just didn't understand how she could doubt herself that much. It must have been her awesome drama skills. Thinking about my therapy junk, and what MC had said, I pushed all anger aside and clapped for her.

"What are you doing?" MC whispered, giving me a wrinkled up, disgusted face.

"I'm clapping my hands."

She scowled at me. *What?* Did she *not* just ask me what I was doing?

"That's not what I meant!" she hissed in a whisper-scream. "You don't congratulate your *competition,* Denny!"

Sometimes I didn't understand her. At times she would build me up and make me a better person, and at other times she would bring me down and get all sly. Was this how true friends *really* were? Or was Mama's Child just acting? Regardless, she was both my best *and* only friend, so I thought I'd keep her.

When the time came for Mama's Child and I to act out our skit, it actually went really well. Sanch was so impressed that she even asked if we would present it again for the whole class. I was floored. This was not what I had signed up for, but MC immediately agreed, probably longing to be in the spotlight.

When we presented in class, in front of *everybody,* I was super nervous, and because of that, I moved a little bit. It shook the cardboard and made the mannequin head fall to the floor. Everyone clapped at Sanchez's orders but with numbingly bored expressions. I reached down to pick up the head that had fallen and realized that Mama's Child had painted the neck of the mannequin red. Wanting to shriek, my brain went over about a million reasons why this was just wrong *and* disturbing. But nothing trumped the fact that she knew I had to put it back in my mom's beauty parlor.

Who would like to see a mannequin head in a beauty parlor with *red paint* dripping off its neck? Even if it had fabulous hair, I was pretty sure many people would totally freak or at least be slightly creeped out by it. I knew I would be! The sight was absolutely *sickening.*

After our performance on the way home from school, I told Mama's Child she shouldn't have painted it red without permission.

"It's okay, Denny." She said this as if it was a fact and shrugged. Now *that* really made me mad.

"How is *that* okay?" I exclaimed, stopping and staring at her. She stiffened, looking offended that I would get mad at her so quickly. But I couldn't help it!

"Because the paint washes off!" she yelled, rolling her eyes and grunting.

"It does?" I asked, a glimmer of hope forming.

"Uh, yeah! I'm not stupid."

"I'm sorry I yelled at you."

"It's fine. Let me get out the bottle to prove it to ya. I know you won't rest till I do."

"Okay."

"Oops," she said, after some careful digging in her backpack.

"What?" I asked, a wave of panic automatically returning, even though I had no idea what her "oops" meant.

"I have two things of red paint in here. The *one* was mine. I musta grabbed someone else's. I honestly don't kner which one I used on our project." Her accent was coming out thick and strong, and I took that as a bad sign.

"Are they the same?" I asked, pleading internally that they were.

"Uh, nerrp! Let's just hope I used da right one."

At my house, we tried to wash off the mannequin in the sink, but it wasn't coming off. Mama's Child apologized again when she saw my grave expression. I had to tell my mother that we borrowed it from her shop *and* we used the wrong paint on it. She gave me two options: pay for another one, or get sent to the grounded room for a couple of days. I picked to pay for a new one, hating the grounded room with a burning passion. I had about $20 saved up in my collection from Easter and other rare occasions. It would cost me $15 for a good one, or at least that's what my mom claimed. After retrieving nearly all of my life savings, I paid her for the dumb mannequin. Part of me wanted to ask MC to pay for at *least* half of it. It had been her fault, after all. But she was poor. Poorer than me, probably. Considering all of this, I let it go.

Chapter 29

MY NEXT SESSION WITH Anthony went as followed:

I told him I didn't think the deep breathing was helping as much as it should. He actually *agreed* with me. Then he told me he would show me how to make a magical ten-bead charm. We spent the start of the session collecting the beads that we liked from his jar. He started to make his first to show me how to make it. I followed suit.

"You must have a lot of these from making them with people." This time I was sitting with him at a small, round table. It was less intimidating, and I liked that.

"Not really. I would have more, but the ones I don't like that well I undo and put the beads back into the jar. I throw away the string if it's not in good enough shape to reuse."

"Oh," I responded quietly, picking up a baby blue bead that was all shiny and metallic like. I gave him the side eye as I held it in my hand, not wanting him to steal it from me just to end up disassembling it or throwing it away later. This bead was lucky. I could feel it.

"How was your day?" he asked calmly, not making eye contact.

"Pretty good today. I got a really good review for my act

the other day with Mama's Child, so that felt good. But…"

"But what?"

"But I had to pay to get a new mannequin head since we messed up the one we were using. So *that* was annoying. Then I missed the deadline, as suspected."

"The deadline?" he asked, raising an eyebrow.

"For asking for a solo on my tambourine." I strung another bead onto my line carefully, paying extremely close attention to detail so they would all be placed perfectly straight and rotated in *just* the same exact manner. They had to be in sync, or else it would just make me more mad.

"Oh. I'm sorry."

"It's fine. I didn't *totally* blow up about the mannequin head, and I was expecting the tambourine mishap. So I could prepare myself much better."

"Good." He offered me a gentle smile.

Anthony then explained how I needed to concentrate on the beads instead of the anger. That I had to count each bead, and when I got to ten, my anger should be gone. He said it may not be one hundred percent effective, but it should definitely help me feel better, reduce the anger, and help me de-stress. It sounded cool, but I told him I still needed therapy, fearing that he would just send me out into the world with a string of beads and think I was cured of all of my problems. That he would try to discard me like everyone else did.

"Oh, I'm not thinking of stopping your therapy, DJ. I think we both agree that you're not ready for that."

Finally, he believed me. He *agreed* with me.

"Good." I let out a sigh of relief and admired my ten, acceptably-colored (no purple or black) beads, which were all placed equally and rotated to the exact same angle. And you know what? They did make me feel better.

The Back to School Dance was coming up soon, and I really wanted to ask Marcus Delon to go with me. But with the way people kept telling me he didn't like me, or telling me how much *everyone* hated me, I didn't want to ask him at the same time. Mama's Child called, saying she wanted me to just go in a group with her. I got distracted and had to hang up the phone because my mom had an announcement for us.

Her sister Sonya was coming to stay for a while, and she adopted a boy from Mexico, named Pablo, who spoke both English and Spanish. *I* wanted to speak Spanish. Sometimes I pretended that I knew other languages, and I'd make up words that didn't really exist. It embarrassed my mom beyond belief. I didn't understand why, though. She was the one who was obsessed with all things Chinese and even pretended to be!

Throughout the next couple of weeks before the dance, I scoured all the stores around town that were in walking distance. I was hoping to find a pretty, affordable dress. When Mama's Child and I stopped in the little dress shop, we scoured the racks. Checking the tag on a cotton dress that was blue and green, I read that it was on clearance and was only seven dollars. *What a steal!* I thought, so I bought it. Mama's Child wanted to buy the same dress as me, so she did. It was annoying in a way, but I was also happy she liked the dress I picked that much.

At the register, the clerk said, "You both must be Tipper children!"

That *really* boiled my clams.

Mama's Child wasn't my sister. Mom did *not* mother every Tom, Dick, and Harry in this town. The lady was *smiling,* too. Did she think it was funny? Or was it not about my mom? Did she assume since we were poor we *must* be Tippers?

I paid for my dress and grabbed my bag, telling MC that I'd see her later. I had to schedule an emergency appointment session with Anthony immediately. My mom would kill me for having another appointment charged to her account *and* for me doing it without her knowing. But I didn't care if I got sent to the grounded room for *weeks*. I needed to see Anthony.

I walked home and chucked my shopping bag on my bed. Then I grabbed my bike.

"Where the *dump* are *you* going, Dennis?" my mother screamed out the window. Did she literally have nothing better to do than watch me like a hawk?

"Don't dumping worry about it," I mumbled under my breath. But knowing better than saying such a thing to her, I yelled, "Be back soon!" instead.

Hoping she didn't hear the rage in my voice, and she wouldn't follow me, I pedaled as fast as my little (big) feet could take me to Anthony's office. How dumb was I? I'd rode past Anthony's for the last couple of years without once stepping a foot inside.

The receptionist told me I couldn't go back to see Anthony. I told her it would be quick, but she didn't care.

"He's busy right now," she said again, her voice completely monotone. She rolled her eyes at me. I stepped around the desk and took a peek inside his office from afar. He had left his door open.

"He ain't busy!" I gave the lady the stank face before continuing, "He's eating a *club sandwich*. I saw him. His door is open."

"I'm sorry, kid. It's his lunch break." She returned to making more clickety clackety noises on her computer's keyboard, but I thought she was faking it so she'd look busy. She probably hadn't even typed a single word.

"It's important!" Getting agitated, I fidgeted, then reached in my pocket and started counting my beads. I got to three then made a run for it, pushing right past her. The lady followed me, but I made it a few steps into the doorway and got his attention.

"Anthony!"

The receptionist picked me up. I didn't want to be manhandled! Reaching for her hands that were death-gripped around me, I screeched at her. Then she screeched right back.

"It's fine! It's fine! Just don't make her any madder," Anthony said, standing up and carefully making his way over to us. He left his sandwich just sitting there on the desk. My mouth watered. *I* wanted a club sandwich. My stomach grumbled.

I yelled at the receptionist to put me down, which she finally complied to. Then she apologized and hurriedly exited his office.

"What's wrong, DJ?"

"A *lot* of things!"

"Well, talk to me. Use your words."

"First thing's first, Mama's Child—"

"—remember, DJ. That's your only friend."

"You're right, but that is not the point. Come on! Listen!" I snapped my fingers at him. "She bought the same dress as me, and I thought it was cool that she liked what I picked out. Like I'm setting a trend."

"...okay?"

"Then the clerk said we both must be *Tippers*. How rude! Am I right?" I widened my eyes at him, hoping he understood the rudeness.

"I don't think she meant to offend you." Anthony frowned.

I frowned right back. "But she *smiled*. What does that even mean?"

"That she was being friendly?"

"OR that she thought it was funny!" I groaned. He was totally missing the point here.

"What was funny?" He cocked his head.

"She thought it was funny that I'm a Tipper. Probably assumed since I was buying a cheap dress, I'm poor. And she probably thought MC was my sibling because everyone thinks my mom has like a gazillion kids and that the whole population under eighteen belongs to her.

"DJ, I think you should relax. Okay? Breathe in, then out. Here, copy me. Like this." Anthony took in deep breaths and was motioning with his hands for me to do the same.

"I already *tried* that! Why does this type of thing always happen to me? Why can't I win? Why do I get blamed for everything? Why—"

"—I think you need to stop analyzing things so much. It's stressing you out." He was eyeing me in that judgy way that I *hated* again.

"It's important to analyze!" How dare he suggest I stop doing something that was so crucial?

"Not like you do. It's not something that you should freak out over all the time. Have you been using the beads?" Folding his hands, he sat down and leaned toward me.

"Yes, I have. And I don't 'freak out'." I rolled my eyes.

"Okay. Well, let's just calm down for now."

I just glared in silence. Everyone knew that telling someone to calm down did anything but make them calm down.

We did some deep breathing exercises, and he put on

some cheesy spa music stuff. It helped. Then we talked about the upcoming dance, and he asked about Marcus Delon. If I was going to ask him. He was being a little nosy, but I told him, "No. Because I'm going to go with Mama's Child."

"Well, that's okay. Groups can be fun. You're so little anyway, you don't need a date."

I narrowed my eyes at him. He was patronizing me again. I could tell he noticed, and he switched the topic to something entirely different.

After my session, I was feeling better, and I rode my bike back home. Mama's Child was sitting on my doorstep when I got there with something in her hands. What was she holding?

"Where were ya at, Denny?" she asked as I chucked my bike to the ground and started walking toward her.

"It's not important," I lied. She took a bite of her ice cream. An actual *bite.* I cringed, but at the same time, I was disappointed she didn't have an extra one for me.

"Well, ya weren't with me, and ya weren't at home. I know, 'cause I been here just a waitin' all day."

"It's fine. I just needed to relax." I shrugged, trying to brush it off.

"Why?"

All this pressure was really getting to me.

"Does it matter that much? *Man,"* I snapped.

"Okay, fine. Be that way." Mama's Child took a great big swipe of ice cream with her tongue, then stood. She walked away without even saying goodbye, and my heart wilted like a dead rose. Why could I never do anything right?

Right before the dance, MC and I both got ready at my house. She tried to convince me to perm my hair like hers but was unsuccessful. I tried my hardest to act like I had actually considered it, when I definitely never did. Our dresses were awesome. We slapped on some Mary Jane shoes and went to the dance. I felt like a rich girl, because even though these were hand-me-downs, they were also the most popular shoes at the moment.

The dance had its hallmark features—the notorious punch bowl, snacks, loud music, and people all dressed up. Oh yeah, and Sanchez of course. *That punch was probably going to get spiked.* I rolled my eyes.

My new cousin was standing beside it, and one of the older kids was talking to him. Probably warning him not to drink it. He was Sonya's newly-adopted son, and she had already come a few days ago and settled in with him. My mom was so annoyed by her being here since she didn't get along with *any* of her many sisters. Dad, on the other hand, didn't mind.

"Is that Pablo in the soccer shirt?" MC asked. We were both jealous of all the girls who had dates, but I told her that Pablo was my cousin, so *don't even think about it.* Marcus Delon came to the dance with Haylee, and Monica went with Mark. I was so annoyed because I should've asked Marcus to come with me. He should have been my date, not Haylee's. And since he was Mark's best friend, I would've gotten to hang out with Monica all night.

Someone came up to us, well actually just to Mama's Child. They tapped her shoulder and said, "Wow! Your style is *great*, Mama's Child. And I like how your friend agreed to dress the same as you, too. It looks cool."

Why the dump did that piece of beef jerky not know *my* name? I thought Mama's Child would certainly tell them I picked the dress in the first place. I scooched closer to her, but she didn't say anything about me and just took all of the credit for herself.

"Mama's Child!" I hissed, after the girl left.

"What?"

"I'm the one who found the dress."

"Well, it was *my* idea to buy the same one." Mama's Child rolled her eyes.

"But *I* was the one who picked it out!" I couldn't believe she was doing this.

"She complimented that we *both* wore them." Mama's Child's eyebrows knitted.

"The thing she was complimenting was *my style.* And you took it as yours!" I threw up my hands and turned to leave the dance. *I couldn't do this anymore.* I was tired of being at the bottom of the food chain. Tired of being frenemies with Mama's Child.

"Denny, wait!" Mama's Child grabbed my wrist to stop me. When she grabbed my arm, she hit my ten-bead charm that was disguised as a bracelet. A snap sounded, and it broke. Every bead that hit the floor *fueled* my emotions. I tried to hold it in. Tried to hold in the rage. Sanch came over immediately. Not because we were fighting, but because she wanted to tell me, "The beads were a safety hazard."

Sanchez swept up my beads, and instead of giving them back to me, she threw them in the trash. In the *trash!* I told Mama's Child she was going to help me go dumpster diving to get them back.

"Classy people don't do that, Denny." MC stuck her nose in the air, as if my beads, the dumpster, *and* me were beneath her.

Then I said something I thought I'd never say to Mama's Child. "But you're *poor!*" I waved my arms, and groaned in frustration.

Tears welled in her gray eyes, and her mouth wobbled,

but she didn't speak. Then she ran out of the dance to go who knew where. My mouth went to ash, and I dug my nails into my palms. But after all this crap, I just wasn't thinking about hurting her feelings.

Doing the dumpster diving myself, and ruining my dress, I fished around for my lost beads for what felt like an eternity. *Please don't let anyone see up my dress,* I thought as I was face down and feet up.

When I got home, feeling *and* smelling like trash, I spent the next half hour finding a string to put my beads back together.

I spent the next couple of days at home, in my room. Trapped in the tragedy that was the inside of my brain, I didn't even go to school. But I did agree to a session with Anthony.

When I walked in, he immediately told me I shouldn't be rude to others because of my rage.

"I'm sorry," I told him, even though he wasn't the person I owed an apology to. Explaining the situation to him, I showed him my charm. It was pitiful. The string was horribly weak and the beads weren't held tightly. They'd fall off any second now, and they were nowhere near being rotated to the exact same angle.

"We can make a new one," he offered.

"It wouldn't be magical anymore."

The rest of the session wasn't too exciting because I was in a slump. I went home and went back to my room. Doing all of my make up work groggily, I sighed deeply. Picking up my tambourine, I practiced for a little while, too. But my heart just wasn't in it.

When I finally went back to school, Sanch yelled at me for being absent without a medical excuse for so many days.

I told her that I didn't *feel* like coming to school.

"Well, neither do I! But I'm the only teacher here, so I have to come *every day*. Why should *you* be any different?" Her words went right in one ear and out the other. Except something wasn't lining up here.

"What are you going to do when you have your baby?" I asked, crumpling my face up.

"My husband is going to sub for a couple of weeks as a monitor. I'm going to explain the work assigned ahead of time. Then I'll be back in about a month." She rolled her eyes as if that should be obvious. But why would my first instinct be to assume that a *police officer* would be our substitute teacher? It seemed more likely to me that she would give birth to her baby in this classroom and raise it here, too.

"It's not really any of your business, anyway!" Sanch snapped. Then she clapped her hands and addressed the entire class.

"Chop, chop, chop! It's French Revolution time!"

"Ugh!" the entire class groaned.

Looks like I didn't miss much.

A week later, nothing else had changed. It was boring every day, and Mama's Child didn't come to my house once. It was weird how we went from enemies to best friends who hung out nearly every day, to enemies then friends *again,* then back to practically strangers. We didn't even *talk.* I used to practically wish for Mama's Child to take no interest in me and leave me alone forever. Now, I kind of missed her. Technically the world was still turning. I assumed it hadn't ended because Rochelle and Lil' Shelbi were still eating corn dogs like usual and I still had all of my memories intact. I just practiced my tambourine a lot more, because I didn't have anything better to do.

When we were eating dinner (inside the living room this time, because it was cold), I thought I had seen MC out the window. *Maybe she's here to apologize,* I thought. When I stood and looked outside, she was truthfully there. Just not for me. She was playing with Mark and Marcus. Mama's Child must have asked if she could join in on their frisbee game. Watching her play outside, I instantly reflected on my entire life. And I couldn't believe that before her, this was what my life was like *every day.*

I couldn't really explain it, but one day out of the blue, sometime after the frisbee game, Mama's Child bumped into me, and we started talking. I apologized, and she did, too.

"'Bout time," she said.

"Are we friends?" A mixture of sadness and hope seeped through those words.

"I guess." Mama's Child shrugged, like it was no big deal, but I caught a hint of a small smile forming on the left corner of her mouth.

I guess being friends with what I liked to call a "half-friend" was better than not having any friends at all.

Chapter 30

ON HALLOWEEN, I SLAPPED on the costume Mama's Child picked out for me. We were both going as Teletubbies. I absolutely *hated* the Teletubbies! But I didn't want to make her mad when I just got her back as my friend. She had asked me if I didn't want to be any specific one. I wanted to tell her that I didn't want to be *any* of them, but I controlled myself and told her my absolute least favorite.

"The purple one," I said.

"Aw!" she pouted. "But that's the one I had picked out for you and wanted you to be!"

I agreed to go along with it.

When Mama's Child showed up at my house my eyes widened, astounded with rage at the fact she *wasn't* dressed as a Teletubbie, or anything else. Not to mention not only was *I* dressed like one, but I was dressed as *the purple one!* I hated the color purple. My *mom's* favorite color.

Mama's Child pouted. "I couldn't afford my costume, and my mom's phone ran outta minutes, Denny. It got disconnected or somethin'." She shrugged and gave me an "I'm completely innocent" expression. But she showed up at my house randomly and unexpectedly all the time! Why couldn't she have just done *that?*

"You have *no* excuse. I don't forgive you. This stuff happens all the time!" I pointed an accusing finger at her, and my rage boiled over the pot that was my brain. "You could've *come* to my house to tell me. You did this on purpose. Don't call me Denny ever again!" I yelled those last words, then ran inside crying.

Even though the door was shut, I could've sworn I heard her laughing. My tears stung on my cheeks, and I was conflicted as to whether my anger or sadness was stronger. After I finished climbing the steps and got to my room, I peeled off my costume and threw it onto the ground. I immediately grabbed my ol' faithful pajamas—the ones that were so faded and worn out they were practically *rags* but were also way too comfy and sentimental to throw away.

"DJ!" my mom hissed, until she realized I was crying. She stopped in the doorway and eyed my costume on the floor. "I still don't understand why you would wear a costume you don't even like in the first place."

I sniffled and met her eyes. "I didn't *want* to. It was to make up with Mama's Child. She claims she couldn't afford *her* costume, so she didn't wear it, but her mom's phone was 'disconnected'—" I placed air quotes around that word. "—so she says she couldn't call me. But I think the whole thing was set up."

My mom's face flushed red, and she hesitated before speaking. She actually got *really* mad.

"I'm calling her mother."

"No!" I whined, but I also kind of wanted her to do it at the same time. It was so unnatural and unnerving that my mom was actually sticking up for me like this.

"I'm gonna put it on speaker," she declared as she forcefully punched numbers into a phone. The ring buzzed through the line, then her mom answered the phone.

"I thought her mom's phone was '*disconnected*'," I mumbled, rolling my eyes.

"Hello?" my mom seethed.

"Yah?" her mom slurred, just like MC did.

"This is Deniese Tipper."

Her mom immediately hung up, so my mom called her back. They yelled and fought for a really long time, then my mom went into a different room. Whatever she was gonna say to her, she didn't want me to hear. A couple minutes later, she came back, no longer on the phone. I waited for her to say something, but nothing would have prepared me for what she said.

"I don't think Mama's Child will be bothering you ever again."

"What?" I asked. The words "*ever again*" rang in my head over and over, on a loop. Sure, I was definitely mad at Mama's Child, and probably would be for a long time, but what happened when I got lonely like I did last time? Mama's Child was my only friend.

"It's for the best," my mom concluded. "You'll thank me later." She turned to leave my bedroom.

"Hey, Mom?" I asked.

She rolled her eyes and groaned, turning back around. Placing a hand on her hip, she blurted "Yah?" Her voice dripped with annoyance.

"Thanks for sticking up for me."

"Mhmm," she said quietly, refusing to meet my eyes. Then she resumed her normal attitude, walking confidently away. Pretending like what she did was strictly to benefit herself and she didn't care about me.

Despite being mad about Mama's Child, and a little *sad* for the same reason, I actually couldn't stop smiling.

Because my mom actually did something *nice* for me, and she *knew* that I knew. Which meant it had to have been incredibly hard for her. She couldn't have people out here thinking she actually loved them! But she did, *didn't she?*

Going back to school after Halloween was difficult. Mama's Child wouldn't speak to me *or* look at me. I sat in my casual, usual, lunch table seat, and she sat at the same table, too! The *audacity!*

Mrs. Sanchez kept trying to partner us up in both normal class *and* theater class. Mama's Child never said anything. She would keep her arms crossed and plaster a blank expression onto her face, just like she was doing today. Her red afro was pulled up into a messy bun, and her eyes were heavy-lidded. I told Sanch that we weren't exactly "best buddies" now and that we both would probably prefer to have different partners. Sanch just acted like what I said couldn't possibly be true, that I was just lying like the liar everyone thought I was. So she turned to Mama's for confirmation.

"Yeah, it's true," MC said awkwardly, not even bothering to look in either of our directions.

Sanch tried to get other groups and partners to split up so we wouldn't have to work together, but no one wanted to. So she told us we could work independently when it was available, but if there were partner activities, we would either have to work together or not participate at all.

"But Sanch!" I whined, my eyes widening like saucers. She just shot me an annoyed look.

The next couple of weeks people continued confusing us as best friends. We both grew tired of explaining, but finally everyone got the memo and quit asking.

When I went to see Anthony, he was surprised to learn that I wasn't friends with her anymore.

"Maybe if you didn't whack down the number of sessions I have, you'd know." I rolled my eyes and folded my hands, staring down at my feet.

"I'm going to ignore that comment. But I'm sorry you're upset."

"Duh, I'm upset!" I exclaimed, pointing at myself. His expression was enough of a warning to tell me to watch it. So I did. "You're practically my only friend, now." I picked at the strings on one of the pillows.

"I thought you said you had lots of friends, DJ." He unclicked his pen and glanced up at me, probably itching to write down that I lied again.

"I just said that to sound cool." I waved a dismissive hand in his direction.

He frowned. "I thought you weren't going to lie in here. But I understand."

Yeah, sure. You "understand," yet you're still writing it down as a penalty.

"Yeah. Well, MC has stolen away everyone from me anyway."

"That stinks. I'm sorry."

"It more than stinks!" I said, raising my voice again. "It's disturbing."

We talked on and on about this stuff. When my session was over, I told him it was time for me to move on.

"From my sessions?" He gave me a puzzled look and picked his clipboard up, walking me to the door. "I thought you just said you were mad that I 'whacked them down'?"

"No, silly! Of course I need my sessions."

He squinted an eye at me, studying me closely.

"I mean from Mama's Child."

Chapter 31

I TOTALLY BEGAN TO see things clearly after that. I told myself I was going to move on, and I did. I was going to look out for myself from now on. No friends meant no responsibility to anyone but *you*. At least that was how I took it.

I began to walk competitively at home, at school, everywhere. No one really seemed to notice but me, but who cared? I was only trying to impress myself now. I ate a big chunky PB&J sandwich as I walked into Sanchez's class. She was going to say something about it, but I stopped her before she could.

"I missed breakfast today, Sanch."

She didn't even respond. I thought her pregnancy was putting her in a better mood lately.

I couldn't wait till she had her baby and her husband would be here teaching for a month. Normally I would think it'd be smooth sailing. That the sub wouldn't know anything. But since he was her *husband,* she informed us all he would be taught our lesson plans. My only hope remained that he was probably way nicer than she was. It'd be pretty hard to be worse than her.

Sanchez passed out a reading assignment on the French Revolution, and I yawned. Rage spiraled throughout the class, but I was fine. I didn't like homework, but I always breezed through anything involving reading.

On the way home, I was pleased to see it was the perfect day for a walk and that the sun was shining. I was *not* going to get splashed by a mud puddle today. After I put all my crap in my room, I headed to our picnic table to eat some Mystery Meet with my family. Lucky for me (and my hungry belly), my mom had decided to have an early supper. When we were finishing up, she told me it was time to milk Ol' Bessie, and I wanted to say it was someone else's turn. But it wasn't worth fighting over. 'Cause I actually had a great day today.

Next weekend I was convinced I saw something outside our house. It was a person dressed in all black. I admit I had totally freaked out, but my family kept telling me they didn't see anything. My first instinct was to call MC or check TownSpy. I had broken myself out of that habit, but in a moment of fear like this, I guess I hadn't. I resisted and didn't call, but I did log onto the chatroom. To my surprise, TownSpy hadn't written anything since their last message a week or so before Halloween. *Mama's Child must've given it up.* Because the only thing currently in the chatroom was:

NiteInShiningArmour: Ladies night tonight
at Bob's Karaoke. ;)
TheCheats: Any girls single out there?
Looking for a date for tonight!
NiteInShiningArmour: Bring your date to
Karaoke, and she'll get in for free!
TheCheats: Are ya implying that I'm cheap?
FootballFever: Definitely coming to Bob's
tonight, anyone else joining? Deniese is up

for a party, and we're bringing some food
with us.
NiteInShiningArmour: You can't bring that
food in. You're just trying to get out of
paying for the food I sell!
FootballFever: What, do you got guards
who check for food now?

I signed out of the chatroom. Nobody invited me to the party at Bob's tonight. That made me a little sad. It probably was just the adults going, but *I* wanted to sing and dance, too! I wanted Marcus to ask me to go with him to it. I knew that was mainly something older kids and adults did, but we could totally have a playdate there, and he wouldn't even have to pay to take me. It'd be awesome.

Hey! If it's ladies night, *I could go by myself without even having to pay!*

I rode my bike to Bob's. Mom didn't say whether I could or couldn't go, but some of my older siblings went. So I was going to go, too.

As I slipped through the door to the club, the music pounded into my ears instantly. Bob had the strobe light on and the disco ball spinning. It honestly was giving me a headache and making me a little nauseous, but I slouched behind objects as I kept creeping around. I was like a spy, because I was on the down low. When I went to turn a corner, I bumped into someone and nearly had a heart attack!

"Hey, Dennis. Didn't see ya there!" Mark Melon snickered.

Back to my invisible superpowers once again.

"Is Marcus here?" I asked, ignoring his comment, and my heart finally slowed back down.

"Uh, yeah. Somewhere! I'm gonna go get a snackaroo.

See ya!" Mark belched then walked away.

The search was definitely *on*.

I walked through the crowd dozens of times but couldn't find him *anywhere*. How could that even be? I had seen practically everyone else in this entire town. The Greens, the Stars, China Lady and Danny, practically all the teenagers, and several kids around my age.

I didn't see MC once, though. So I went to the bathroom to pass time, hoping the crowd would thin out and I'd be able to begin the search again. As I exited the bathroom, Marcus was standing relatively close to me, beside Haylee and Mark. An unusual burst of confidence struck, and I went over there to try to be friends with all of them. When I got within about a foot's range, however, my mom called for me.

"DJ! I need ya to get over here, now!"

Ugh, of all times!

I made my way to Mom, and when I looked over my shoulder, Monica was standing with the other kids now, along with her brother Cameron. They were all laughing like they were having so much fun.

"Yeah?" I asked my mom, not bothering to hide my annoyance.

"Can you go home and get my spare car key? I locked myself out of my car!" Mom rushed the words so quickly she sounded frantic.

"You're ready to *leave?* Already? How long have you even been here?" I asked. Normally my mother would have told me off right then and there, but she didn't.

"I've been here about…" She counted on her fingers. "Uh…two hours? How long have you been here?" Her lazy and dreamy looking eyes focused, and she pursed her lips for half a second. Probably realizing that I came here without telling her.

"Uh…" I muttered, looking away, and mom snapped right back to the happy-go-lucky state she was strangely in.

"Okay, look. It doesn't matter." She waved a dismissive hand at me. "I just don't want chu out there at dark. So can ya go get mah keys? While it's still. Uh. Light out?" Her words were getting all slurred.

"Yeah."

Glancing back at the group of populars, I exited the club and grabbed my bike, then pedaled back to our house. Something caught my eye, and I blinked a couple times, trying to will the person in black back to my vision. But nobody was there.

"I must just be tired," I muttered out loud to myself.

Throwing my bike down, I went inside the house and retrieved the keys. It really bothered me that we didn't lock the door to our house, but it was also good because there was no other way I'd get in. Mom didn't trust me to have my own house key, and she refused to tell me where the spare one was. Like I'd steal it or something. I started my ride back to the club.

"Thanks, DJ!" my mom exclaimed, looking like she wanted to kiss me. I dropped the keys in her hands, and she acted like I'd just given her gold. "You can stay as long as you like now, as long as you don't go home by yourself." She patted my arm and nodded, looking like she was gonna fall asleep. "But if it's light outside, you can go alone."

My mom patted my shoulder this time, in the same patronizing manner. That was when I put all the clues together and concluded she was obviously drunker than a fish.

"It'll be dark in a half an hour," I stated.

"Yeah."

"Well, who am I going to go home with?"

"You probably should just stay for a few minutes and come back home." She smiled.

"I'll just go home with you. Can I load my bike into the back of your bug?" She swayed back and forth to the music, mumbling the lyrics to herself like a lullaby.

Met with no response besides undecipherable singing, I was going to do it anyway. So I turned to go, but she snatched my wrist and threatened, "*Don't* get any dirt on the seats. Or *else.*"

"Oh…okay," I stammered.

I went outside and lifted my bike up, being super careful to not get any dirt on the seat. The bike was nearly bigger than me and weighed a billion pounds. As challenging as it was, I knew I couldn't have ridden it back. My thighs were numb from all the pedaling, and I was exhausted. I shut the car door before going back inside the club to sit and wait for the effects of my mom's drinking to wear off. This might be a *very* long night.

Chapter 32

"*IT'S BEGINNING TO LOOK a lot like Christmas*!" my dad sang loudly upstairs.

"Dad!" I hollered back. I was sitting at the bottom of the steps, and my mom had already passed, threatening me about not falling asleep.

"Yeah?" he called.

"*Thanksgiving* is this week. *Not* Christmas!" Rolling my eyes, I propped my chin up with my hands, yawning. What was it about this spot?

"Can't we just skip that? It never works out well. Let's just skip straight ahead to Christmas." My dad nearly tripped over me, and I questioned his intelligence level instantly. Was he really that oblivious? Or was I really *that* invisible?

"I agree." My mom waved a hand in the air.

I gasped, my eyes shifting between the two of them.

"What?" I shrieked. I *loved* Christmas. But I was all about celebrating *every* holiday. There would be no skipping around them. That was just sick! And Thanksgiving had amazing food! My mouth was watering just imagining it.

"Yeah. Let's just skip it." My mom leaned against the banister, and the two of them were practically having a conversation over top of my head. I really did seem to be invisible.

"But what about the food?" I whined. "You've got to be joking."

My mother's lips and eyes frowned down on me, and she shook her head in annoyance. "I don't feel like cooking nothin'."

"I'll cook!" I pleaded with little begging prayer hands. I tried to look as adorable as possible, even though everyone acted like I was ugly. It was worth a shot.

"DJ, you're only seven years old! You'll burn the house down if you're not careful!" My dad rubbed his beard nervously and glanced at Mom. She didn't say a thing. I was honestly surprised they even remembered my age.

"*Please?* Please let us have Thanksgiving! I look forward to that stuff. Take pity on your child's boring life!" I groaned dramatically and pretended to fall against the steps, as if I had fainted.

"*Boring?*" my mom scoffed. "Are you saying we don't entertain you enough?"

I straightened. Crap. I'd made it personal now. "No! No. Not at all. Can we please just have a Thanksgiving meal?"

"Fine."

"Yes!" I clenched my fist and brought it down in a triumphant motion.

"But your dad is cooking." My mom's face remained flat, but my dad started laughing.

"Oh ho ho ho ho. No. Nada. I am not doing that." His ponytail swished with each shake of his head.

"Then your older siblings are."

I was surprised she let my dad out of it. How dare he tell her no? Everyone knew that *she* was the boss around here. I swear—*everyone* suddenly got out of bed and rolled their eyes so far back into their heads that they'd never see the light of day again. All the doors in our house seemed to open in one fluid motion.

"No way!" they all yelled. "Are you kidding?"

"Freaking DJ," one of them scoffed. "What the heck?"

"Y'all are cooking!" my mom hollered up the stairs at them.

And that was that.

On Thanksgiving the food was decent. Pretty *good*, actually. Some of the older kids were impressed with themselves so much that they were actually happy about it. But some of them were still mad at me because they had to cook. The doorbell rang, and I volunteered to answer it. As good as the food was, I had already had about three plates full, and the dirty glares from some of my siblings was making me way too uncomfortable. When I got to the door, nobody was there. It was so odd.

"Who was it, DJ?" asked my dad as I returned to the table.

"Yeah, who has the *audacity* to bother us on Thanksgiving?" asked my mom, stabbing at her green beans.

"There was no one there."

"Of course there was someone there, idiot!" My mom dropped her fork to her plate and raised her hands to her temples. "Someone done rang that doorbell. I'm not crazy."

"Ya got ding-dong ditched, Mom." Rochelle faked a cough to cover up her snicker.

"Ha!" Lil' Shelb laughed so much that a piece of her turkey flew out of her mouth and hit my cheek.

I gagged and groaned, "Ew!" Reaching for a napkin, I wiped it off and shuddered. That was *so* germy.

"Mom, come to think of it, I saw that person in all black

again the other day. It was on the way back to get your car keys."

My mother narrowed her eyes and cocked her head like she had no recollection of what I was talking about.

"You 'member? It was when we all went to Bob's Karaoke Club. Ladies night." I searched Mom's face for any sign of recognition.

"You went to *ladies night?*" Rochelle laughed so hard I thought she'd die, and I rolled my eyes. I didn't have to explain my choices to her.

A knowing expression finally crossed Mom's face, and she sat straight up in her chair. "Dennis! Why didn't ya say something? I think I know who ding-dong ditched us." My mom glanced frantically toward the door, then back to us.

"Who?" we all asked in unison.

"Beverly Hill."

Next time it was my mom who saw the person in all black, not me. She confronted them, and she was *right*. It *was* Beverly Hill. She was standing in our front yard, and I happened to be outside. I hid behind the side of the house to eavesdrop as my mother approached the woman.

"What do you want?" My mom sighed, her voice filled with exhaustion.

Beverly responded, but I couldn't tell what she was saying. Straining my ears, the only thing I could make out was something about her being angry, coming home, Bev, and Mexico. Unable to decipher anything else, and honestly being a little (okay, a *lot*) terrified of her, I snuck around the back and went back inside.

The next couple of days, nobody saw her again. I didn't have a clue where she went, and my mom refused to talk to anybody about their conversation.

Glancing out the window at school on an early December day, I hoped it would snow again. But it didn't even get close. It was unusually (or I guess I should say *usually*) warm. Last December's snow had spoiled me, and it rarely snowed here in California. All I wanted was a little Christmassy weather. I sighed and wished on every shooting star (or airplane—*thanks for crushing my dreams, Rochelle*) that my desires would be granted and it would snow like no other.

A week later, I got exactly the *opposite* of what I wanted. When I looked out the window, the sky rapidly turned almost black from thick clouds. A lightning bolt struck, rain downpoured, and thunder rumbled louder than my mom's stomach after she ate Mexican food.

Sanchez came down from her attic-home breathing extremely hard. Officer Pete followed her with a suitcase. They got inside their car and faded as they drove away until they were nothing more than a little dot in the distance. Some of the older kids came downstairs and made me step away from the window. I didn't want any of them telling my mom I was snooping, so I pretended to act casual. They murmured and whispered jokes about Mrs. Sanchez, and some of them made comments about her baby coming early and that they were going to the hospital. Orange waddled down the steps with a basketball shoved up her shirt and clutched her stomach. She started panting heavily, and all the other kids bursted into giggles.

A loud crash outside distracted me and drew me back to the window to find a raccoon heading for one of our trash cans. Cramming my big feet into my horribly beat-up sneaks, I flung open the front door and took off running in the downpour. I chased that sucker all the way across the street before someone must've ratted me out.

My mom screeched at me from our front door, demanding that I get inside. "Are you *dumb?* You're gonna get rabies! You idiot!" I closed the distance between us and met her at the door. She wrapped an arm around my drenched shoulder and shoved me inside. Her eyes scanned the street before shutting the door, and I couldn't tell if she was paranoid about her mother or if she was worried about her reputation if anyone saw her child chasing after a raccoon during this monsoon of a storm!

The weather intensified, and I was beginning to get nervous. It wasn't that I necessarily had a *fear* of storms. But the lights were flickering, and I just had an extremely eerie feeling that something was definitely wrong. The sound of glass breaking filled my eardrums, and I screamed, thinking someone was breaking into our house. But it had just been a tree branch that shattered the window. I stepped away from the glass, and that was a smart decision because my mom immediately directed us to split up into the few rooms we had without windows. She wanted to be cautious in case there'd be another tree branch or something. My mind instantly went to the scene in *Snow White* when all the trees came to life and tried to kill her.

Sitting crammed next to my mom and about half of my siblings in a windowless bedroom, I strained my ears to make out the news on the staticky radio. The person talking was making comments about staying off the road and finding shelter. My mom switched it off. She had this thing where she thought if any electronic device was on during a storm it would get fried, so she only turned it on for brief periods. I didn't know if scientific evidence existed to back her theory up, but we all knew better than to question my mother.

"Poor Sanch! *She's* on the roads, and she's having her baby!" Shaye shook her head with a solemn frown.

"Ew, why are you feeling bad for Sanch? She's the worst," Rochelle groaned.

We all straightened our spines when the sound of tires screeched outside. I wished I could look out a window to see what was happening. Someone was obviously speeding. What ignoramuses! Did they not have their radio on? Did they not know they could *die* out there?

Whoever it was seemed to not care what was happening around them. They were on a mission, and it was clear that nobody and nothing would stop them.

Chapter 33

TOMORROW WAS MONDAY, and Mrs. Sanchez had been labeled "missing" for a week. As in *missing*. She should have been back at school by now. I wondered if she would be in class today. Part of me also wondered if Mama's Child had kidnapped her. She had made worried remarks about failing again, but she hadn't reached out to me for help yet because of our fight.

Officer Pete was getting his certification, so he could be the teacher here permanently. Someone was brave enough to ask about his and Sanchez's baby. He said that China Lady was watching her. I couldn't believe that Sanch went missing in the first place. *Or* that she left the baby behind. Nobody knew where she went! I figured she'd want to come back as soon as possible to teach us more about the French Revolution. That was what she *lived* for.

Mama's Child was talking really loud in the lunchroom, sitting at a different table. I naturally stayed at my casual, usual lunch table in my casual, usual seat. Overhearing her gossiping, I tried not to look too interested as she explained to a few other kids, "Sanch left Officer Pete! She ran off to protect 'er own soul. Didn't even think *twice* 'bout dat baby!"

When I went to throw my trash away, Rochelle, Shaye, and Nicole were doing the same thing. Rochelle leaned real close to them and whispered, "Sanch went to *France* because she finally cracked off and wanted to live out her own French Revolution."

I shook my head at all of the nonsense. I didn't buy *any* of those stories.

When I walked home that day, I'd admit it. I searched for Sanch everywhere and found nothing. With my detective skills, she couldn't possibly be within our area. I never really liked her, so I didn't know why I even cared so much. I talked about her with Anthony, and he kept telling me that everything would be fine. That I "didn't need any more stress in my life" and to "forget it."

The next couple of days there was no theater practice. So I approached Officer Pete's desk after school and asked him what was up.

"Well, I just don't know much about theater. And besides, I have *a lot* on my plate right now, Deidre." He motioned toward some paperwork.

"It's Dennis!" The *audacity! Wait. Was I* really *calling myself Dennis now?* Not even bothering with Deniese?

"Oh, sorry." Blinking, he continued, "So, why do you care so much about theater?" He put his pen down and gave me his full attention. It was a welcomed change, even if it *was* a stupid question.

"Uh, duh! 'Cause I'm in it!" Waving my arms around, I wanted him to get the point here.

"Yeah. But do you feel that you really *need* theater?" He put a huge emphasis on the word "need," and it made me feel silly.

"Well," I paused, needing a second to consider. "No. I guess not. But how am I gonna be awesome if you're whacking down all the clubs?"

He gave me a slight smile that quickly faded back into his flat frown. "I don't know. I'm just not sure when Sanchez will be back. I'm sorry. I don't wanna take over her club if she's going to be right back. She might get upset over me teaching you guys a different thing than she wanted to."

Did he seriously just refer to his wife as *Sanchez?* Did she even have a first name? I shrugged and told myself it was none of my business. This guy surprisingly didn't seem to hate me, and I'd like to keep it that way. So I tried to be understanding and patient, settling for just the words, "Okay, then."

Having Officer Pete as a teacher was kinda awesome. He had been teaching us for a few weeks and kept teaching on the French Revolution for Sanch, but he looked good while doing it. Did I *mention* he was cute? Everyone thought so. I mean, for a teacher that was. He was really young with wavy dark hair.

"How'd Sanch get *him?"* people kept murmuring. I'd admit I jumped on the bandwagon. I didn't think he was that cute at first. But all the girl teens did, so all the younger girls naturally copied them.

Mr. Sanch then announced that he came around to the whole "theater club" idea. He stated he was preparing for a play—a musical, in fact—and any of the younger kids could come audition.

"All of the older kids in the theater club can work the stage. Then when we have a play for older kids, we'll flip flop, and the younger kids can work on the stage. If we ever have a joint one, I'm sure we could get parents or volunteers to work the stage."

"Yas!" screamed MC. "*I'll* be there!"

He asked for suggestions for what musical we should do. Haylee raised her hand and he called on her.

"*West Side Story!*"

"*Phantom of the Opera!*" Monica piped up. I had no idea what either of those were.

Then all of a sudden, someone cleared their throat.

"*Chicaaaaaaaaaaaaaggooooooooooooooooooo!*" screeched Mama's Child for what felt like an eternity. She stood on her chair with her arms up in the air. I thought she was doing jazz hands.

My mouth dropped open, and a lot of the older kids laughed.

"He'll never allow it," Shaye muttered from the back of the class.

"*Chicago?*" Mr. Sanch asked, rubbing his chin. "Ain't that the one with the song *All That Jazz?* I like it."

Mama's Child whooped and hollered, and everyone else was astounded. Including me!

At auditions, we all sang the same song—*All That Jazz.* It was slightly inappropriate. Then we had to read a little bit of script. Mr. Sanch told us he was gonna post the role list outside the school later that evening. I wrung my hands. For some reason, singing and dancing didn't give me anxiety like public speaking and acting did. Knowing that most people usually hated me, and that I was invisible, I didn't expect much. Didn't wanna get my hopes up too high.

"I'm happy to announce that *everyone* who auditioned will get a part in the play. There's enough spots for everybody." Mr. Sanchez was smiling a real smile. Practically his first ever since Sanchez vanished into thin air.

"It's okay. There are no small parts in the *ensemble*," Mama's Child patronizingly crooned in my direction.

Was my audition really *that* bad? Saying nothing, I walked home with my fingers crossed. My hopes kept rising higher and higher, even though I kept telling my brain to *stop it!* I waited about an hour before I grabbed my bike and rode it down to the school. I must've rode past the building about a gazillion times waiting on that list to be posted, and my thighs were jelly mush that would give out on me any second.

Finally, a piece of paper taped to the school door caught my eye, so I rode my bike onto the sidewalk and chucked it down in the grass. I flew as fast as my little (big) feet could take me. Sliding my finger down the list, I went straight to the bottom and worked my way up, looking for ensemble first. I scanned it like I was cramming for a test but didn't see my name. I didn't even get *ensemble*. He said that *everyone* would get a part! Did he forget me? *Probably.*

I knew it was probably pointless, but I kept reading anyway. Feeling an extreme rush of adrenaline, I kept looking and looking until I was astounded with glee. Because the list read:

Roxie: Dennis June

Velma: Lil Shelb

Amos: Marcus

Billy: Cameron

Mama: Mama's Child

Mary Sunshine: Jillian

Fred: Nigel

Cop: Mark

Liz (Pop): Monica

Annie (Six): Hallee

June (Squish): Haylee

Hunyak (Uh-Uh): Krissy

Mona (Lipschitz): Dominique

Judge: Josh

Ensemble: Jade, Ambrosia, Joe, Pablo

Kitty: Kayla

I smiled until someone shrieked behind me. It totally broke me out of all my thoughts about how some of these kids weren't even in school yet, and how I had just gotten a big part!

"There is no way that *Dennis* got the lead." Katrina's face was as pinched up as ever.

The lead?

Looking her right in the face, I snarkily remarked, "What do *you* care? You're too old to be in it, anyway."

More kids started showing up to check the list. Mama's Child gave me a cold congratulations, but that wouldn't be the end of it. It *never* ended with MC. She bragged about how she got the role that she wanted.

"I don't even have to worry about memorizing *my* stage name. I am Mama, and Mama is me. We are one in the same."

"What are you doing?" I asked her, wrinkling my nose up.

"Getting into character."

That girl *really* gave me the creeps.

Mr. Sanch said we all had to have signed permission slips. Now I had to convince my mom to sign a permission slip for me to play in *Chicago* (*Junior*). I'd worry about that part later, though. Rereading the list, I almost fainted.

Marcus Delon was playing my *husband.*

At my house, I thought I'd have to try real hard to convince my mom. But it wasn't as hard as expected, because she couldn't care less, and all the other kids had permission slips, too. I told her that I got the lead, smiling ear to ear.

She just laughed. "*Really?* Just let me sign your ensemble slip, Dennis." The words stung, but I didn't say anything. I didn't want to let anyone ruin this day, so I silently watched her signature float over the paper.

My mom gave me a pity-filled smile. "There are no small parts in the *ensemble,* Dennis."

Internally, I was screeching from rage. I just felt like my whole life up until this moment was defined by the word "ensemble" and what it meant. That I wasn't important, basically invisible, and sort of just *there.* No one could distinguish me from anybody else, and no one remembered me. Why did *everyone* keep telling me that I was an "ensemble"? I'd show them.

I studied my script like I was studying for a test. The musical wouldn't be for a long time, but *still.* If I was the lead, I got to be on my A-game. Especially when everyone was expecting me to screw it up like everything else. Roxie was supposed to be pretty, skinny, and blond. That meant I better go on a diet. No more Mystery Meet for me! *What?* Did you think I'd honestly give up my Debbies? *HA. No.*

It didn't take me too long to read through the script, and I was disappointed when I found that ironically even though

Marcus was playing my husband, there was no kissing or hugging scenes. Zero! I did get to kiss someone though. His name was Nigel, and he was Monica's cousin. It would be my first kiss, *ever!* I was going to kiss a boy. This was amazing. If it wasn't for Marcus Delon, Nigel and I could get married. I giddily jumped on my bed, the script pages flopping around.

"Dennis!" my mom screeched from down the hall.

I stopped immediately and stood still.

"What do ya think you're doin' in there? You're making a terrible racket!"

"I'm just reading," I told her, plopping down on the bed. She groaned loudly. For all I knew, she might've been coming for me with one shoe already off. I bet it was the left one.

"Dumb," my mom slurred, passing my open doorway. She didn't even look in as she reached for my doorknob and slammed the door shut.

Chapter 34

EVEN THOUGHT IT WAS winter break now, we still had theater practices nearly every day. I was beginning to get a little sick of it, but I didn't say a word. Actually being a part of something—a *big* something—made me feel great. Complaining might just ruin it. Mr. Sanch had to know how dedicated I was to this production. That was what we called him, by the way. *Mr. Sanch.* Apparently *he* took *her* last name when they got married.

"Choreography day today, folks!" Mr. Sanch smiled at all of us but quickly regained his stern expression when we began goofing around. I snapped out of my goofing immediately. Okay, I hadn't been goofing off in the first place. It wasn't exactly like I had anybody *to* goof around with. He told us we better shape it up if we wanted our dance moves to be correct, and I really wanted to wow everyone. I had the most to prove here out of anybody, so I followed all of his instructions one hundred and ten percent. Sweating like a pig, I collapsed onto the stage floor when we were done.

As I lay on the stage floor (that smelled like feet, *gag!*), I could tell I was drenched. *Would I sweat like this on stage?*

Would it be noticeable? About a million horrible thoughts entered my head—including the fact the floor was probably infectious. I sat up immediately, grabbed a towel to dry off, then got a water bottle from Mr. Sanchez. Since the next number to practice didn't include me, I got to take a little break and sit it out.

About to head home, I was saddened once again by the fact no snow glistened the ground. Snow was my favorite weather, yet I lived near Malibu and rarely got to experience it. And, I'm sorry, but winter was not winter, and Christmas was not Christmas without *snow.* That was just the way it was in my brain. Feeling like something was watching me, I nearly jumped out of my skin when I looked over my shoulder, and it was Mama's Child.

She approached me, and I was shocked. She talked to me yesterday about the play, and now it seemed like she was going to talk to me today, too. I was under the impression we weren't on speaking terms. My mom didn't want me hanging out with her, and *her* mom didn't want her hanging out with *me.*

"Hey, Den." Mama's Child said the name she had bestowed upon me as if it was a common phrase.

"Hey," I responded, paying close attention to how I said it. I wanted to try to be friendly, but my cold facial expressions were probably betraying me. It had been said I was an open book, and I was beginning to understand what that meant.

"Did you like my run-through of my solo?"

"Oh, yeah. Good job."

Was Mama's Child just trying to make small talk, or was she out here fishing for compliments? 'Cause I was going to walk home.

"Thanks." The words came out clipped, but she gave me

a close-mouthed smile. I could tell it was fake.

"Yep."

"Well, you know we have lines together. We can't act like we ain't friends. I mean, we ain't really friends in the play, but if you act mad at me? Peeps will know somethin' is off." Either Mama's Child had been working on her speech or her mom was helping her. The twang still came out, but she was starting to lose her accent. It made me sad, and I didn't know why.

"I didn't think I was acting mad at you. Mr. Sanchez didn't say anything."

"Yeah, but you could sense all the awkwardness, Den Den."

I hesitated. I hadn't thought I'd acted any different with her than I did the other people in the play. Except for Marcus, but I couldn't help myself! I always did something embarrassing. Or at least that was the way I felt when I was around him. Like I couldn't even tell my left from my right.

"I think we should start hanging out again…"

This snapped me right out of my thoughts and earned her my full attention.

Here we go again, I thought. *It was always like a rollercoaster with her.*

"Ya know. To practice our scenes." Mama's Child shrugged and looked away like it was nothing. But it was never nothing with her.

"Well, okay. I don't see a problem with—"

"—can I stay the night?" Mama's Child asked hurriedly, cutting me off. Her eyes were almost pleading, and it was like they were boring holes in my soul.

I knew my mom would flip, but I couldn't say no. That would be so mean!

"I guess," I decided, trying not to act like it was my idea

in the slightest. I didn't want to be blamed for anything that might result. "But you *better* not get me in any trouble."

"I would never get you in trouble, Denny." Her Cheshire grin lit up her face, her freckles leaping with joy.

"I mean it this time, Mama's. If you get me in trouble— You. Are. Out." I paused between each of the last words to make sure she got the idea loud and clear.

"I'll be on my best behavior," she cooed at me.

"You better act like a *nun.*"

Mama's Child reached around, grabbed the back of her shirt, and pulled the head hole up over her head. Then she laughed and did the thing Catholics do with their fingers. Where they move them around their face while they're praying. I didn't know what it was called because I wasn't Catholic. But Mama's Child wasn't *either.*

I raised my voice at her and gasped. "Mama's Child! You can't do that. You're not a Catholic. That's disrespect!"

"You said to act like a nun!" She bursted into giggles.

"Not literally!" I glanced around, hoping there weren't any Catholics nearby.

"I don't know what you want from me, Denny."

"Just come on!" I smacked her arm lightly with the back of my hand and rolled my eyes.

We began walking.

"Hey, Den. I forgot to turn in that assignment that was due before break."

I narrowed my eyes and glanced at her, watching her cautiously out of the corner of my eye. "Then turn it in," I responded flatly.

"It's not all the way done. I need help."

I got an uneasy feeling in the pit of my stomach. "How much is done?" I dared to ask.

"…one sentence."

"No!" I stopped walking, and she did too.

"But I'll fail if you don't help me! And then I won't be allowed in the play. And no one knows my lines, my song, they'd have to cut *everything* I'm in! So, if ya think about 'er, that means that half a yer scenes are just gone!" Her eyes widened, and she waved her hands rapidly in the air to make her point. I hated how she manipulated me like this.

"Ugh!" I groaned. She just watched me until I couldn't take it anymore and caved. "Fine. Let's go. This is gonna be a *long* night."

I should have known she didn't want to be my friend again *just* to be my friend. There was always something when it came to her.

I was actually glad to hear we didn't have practice on Christmas Eve *or* Christmas. After the late night with Mama's Child last weekend, I was ridiculously tired and could not seem to get caught up on sleep. So I took a major snooze and wasn't planning on getting up till at least after twelve p.m.

You can only imagine how surprised I was when I went downstairs and saw that the calendar tacked to the kitchen wall said it was the *26th of December.*

I literally slept through Christmas. And no one in my family even woke me up. No wonder I had to wazz like a racehorse this morning! It'd been marinating in my bladder for over *twenty-four hours.* When I finally decided this wasn't something I could logically think my way through, I became infuriated. I walked out into the living room and slammed a hand down on the banister. Hollering for everyone in the entire house, and possibly even our neighbors, to hear I shrieked, "Y'all let me miss *Christmas*! That's just *mean!*"

"Dennis!" my mom bellowed back immediately.

My rage was so bad, though, that I wasn't even *scared.*

"I can't believe it!" I whined, like I was dying. "My favorite holiday just up and ran away!" When the tears started spilling over my chunky cheeks, they weren't pretend. This was absolutely awful.

"We thought you knew it was Christmas." My mom's high heels clicked as she stomped down the stairs.

"I was *sleeping!*" My nasal and high-pitched voice echoed off all the walls. Like a fire siren.

"If you don't watch it, you're gonna get yourself in *big* trouble. I ain't playing witchu today!" Her eyebrows arched, and she crossed her arms. It made her chest pop out of her low cut top, and I wrinkled my nose up in disgust.

"Why?" I blurted.

"Back talk."

"Fine." I could cross my arms, too. I padded up the steps and returned to my bedroom. I plopped on my Santa hat and dug out my old candy cane pajamas. Then I whirled back around and went downstairs to the living room. The anger and sadness were enough to overpower my disinterest in exercise.

"Mom!" I could hear her sigh clearly even though she was all the way in the kitchen. "Did Santa at least leave me gifts this year? Are there any leftovers from Christmas dinner? Is there any candy? Did it snow? Did you guys sing Christmas carols without me? Did—"

My mom clodhopped her way into the living room, groaning with every step and slouched over like a teenager. "Dennis! Calm down. How am I supposed to answer any of that when you're barely even breathing? What is this? Twenty-one questions?"

"Sorry."

"You did get a stocking." She sighed, placing a few fingers to her temple. "There probably *was* candy in it, but ya know what they say."

I just stared at her.

"Finders keepers."

"Did *you* eat my candy?" I asked incredulously, placing a hand on my hip and frowning.

"There are a few dinner leftovers in the fridge, but let me just tell you, it was *nassssstay.* "

I noticed she still hadn't answered my question about the candy, and I eyed her like she was a suspect. Detective DJ was on the hunt once again, and she was at the top of my list. Especially when chocolate was involved. The hustler. What deception! You couldn't even trust your own mother in this world.

"There's a present under the tree for you," she considered, "but quite honestly, I don't think you deserve it."

I dropped my mouth open in shock.

"Ain't nobody out here singing Christmas carols, with or without you. And there was no snow. What is wrong witchu? Did you not check the weather this week? It was supposed to be like seventy degrees outside." She looked absolutely disgusted to have birthed me.

"Thanks!" I yelled, running to get my gift. I should've given her my two cents about her rudeness and sass, but I didn't put it past her to steal my present from Santa either.

I unwrapped the gift as fast as my little pudgy fingers could get the paper off, ribbons flying everywhere. I would clean that up later. *You have to clean that up* now*, DJ. You cannot leave scraps of paper on the floor. Someone could slip on them and* die! Shaking my head no, I told my brain to shut up and let me enjoy my present.

When it was completely unwrapped, *there she was.* Just like I had asked him for. A new, bedazzled tambourine. I couldn't believe what luck (other than the fact I missed Christmas, of course). Smiling, I was relieved that those farts didn't steal my gift. Deciding to check my stocking, I hefted it down off the coffee table and plopped it onto the floor where I was sitting. There were two mini-sized chocolate bars, three candy canes, and one of those fake lumps of coal. I shook the stocking upside down a few more times just to be sure, praying that there weren't any more candy canes in there—lest they break. Even though some of it was clearly missing (my mom wasn't clever *or* clean enough to remove the *wrappers* from my stocking, eye roll), I jumped into the air and yelled, "Thanks Santa!" at the sky.

I was convinced that even though Santa lived at the North Pole, he must be in Heaven, because nobody knew where the North Pole was. He lived up there, and him and God were best friends. That was how he knew if you'd been good or not. Because *duh,* Santa couldn't just *know* those things. That was totally unrealistic. He might as well not even exist if you went on *that* theory—ha! Thank goodness I knew the truth. I shook my head, thinking about the poor suckers who had been deceived.

Snagging out a chocolate bar, I decided I could totally skip out on my diet in order to eat it. If I didn't eat it now, it'd get eaten by one of my siblings who couldn't keep their greedy paws off my stuff! Or my mother. She was worse than all of them.

After getting those gifts, and a few days to simmer off, I was finally one hundred percent over missing Christmas. Mama's Child called me and asked (well, practically *demanded*) that I come to her mom's diner on New Year's Eve. I tried to explain it was going to be my twin sisters'

Katy and Maria's first birthday.

"So?" she asked rudely. "Don't ya got enough siblings that they'll feel loved enough?"

"I guess, but still." I twisted my mouth. Would it really be okay?

"It's gonna be *awesome,* Denny. We could shoot off fireworks from the roof!" She was speaking so brightly and sing-songy that I knew she was trying to hook me on the idea like a fish.

"That sounds like trouble. Plus, I thought your mom hates me. Not to mention you and I have no idea how to set off fireworks. We're seven, MC."

"No, *you* may be seven. I be six."

"That's even worse!" How was that supposed to make me feel better?

"Den, it will be awesome. Just come." She hung up the phone, and at this point if I didn't go, she would act like I stood her up. Mama's Child had this annoying habit of hanging up before you could say no. That way you *had* to do whatever she asked you to.

It was New Year's Eve, and I made my way over to Mama's Diner, passing Marti's and Megan's houses to get there. I was not gonna lie and say I didn't sneak a peek in the Stars' window. But I wished I hadn't. Marcus was there. As in, he was in *their* house, dancing with *Haylee.* I stepped backward and decided not to peek in anybody else's windows tonight. It would just be too painful.

This was all after two hours of me repeatedly asking my parents if it was okay for me to go. My mom officially hated Mama (I had no idea what MC's mom's name was) more than I had hated Mama's *Child.* My dad didn't give a crap who I hung around with, as long as it wasn't Bob Waltzer.

But he wanted me to be there for the birthday party, and he made a big deal about how I always watched the ball drop at midnight with him. In reality? *I* always watched the ball drop at midnight while he was on the toilet for what felt like three hours.

My mother's words kept playing over and over again in my head as I walked to the diner. "*You better not do anything stupid. I* mean it! *I'm letting you go to the party, so it'll be a lighter work load for* me. No *other reason.*"

I arrived at Mama's Diner to realize it was an empty restaurant. Mama's Child sat in the middle of the floor with party streamers and a few little kid fireworks, such as party poppers. Her mom was in the back kitchen cooking fish tacos, from the smell of it. The aroma floated through the air, pungent and strong. It was deadly and smelled like fried toe jam.

"Hey, Denny!" Mama's Child reached up and adjusted her pink munchkin hat.

"What's up with the chairs?" I asked, motioning to the walls. A spacious amount of floor room flooded my eyes, the tables and chairs all pushed up against the sides.

"It's closed," she said bluntly, giving me a dumbfounded look. "This is what a closed restaurant looks like. Duh." Her eyes rolled up, down, and side to side.

"It's kind of creepy being in a restaurant at night with no tables or chairs."

"No, it's not!" Her eyes widened, like I was crazy. "It's *cool.* Gives you the whole place to yourself."

"Why's your mom back there cooking fish tacos if there won't be any customers?" I asked, furrowing my eyebrows and sitting down in front of her, crisscross applesauce.

"For us!"

"But...I don't *like* fish tacos."

"I can't believe you're complainin' when you eat that Mystery Meet all the time. Like you be too good or sumtin'."

I could tell I was getting on her nerves by her accent crawling out of the woodwork.

"Are you two *fighting* out there?" her mom hollered. "If you are fighting, you can just go on your separate ways, and there won't *be* a party. I'm tired of this drama!"

I glanced around, but couldn't get a glimpse good enough to see her. She must really have the ears to be hearing us over that grease popping.

"Sorry," we both said in unison.

Her mother grunted, and it was hard to tell if it was at us or if she got burnt by a splash of fatty fish grease. I tried not to gag thinking about it. Because that would *really* set MC off.

Mama's Child turned on the TV on the wall, and New Year's parties were on tons of channels. We picked the one that had the ball drop and good music to watch while her mom served us food. Then we went outside and set off the party poppers.

"Ow!" I yelled, a spark from hers bouncing off my hand. She just laughed. We reached into her bag, and one last party popper remained.

"I wanna set it off!" she stated immediately. "My mom paid for them, after all." Her intensity turned into a look of sadness, and I thought it was probably 'cause they didn't have lots of money. It struck a chord inside me somewhere that she had spent money on fireworks just so I could have more fun.

"Thanks for getting the fireworks, and for inviting me."

"And?" she asked.

I grimaced, touching my upset stomach. "And thanks for

the fish taco," I muttered through a half-smile, half-gag.

"Don't worry 'bout it."

Well, if I didn't have to worry about it, then why did I have to thank her? I censored that thought and didn't speak it out loud.

Mama's Child and I stayed up till the ball dropped, then she fell asleep. I was slightly annoyed because we were supposed to have lots of fun. It *was* fun. But I had thought we were going to pull an all nighter. I actually got so hungry that I ate *three more fish tacos* after she went to sleep. My stomach spoiled like milk just thinking about it. But it was all that her mom had provided for us, and I wasn't allowed to go back in the kitchen.

I threw up in the bushes at the crack of dawn, wondering just how long them tacos had been sitting out on the counter. The thought of food poisoning weaseled its way inside my head, and I denied my brain the privilege of trying to calculate that. Because I honestly didn't *want* to know. Music boomed down the street, and I could only assume it was coming from the Stars' or the Greens' house. Walking back inside the diner, I lay down on the cold, hard tile and fell back to sleep.

In the morning, I woke, lying on the floor with tables all around me. I blinked multiple times when I saw people sitting at a table by me and almost *shrieked* when Mama yelled, "Order up!"

I scrambled up to a sitting position and scanned the diner. I didn't see Mama's Child anywhere. Gathering my stuff, I went outside. It took some looking around, but I finally found her playing with one of those toys where you have to catch the ball on a string in a cup.

"Mama's Child!" I hissed.

She turned around.

"Why didn't you wake me up?

"Pays to be an early riser, Den. Ya gotta re-route your internal alarm clock. Think yers must be broken!" She chuckled and continued playing with her toy.

"What?" I yelled, growing angrier by the second.

"I think you are gettin' the rage from bein' an over sleeper."

"Are you *crazy?*" I took a few steps toward her and stopped in front of her.

"No, are *you?*" She looked straight at me with wide, crazy eyes. Then she chuckled again. I grumbled unintelligible syllables under my breath, then pulled myself together. *This ain't good for my rage.*

"Well, I think I'm gonna go home," I said, trying to stop while we were ahead.

"What? Are ya mad, Denny?" She turned toward me and placed a hand on my arm.

"No," I lied. "I just gotta go home before practice. The play is tomorrow." I shrugged and kicked at the dirt.

"Okay, did ya have fun?" Her eyebrows raised hopefully, and a small smile tugged at the corners of her mouth. Her freckles did their familiar dance across her cheeks and eyelids.

"Yes. Thanks for not causing trouble." I didn't want to get in a huge fight with her before the musical and get myself all freaked out over it. I'd mess up for sure.

"You're welcome." She laughed.

As I turned to go home, a few diners pointed and snickered at me, and I shook my head in dismay.

I couldn't believe she literally let me wake up on the floor of an *active diner.* I blew hot air out of my mouth, making a sound similar to that of a horse.

It wasn't worth it, DJ. Keep on keeping on.

Chapter 35

STANDING BEHIND THE RED plush curtain of the stage exactly fourteen minutes before the show was supposed to start, I could feel my heartbeat in my ears. And something was up with my stomach because it felt like it had leaped up into my throat. I turned around, and all the other kids were showing up, dressed and ready in their costumes. Mumbling some of my lines under my breath, I also muttered a silent prayer that I wouldn't forget any of them.

"Are you done talking to yourself *again*, DJ?" Rochelle rolled her eyes and messed around with some ropes and such.

"I'm practicing my lines," I said flatly. I did not need her psyching me out this close before the production.

"Well, your mumbling is distracting me from my work. And quite frankly, I'm getting tired of your attitude."

Gawking at her in disbelief, I wondered what her problem was. I didn't think I was having an attitude, and she didn't even look like she had *that* much work to be distracted from. Who did she think she was, anyway? Our mom?

"I'm sorry?" I said the words as a question. Because I

didn't think she deserved them in the form of an answer.

"Yeah! You better be. I don't wanna be here in the first place. I had to skip my shift at the factory for this crap, because if I didn't show up, I wouldn't get participation points. And we all know I'm gonna need them."

I *did* know that she needed them.

"But wouldn't you have come to watch Lil' Shelb anyway?" I squinted at her. Lil' Shelbi was her entire world.

"Um, of course! But this way I have to work instead of being in the audience relaxing. It sucks, Dennis." She spit on the floor, and I wrinkled my nose. That was so disrespectful and nasty. I figured this conversation needed to end for both of our sanity. Rochelle and I just rubbed each other the wrong way.

Turning back around, I peeked behind the curtain— something that everyone said *not* to do. They said it made you more nervous, but I wasn't buying it. Had to find out for my own curious self. Okay. Turned out they were right. A flush of heat coursed through me at the countless eyes peeled to the stage, waiting.

I gulped and paced back and forth. It was hard to believe this was real, even this far into the production. How did I actually get placed as the lead? I should've made an appointment with Anthony to tell him the great news and to practice calming exercises. I'd been so busy, I had forgotten all about Anthony.

Mama's Child strutted across the stage in full attire as I was getting a drink of water from the fountain.

"Break a leg, Den!" She slapped me on the back, and I choked, hacking water all up onto the floor.

"You should really drink more slowly, Dennis." I clenched my fists, and tightly shut my eyes. Mama's Child always thought she knew everything, and she always had a solution. Even if *she* was the problem in the first place. Taking deep breaths, I cooled my rage down.

After each number, we got a vibe from the Stars that they weren't appreciating the language choices of the songs and lines, and that they didn't particularly approve of the outfits, either. It made me uncomfortable, being on the stage while Marti sat there gasping the whole time. She was distracting me. Thinking about the content though, I couldn't believe this was allowed either.

My mom sat there just a hee-hawing and clapping. I thought I even heard her say, "This is really hitting home." I was very curious as to what that had meant. Part of me wondered if she had done some of the things in this musical or acted this way when *she* was a teenager. Or maybe she had just showed up after a few drinks. It was honestly hard to tell with her.

The Greens hadn't seemed to care one way or the other. Megan pulled out a video camera every time her kids were on stage. My cheeks had turned hot and red in the spotlight, and I kept getting self-conscious, thinking about how I would be in pieces of their family video—for *eternity*. Monica had done brilliant singing the "Cell Block Tango." It was unbelievable! Like she had special training in acting and singing.

Mama's Child sang her solo, and I laughed a little. She *really* milked it for all she could. The crowd greatly applauded, except for my mom. She was definitely still holding a grudge over her being Mama's daughter and about her setting me up on Halloween. My mom had a very selective memory, and she could probably tell you exactly what you did to upset her for any specific date and time of any year. Maybe she had a filing cabinet somewhere just chock-full of everything anyone had ever done to make her mad or hurt her.

I surprisingly did not forget any of my lines, but I did stumble during a dance number. Since nobody laughed or made hateful comments like they normally did anytime I did *anything* incorrectly, I assumed nobody had noticed. When Nigel and I got to the kissing scene, I was so shocked, thinking, *Oh wow. This was going to be my first kiss*—ever. But I wasn't very happy with how it had ended. We hadn't practiced this scene, because Mr. Sanch didn't want us to be uncomfortable. It was supposed to be a quick peck on the lips. You know how it was, a *real kiss!* But when he leaned in, he kissed me on the *cheek* instead. What was *that* supposed to mean? I would have to make an appointment with Anthony for sure now.

I met up with my family after the show, and *nobody* told me that I was awesome. Choking back tears that were welling up inside my eyelids, I rubbed away the lump in my throat. Megan Green took a few steps in our direction, and I tried not to stare or be embarrassing. She was probably just coming over to gossip with my mom. But then she tapped my shoulder and told me I did great. She handed me a bouquet that smelled like *Chanel No. 5.* Smiling ear to ear, I thanked her, feeling like a VIP. Granted, she gave every kid a bouquet. But that wasn't really anybody's business but my own.

My dad's face was pinched, and I asked him what was wrong.

"Well, it's just that I called off work at the factory for this." He grunted a sigh, but said nothing more. I was *astounded.* He called off? Oh my gosh, that was a big deal.

"You called *off?*" I asked, my jaw hitting the floor, thinking he must have called off so he could see me play the lead.

"It's the first time I've called off in a *long* time. I was invited to go see *Chicago,* but I was under the impression it was being put on by professional actors. *Not* little kids." He glared at my mom out the corner of his eyes, and his lips turned down at the edges. My mom looked right at him and smirked. Immediately, I knew she had been behind this.

"Well, I'm glad you came, Dad."

"You're welcome," he muttered, barely even making eye contact with me. It was almost like he was here, but his mind was somewhere else.

"When I get home, I'm going to eat my leftovers and go straight to bed for a nap. I got a triple shift to work tomorrow—" His eyes focused on something behind me, and when I glanced over my shoulder, Krissy and Dominique were running past the crowd of other kids and our direction. My dad's face and voice brightened immediately.

"Great job, babies!" he cheered, wrapping an arm around each of them and pulling them in for a big bear hug. He lifted them up off the ground and swung them around. He was laughing, and they were giggling like it was the time of their lives. I'd admit that I was jealous. I'd admit it. It sounded terrible, but *that wasn't even their dad.* Why did they get such special treatment and love? Rage bubbled beneath my skin, running hot as a fire in my veins, and a dark thought crossed my brain. *He should treat them like the little orphan Annies that they are.* Then I punched myself in the stomach and mumbled, "Anthony would be so disappointed in me right now."

You are a terrible person, my brain told me. *You deserve to be treated this way.*

Rochelled dragged her feet as she slouched her way over to us. She looked me dead in the eyes and said, "Don't worry, Dennis. You don't have to punch yourself. *Fat people can make it as actors, too.*"

Struggling to discern whether that was an insult or a compliment, I glanced down at my stomach, which was starting to hurt from that punch. I shouldn't have done that. I winced as the other kids ran around like hooligans, not even caring or appreciating the hard work and the nice show we just did. It was bothering me; it was too much. Too loud, too busy. This production was huge. Why did nobody else seem to care? This would look great for us in the future if we wanted to be actors or anyone popular.

Popular.

Wait a second, I was the lead. Why did I not feel more popular? Shouldn't this have made a difference? I had a great moment just now in my life, and I wasn't getting to share this awesomeness with *anyone*. Because everyone just thought of it as a stupid play.

On a Wednesday afternoon, I strolled into Anthony's office.

"Well, DJ." He shut the door behind me as I walked in and took a seat in front of his desk.

"Yeah?"

"I'm sorry to have to see you here again." He noticed my frown, and clarified, "I mean, it's good to see you. But I had just thought you were making some real progress."

"Don't you get paid for me being here?" This was his job, after all.

"Well, yes. Yes, I do." He rubbed his chin like he did when he was considering what to say to me.

"Then shouldn't you be *happy* that I'm here?"

"The world's not about money, DJ."

"It is in my mother's opinion," I muttered. It was silent

for a few seconds.

"How…is your mother?" He looked down at his desk and tapped his pen lightly.

"Married." I gave him the side eye.

"That's not what I asked, DJ. Is there a problem? I sense some tension."

I shifted in my seat.

"And last I heard, she was divorced," he muttered more to himself than to me.

I sat up straighter in my chair and raised my voice. "Well, she's not anymore, so you can just mind your own business, sir!"

Anthony chuckled, which dumped me off even more.

"Why are you laughing?" I demanded.

"It's just that you gave me a lot of strong attitude there, DJ. But you politely ended your sentence with the word 'sir'."

"Oh," I said shortly. I still didn't see how that was funny. People tended to laugh at things I said and did often, even if I didn't sense any humor in them whatsoever. "Can we talk about *my* problems now?" My voice came out a little more sassy than I would have liked, but Anthony made no comment verbally or on his little clipboard.

"You know how there was this *big* play? You might have heard of it. It was a pretty big deal. It was called, '*Chicago Junior*'?"

"Um, no I didn't."

"Well, it was *big.*" I widened my eyes and nodded, so he would get the picture.

"Okay."

"And I was the lead in it."

"Dennis, I thought we had already decided we were not going to be lying to each other—"

I screeched, a loud scream. No words. Just a scream.

"I'm not going to judge you for being in an *ensemble*."

The word cut through me like a knife. I stood and lost it. I threw his vase. It was hard plastic, so it didn't break, and I was very disappointed. More disappointed than Anthony was in *me*. Something needed to be *smashed*. When he calmed me down, I showed him a video of me singing *Roxie* on my mom's phone (which I had stolen from her this morning for this very purpose).

"Congratulations," was all he said.

I rolled my eyes. "I told you I wasn't lying."

"I said congratulations, DJ."

"I know, but nobody thought it was as cool as me." Plopping back down in my seat, I huffed a loud sigh.

"Did they tell you that?"

"No, but I know they were thinking it."

"What makes you say that?"

"Because nobody brought it up. It's kind of like it was over, and everyone stopped talking about it. It felt just like the day after Christmas, when all the fun and excitement and happy feelings are just up and gone. You come down off the high. But it was so *important* to me. Now they ruined it, and it's like it was nothing but another day." I stopped and held my head in my hands.

"Well, if they didn't actually *say* anything about it, they may have *thought* it was awesome. You might just not know because you didn't bring it up to them."

"It shouldn't have to be my job to bring it up. If *I* did that, it would be like bragging."

"No, it wouldn't. Think of it as a conversation starter." He cocked his head to the side and tried to appear interested. I felt like he wasn't though, and he was just doing things he learned in his fancy *How to be a Therapist* books.

"It'd be like word *vomit*. I started talking about my new tambourine one time, and then I kept wanting to talk about it. Everyone eventually got annoyed. Like they always do." My breath was shaky as I squirmed in my seat. I swung my legs and kept glancing around the room. Anywhere but at him.

"Have you been stressed lately?" he asked in a soothing voice. "Are you using the exercises?"

"Yes."

"Are they working?"

"Most of the time," I murmured quietly.

"So you won't need to see me anymore, unless needed, right?"

I finally brought my eyes back to his. "No, I didn't say that!" I exclaimed. "I think I need to have *more* sessions again."

"Why?"

Just another person trying to get rid of me, I thought. *Just be honest.*

"'Cause then I can talk about whatever I want, and someone *has* to listen. It will ensure that I'll have a friend. That I won't get bored and lonely." My entire body flushed from embarrassment. How pitiful was I?

"DJ, insurance won't cover your sessions for a reason like that." He didn't crack a smile in the slightest, and I didn't think he liked me anymore. He probably never did.

"Insurance?" I asked. "Don't people pay for that?"

"Yes, you have to pay for insurance."

"Well, then it doesn't matter. We probably don't have that anyways. If it costs money, I doubt we do."

He ignored this and changed the subject. "What about Mama's Child? Isn't she your friend?"

"We have a love-hate relationship, I guess." I shrugged.

"I don't know. What can I say? It's like we are best friends one minute, and she's out to get me the next."

"What?" He rubbed his forehead, so I tried to be more direct.

"Yeah, I think we're currently friends. But we don't really talk a lot."

"Okay." A puzzled look crossed his features, and he pushed his glasses up on the bridge of his nose.

"DJ, *whose* phone was that you showed me?"

I flipped it open in my lap, and the screen lit up. It said *Deniese* in fancy writing. "Mine!" I said, quickly.

"No, it's not."

"It has my name on it."

"Is that your *mom's* phone?" he demanded.

I hesitated, my pulse quickening. "Maybe."

"I'm gonna have to tell her."

"Yeah, you'd like that, wouldn't you?" I raised my voice at him, standing up and holding the phone with a death grip. "You'd like to have a reason to call her. I know when I'm in these sessions you look at me, but all you see and think about is *her.*"

"What?" Anthony's face flushed fire hydrant red.

"You heard me!"

His mouth opened and shut like a fish gulping for air. "I-I-I don't know what you're talking about."

The little bells went off, signaling someone had entered the reception area, followed by a knock at his office door.

"DJ," Anthony lowered his voice, "your session is over."

"I'll leave."

"DJ!" my mom's voice called sweetly. It was sickeningly sweet, like thick molasses. It made me sick at how fake it was.

"Bye," Anthony said, watching the door.

"Married." My tone was blunt, and I gave him the side eye as I left. I didn't trust him not to come out here and run off with my mother.

Mom and I walked out of the office, and she drove me home. Her hair and makeup was immaculate as always, and she was wearing a low-cut top. She probably thought she'd be seeing Anthony today and wanted to dress up. But Anthony didn't even walk me out. He stayed in his office, and I was glad he had gotten my message.

"DJ," my mom said, after driving in complete silence for a few minutes. She fluffed up her hair and eyed herself in the mirror instead of watching the road.

"Yeah?"

"Don't you have homework or somethin'? I haven't seen you doing any lately."

"Mr. Sanch gave us time off."

"Mr. Sanch? You mean Officer Pete?" She wrinkled her nose up and squinted.

"No, when he married Sanch, he took her last name."

"There's no way," my mom said, in a tone that told me she totally thought I was lying through my teeth.

"Yes-huh."

She slammed on the brakes, and I flung forward in my seat. "DJ, you are lying straight to my face."

"No, I'm not. I promise. Everyone calls him that." Staring at her eyes in the mirror, I crossed my fingers that she would believe me. The car started moving again, and I took that as a good sign.

"Well, what's wrong with this dude if he took his *wife's* last name in place of his own, quit his own job to become a substitute teacher, *and* he's not giving you *any* homework?"

I shrugged. "I know, it's lots of drama."

She was quiet for a second before eyeing me and saying,

"You don't get this kind of info on my favorite radio talk show—*Gossip Girl 411*."

"Yeah?"

"Yeah."

Sitting in the car with just the two of us seemed an awful lot like a bonding moment. I kind of smiled but didn't say anything. She'd never admit that she liked bonding with me. But maybe deep down she actually did.

"DJ, why you be smirking, huh? You crushin' on a boy?" She grinned eagerly.

"Mooooooooooooooom!" I whined, blushing.

"That'd be a yes."

"What? I didn't say that—"

"—ooooooooh, girl. You better be dishin' the deets!"

"Deets?" My eyebrows knitted into what I imagined would look like a squiggly ferret.

"Duh! The *details.*" She slapped the wheel a few times before rolling down the window and yelling, "MOVE! The light is green, idiot!" at the person in front of us. They started moving.

"Mom, I won't tell you. You'll just embarrass me!"

"Is it the boy that kissed your cheek in the play?" she asked, watching me carefully.

"You noticed that?" I shrank in my seat. Here I thought she didn't even *care* that I was in the play at all.

"Um, duh! I was there!" She slapped the wheel, like I was wasting her time.

"Yeah, I don't know what that was about. He was supposed to—" I stopped, suddenly unsure if this was something I could talk to her about.

My mom quirked an eyebrow like she was going to ask me what I meant, but then she straightened and turned up the stereo's volume.

"This is my *jam!*" she yelled at the top of her lungs. Then she started dancing and swinging a sweat belt that was sitting next to her on the middle seat. I was laughing, but she was so into the music that I didon't think she even noticed.

Chapter 36

WALKING ON THE SIDEWALK and avoiding stepping on any cracks, Mama's Child and I were on our way to Izzy and Chad's wedding. It wasn't anything new or unique. I shouldn't have been surprised that their date choice was *also* on Valentine's Day. Cherry and Izzy had done everything together; they might as well share anniversaries, too. So much romance and mush in the air. You could almost smell it. Oh, wait. Nevermind. That was just the smell of old rain on the pavement.

"Hey, Mama's Child?" I asked, gently swinging my purse as we walked.

"Yah?"

"What is love?" I was being completely serious, but Mama's Child apparently wasn't.

She replied in dramatic song, *"Baby, don't hurt me! Don't hurt me! No more!"*

I stared at her like she was an idiot, but she just screeched "Gotcha!" and punched me in the rib.

"Ow!" I screamed, lifting my shirt up to find a bluish bruise already forming. I put it back down and did my deep breathing exercises. "I was being serious!" I threw my hands up in the air and cringed, grabbing at the searing pain in my rib. It hurt to raise my arm on that side now.

"You'll know when ya know," she crooned softly, slipping her arm around my shoulder. We swayed back and forth as we walked, the best of buds.

"Mama's Child, can I tell you something since we are friends again?"

"Yeah."

"My hot therapist has been calling my mom's phone all week and sending her winky face text messages. I haven't answered any of them, so he's been sending a bunch. I may be slow when it comes to socialization, but I'm thinking there's something going on between them."

Mama's Child gasped. "Scandalous! What juicy gossip, Den." Her Cheshire Cat grin reached both of her ears, and she held an arm out in front of me to slow me down. "Wait, why do you have your mom's phone?"

"I took it to get on the group chat when the computer doesn't work," I lied. I couldn't tell her that I took it to prove to Anthony that I was a rock star in a musical. *Or* that I didn't have an opportunity to put it back because my mom's been scouring our house for it and would notice. That would be embarrassing for one thing, and for another? She might *tattle* on me and get me in trouble.

"Watch that puddle!" Mama's Child exclaimed, pushing me out of the way.

The contents of my little purse spilled everywhere. I had felt so cool bringing my own purse, and look at what happened! I shoulda just went in pants with pockets. But Mom insisted *that* would be embarrassing for her. I didn't see why it would be. It wasn't like she would be wearing the pants with pockets, and why did it matter anyway? Pockets were handy. Much better than a skirt.

Bending to gather my things, I scanned the mess.

Mama's Child crouched and helped me. "Oh no, Denny. Some of your stuff fell in the puddle! There's no use digging in it, you'll get a *disease!*"

Oh no. I'll get a disease. She was right. I hated when she reminded my brain to freak out. *You'll get a disease and die,* my brain told me. Then it tried an even scarier tactic. *What if there's a mouthful of teeth attached to some scary water swamp monster? What if it bites me and I lose my hand? What if—*

Mama's Child's hands were in her back pockets, and she shifted around, looking at our surroundings.

"What's wrong? Did ya see something?"

"No," she answered quickly.

I fished around in my purse and checked to see what was missing. My nerves bundled into one huge knitting ball of yarn. I checked my purse a third and fourth time, and it wasn't in there. Maybe my mom's phone had fallen in the puddle. Eyeing the deep abyss, I couldn't see anything unless I put my hand in there. And I couldn't do *that.*

"Come on, Den. We're gonna be late."

"But, Mama's Child! I'm missing my twenty dollar bill *and* my mom's phone!"

Spaghetti. The ball of yarn had turned into big, wet, noodly spaghetti.

"Puddle just gobbles up what it wants." She shook her head and shrugged. "It's probably karma getting ya back for takin' yer mom's phone." Her accent was coming out, and I eyed her suspiciously. Glancing at the puddle once more, I sighed. It wasn't worth losing my hand to a swamp monster, and it wasn't worth getting an infectious disease. I had to leave it. At least now my mom wouldn't think I took it, and it wouldn't be found with me.

❖

The wedding was absolutely beautiful. It was like a rock concert—so cool and so unlike Cherry and Derek's. I had to give Izzy *that* much. She wore a short white dress with black studded boots. All of the bridesmaids had purple streaks put in their hair, just like Izzy's. Cherry was the maid of honor, and Monica was the flower girl. And Monica looked *great* with a purple streak in her hair. *I* wanted a purple streak in *my* hair. I couldn't tell MC I thought it was awesome though, because she'd probably flip out on me like all the other times when I talked about Monica.

The reception had no slow songs, so I rocked out with my BFF, Mama's Child. She kept zipping her pockets up, and one of them bulged like she had a wallet back there. *Couldn't be,* I thought. *She's poor.* I suddenly felt both a little jealous that MC's mom let *her* wear pants with pockets and a little bad that she didn't have any money. I offered to grab her another burrito from the bar, thinking it'd make her feel better. She declined and told me she was watching her weight. Maybe it was because I had been on a diet? She wanted to be just like me, and I knew it. It wasn't like she tried to hide it; she copied everything I did. Except why was *her* diet working? She was looking thin. I patted my stomach and smoothed down my shirt.

Wanting to think about something other than myself, I did some observing. I liked to know things. Little Shelb was dancing with a burrito in her mouth and two in her hands. Rochelle was smoking a cigarette in the doorway. My mom was half drunk at the bar, slurring, "Slap me up another beer!" Bob Waltzer was sleazing on my mom.

I gave him the side eye, my gaze stopping at his nearly-white hair. He *did* have hair kind of like mine. It made me uncomfortable, wondering if what my mom said about him being my dad was true. I shook my head. That was stupid and complete nonsense. Mom made inappropriate jokes all the time. That was all it was.

Megan Green was toasting with some relatives. Ashley hadn't come because she was babysitting all the little kids, and my dad was at work.

Just then, an eerie feeling that someone was watching the party, or even me, came over me. Goosebumps prickled every inch of my skin. The music got quieter, even though no one turned it down. Was this a panic attack? My breathing became short and fast.

Mama's Child whispered in my ear, "Do you have that *feeling* again, Den? I can see it in your eyes. Smells like fear."

Footsteps in the distance seemed to drown out everything else. They were getting closer and closer. What was happening? What was happening to *me?* I wanted to scream. Mama's Child had left my side. I was frozen in fear.

A deep alto voice murmured, "Hello, Deniese."

"No!" I screamed and turned around.

My eyes were closed shut, clenched as tight as possible. I reached out my hand and slapped the person's leg before I even saw who it was.

Panting, my mom stumbled out of the bar, yelling, "*Deniese.* What have you *done*?"

I knew whatever had happened was bad. Whatever I *did* was bad. She used my real name. *Her* name. Aware my eyes were still shut, I summoned the courage to open them, hiding between a few cracks in my fingers. And when I did, I saw bright blue stilettos.

Tight blue pants.

Tight, *electric* blue, leather pants.

Then I looked up.

Expensive, name brand, silver jacket.

Sleek, blond, highlighted hair.

I took in a deep breath. Then I said, "*Who the dump are you?*"

My mom shrieked and passed out. A few people turned to see if she was okay. Namely, Bob Waltzer.

"I. Am. Morgan."

…?

"…I. Am. Dennis?" I asked in a robot voice. I tried to copy her tone exactly. Then I snickered, thinking about how quick I came up with that one. I did the robot dance move, and the whole room got quiet. People were staring at me.

Mama's Child rushed over to my side. Her footsteps were the only sound in the entire building, despite being filled with so many people. They echoed.

"That's *Megan's mother*," she whispered in my ear. "Some people call her '*Boss*'."

Instant fear set in.

I didn't know what to say, so I ran into the porta potty and hid in there until the party was over. My cheeks were red hot, and I had a feeling that the other pair was going to be too when I got home.

Chapter 37

NOTHING HAPPENED FOR the rest of February. You know, considering I was in *the grounded room* for the *rest of that whole month!* I had nothing in there except for pencils and papers to write an apology letter with. Apparently, "Boss" was the CEO of Disney Donuts. Which was *also* the place where Mama's Child and I got in trouble (a few journal entries back). Not to mention she was *Monica's grandma*! She was never going to speak to me again, I just knew it.

Sigh. I really needed an appointment with Anthony. Wonder if my mom ever found her phone? It probably wouldn't work at this point. No amount of rice could fix *that.* That was a weird fact I stumbled upon on the computer one day. That putting wet electronics in rice could sometimes fix them. Weird.

I was allowed to get out of the grounded room today, and I wasn't really all that excited. I mean, I was. You could only stare at the same old, dirty four walls for so long. It smelled musty in there. But I was kind of afraid, thinking it was no doubt a *fact* that everyone hated me. Mama's Child hadn't even found a way to get in contact with me this time.

And she was *Mama's Child.* She knew *everything.* My mom could be dating Anthony now for all I knew.

When I exited the grounded room, and my mom and I were both aware it was my last day, she was clearly still mad at me. Her cold shoulder was almost worse than her abusive insults. I tugged on her shirt tail. Pouting my bottom lip out, I told her, "I'm sorry!"

And I had meant it!

She didn't answer.

My dad didn't talk to me either. I was assuming he was filled in when he got home from work that day. When my mom left and disappeared into the kitchen, I picked the house phone up off the coffee table. The line rang a couple times, searching for MC on the other end. She didn't answer, so I called again.

It rang multiple times, and still no answer.

On the fourth call, her mom picked up and hissed, "If this is *Dennis,* I'm extremely disappointed in you and want you to quit calling my daughter. You are a bad influence on her."

She hung up the phone, and I gasped. How could I possibly lose *everything* over one teensy mistake? I had no idea how to deal with these feelings, and part of me said to go on a walk. But instead, I went over to the newest place in town—iHOP.

They had just built it, and rumor had it they had an all you could eat pancake deal for three ninety-nine right now! I reached into my pocket and scrunched my wilted five dollar bill. The money had been laying under the bed in the grounded room, so naturally, I took it. Maybe it was a gift to make me feel better? Or maybe it was magic? I didn't know! I was bored, so I started looking at other things besides the four walls. The only piece of furniture was the bed, so I searched under it. And there she was! Ol' faithful! I placed the money back in my pocket and finished the trek to the restaurant.

The door chimed as I walked in, and I took a seat at the counter. I was about to order when I did a double take upon seeing my *mom and dad* here! It was a Saturday, and my parents almost always worked. But I hadn't even seen them leave. They were too sneaky. What else did they do that I didn't know about?

One of my siblings must have tagged along, and I squinted to see who it was. And to my amazement, sitting there in between my parents, was *Mama's Child.* What in tarnation was *she* doing here? I was seething with anger.

So! She had enough time to hang out with *my* parents, but she wouldn't call me back?

Dude Green walked in and took a seat. My dad scooched down so he could sit next to him. I stood and crossed over to them, then sat right down next to MC since there now was an open seat.

"I hate you," I told her. "You saw Morgan coming, and you *ran* instead of telling me who she was. And now you're ignoring me? You didn't even answer my phone calls."

Just then, someone slapped a plate of what appeared to be fifty pancakes in front of me, and everyone else who was at the counter. I took in the humongous stack, and my stomach growled. They did look delicious, but *nobody* could eat that much! What was going on?

"You have ninety minutes!" someone yelled from the back of the kitchen.

"What the dump *is* this?" I screeched.

A waiter walked out and said, "Thank you to everyone who decided to celebrate our grand opening with a pancake eating contest! Whoever can finish these pancakes first gets a free, brand new cellphone!" The other diners in the restaurant cheered. I couldn't believe my parents hadn't noticed me. Or if they did, they didn't care.

My parents, Dude Green, Bob Waltzer, Rochelle, and MC started chomping down their pancakes. I fumbled with my silverware and tried to grab my fork. When my fingers could properly handle it, I started shoveling them pancakes into my mouth! I was winning that phone. If I had to participate, *I was going to win.*

I was fifteen pancakes in, and I had to stop to unbutton my pants. I regretted this so much, but I just kept shoveling them in! It wasn't exactly like I could back down now, and after glancing at my competition, I knew I was in trouble. My mom was still going strong. But Mama's Child was now sitting in a corner booth, watching me icily. She had only eaten one pancake before bowing out.

I finished pancake number twenty and went to wipe my mouth with my napkin. When I picked it up, a written on napkin lay crumpled beside it. So out of curiosity, and not fearing germs since I knew it was MC's, I opened it up and read it. It was a note that had the following words on it:

"I hop u enjoy dem fluffy pankakes with all dat melded budder! I imagine dat u r drownin in sirup. Not gud 4 ur wait watchers, DENNY!"

Had she set me up once again? I growled, realizing that MC probably sat in this seat on purpose. She knew I'd confront her, and she wanted me to be stuck in this competition so I'd get *fat.* Standing up, not even caring about the phone, I stormed out of there *steaming*!

Bumping into something hard, I backed up, and to my embarrassment it was none other than *the* Marcus Delon.

"You, um. You've got some syrup on your face, Deniese."

I ran away crying, and about halfway home, I realized he still wasn't calling me Dennis. It made my heart flutter.

At home, I pulled out my workbook and started scribbling *Mrs. Deniese Delon* all over it. Thinking about Marcus's ocean blue eyes and wavy blond hair, I sighed dreamily. My full belly plopped out with the sigh, and I groaned. *Why* had I eaten so many pancakes? Placing my hands on my stomach and rubbing it regretfully, I hit my pants button. Looking down, I realized that I had been walking around with my pants *unbuttoned* since I left the restaurant. Which meant…oh, no. My pants had been unbuttoned in front of Marcus! I wailed aloud and decided I needed to call Anthony.

Squeezing my belly and sucking it in, I tried to get my pants to button, but they wouldn't. I couldn't handle this stress. Padding down the stairs as quickly as possible, I grabbed the phone and dialed the familiar number.

"Thank you for calling Better Future Therapeutics, this is Mindy. How can I help—"

"—I need to speak to Anthony!" I cut her off.

"One moment, may I ask who is calling?"

"Tell him that it's Deniese Tipper and I need to see him *immediately*!" My breathing was too short, too fast. I grew lightheaded.

After a few moments of silence, someone picked up the phone.

"Hey, *baby*. How was the pancake contest? Did you win?"

I screamed and hung up. I was surprised I didn't die from a heart attack when my mom kicked open our front door and yelled, "Who the *dump* is screaming in *my* home?"

I threw the phone down on the couch and ran up the steps, not wanting to get the shoe. I needed answers, but I didn't need them like this. Opening my door and quickly swinging inside, I ran to my bed and flopped down on my belly, crying into my pillow once again.

I was so stressed that my mom scheduled me an appointment with *Anthony*. The nerve! I walked out of the house and kept walking. In no dumping world would I go see *him* after all that had happened! I needed to calm myself down. Today was the shamrock party at school, and I wanted to be in a good mood so I could enjoy it.

Realizing I had forgotten to wear green, I tried not to panic as my eyes took in everyone *else's* green apparel. Monica was fashionable in bright green leggings and a black sweater. I was in a brown shirt with cookies on it that said *"Bite Me!"* Mark Melon took it as a direct order and bit my arm, leaving a mark. I screeched at him like one of them howler monkeys, and Mr. Sanchez told us to knock it off and sit down.

When I spotted Mama's Child at recess, I was still so mad at her that I couldn't help myself. I snuck up behind her and pushed her off the swing. She screamed a bad word, and we both got sent to the principal's office. Turned out, I got an after school detention for violence and so did she for saying that word, which I will not recite.

On my way out of the principal's office, a wave of nausea swept over me so strongly that I threw up my lunch in the nearest trash can, barely making it. We had them fake cheeseburgers for lunch, and it was worse than Mystery Meet. You know, for a private school, this place was *disgusting*. It was probably Mrs. Sanchez's fault.

I walked to detention a few hours later despite trying to go home "sick" and sat down to hear the most disgustingly familiar sound. Yup, you guessed it. There sat *Mama's*

Child, chewing and slurping on her pencil.

She gave me the side eye and raised her hand. "Mr. Sanch?"

"Yes?"

"I think my knees need more Neosporin!" And with that, she flashed me a wicked grin. She excused herself to go to the bathroom. When she came back, her hands were dripping wet, and I cringed. As she passed me to go to her seat, she pulled my shirt collar back and shoved something wet and slimy down my back. I reached down my shirt immediately, and it was a *toilet paper wad*! Gross!

I stood, flipped her desk over, and screamed, "What's your *beef,* Mama's Child? What the dump did I ever do to make you so mad?"

Her eyes widened, and she said nothing.

"If anyone should be mad, it should be me!" I stabbed a finger at my chest.

"Dennis June, sit down. *Now.*" Mr. Sanchez helped MC set her desk back up, and I took my seat, heaving dragon fire breaths. He returned to his desk and put his feet up, grabbing his magazine and reading it.

I stared straight ahead until I felt her eyes on me. When I turned to her, she looked me straight in the eyes, and for once I felt like she was telling me the truth when she said, "You *know* what you did."

She then pretended to cough while flipping me off so the teacher wouldn't notice. I stiffened and stared at her, cocking my head. Did I do something and didn't remember? If I didn't do anything, then why did I feel embarrassed? And why did I feel like she was telling me the truth?

MC slapped a hand against her desk and stormed out of the room.

I stood and followed her, screaming, "Mama's Child, talk

to me!"

"No," she said, and kept on walking. She didn't even bother to turn around.

I asked her nicely two more times and received the same one-word answer. So I had to go for a low blow and try another method.

"Tell me what I did, or I tell the whole school you're poor!"

She wheeled around and bared her teeth at me. "Wouldn't surprise me if ya did, Chubs! You're turnin' into one of *them.*"

"One of who?" I asked incredulously.

"The *populars*!" Her foot stomped against the ground, as if she was a two-year-old throwing a tantrum.

"What the duff?" I asked, incredibly confused. I wrinkled my face all up and gulped like a fish out of water. "They *hate* me!"

"No, they don't!"

"I slapped Monica's grandma!" How in the world would that make them *like* me?

"I know, ugh!" she groaned. Taking in a deep breath, she continued, "I was at the playground when you were in the grounded room. I was talking crap about you to Monica and her squad—"

"—*excuse* me?" She had been talking *crap* about me?

"Shut up!" she snarled. "I was talking crap, like I *said.* Anyway, I said, 'Can't believe that toaster strudel slapped yer grandma, girl. What a joke!'. Then Monica said, 'She didn't know, it was an honest accident.'. So then I *knew*, Denny. I knew that you were lyin' to me and hanging out with the popular squad. You were thinking you could get popular and dump me like the massive poop you took after you ate all those pancakes."

"What?" I shrieked.

"You *lied*, Denny!"

"*You* talked crap about me before you even knew. You just admitted to it. And I honestly haven't been talking to *any* of them!"

Mama's Child flipped her afro and walked away.

Mr. Sanch came out into the hallway and told me to quit talking to myself and come back inside.

"What?" I asked.

"Come back inside."

"I was talking to Mama's Child."

He didn't believe this. "She's not talking to you right now."

Sighing, I went back into detention. Did he just entirely forget that MC was supposed to be in here too? Or did he not care? Where did she even go? I mulled it over for the rest of detention.

Chapter 38

THE BEGINNING OF SPRING. Bliss for some—*crappy* for me. Mama's Child was still infuriated with me for no good reason. I was finally getting back on the right track with my family after the Morgan incident, and Mama's Child had to go throw me off my groove. I had a B- overall in school right now. That was *horrible*. That was like a failure for the rest of my entire school career. I hung my head in my hands and groaned. My mom was gonna be ticked. I was used to having an A.

I could smell and hear that everyone was having their Saturday morning breakfast as I approached the kitchen. My mom exited as I was about to enter, and I stopped. She was turning on the TV. I was about to grab some food when the TV boomed, *"Breaking News! An update in the Sanchez missing person story."*

Everyone within earshot stampeded their way out of the kitchen. Some of my younger siblings had milk dribbling down their chins, and Ashley was brushing toast crumbs off her shirt. My dad pushed himself through the crowd, and they parted out of his way. He turned up the volume, and everyone quieted.

"A ratty old ballet slipper was found hanging from the jungle gym at the Crab Cove Private School. It had a note pinned to it, saying, 'You'll never find me...alive.'. Investigators claim that it was signed 'Sanchez'," stated the newscaster.

Mr. Sanch was on the TV screen, crying. He officially had resigned from being a cop, saying in his interview that "it was hitting too close to home." The newscaster informed viewers that he had taken a full-time position at the school and was now going to be our teacher *permanently*.

My mom quickly reached for a remote and turned the TV off. She tossed the remote onto the coffee table with a clatter, and everyone got out of her way as she moved to the kitchen. I followed behind in the parted trail she left, my stomach growling. My mother went to the stove, picked up a pot of what looked like oatmeal, then slammed it back down.

"I *swear* this has my mother written *all* over it." My mom placed her hands to her temples, then leaned on the counter, bending forward like it was the only thing holding her up. She burned her palm on the stove and winced, shaking her hand.

"Maybe we should all sing 'Beverly Hills' together." Rochelle laughed.

"Beverwy Hwills," Frogster screeched from a cluttered highchair. My mom *fumed* and demanded that Chelle go to her room. I didn't blame her.

Taking a seat at one of the few seats available, I pushed someone else's breakfast out of the way and munched on a piece of toast with grape jelly. I sat there in a shocked state as everyone began to go on about their Saturday. A shadow passed across one of the kitchen windows, and I didn't know if it was really there, or if I just saw it because I was scared.

I counted to five and took another bite of toast. Nobody else mentioned it.

I smacked my hands together to brush off the crumbs, then headed upstairs to work on my homework. Lil' Shelbi was in my room making paper airplanes out of my papers, and I was about to lose it. Calming myself down once again, I decided I'd just start over.

Anything I wrote on that homework at two a.m. is probably crap anyways, I thought to myself.

The telephone rang, and wanting any excuse to stop doing my homework, I ran downstairs at the speed of light to answer it.

"Hello," I said. When only hot breath and a buzz were on the line, I got so creeped out that I hung up the phone. I just about jumped out of my skin when they called back. *Scare them before they can know they scared you.*

"Hello?" I asked in as angry a voice as I could muster up.

"…is this Deniese?" they asked.

"Yeah, it is! Why?" I demanded.

"This is Marcus."

I almost hung up the phone because I was extremely nervous, and my heart was going super fast. Oh no, I had just *yelled* at him.

"Hi." I adjusted the tone of my voice to make it more friendly, but it cracked and came out all squeaky. I rolled my eyes up in my head and slapped my forehead.

"I need help with my French Revolution paper. I was wondering if we could meet at iHOP. You know, since you like it so much." His voice sounded like melted butter, and I just about cried. *He knew my name, what my voice sounded like,* and *that I liked* iHOP.

"Tha— that sounds great!" I stammered, giggling nervously.

Fast forward two hours, and I was sitting across from Marcus Delon, unable to believe what I was seeing. He ordered for *us* those pancake bites. He also got *extra* cream cheese dip. Smart man.

Mama's Child entered the restaurant and immediately met my eye.

"Denny!" she screamed. "You continue to lie to me!" Then she stormed out.

"Uh…" Marcus muttered.

I was about to explain myself when Mark sat beside us, followed by Haylee, Hallee, Cameron Green, *and* Monica. I pinched myself to make sure it wasn't a dream.

It wasn't.

"Thank you so much, Deniese, for agreeing to help *all* of us with our assignment!" Monica said.

"You're welcome." I smiled. Then it dawned on me. "Wait— *What?*"

"Marcus said you wanted to come to iHOP to help us with the homework assignment!" she answered cheerfully.

I didn't know what to say to this, so I just said, "Oh. Yeah."

Marcus smiled, but I no longer thought it was because he liked me or wanted to be my friend. It was because I was helping him *and* all of his friends. Normally, I would think, "Who cares? I'm sitting at an iHOP with the *popular* squad." But now I just had this nagging thought about whether or not I should go talk to MC and try to make things right. Did I stay? Or did I go?

I decided to stay and live it up with the popular squad. Mama's Child had no right to be mad at me anyway, *right?* I technically didn't *lie* to her. Deciding to help the populars, I tried to scratch off the creepy-crawling, dirty feeling that came over me.

"So. The French Revolution started when—" I began.

"—I like that shirt, Deniese," Monica pointed out. My face turned as red as her auburn hair. I had dressed extra spiffy for Marcus, wearing only my *best* hand-me-downs. But it paid off since I ended up in some surprise get together with all of the popular kids.

"Thanks," I mumbled awkwardly, not knowing how to accept a compliment.

Monica flipped her hair, and Hallee said, "I'm *really* craving some movie theater popcorn right now! We should totally catch a movie. My mom's treat. Who's in?"

I didn't say anything, 'cause I didn't know if I was invited or not. Mark, Marcus, and Cameron all said they wanted to go.

"Deniese and I will go, too."

I couldn't believe that Monica had said *both* of our names in the same sentence. We all packed up our stuff. Now I *really* got to thinking that Mama's Child may have had a real point.

Marti dropped me off at my house after the movie at six p.m., and I realized that I never got to teach them *anything* about the French Revolution. I also realized that I didn't even write my *own* French Revolution paper. I tried to write it immediately, but I couldn't focus. So I went to bed, against my better judgment.

Chapter 39

I GOT ON THE BUS the next morning and sat next to Mama's Child because I wanted to. It was also the only seat left, so I had an excuse. She turned to me, and her eyes were as cold as death.

"Sit on the floor, *Dennis*. You've got to pick. Me or them." Her words cut me like a knife. But I sat on the floor, despite the laughter and the embarrassment. MC placed her backpack up on the bus seat beside her and frowned down at me. I couldn't give up my chance at popularity with Monica for Mama's Child, no matter how long we had been friends. She'd just been *way* too rude to me too many times. She'd stabbed me in the back more times than I could count. But it still felt...*wrong.* I didn't know what I was going to do.

At school, the teacher asked us to turn in our assignments. Everyone turned one in but me. I was in absolute shock as he collected a paper from every single one of the popular kids' desks. They all must have worked on it when they went home from the movies. I had been distracted and too worried to even think! My brain had been running on fumes last night after all of that excitement and strangeness.

"Why are your grades slacking lately?" Mr. Sanch asked me after school.

"Mr. Sanch, I'm becoming distracted by my newly acquired popularity."

He cocked his head in confusion, and a hint of a smirk glimmered on his face. Until he registered that I was being serious. I didn't know how to have friends and live my life at the same time.

"Don't let it get to your head, Dennis," he said flatly.

The next morning, I walked to school. Yep. I *walked*. If I was going to be part of the popular squad, I would have to get fit. I also brushed my ratty hair into a frizzy ponytail, trying to make it look like the other girls'. Wearing a Goodwill skirt and knockoff Mary Jane shoes, I felt more confident than I usually did, but also totally unlike myself at the same time.

Hallee and Haylee complimented my appearance at school, and I felt like a celebrity. Usually nobody even spoke two words to me, unless it was something about me being in trouble or MC whispering some rumor she heard. A sorrowful pang wounded my stomach, and I tried to shake it away.

Noticing that what I called *The Queen Bees*—the popular older girls—were all sitting with their ankles crossed, I crossed my ankles, too. Mr. Sanch assigned us some reading homework, and then we went to lunch.

At recess, I walked over to Monica and the other girls, and said, "Hey, girls!" I waved at them like other people did with their friends. Mama's Child jumped in a mud puddle that was nearby, and it splashed me. It completely *ruined* my pink Mary Jane knockoffs. Katrina came over just as I asked the other girls if they wanted to do the reading homework with me tonight. I wasn't good at asking people to spend time with me.

"Actually, *Dennis the Menace,* we're having cheerleading practice tonight and then a slumber party at *my* house. I invited all of them. I *would* invite you, but your shoes are *filthy,"* Katrina crooned. Her voice was angelic, but her words were purely hateful. Everyone looked at my shoes, and heat rose to my cheeks. I clenched my fists and curled my toes down, willing myself to stop showing my embarrassment. Feeling mud squishing between my toes, I wanted nothing more than to take these shoes off—for more than one reason. My top reason being to chuck one at Katrina.

"They would just ruin my mom's *five thousand dollar white rugs."* She flipped her ponytail and walked away.

"Sorry, Deniese." Monica shrugged. "Duty calls."

And with that, I was left *alone,* with nothing but a snickering Mama's Child and ruined shoes.

Chapter 40

IT WAS APRIL FOOL'S DAY, and I groaned as I got ready for school. I figured there would be tons of people ready to prank me. I'd been through a major dry spell. Ever since that day when MC ruined my shoes, I hadn't been nearly as popular as I was. I wasn't sure if I ever actually *was* popular to begin with. Maybe I made it up because I wanted it to be true.

At school, Mama's Child passed out cupcakes. She even handed me one. Still feeling a little bitter from her actions, and not entirely trusting her, I asked, "What'd you do, spike 'em with rat poisoning to fool me on April Fools?"

Her face instantly fell. "Are you *serious,* Dennis?" It seemed as if even her freckles were frowning, and she sounded incredibly hurt, not mad.

"What?" I asked awkwardly. I had no idea why else she would be passing out cupcakes.

She sat in her seat, and I studied her carefully, holding the cupcake in my hand. When Mr. Sanchez led the whole class in singing "Happy Birthday" to her, a major lump formed in my throat, along with a crappy feeling all over. I couldn't believe I had actually *forgotten* Mama's Child's birthday. I was such a crappy friend, and I hated myself for it. Even if we had been fighting, I still should have remembered something like that, right? I knew how horrible it felt to have your birthday forgotten, and if I had *known,* I would *never, ever,* have acted the way I did. No matter what we were dealing with, I would have told her "Happy Birthday." I didn't know much about relationships, but I knew that you told the people you love "Happy Birthday." It was as simple as that.

I should never have hung out with the popular kids that day. Now I wasn't only unpopular but I also had *no* friends at all. My only real friend hated me. And I deserved it. Nothing else could be said. This was an unredeemable, unjustified mistake. I took a bite into the funfetti cupcake I didn't deserve and tasted nothing but regret with every crumb that slid down my throat.

After school, I went to my room. I called for a therapy session, then I remembered about Anthony and my mom.

"Tell Anthony that it's Deniese Tipper," I said, after the lady picked up the phone.

Anthony got on the line.

"Hello, Deniese. You've been kind of distant lately," he said.

I tried my hardest to impersonate my mom's voice. Taking a deep breath, I began, "I know, I've been having a rough time."

"Uhh...have you decided on what to do with whether or not you want to get divorced?" he asked. *What?* He *actually* thought it was my mom on the phone, and he was talking about a divorce? I had to do something.

"Yes," I answered, "I am *not* getting a divorce." I spoke the words firmly, even though I was shaking.

"I gotta tell you, I was surprised that you lied to me in the first place. I thought you guys were already divorced." He sounded a little annoyed.

"I want to stay with my husband," I answered, not knowing what else to say.

"You don't sound like yourself. What about Bob, then? Are you getting rid of him?"

Bob? Bob! I tried not to fly off the handle.

"Um, yeah. I'm kicking him to the curb!"

"So, where exactly does that leave me?"

I hesitated, not knowing what to say. Nearly having a heart attack, I closed my eyes when my mom picked up the other landline. *This is it,* I thought. *Busted. You're going to be in the grounded room for all eternity. You will probably die there.*

"I don't want to order *no* girl scout cookies this year! Quit calling!" my mom's voice was incredibly brassy, and she hung up. It also hung up my end of the line, and I was slightly relieved that this was settled once and for all.

Then I remembered that I never even made an appointment. Oh, well. After *that* conversation, I didn't really want to see him. I was mad at him for trying to split my parents up. Reaching for the phone again, I slowly and carefully punched in Mama's Child's phone number. It rang several times with no answer. I called again. And again. She didn't answer.

I got in the chatroom and typed a message, saying, "Happy Birthday, Mama's Child. May you have a great day!" and I even put one of those little smiley faces at the end. It took me forever to figure *that* out. But she didn't respond to that, either.

Maybe I should wait, I thought. *She needs time to cool off.*

When she didn't respond within two hours, I called again with no answer.

So I gave up for the night.

❖

In the morning, I got up and checked the chatroom. While people were writing in it, there had been no response from who I wanted to hear from.

At school, she showed up late, *and* she ignored me. And during recess, I couldn't take it anymore. So I went up to her.

"Hey," I said. She turned her back to me and looked the other way.

"Mama's Child, I'm sorry." I took a seat beside her, the two of us sitting on the grass in front of a small pond-like area.

"I got caught up in the popularity," I tried to explain. Reaching for a small rock beside me, I picked it up and tried to skip it. It just sank in the water. In some strange way, it reminded me of exactly how I felt inside.

I didn't get any answer from her.

"Look, I know that I messed up. But you won't even *talk* to me."

No answer. I sighed deeply.

"Okay, I know I shouldn't play the blame game and put it all on you. It was my fault."

I picked up another rock.

"Try to understand," I continued. When I tried to skip it, it just failed again and sank to the bottom.

"I know I made you sad. And certainly *angry,*" I added, as I picked up another rock. "You've always wanted to be popular, too." This rock sunk, too, even though I had thrown it differently.

"Are you ever going to forgive me?" I asked, picking up

the last rock near me.

She stood and walked away. I looked down at the rock in my hand, and a single tear fell from my eye and splashed against its cool, gray surface. After I tossed it weakly, it sank too.

Chapter 41

IT'D BEEN THREE WEEKS since MC last spoke to me. I'd been too down in the dumps to write anything. So I put all of my effort into the tambourine. Wanting to be president of the band next year, even though it wasn't likely, I figured it was worth a shot. Not like I had anything better to do.

I pulled out an old picture in my drawer of me and Mama's Child. There weren't very many photos of me, and I had no idea when or even where this had been taken. I'd admit it. I cried a little. She was my only friend, and I didn't even act like it. Taking her for granted, I'd lost her so many times already. But she always came back, and *I* always came back. This time I really blew it.

I needed to try to make a new friend. Somebody who wouldn't be popular, so they wouldn't make MC jealous if she came around. I needed someone who would be beneficial to me and not use me. So I thought about a girl named Jade. She was one of the Star kids and was super quiet. Jade was an A student, only a year or so younger than me, so she fit the criteria. I went to the Stars' house and knocked on their door. She was only a year younger than me. It wasn't that big of a difference.

Katrina answered the door, and my heart sank. *Of course,* I thought.

"What are *you* doing here?" she asked, snottily as ever. I just stood there, not knowing how to respond. Feeling like the dirt that I was.

Haylee and Hallee saw me as they passed behind Katrina, and they called, "We're playing Barbies and having ice cream. Do you want to join?"

"Um, no thanks," I said, even though I *really* wanted to. That would definitely be crossing Mama's Child. I knew where that line stood now.

"Is Jade here?" I asked, then heard Monica's unique giggle. *Man!*

"Um, like, why?" asked Katrina, blocking the doorway.

"Um, because, like, I want to talk to her, uh, duh!" I mocked.

"Drop the 'tude."

"Not till you drop it first!" I retorted.

"Go eat a *raccoon,*" Katrina hissed, slamming the door in my face.

Okay, so maybe I deserved that.

I walked home and stopped at the pig pen.

"You still love me, right?" I asked him.

His pink snout wiggled, and he oinked in reply, evoking a sad smile.

"Thanks, Beanie." I patted his head before heading inside.

My mom asked me what I wanted to do for my birthday. It wasn't even for four more weeks. How did she even remember that when she didn't remember it on the actual *day?*

"Nothing," I muttered, defeated.

"*Excuse* me?" asked my mom.

"I don't want a party. Just want to stay home with you guys." I didn't even make eye contact with her and kicked at the snags in the living room carpet.

"Are you sure? What's up with *that?*"

I didn't have to look at her to tell she was frowning at me.

"Yeah, I'm sure."

"I'm giving you another chance, just cause I'm feeling nice, today." She grabbed my chin and forced me to look up at her. "Are you *sure?*"

"Yes."

She sighed, like she couldn't believe it. Shrugging and letting her arms slap to her thighs, she said, "Okay, if you say so. Less money for me to spend."

As she walked away, I couldn't believe she had offered to do something for my birthday.

My birthday had always landed on the last day of school. Once again school would be wrapping up and I would become a *third grader.*

How exciting! I told my brain. *This is going to be the best summer ever.*

I knew I said that every year, but as low as I felt now, I wanted to seriously try this time.

Despite my best efforts not to, I checked the chatroom. Nothing was written by Mama's Child.

Quit thinking about her, I thought. *There's no need stressing over a friendship that she's not even* trying *to save.*

And with that, I signed off.

Chapter 42

MR. SANCH WAS WRAPPING up the school year and told us that he was already thinking of what next year's musical would be, and that he was considering *HAIRSPRAY!* Mama's Child didn't look the slightest bit enthused. I was in too much of a slump to even process the words.

Stephanie and Orange were going to graduate, so they didn't care, and nobody else besides me was really even that into acting.

After school, I walked home and tried to start a conversation with my mom, asking her what she knew about the musical. But she didn't care and didn't answer me. So I worked on the finishing touches for a project due the next day. I sat on my bed and counted my new (not-magical) beads, trying to calm myself down. The strand of beads had practically been forced upon me. *They didn't feel special to me, so how were they supposed to work?*

I went to bed early.

Tomorrow is another day, I thought.

In the morning I walked to school with an art project

Sanch had assigned, avoiding all of the puddles and everything that could damage it. It had been hard trying to watch for the cracks in the sidewalk when my hands were so full with the popsicle house sculpture. I got there exactly one minute before the bell rang, so I set my project on my desk and sat down. Sanch quickly went around and collected the projects. After he marked down all of our work in his little gradebook, he said he had an announcement. Everyone got quiet.

"I am pleased to say that nobody failed this year and that you will all be moving up."

A few of the older kids clapped in a mocking way.

Mr. Sanchez rolled his eyes. "Stephanie and Orange, would you like to share with us what you two are going to do when you graduate?" he asked.

We all turned around, including me, and waited for their responses.

Stephanie stood and smoothed down her extremely short, sparkly miniskirt. Flipping a blond curl over her shoulder, she spoke brightly, "Yes. I am going to travel the world. I will not be going to college, because that is just *too much work.* I'm going to become rich, so I don't have to have a job."

I glanced at Orange, who sat beside her. She rose and went ashen like she was going to faint, but managed to say, "Whatever."

"Okay, then..." Mr. Sanchez sounded incredibly unsettled.

Orange had apparently told our mom that she was going to become a nail stylist. I never heard her say such things, but then again, I never heard her say anything other than *"whatever."* My mom told her later that night at dinner that she could not work in her shop or open up one close to her salon, because it'd be bad for her "beauty shop business." My dad had just grumbled, "I'm going to work. Congrats on picking a job, even if it *is* a stupid one."

I thought, in all honesty, he would never be satisfied with any job any of us got unless it involved *football, being a mother to a million children,* or *working at the factory.*

On the last day of school, my *birthday,* I got up so excited. I was eight years old today! I wasn't going to fail school! Mama's Child didn't fail either!

Oh yeah…*Mama's Child.* I forgot. I walked downstairs and ate a pancake that was leftover from when my mom got iHOP to go the night before. I got a few "Happy Birthdays" (specifically from Ashley, Mom, and Ambrosia, who was at our house for whatever reason). I was going to keep track now, because I was tired of people not telling *me* "Happy Birthday" then getting mad if I didn't tell *them.*

At school, I sat down, and we all were handed our report cards. Mine said that I had an A- overall for the whole year. Ugh. Not my best work, but I'd take it. It was still an A. I couldn't believe I had managed to get it up from my lowest point *ever,* a C+. I will admit that I apologized to Mr. Sanch and turned in my French Revolution paper late with an extra and unnecessary page stapled to the back (which I was sure to point out to him) and got five points of extra credit for staying after school to clean up after arts and crafts day. Mama's Child sighed loudly from her seat, and I knew she hadn't done bad enough to fail, but that she must not have gotten a very good grade.

At lunch, I sat at my casual, usual, lunch table, and nobody said "Happy Birthday" to me. That was okay, though. Sitting at my table with me (at the very end, as far away from me as possible) was Mama's Child. As I ate an iced cookie, I felt kind of pathetic. I had gotten it after I repeatedly told the lunch lady it was my birthday. Either she felt sorry for me or she just wanted me to leave her alone and shut up.

On the way home, I was so pumped that it was summer. I went in my house and threw my backpack in my room. Dumping all of my stuff on the floor, I threw away all of my old assignments while singing, "*Oh, Happy Day!*"

As I dug through my things, I found the yearbook I got. I hadn't even looked at it yet, I'd been too sad and stressed. It contained pictures from the dances, all of the popular people, the sports teams, etc. When I got to the band page, my spot in the picture was right in the crack of the book, so you couldn't even tell it was me (other than from my beat-up sneakers and my hair). I tried to brush off my anger and annoyance. Flipping through the pages, I found two good pictures of me. The *only* other two pictures I was in throughout the entire book. But both of them were of me and Mama's Child from earlier in the school year.

Just then, my dad yelled from the kitchen, "A celebration is in order!"

I got so excited, that I abandoned all of my junk *and* the yearbook on the floor. Running down the steps, I couldn't help but think, *Oh, those guys!*

I had told them that I didn't *want* a party, but I was still excited, nonetheless. A party was a party, and this one was for me. When I reached the kitchen, and everyone gathered around, I didn't see any cake.

That's odd, I thought. *Cake is the best part of having a birthday.*

Let it go, DJ. Let it go.

"Your mom and I have an announcement to make," my dad grinned.

Okay…

"I'm pregnant!" blurted my mom.

"What?" I yelled. Everyone else seemed to yell the same thing. Some of them clapped, some of them cried.

Orange said, "Whatever," and I stood there, shocked. It felt like all the blood had been drained from my body. *This* was the surprise? *This* was the *celebration*? *Today*?

"Tell 'em, babe," my dad encouraged my mom.

I felt like I wasn't even in my body.

"Tell us what?" I heard my own voice asking.

"This pregnancy is different," muttered my mom, unenthusiastically.

"What do you mean?" My lips were moving, but I wasn't entirely sure I was alive right now. The grin on my dad's face, and the lack of color in my mom's, made me nervous.

"Is it twins?" Dominique and Krissy giggled in unison. They were clearly excited, and I had no clue *why*. This was *horrible* news.

"No," said my mom. The room was quiet for what felt like a torturous eternity.

With a smile bigger than the sea plastered across his face, my dad pumped both fists into the air and bellowed, "It's *quintuplets!*"

"What?" I blurted, my jaw dropping.

I didn't understand. Then he said something that absolutely floored me—

"That means five!"

Coming Soon…

One Demerit, Two Demerits

part of the Tomorrow Is Another Day series.

Acknowledgments

There's just something about a blank piece of paper and a blinking cursor, or a freshly inked pen, that calls my name. Something about the unknown. The adventure. The endless possibilities. Something that is felt and experienced with the whole entire body, mind, heart, and soul.

I would be lying if I said that writing this novel had been an experience that consisted of one hundred percent, solely joy-packed moments. It was easy, yet it wasn't. It was fun, and it was frustrating. There was laughter. Crying. Happiness. Stress. Times I thought I couldn't do it. I'm *just* me. I couldn't *really*, possibly fathom that I could write my own novel, right? Wrong.

Writing really is as simple—and as hard—as beginning. Just starting. This novel began long ago, when I first was introduced to writing. No, I don't mean writing homework. Writing words? Spelling? No. What I *mean* is actually being introduced to the world—or should I say galaxy, even universe—that writing truly is.

When I was ten years old, I remember specifically that

there was a day I was so bored and impatiently waiting on one of my three siblings to play with me. (Specifically, Lindsey, whom this novel is dedicated to.) Rumour has it, as she likes to say, *I* was born *for her*. She is roughly two years older than I, and constantly reminded me as a child (and occasionally still does today) that *she* called the shots and that *I* was to answer to *her* requests—not the other way around. Siblings, right?

Anyway, I was—and still am, completely—head-over-heels, *obsessed* with the art of creating your own stories and characters and escaping to your own world. Little did I know, this is what I had been doing all along. See, back then, this was expressed through the fun of playing with Barbie dolls—which has a whole other deeply-rooted connection to my novels. To remain elusive for now.

After a while of pestering my sister to play Barbies with me, and her repeatedly telling me no, I decided to ask her what she was doing. She responded to me that she was writing. This piqued my curiosity, and I asked her a bunch of questions and kept pestering her, as annoying little siblings have a knack for doing. She finally told me as a sort of "cure" for my boredom that I should write something too.

What? *Me? I* should write something? How? That's a thing? "But what would I write?" I asked her, or something along those lines. Off the top of her head, she instantly suggested that I write about the characters we made up when we played Barbies. But I wouldn't even know where to start!

Lindsey gave me a few ideas, telling me to just explain briefly who the character is. Give the name of the town. Make up the setting. See where it goes from there. She handed me a piece of notebook paper and a pencil, and off I went. Did she have a feeling I would be able to write something worthwhile? Did she think I could *really* write a story? *An entire book?* Was she just trying to keep me busy so I wouldn't bother her? I haven't asked. Maybe she'll tell me when she reads this.

After I wrote a paragraph or so, I instantly came back into the room, all giddy and excited to share what I had written. I read it to her, and there was something in her facial expression that I captured. I will always remember it, and carry it with me for the rest of my life. Was it joy? Not exactly. Was it laughter? Not necessarily. It was an emotion that I am still to this day unable to describe. Funny, right? A *writer*, unable to express something through words. But…I knew I liked it. Somewhere inside, I knew that I had created that. Yes, the written work, but more importantly, that indescribable emotion. And I knew that I wanted to create it again.

She immediately encouraged me to keep going. Soon, I had several pages of pencil-written, smeared pages. Misspelled words, horrible grammar, incorrect uses of "your" and "you're," "to," "too," and "two," and well, you know the gist. So I eventually decided to read a small amount of my work to my mom, grandma, and grandpa. They laughed and seemed to enjoy my story too, with a similar reaction to the indescribable one of Lindsey. Not only could this be created in her, but in others. I treasure reactions like those greatly, and it gives me great pleasure and a purposeful feeling in life. One that I was not aware was possible or existed at that age. It's one of the many reasons why I love to write.

The novel itself was a great escape for me, and I enjoyed

writing it. School got in the way, stress, life in general, and growing up. Plenty of excuses, plenty of procrastination and forgetfulness. Losing sight of the simple joys and forgetting the importance and rarity of that feeling I created in others and myself through writing and reading my story. Almost quitting writing for good because of some negative or discouraging comments and opinions. Being told my work wasn't good enough. That being an author is unfathomable. Unrealistic. I could go on and on with reasons and excuses for not writing, but I won't. I took quite a few, way-too-extended, hiatuses from writing this novel. Because of this, it could probably be said that it took me a little longer than it should have to write it. Try ten years.

Despite me getting discouraged, lazy, busy, or whatever else prevented me from writing, Lindsey was always there to get me back on track.

"You know what you should do again?"

"What?"

"Write."

"Write?"

"*Your novel.*"

Although there were times I was annoyed, or really just did not want to write, I really appreciated her pushing me to just do it. Just start. Like I said, it was really *that* simple— *and* really *that* hard.

"All you need to do is start. Then it will come back to you. Just begin. It will all start flowing again. It's *you*…"

These words she spoke are some of the truest words I have heard. That really *is* all that it takes. Anyone can write —anybody. *Really.* If you want to write, do it. Just begin. You can. As soon as I would begin again, the words really *did* start flowing again. Like I never missed a beat.

With that, I can honestly say that I would probably never have discovered that I could write anything other than what I had to. Nothing creative. Nothing of my own imagination or free will. Certainly not that young. Not without Lindsey. Without her, I probably wouldn't have even *finished* this novel. I probably would've let other things distract me, discourage me, or take for granted the story we created, all those years ago. And for that, I would like to genuinely say thank you, with much love—from the bottom of my heart.

I would also like to thank God, my mother, my siblings, my grandparents, and anyone else who has free-willingly (or not-so-freely—cough, forcedly, cough) listened to the hours- (and days-) long reading sessions of my novel. For supporting me, for laughing, encouraging me, shaping me into who I am today, and helping me believe I can do anything that I set my mind to.

To those who have never forgotten me during my hardships: my Uncle Dave, my lifelong childhood-friend Shirer, my pastors, and Steve Dixon. A thank you is simply not enough.

My deepest sentiments to my FFFL, Anne Stryker. Thank you for the guidance, advice, friendship, and late night chats. For loving Beans. For helping me turn my dreams into reality. For your prayers, and the magic you bring to my life and countless others. For always being willing to do the hard work while letting me have the fun. Your kind and selfless heart warms me in ways I cannot express, and you have been such an incredible blessing from God. Thank you.

Thank you to Orian Graphics, for putting up with my

pickiness to get *the* cover. For letting me use ~~my own~~ DJ's sharpie doodles, and creating something absolutely perfect and beyond my wildest dreams! You're amazing!

Thank you to the readers, for giving my novel a chance, and to my fans, who will read my future novels, speak kindly of my work, and patiently wait for more. Thank you.

Tomorrow Is Another Day has been, and will always be, the journey I always wanted to be a part of but was too afraid to go on. The story I always wanted to tell but was too shy to do so. The chances I wanted to take, but didn't. The things I wanted to say, but couldn't. The friends I wanted to have, but wasn't granted. Because I was too shy. Too quiet. Too nervous. Too scared. Too doubtful. Too different. Too…me.

Through everything I have been and become, I have realized that being me is okay. I hope you do too.

God bless, and happy reading.

-T. R. Prouty.

Author Bio

Tomorrow Is Another Day serves as a debut, introducing author T. R. Prouty. T. R. is a self-taught author, beginning her work in the year of 2008, at ten years of age. Since finishing this work, T. R. has gone on to write additional novels, with plans and progress on publishing them and creating more.

If you loved *Tomorrow Is Another Day*, then good news! T. R. has continued the tale of Dennis June in the gut-busting sequel, *One Demerit, Two Demerits*. That's right—a sequel! Dennis June is back at it again, and this next novel is sure to bring a smile to the faces of young and old alike with the nostalgic feeling of childish shenanigans. Coming soon!

You can follow T. R. Prouty on Instagram at @regallywritten, or email her at regallywritten@gmail.com.

Lightning Source UK Ltd.
Milton Keynes UK
UKHW040419171220
375384UK00001B/5